Praise for **The Afrika Reich**

'[The] plot is clever, imaginative and, in its finale, wholly un-expected. In a crowded field, *The Afrika Reich* stands out as a rich and unusual thriller, politically sophisticated and hard to forget' *Economist*

'A thoroughly enjoyable and compelling read' *Sun*

'This graphic, pacy alternate history thriller is scarily convincing' *Australian*

'An enthralling look at the horror that might have been if Germany was not defeated' *Sydney Daily Telegraph*

'Guy Saville's scorching debut novel [is] a terrifying account of the way things might have been . . . When this dark and dystopian world is coupled with a cast of credible characters, Machiavellian plot twists, cinematic action scenes and pulsating suspense, the story becomes irresistible . . . Immaculately researched and with accompanying notes to put the story into its context, *The Afrika Reich* is an exciting first novel which blends history and fiction into an unforgettable drama' *Lancashire Evening Post*

'Don't miss this explosive blockbuster . . . a blood-pulsing and convincing read' *Peterborough Evening Telegraph*

'Gripping, well-researched and terrifyingly plausible, this is a fast-paced, ambitious book that paves the way for its sequel with a jaw-dropping twist' *Lincolnshire Echo*

Guy Saville was born in England in 1973.
He has lived in South America and North Africa
and is currently based in the UK. THE AFRIKA REICH
is his first novel.

The Afrika Reich

GUY SAVILLE

HODDER

First published in Great Britain in 2011 by Hodder & Stoughton
An Hachette UK company

First published in paperback in 2011

2

Copyright © Guy Saville 2011

The right of Guy Saville to be identified as the Author of
the Work has been asserted by him in accordance with the
Copyright, Designs and Patents Act 1988.

A CIP catalogue record for this title is available from the British Library.

ISBN 978 1 444 71066 3

Map drawn by Martin Collins

Typeset in Monotype Sabon by Ellipsis Digital Limited, Glasgow

Printed and bound in the UK by Clays Ltd, St Ives plc

Hodder & Stoughton policy is to use papers that are natural,
renewable and recyclable products and made from wood grown
in sustainable forests. The logging and manufacturing processes
are expected to conform to the environmental regulations
of the country of origin.

Hodder & Stoughton Ltd
338 Euston Road
London NW1 3BH

www.hodder.co.uk

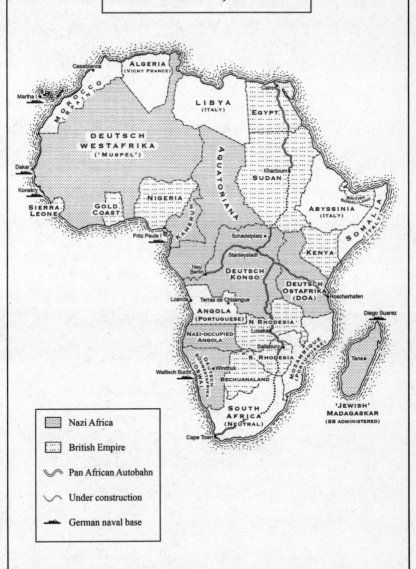

AFRICA, 1952

Martha I.

Casablanca

MOROCCO

ALGERIA
(VICHY FRANCE)

LIBYA
(ITALY)

Cairo

EGYPT

DEUTSCH
WESTAFRIKA
('MUSPEL')

Dakar

Konakry

SIERRA
LEONE

GOLD
COAST

NIGERIA

Khartoum

SUDAN

British
Somaliland

ABYSSINIA
(ITALY)

SOMALIA
(ITALIA)

AQUATORIANA

KAMERUN

Fritz Paula I.

Schädelplatz

Stanleystadt

KENYA

Neu
Berlin

DEUTSCH
KONGO

DEUTSCH
OSTAFRIKA
(DOA)

Roscherhafen

Diego Suarez

Loande

Terras de Chisengue

ANGOLA
(PORTUGUESE)

Nazi-occupied
ANGOLA

N RHODESIA

Lusaka

Tana

MOZAMBIQUE
(PORTUGUESE)

Salisbury

S. RHODESIA

DEUTSCH
SÜDWESTAFRIKA
(DSWA)

Walfisch Bucht

Windhuk

BECHUANALAND

'JEWISH'
MADAGASKAR
(SS ADMINISTERED)

SOUTH
AFRICA
(NEUTRAL)

Cape Town

Nazi Africa

British Empire

Pan African Autobahn

Under construction

German naval base

For my own Cole
okunene okuhepa

Throughout the book Berlin is referred to as 'Germania'. If Hitler had won the war this is what he planned to call the capital of his new empire, as he stated in 1942: 'The name "Germania" will give every member of the community, however far from the centre, a feeling of unity and close membership with the Fatherland.'

On the day when we've solidly organised Europe,
we shall look towards Africa

ADOLF HITLER
Speech to the SS, 22 February 1942

There will be no great conflagration with the blacks.
The true battle for Africa will be White against White

WALTER HOCHBURG
Memorandum to Reichsführer Heinrich Himmler,
15 October 1944

Saltmeade Farm, Suffolk, England
28 August 1952, 05:50

HIS father had a special name for it: *Hiobsbotschaft*. From the Old Testament, Job's news. The type of news you didn't want to hear. News brought on the wind of shipwrecks. Or by breathless messengers arriving with the dawn.

In an instant Burton was awake. He had never slept well, not since he was a child. Outside he heard the sound again.

Whump.

He moved to the curtains, drew them open a sliver, and peered out – like an archer at the window of a besieged castle. The sun was pink and fresh on the horizon. It had rained again in the night.

Another w*hump*: the sound of wheels as they hit potholes in the driveway. Burton had been meaning to fill them in for months, to make everything perfect for Madeleine. Except now maybe she wasn't coming. Why else would someone be driving to his door at this hour unless to bring bad news?

The car was a Daimler, the latest model, its paintwork brighter than vinyl. As it approached Burton made out two figures inside: a chauffeur and passenger in the back. The passenger's face was obscured by a newspaper. Or maybe a large, unfolded map.

Burton let the curtains close gently, so as not to draw attention to the movement, and picked up his clothes from the floor.

Corduroy trousers (no time for smalls), yesterday's shirt. He strode to the door – then hesitated.

These people could be anyone. Maybe they'd come to repay some act of violence. Maybe they were just a diversion: shiny car at the front while men with balaclavas and pistols sneaked round the back. That's how Burton would have done it.

He reached underneath the bed to a jewellery box: there were no gems inside, just his gun. It was a Browning HP, one he'd acquired in French West Africa years before. Not that there was a French Africa any more. Nowadays it was marked red, white and black on the map; a forbidden territory of sand dunes and hearsay.

The Browning felt solid in his hand. Reassuring. Its grip was made from engraved ivory.

Madeleine had kept asking him to get rid of the gun before Alice came to visit again. She didn't want a weapon in the house with a child, even if it was hidden. Burton agreed but never quite got round to doing it. For once he was glad of having too many chores. There was no clip, but he hoped to rely on its effect rather than actually pulling the trigger.

The car was close now.

Burton tucked the gun into the waistband at the back of his trousers, hiding it beneath his shirt, and hurried downstairs.

By the back door he paused to yank on his boots, then slipped out into the morning. The air smelt of dewy grass and cattle; there were no masked men waiting. With only a shirt on Burton felt his skin prickle and shrink; he ignored the sensation. He half crouched and using a low wall for cover darted to the front of the house, thinking how ridiculous he'd look if his visitors were making a social call.

The Daimler had come to a halt outside the farmhouse, the chauffeur already opening the door for his passenger. The man in the back got out. He was dressed as sombre as a banker, had silver, brilliantined hair with a razor parting. Only his skin suggested a life beyond a desk. The man strode to the house and rapped on the door.

'Major Cole!'

Burton recognised the accent at once: Rhodesian, possibly South African, somewhere from the Transvaal. As far as he knew Madeleine had no connection with the colonies. Perhaps it wasn't anything to do with her. He adjusted the Browning in his waistband.

'Maybe he's not up yet, sir,' suggested the driver. 'It's still early.'

'These type of people never sleep. Too much on their conscience. And never enough under the mattress.' The Rhodesian chuckled at his own wit. He knocked again, harder this time. 'Major Cole!'

'Actually, I sleep very well,' said Burton, appearing from behind the wall.

If the Rhodesian was startled, he made no show of it. Instead he turned deliberately from the door and appraised the man opposite.

Burton imagined what he saw: old, army-issue shirt, trousers spattered with mud and creosote, wheat-blond hair far too long to be respectable. Five days of beard; Burton loathed shaving. Only his eyes might suggest something of his background. They were blue-grey, the colour of an autumn afternoon. Calm but alert. Hard as a rifle butt.

'Burton Cole?'

'Yes.' Burton's own voice was soft but growly with the nowhere accent of his upbringing: English, German, African.

The Rhodesian moved to greet him, sending out a waft of citrus cologne. 'My name is Donald Ackerman. I wish I didn't have to call so early but I've important business.'

Burton felt a sudden tightness in his chest.

There was something about the way he'd said 'important business'. Burton had a flash of Madeleine lying cold and colourless, Alice tugging at her hair not understanding why Mummy was so still. *Hiobsbotschaft* after all. He took Ackerman's hand and shook it. It was warm and chalky.

'Is there somewhere we can talk?' Ackerman motioned towards the house. 'Somewhere private.'

Burton didn't move.

He'd bought the farm wholesale, complete with its cracked-brick floor and old man's furniture. Had no choice but to keep everything (except the crucifix above the bed). Maddie never seemed to care, but if there was a connection between her and the Rhodesian, Burton didn't want him to see the interior and make any assumptions. Assumptions that he couldn't provide for Madeleine, especially after the luxury she was accustomed to.

'Come with me,' said Burton, leading him away from the door.

Ackerman lingered for a moment, then followed.

Physical discomfort was something Burton had long grown used to. The one thing he couldn't bear, however, was boots without socks. In his rush to get outside he hadn't put any on. Now, with each step, he felt his soles rub against grainy leather, felt his nails catch on the toecap. The boots themselves, like the Browning, were another acquisition – this time from the carnage of Dunkirk. He'd pulled them off a dead German paratrooper and they fitted as if measured for his own feet.

'You don't seem like your average farmer,' said Ackerman as they trudged towards the orchards. Ahead were rows of vranja quinces and apples; ravens watched them from the branches.

'It's a new life,' replied Burton.

'And you own this place?'

Something about his tone made Burton suspect the Rhodesian already knew the answer. He came to a halt by a quince tree. 'Like you said, Mr Ackerman, it's early. And I've got a lot to do. What is it you want to talk about?'

'A business proposition.'

So not news about Madeleine. 'Unless it's about my crop,' he said, 'I'm not interested.'

'I haven't come all this way to buy fruit, Major. Besides, your quinces aren't ready yet.'

'Another month, I know.' It never ceased to amaze Burton how the details of the seasons had come to capture his enthusiasm.

That was Maddie's doing, she made him see the world like a child once more.

Ackerman spoke again. 'I represent certain . . . "interests" in Northern Rhodesia.' He said it as if struggling to find the right word, though Burton guessed this was a long-prepared patter. 'LMC, to be precise. Lusaka Mineral Concessions. We need you to do a job for us. Head up a team of commandos—'

'I've already told you, I'm not interested.'

'An assassination.'

'Assassination? What are you talking about?'

'Come, Major. You have a certain reputation – Dunkirk, Tana, Stanleyville to name but a few. Why do you think I'm here?'

Definitely not about Madeleine. If she were here she'd already be yelling at Ackerman, her fists in balls, black hair flying.

'Mr Ackerman, I suggest you leave. Now.'

'You will of course be paid . . .' again he searched for a well-prepared word, '"handsomely" for your services.'

Burton laughed. 'There's nothing you could pay me.'

Ackerman didn't reply. Instead he reached inside his jacket and withdrew a small leather box. He handed it over. 'My business,' he said.

Burton opened the case and fought the urge to gasp.

'That's just a down payment. To secure your interest. You'll get the same again on acceptance of the job. Double if you complete it . . . "satisfactorily".' He made it sound like homework.

'How do I know they're not fakes?'

'You don't.'

Burton looked at the diamonds. There were five of them, each the size of peas.

Five plus five plus ten. A fortune.

He could pay off the loan on the farm. There'd even be enough for new furniture. No more making love on that mildewy mattress for him and Maddie. And he could buy her a dressing table, something antique, French, none of that imported German kitsch. And chesterfields for the drawing room. And a pony for Alice so maybe she wouldn't hate coming here so much . . .

Burton closed the box and handed it back. 'It's a very generous offer, Mr Ackerman. A few years ago I'd have taken you up on it quick-flash. Not any more.'

'It's not enough?'

'My life is here now, no more killing. At any price.'

The Rhodesian chuckled to himself. 'You're going to give mercenaries a bad name.'

'I'm sorry to disappoint.'

'Nevertheless, I still expect you to head up our team.'

'I'm not heading up anything. I want to stay here, work the land.' Burton suddenly thought of his former comrades and the ribbing he'd have got for declaring that. 'Maybe even settle down.'

'That's all very endearing, Major Cole. But I think marriage is perhaps a fantasy too far.'

'What do you mean?'

'Madeleine. I'm sure her husband won't give his blessing. I hear he's a very jealous man.'

Burton clenched his hand together until the knuckles stung. In his mind he saw himself grab the Browning. Force the gun hard against the Rhodesian's gullet. Cock the trigger. Demand to be told how he knew. Instead, he remained impassive except for a slight tic in his jaw.

'So that's why you're here.'

'No,' replied Ackerman. 'The Kassai diamond fields, German Kongo.'

'Kongo? I don't want anything to do with Africa. Not any more.'

'How very British of you.'

'The Nazis fucked it up . . . and we let them.'

'Exactly why your talents are required now.'

'You want me to kill someone,' said Burton. 'Why? There are a thousand men out there who could do it.'

'But none so good.'

'There are plenty better. Pulling the trigger was always my last resort, not profession.'

Ackerman snorted. 'Now you're just being modest.'

'No cold blood. Ever.'

'Hot blood, cold blood. It's still blood. Besides, we feel you'd be more "committed" to the task than anyone else, especially when you learn the target.'

'I told you: I'm done with all that.'

'You'll change your mind.'

'Mr Ackerman,' said Burton, struggling to find some gritted patience, 'I don't want your diamonds. And Madeleine and me is my business. I want you to leave. Now. I'm not going to tell you again.'

But when the Rhodesian failed to move, it was Burton who turned and strode away. The Browning felt sweaty against the small of his back.

Ackerman called after him: 'I've got news of an old acquaintance of yours, Major. A friend.'

'They're all dead.'

'Not this one.'

Burton ignored him.

'The man we want you to kill is – Walter E. Hochburg.'

Burton stopped solid.

It was as if his entire body – every muscle, every sinew, every pulsing vein and nerve – had turned to stone. Although the sun was continuing its ascent everything suddenly seemed darker: the fields, the trees, the farmhouse he so desperately wanted to make a home for Madeleine. The thought of her in front of the fire, toasting crumpets, flickered through his mind; they were both looking forward to their first autumn here. He pushed the image away. As far away as he could. So help him, God.

Very slowly he twisted to face Ackerman. 'What did you say?' He spoke as if his breath had been stolen.

'I think you heard me well enough.'

From close by came the croaking of a raven.

7

Burton tried to laugh. 'It can't be. Hochburg died years ago. In a fire.'

'Let me assure you, Major, he's still very much alive.'

'No.'

'Alive and now the Governor General of Kongo—'

'I'll do it,' said Burton. There was the slightest catch to his words.

'Don't you want the details? What we're proposing is danger itself. And what about your quinces?' He might have been joking with him now. 'And Madeleine? She's arriving later today, isn't she? I rushed to get here first.'

But Burton was deaf to everything Ackerman had to say.

'I'll do it,' he repeated.

This time his voice was unflinching.

Part One

GERMAN KONGO

Never wage war with ghosts

AFRICAN PROVERB

Chapter One

Schädelplatz, Deutsch Kongo
14 September 1952, 01:14

NINE minutes. He had nine minutes to exorcise a lifetime.

Burton Cole sat at Hochburg's desk, sweat trickling behind his ears. He was dressed in the uniform of a Sturmbannführer, an SS major: black tunic and breeches, Sam Browne belt, jackboots, swastika armband on the left sleeve. His skin crawled beneath the material. To complete the look his hair had been cut short, beard shaved; the skin on his cheeks felt raw and exposed. Chained to his wrist was an attaché case empty except for two items: a pouch fat with diamonds and concealed inside that, a table knife.

The knife had been his mother's, from a service used only for best. He still remembered the way she would beam as she laid the table for visitors; the flash of silver. That was – what? – when he was eight or nine. Back then he used to struggle to slice meat with it, now it was as deadly as an ice pick.

He'd spent years sharpening it to a jagged point for this very moment, never once believing it would come.

But just as Burton opened the case to grasp the knife, Hochburg held up his hand. It was an immense, brutal paw that led to an arm straining in its sleeve and the broad shoulders of a swimmer. The movement itself was languid – a lazy version of Hitler greeting the ranks.

11

'The diamonds can wait, Sturmbannführer,' he said. 'First I must show you something.'

Ackerman warned him this might happen. Hochburg had shown all the previous couriers, showed everyone, no matter what their rank. It was his great pride. *Indulge him*, Ackerman advised. *Do nothing to arouse his 'suspicions'. There'll be plenty of time for the kill.*

Burton glanced at his watch. Everything had gone wrong that night; now he felt crushed by the lack of seconds. This was not how he had envisaged the moment. In his dreams time stood still, there was opportunity for talk and torment.

And answers to all his questions.

Hochburg rose from his desk. The office around him was austere. Naked wooden floors, simple furniture, white walls that smelt of damp and rubbing alcohol. There was a gun cabinet in the corner and shelving for hundreds, possibly thousands, of books – though not a single volume filled them. Overhead a fan remained motionless despite the humidity of the night. Although dark patches were spreading across Burton's shirt, Hochburg looked as if his body were chilled to the bone. The only decoration in the room was the obligatory portrait of the Führer, another of Bismarck, and maps.

Maps of Aquatoriana, Deutsch Ostafrika, DSWA, Kamerun, Kongo, Muspel: all the dominions of Nazi Africa. The cartography of enslavement, thought Burton. Every last hectare pored over, charted, claimed. In the first years of conquest they had been governed by the Kolonialpolitisches Amt, the KPA, a haphazard civil administration. Later the SS took control.

Hochburg moved towards the opposite end of the room where French doors led out to a veranda.

'But your diamonds, Herr Oberstgruppenführer,' said Burton, remaining in his seat. He didn't relish the idea of killing Hochburg on the balcony in full view of the camp.

'I said they can wait.'

Burton hesitated, then got to his feet and followed. His jackboots pinched with every step.

Hochburg was already on the veranda. Above him hung a silent wind-chime. He spread his arms with a messianic sweep. 'Magnificent, isn't it?' he declared in a baritone that sounded raw from cognac, even though Burton knew he was a teetotaller. 'A thing of wonder!'

The official headquarters of the Schutzstaffel, the SS, may have been in Stanleystadt – but this was the real powerbase of Deutsch Kongo. Burton had arrived through the front entrance, past the cranes that were still erecting the imperial façade. The quadrangle below him was at the rear, the hidden part of Hochburg's fiefdom, used for ceremonial occasions. No one but the SS were allowed here.

It was the size of a parade ground with several storeys of offices on all sides and, according to Ackerman, cellars that went as deep below as the floors above. Bureaucracy and torture: two pillars of Nazi Africa. There were guard towers on each of the corners; a patrol stalking the perimeter with a Doberman. Enough barbed wire for a concentration camp. But it was the ground that most caught Burton's attention. Searchlights dived and soared over it. For a second he stood dumbfounded at the sheer scale of it. The sheer barbarity. His father would have wept at its sight.

Then his stomach curdled.

'A wonder!' repeated Hochburg. 'You know, when the Reichsführer first saw it he clapped his hands in delight.'

'I heard that story,' said Burton. 'I also heard he filled two sick bags on the flight home.'

Hochburg stiffened slightly. 'The man has a poor constitution; we gave him a sumptuous dinner.'

Burton glanced at the square again, then turned his eye to the murk of the jungle beyond. Somewhere out there, concealed among the symphony of cicadas and tree frogs, were the rest of his men. He imagined them: hearts jumpy but mouths set, faces thick with camouflage, counting down the final minutes on their watches. Patrick would already be slowing his breath to maximise the accuracy of his shot . . . Assuming, of course, they were even there. The team had gone their separate ways twenty-four hours earlier and Burton had no way of knowing if the others had made it to their positions. It was the one flaw in the plan. He might be about to leap into the abyss – with only darkness to break his fall.

'How many would you say it took?' continued Hochburg.

'I've no idea, Oberstgruppenführer,' replied Burton. 'A thousand?'

'More. Much more.' There was a gleam in his eyes. They were the colour of coffee beans and not how Burton remembered them. When they glinted in his nightmares they were black – black as the devil's hangman. But maybe that was just the years in between. It wasn't the only difference. Hochburg had also lost his hair, every last follicle of it.

Burton offered another guess. 'Five thousand?'

'More still.'

'Ten?'

'Twenty,' said Hochburg. 'Twenty thousand nigger skulls.'

Burton looked back to the quadrangle and its gruesomely cobbled square. It gave Hochburg's headquarters their name: the Schädelplatz. The square of skulls. Inside him something screamed. He saw children torn from parents, husbands from wives. Families left watching the horizon for loved ones who would never return home to smile and bicker and gather round the fire. Every skull was one more reason to kill Hochburg.

He saw the view of his childhood, the dark jungle of Togoland. He saw his mother's empty room.

Burton struggled to keep his voice level. 'Can you walk on it?'

'You can turn panzers on it.'

'How come?' His brain could only supply nonsense. 'Have they been fired? Like tiles, to make them hard.'

'Fired? Like tiles?' Hochburg stiffened again . . . then roared

14

with laughter. 'You I like, Sturmbannführer!' he said, punching his shoulder. 'Much better than the usual couriers. Obsequious pricks. There's hope for the SS yet.'

With each word Burton felt the breath wrenched out of him. He suddenly knew he couldn't do it. He had killed before, done it so many times he'd grown indifferent to it. But this – this was something else. Something monumental. The desire to do it had been a part of his life for so long that the reality was almost like turning the knife against himself. What would be left afterwards?

Burton tried to glance at his watch but it caught on his sleeve. The minutes were counting down: he was running out of time. On the veranda the wind-chime tinkled briefly.

He must have been crazy to think he could get away with it, that Hochburg would reveal his secrets. Here was a man dedicated to making silence from living, breathing mouths.

Then the moment passed.

At 01:23 the north of the Schädelplatz would vanish in a fireball. By then he'd be on his way home, justice done, Hochburg dead. He'd never have to look backwards again. The future would be his for the taking.

'Your diamonds,' Burton said, moving decisively towards the study.

But Hochburg barred his way, his eyes drained of humour. He seemed to want reassurance, to be understood. 'We have to cleanse this place, Sturmbannführer. Let the flames wipe Africa clean. Make it as white as before time. The people, the soil. You understand that, don't you?'

Burton flinched. 'Of course, Herr Oberstgruppenführer.' He tried to pass.

'Any fool can pull a trigger,' continued Hochburg, 'or stamp on a skull. But the square, that's what makes us different.'

'Different from who?'

'The negroid. We're not savages you know.'

In his mind Burton could hear the precious seconds counting down like a tin cup rapped on a tombstone. He tried to move forward again. This time Hochburg let him through – as if it had been nothing.

They resumed their positions at the desk, the smell of rubbing alcohol more potent than before.

Hochburg poured himself a glass of water from a bottle in front of him – Apollinaris, an SS brand – and downed it in a single, gulpless motion. Then he reached beneath his black shirt for a chain around his neck. He seemed greedy for his loot now. On the chain was a key.

Burton released the attaché case from his wrist and set it on the desk between them, feverishly aware of the blade hidden inside. He thought of the fairy tales Onkel Walter (his gut convulsed at the words) used to read him at night, of Jack lifting the ogre's harp and it calling to its master. For a moment he was convinced the knife would also speak out, warn Hochburg of the looming danger, its loyalty to Burton forgotten in the presence of the hand that once grasped it.

Hochburg took the case, placed the key from his neck into the left-hand lock and gave it a sharp turn, like breaking a mouse's neck. The mechanism pinged. He swivelled the case back. Burton inserted his own key into the second lock. Another ping. He lifted the top and slid his hand in, finding the bag of diamonds. He took it out, the knife still hidden inside the pouch, and stared at Hochburg. Hochburg looked back. A stalemate of unblinking eyes.

Ask, a voice was bellowing in Burton's head; it might have been his father's. *What are you waiting for? Ask!*

But still he said nothing. He didn't know why. The room felt as hot as a furnace, Burton aware of the sweat soaking his collar.

Opposite him, Hochburg shifted a fraction, clearly not used to such insubordination. He ran a hand over his bald head. There was not a drop of perspiration on it. In the silence Burton caught the prickle of palm against stubbly scalp. *So not bald, shaved*. Any other time he might have laughed. Only Hochburg possessed the arrogance to believe his face needed something to make it more intimidating.

Burton's fingers curled around the handle of the knife. Very slowly he withdrew it from the pouch, all the while keeping it out of sight.

Hochburg blinked, then leaned forward. Held out a grasping claw. 'My diamonds, Sturmbannführer.' He offered no threat, yet there was confusion in his eyes.

Burton spoke in English, his mother's language; it seemed the most appropriate. 'You have no idea who I am, do you?'

Hochburg's brow creased as if he were unfamiliar with the tongue. 'Do you?'

'*Was?*' said Hochburg. '*Ich habe nicht verstanden.*' What? I don't understand.

In those restless nights before the mission Burton's greatest anxiety was that Hochburg might recognise him. It was twenty years since they'd last seen each other but he feared that the boy he'd been would shine through his face. Throughout their whole meeting, however, even with their eyes boring into each other, there hadn't been the slightest tremble of recognition.

Now something was creeping into Hochburg's face. Realisation. Alarm. Burton couldn't decipher it. Hochburg glanced at the portrait of Hitler as if the Führer himself might offer a word of explanation.

Burton repeated his question, this time in German, revealed the knife as he spoke. The blade caught the lamplight for an instant – a blink of silver – then became dull again. 'My name is Burton Cole. *Burton Kohl*. Does it mean anything to you?'

The faintest shake of the head. Another glimpse towards the Führer.

'My father was Heinrich Kohl. My mother—' even after all this time her name stumbled in his throat '—my mother, Eleanor.'

Still that blank look. Those empty brown eyes.

If the bastard had hawked their names and spat, if he had laughed, Burton would have relished it. But Hochburg's indifference was complete. The lives of Burton's parents meant no more to him than those pitiful, nameless skulls on the square outside.

He had planned to do it silently so as not to bring the guards hammering at the door. But now he didn't care.

Burton leapt across the table in a frenzy.

He crashed into Hochburg, hitting the bottle of water. Shards of it exploded everywhere. Burton grabbed the older man's throat but Hochburg was faster. He parried him with his forearm.

They both tumbled to the ground, limbs thrashing.

Hochburg swiped ferociously again, snatched at Burton's ear as if he would rip it off. Then he was grasping for his Luger.

Burton clambered on top of him. Pushed down with all his weight. Pointed the knife at his throat. Hochburg writhed beneath him. Burton slammed his knee into his groin. He felt the satisfying crush of testes. Veins bulged in Hochburg's face.

Outside the room there was shouting, the scrape of boots. Then a tentative knock at the door. It locked from the inside and no one was allowed entry without the express command of the Oberstgruppenführer, even the Leibwache – Hochburg's personal bodyguards. Another detail Ackerman had supplied.

'You recognise this knife,' hissed Burton. All his teeth were bared. 'You used it often enough. Fattening yourself at our table.' He pushed the blade tight against Hochburg's windpipe.

'Whoever you are, listen to me,' said Hochburg, his eyeballs ready to burst. 'Only the Führer's palace has more guards. You can't possibly escape.'

Burton pushed harder, saw the first prick of blood. 'Then I've got nothing to lose.'

There was another knock at the door, more urgent this time.

Burton saw Hochburg glance at it. 'Make a sound,' he said, 'and I swear I'll cut your fucking tongue off.' Then: 'My mother. I want to know. I . . .' He opened his mouth to speak again, but the words died. It was as if all Burton's questions – like wreaths or phantoms – had woven themselves into a thick cord and pulled tight around his throat. He made a choking sound and became deathly still. The blade slackened on Hochburg's neck.

Then the one thing happened that he never considered.

Burton began to weep.

Softly. With no tears. His chest shuddering like a child's.

Hochburg looked more bewildered than ever but took his chance. 'Break down the door!' he shouted to the guards outside. 'Break down the door. An assassin!'

There was a frantic *thump-thump-thump* of boots against wood.

The sound roused Burton. He had never expected to get this opportunity; only a fool would waste it. He bent lower, tear ducts still smarting. 'What happened to her?'

'Quickly,' screeched Hochburg.

'Tell me, damn you! I want the truth.'

'Quickly!'

'Tell me.' But the rage and shame and fear – and in the back of his mind the training, that rowdy instinct to survive – suddenly came to the fore.

Burton plunged the knife deep and hard.

Hochburg made a wet belching noise, his eyelids flickering. Blood spurted out of his neck. It hit Burton in the face, a slap from chin to eyebrow, geysered on to the walls. Burning hot. Scarlet.

Burton stabbed again and again. More blood. It drenched his clothes. Spattered the maps on the walls, running down them. Turning Africa red.

Then the door burst inwards and two guards were in the room, pistols drawn. Faces wide and merciless.

Chapter Two

T was called *dambe*. Burton had learned it as a kid on the banks of the River Oti, in Togo, taught by the orphans his parents were supposed to redeem. Learning to kick and punch and headbutt with the unbridled ferocity of a fourteen-year-old. But always at night, always away from Father's soulless eyes. Inventing excuses for the splits and swellings that blotted his face. Soon he was beating the boys who instructed him. They said he had the *yunwa* for it – the hunger. That was after his mother had left them.

The Leibwache glanced down at Hochburg, their mouths sagging with disbelief. Blood continued to gush from his throat, weaker with each spurt.

Burton sprang up. Three strides and he was at the door, his left hand held out in front of him straight as a spade, the right curled into a ball of knuckles tight at his armpit, legs bent like a fencer.

He stamped his boot down on the closest Leibwache's shin. The man buckled as Burton lunged forward and – *snap* – fired his fist into his face. A headbutt and the guard was rolling on the floor.

The second Leibwache spun his pistol at Burton and fired, the shot missing his head by a fraction. Burton felt his eardrum thunderclap and muffle at the closeness of the bullet. Oblivious to it, he twisted low and rammed his elbow into the Leibwache's chestbone. The guard doubled up, his pistol skittering across the floor.

Past the open door Burton heard the sound of boots on stairs.

The winded Leibwache lurched towards Burton who slipped underneath him and thumped his wrist, the *hannu*, on to the back of his neck where vertebrae and skull connected. The man dropped lifelessly.

In the room beyond, another guard appeared, roused by the gunshot. For an instant his eyes met Burton's. Then Burton slammed the door shut.

The click of the bolt.

There was no double-locking mechanism so Burton dragged Hochburg's desk to the door, stood it on end and jammed it hard against the frame. It would buy him a few extra seconds. He was lathered in sweat, even the material of his breeches sticking to his thighs. He undid his top buttons and tried to breathe. The smell of rubbing alcohol burned his nostrils.

His watch read 01:21.

Burton reached down for one of the Leibwache's Lugers. He wished he had the reassuring handle of his Browning to grip, but the pistol was in Patrick's care. The Luger would have to do. He checked its firing mechanism and clip (seven shots left) and hurried towards the veranda.

Burton hesitated.

He looked back at Hochburg's body. The bleeding had stopped. He was completely still except for his left foot which twitched sporadically. It looked almost comic. His features were a mask of scarlet. Burton thought of Ackerman: *hot blood, cold blood. It's still blood.*

He needed to make sure.

Burton returned to the body, knelt and checked the pulse. Nothing. There was no breath from his nostrils either. He reached to retrieve the knife still buried in Hochburg's throat . . . then decided against it. His last chance of knowing about his mother – why she'd vanished, what had happened – was gone for ever. Even the killing itself had been pleasureless, with none of the satisfaction he had envisioned. A numbness was spreading through his mind.

He stood, feeling he should mark the moment he had craved all these years. What would Father have done? Make the sign of the cross? Say a few words about the need for forgiveness? Maybe. Or maybe he'd have sucked on his lungs and spat.

Burton left without a backward gesture.

On the veranda the night was still; the sound of the gunshot obviously hadn't carried. Burton was grateful for that. He lowered himself over the side and shinned down one of the supporting posts, his feet finding the nameless skulls below. Inside his boots his soles arched as though he were barefoot in an abattoir.

Burton marched out into the square. The searchlights moved idly; the Doberman patrol at the far end walking away from him. If the rest of his team had been captured, or if Dolan was still nursing his grudge and chose not to hit the detonator, this might be the shortest walk of his life. A ten-second stroll through a firing range.

He headed towards the far gate, resisted the urge to sprint. For some reason an old barrack-room tune sprang into his head:

> *Went to war for the Poles, the Frenchies and Slovaks*
> *What for, Winston?*
> *Dead chums and kingdom come*
> *We ain't fighting for no blacks—*

An alarm began to sound. A wailing, mechanised klaxon.

The searchlights froze, then began to scour the square. They both found Burton. Ahead he saw the Doberman patrol halt and turn in his direction. The dog growled.

Burton motioned impatiently towards the guard towers, a gesture that said *get that fucking thing out of my eyes or you'll be on punishment detail for a month*. He hoped they wouldn't be able to make out the bloodstains on his face and hands.

A voice cried out from the darkness: 'Apologies, Sturmbann-führer. Is it a drill?'

Another alarm started up.

Through the cyan-white glare Burton made out two guards in each tower, one with the light, the other pointing an MG48 machine gun, enough to turn a man to bonemeal in seconds. 'Search the perimeter,' Burton shouted at them. 'Then stand down.'

The lights did as they were told. Burton continued towards the exit.

'There!' came a voice from behind him.

He spun round to look back at the veranda. Standing on the balcony was a Leibwache, arm rigid in his direction. 'Stop him. Fire!'

Burton ran.

Immediately the lights were back on him. The ground erupted in bullets, fragments of skull bursting upwards. Burton zigzagged wildly, lurching to the left, next second doubling back on himself. Anything to avoid the onslaught.

Where was Patrick? Where was that damn explosion?

There was a crackle of gunfire from the balcony. Another from the nearest guard tower, close enough to singe the leather of his jackboots this time. The light was relentless.

Burton slipped, his hands flailing. He imagined the guard in the tower seizing his chance. Burton had done it enough times himself. Wait for the target to stumble, line up the sights and squeeze the trigger: an easy kill-shot.

At least I got Hochburg, he thought. I'll be able to look Father in the eye – before St Peter turns me away.

Then the searchlight was gone. Burton squinted into the darkness. The beam was pointing upwards, vanishing into the sky. The tower empty.

Across the square, the other tower aimed its light at him before it too jerked away. Burton could make out a guard gripping the MG48, aiming it at him. Suddenly he snapped back in the shape of a starfish. Dead.

Not for the first time Burton whispered a thank you to Patrick Whaler and his sniper rifle.

The two guards and the Doberman were now belting towards him. There was another silent blast from the darkness and the guard with the dog stumbled. He unleashed the animal and encouraged it on with the cry, '*Angriff!*' The Doberman galloped forward, fangs snarling.

Another shot, then another. Both guards dropped.

Fuck the handlers, thought Burton, *shoot the dog!*

The ground splintered and spat near the Doberman – but the animal was moving too fast for Patrick.

Burton came to a halt, concentrated on the dog. In his mind he was back at Bel Abbès, the Legion fort where he'd trained as a soldier. A *sous-officier* was pointing at a blackboard; afterwards they'd practised on crude models made from jute and straw.

Patrick fired another shot. It clipped the Doberman's tail, stoked its ferocity.

The dog was no more than ten yards away.

Burton crouched low like a sprinter at the start of a race. His chest was straining, the roof of his mouth dry. He was dimly aware of more alarms ringing, more gunshots from the balcony.

At the last moment – just as the dog leapt to attack – Burton sprang upwards and grabbed the animal's front legs. Teeth gnashed inches from his face. With a single, vicious movement he wrenched its limbs apart.

There was a crack as the breastbone broke, then Burton flung the Doberman away. He forced himself not to hear its whimpering.

Another torrent of bullets – from behind this time.

Burton turned to see several Leibwache gathered on the balcony shooting at him. He fired off several rounds from his Luger, none of them finding their target but enough to make the guards duck out of sight. Then he ran again, sprinting to the gatehouse.

The barrier was down but there were no guards. As Burton approached he saw them slumped on the ground, haloes of blood pooling around their heads. The window of the gatehouse had a single bullet hole in it; inside, another guard looking into distant space. Whatever else might have happened to Patrick his aim was as straight as ever.

The gunfire continued remorselessly. There was a heavy-calibre retort mixed into it now. The Nazis were coming to full alert: another thirty seconds and he'd never get away.

Burton dived to the ground and crawled round the edge of the gatehouse. The window above him exploded, showered him with glass. Looking back across the square – through the bursts of machine guns – he saw an open-backed lorry roaring towards him, laden with Waffen-SS troops. There were more men behind it on foot. Enough firepower to quell an uprising.

Burton struggled to move forward, using the corpses around him as sandbags. At that moment he'd have signed away the entire farm for a single hand grenade.

The headlights of the lorry shattered. Then the windscreen. The driver slumped forward, the vehicle twisting to a halt. Troops immediately poured off it. Fifteen, twenty of them. More than a match for Burton's pistol, more than even Patrick could take out.

He fired off the final shots in the Luger, scrambled up and ran. Gunfire streaked around him like angry red hornets.

The troops were closing in. *Oh, Maddie*, he thought.

Burton was knocked off his feet. It felt as if a huge, hot fist had slammed against his back. The skin on his scalp contracted and stung.

A fireball rose into the sky. A gulp of night air – and then another, even bigger blast.

Debris rained down on the Schädelplatz: burning lumps of metal, oil drums that landed with hollow booms. At the front of the complex a crane toppled over. The troops darted for cover, turning their weapons in the direction of the explosion. From the opposite side of the square came a sputter of phosphorous blobs. It sounded as if an entire regiment were attacking the camp: Dolan, and his 'box of tricks'. Burton almost grinned. The phosphorous fell to the ground igniting everything it touched. The stench of tarred wood swirled round the square.

Burton got back on his feet, a few sporadic shots whistling in his direction. Among the dead guards he spied the distinctive shape of a BK44 rifle. He scooped it up and ducked below the barrier that separated the camp from the jungle road beyond. It was lit for a couple of hundred yards before being reclaimed by the darkness; three hundred miles later it reached the Doruma garrison and the border with Anglo-Sudan.

Still running, Burton searched for a sign of the others. Nothing. He tried to visualise the direction Patrick's shots had come from. There was another explosion behind him. The lights along the road flickered – buzzed – and died. An instant later the entire camp was extinguished.

'Fuck it,' snarled Burton. 'Patrick?' he called out. 'Patrick?'

Only the chaos behind him answered.

Burton kept pushing forward, moving at an unsteady trot. The tarmac beneath his feet shimmered with a fiery light but the trees either side remained black.

'Patrick?' he called again. This was absurd! He hadn't survived everything to get lost in the dark.

Somewhere to the left the undergrowth shook. Burton stumbled in its direction. An engine fired up, high-powered and urgent. Seconds later a vehicle roared forward. It executed a sharp U-turn and ground to a halt.

It was a Ziege jeep, the Nazis' workhorse in this part of the world, built at the Volkswagen factory in Stanleystadt. On its bodywork was the skull and palm tree insignia of the SS in Africa.

Burton raised his rifle, flicked off the safety.

Then a voice: 'Major. Get in.'

It wasn't Patrick – but it would do.

Chapter Three

'WHERE'S Patrick?' shouted Burton. The gearbox was howling. 'Where's Patrick?'

They were reversing down the road, back towards the camp, Lapinski gripping the wheel as if he would strangle it. His eyes gleamed in the darkness like a cat's. They drove without lights.

The Ziege screeched to a halt. There was a thump as something landed on the roof. Lapinski hit the throttle again. They lurched forward, rapidly picking up speed. Burton turned round in the passenger seat, his rifle drawn. A figure manoeuvred itself from the roof into the back of the jeep. It was dressed in a suit sewn with leaves, on its head a bulky brass helmet and goggles encrusted with tubes: night-vision equipment. Beneath the contraption Burton could just perceive the face. Lean and wrinkled; smears of camouflage paint; a sharp nose that had once been broken and now twisted to the left.

It was Patrick Whaler.

'I'm too old for climbing trees.' He rubbed the small of his back, winced, then jerked his head upwards. 'But the line of fire was better up there.' In his other hand was a customised rifle with oversized butt, silenced muzzle and telescopic sight the size of an artillery shell. Carved on to the stock were the words, *für Hannah*.

27

'You're still the best shot I know,' said Burton.

'I missed the dog,' replied Patrick. His voice was Boston Irish churned with two decades of French desert. 'Once I wouldn't.'

'I got out, didn't I? Relax, the hard part's over. We're almost home.'

'That's what you said at Dunkirk.'

Patrick was one of the few conditions Burton had insisted on with Ackerman. He needed someone he could trust completely on the mission. The two of them had known each other for twenty years, back since their days in the French Foreign Legion when Burton had been an angry teenage volunteer, Patrick his commanding officer. He wasn't the man he'd been though. Prison had changed him – as if something grey had been mixed into his blood.

Burton turned to face the front. They were hurtling through the jungle, Lapinski leaning over the wheel, face set into the gloom.

'I can't see nothing,' said the driver.

'No lights,' said Burton. He flicked a look in the wing mirror: plumes of fire were reaching into the sky. 'We're still too close.'

'We'll miss the turning.' Lapinski's nose was almost touching the windscreen.

Patrick's head appeared between them. With the night-vision equipment he resembled a gigantic fly. 'There!' he said. 'On the left.'

Lapinski squeezed the brakes and turned sharply. They crashed through thick foliage – then a rotting wooden barrier – before joining another road parallel to the one they had left. This was the dirt highway from when Belgium had been the colonial power. Neglected since the Nazis conquered Kongo, it was now hidden from pursuing eyes by a canopy of vegetation. Vines clawed against the jeep.

'Lights?' said Lapinski.

The jeep was bouncing up and down like a rowing-boat in an Atlantic squall. Burton felt his brain bash against his skull. 'We can risk it.'

Lapinski flicked a switch, headlights illuminating the way in front. They were in a tunnel of trees – green, grey, black – the road as potholed as a lunar surface.

Burton felt a hand on his shoulder, Patrick motioned at the track behind. He turned to see another pair of headlights following them. The lights were closing in. Patrick reached for his rifle.

'Wait!' said Burton. 'It might be Dolan. Signal first.'

Patrick grabbed his torch and began flashing letters in Morse code. V-R-A-N-J-A. Vranja, the quince variety in the main orchard back home. Burton could see them now, the fruits already fat and yellow. He hoped to make a good living out of them one day – it had to be better than all this! The first thing he'd do when he got back home would be to go with Madeleine and pick one. Inhale its perfume.

No reply came from the other vehicle.

'What if their torch got broken?' said Lapinski.

Patrick shouldered his weapon. 'What if they're about to blow us off the road?' He put his eye to the scope.

The jeep hit a pothole, jolting the vehicle. The muzzle of Patrick's rifle flayed in the darkness.

'For fuck's sake,' he growled. 'Can't you keep this thing straight?'

Lapinski snapped back: 'Any time you want the wheel—'

'They're flashing their headlights,' said Burton. 'W-A-L-L-O . . . Wallop.' Dolan's call-sign. 'Everyone just relax and we're out of here.'

Patrick grunted.

Burton settled back into his seat. It was only then that he realised he was gripping the stock of his BK44. Gripping it so hard his wrist stung.

It took them forty minutes to reach Mupe, exactly as they had planned. Burton spent the time wiping sweat from his eyes, trying not to think of the tears he had shed in Hochburg's study. He kept glancing in the rear mirror, but there was no swarm of

German lights. Lapinski remained hunched over the wheel. With his thin moustache and slick hair he could have been a spiv's apprentice. Like all the team he was wearing an SS uniform, the cloth clearly distasteful to him. Every now and then he muttered something in Polish. Prayers or complaints, Burton couldn't tell.

Mupe was a disused airstrip on the flight path from Stanleystadt to Irumu in the east. When SABENA, Congo's original airline, had set up its network of airfields in the 1920s it also built emergency landing-grounds dotted through the jungle. These were now shrinking back into the trees, ideal for covert extractions. The Nazis had abandoned most of the old Belgian infrastructure to construct bigger, better facilities: monuments to conquest. A network of airports connected the six colonies of German Africa, with hubs linking the continent to the Fatherland. In the Schädelplatz region every aerodrome was now redundant to the new international terminal at Kondolele that could accommodate military aircraft and the latest Lufthansa Junkers. Private jets also used the tarmac, whisking in SS dignitaries who marvelled at Hochburg's square before flying out again vowing never to return to the squalid heat of Africa. Burton had flown into Kondolele earlier that evening; already it seemed a lifetime ago.

'Keep the engine running,' said Burton when they reached the airfield. He slipped out of the jeep, Patrick following, his face still obscured by his insect-head. The two of them jogged to the tree line.

Behind them, Dolan's vehicle ground to a halt. At the wheel was Vacher – the fifth member of the team, a Rhodesian. Burton motioned to both of them to stay put. Dolan threw up his hands in exasperation.

'Looks smalty enough,' said Patrick, scanning the silent perimeter of the airfield. 'How long?'

Burton glanced at his watch, struggling to read the dials in the swamped light. Their plane was scheduled to touch down at 02:20. 'Another ten minutes.'

'Assuming they even left.'

'Ackerman wouldn't dare,' replied Burton, trying to reassure himself as much as Patrick. 'I'm going to check out that building. You keep the others here. I don't want Dolan thundering around.' He left the cover of the trees.

'Wait!' said Patrick, fishing inside his pocket. 'You might need this.' He tossed something towards him. Burton caught it. It was his Browning, still warm from Patrick's body.

Burton nodded, then put the pistol into his waistband. With the BK44 in the other hand, he crouched down and moved silently to a caved-in building on the far side of the airfield. It reminded him of the apple store back on the farm.

There was no door, just a frame. Inside it smelt of orchids and wet plaster; cockroaches teemed on the floor. Everything of value had long since been stolen. Screwed to the wall was a portrait of Leopold III of Belgium, former ruler of the colony. Someone had added a toothbrush moustache and engorged penis to the picture; another, a hangman's noose. There were swastikas daubed on all the walls, but crudely as if drawn by children.

Burton moved to what was once the control room. Broken windows looked out on a runway of compacted dirt. They'd need to light some markers for the pilots. Even with night-vision sights a landing like this was fraught with—

A noise.

Burton strained to hear it. For an instant his spine turned to ice. It sounded like Hochburg. The gait of his step as he strode in for dinner. Then it came again, something much more earthly: the clink of webbing. Burton pushed himself hard against the wall. Raised his hand, ready to swipe any intruder off his feet and slam the hard bone of his wrist on to their neck. The *hannu* was as effective as a club.

A footfall. Then another. And a broad figure lumbered into the room. Burton had him on the floor faster than a heartbeat, raised his hand to strike.

'It's me!'

He recognised the booming Welsh voice at once. 'You were supposed to stay with the others.'

'Bah! That's what the old man said.' Dolan had developed a wary lexicon of contempt for Patrick: old man, Yank, (if he was out of earshot) chickenshit-bollocksucker. Their dislike had been instant and mutual, the type of animosity that only kindred spirits can find. That America had stayed out of the war seemed to affront Dolan further, as if Patrick were personally responsible.

Burton helped him off the floor. Even in the darkness, even with his face covered in camouflage cream Dolan still looked ruddy. 'Keep your voice down! *Major* Whaler was acting under my instructions.'

'I needed to know. Did you get the Kraut bastard?'

Burton had a flash of tears and blood. That curious belching sound as the knife tore into Hochburg's windpipe. An unanswered question.

'He's dead.'

In the darkness, Burton could make out Dolan's teeth as he grinned. He had too many of them, set like pillars in his mouth; a cannonball head; body as wide as two kegs roped together. The Welshman, an explosives expert, had been the original team leader before Ackerman visited the farm, something he bore with resentful good grace. At that moment he chuckled and gave Burton a triumphant thump round the shoulder. 'Did you catch my handiwork? BOOM! Must have bagged at least twenty Krauts with that.' He chuckled again.

'There'll be time for that later,' said Burton uncomfortably. 'For now, I want two flares. One at the top of the field. Another at the opposite end. You and Vacher get to it.'

A mock salute. 'Yessir.'

Burton watched him hurry away. He had known soldiers like Dolan before, boys who had never seen real combat, who considered the 1939–40 conflict a disgrace. They thought war was a rough and tumble game. Bulldog with grenades. In the Legion the *sous-officiers* would have had him spitting teeth by the first night but now, with all the wars over, discipline was slipping.

Following Hitler's surprise attack on the Low Countries and France in the spring of 1940, the British Expeditionary Force had been encircled at Dunkirk. For a few brief hours it was hoped that the troops might be evacuated, then came the order from Führer headquarters to smash the British into the sea. Forty-five thousand were killed, almost quarter of a million taken as prisoners of war, with fewer than five thousand managing to escape. 'The whole root, core and brain of our army destroyed', as Churchill admitted after he was forced to resign as Prime Minister.

In his place came Lord Halifax – cool-headed, pragmatic – who judged the public mood of dread and proposed a summit with the Führer to decide the future of Europe; there was no appetite for a protracted war, no repeat of 1914–18. Hitler agreed, declaring, 'If there's one nation that has nothing to gain from this conflict, and may even lose everything by it, that's England'. Despite rumbles of protest, Halifax's position was strengthened by the press and their 'Bring 'em Home' campaign. All that summer, as Spitfires and Messerschmitts battled over Britain, headlines called for the return of the Dunkirk POWs in exchange for peace. Mothers and wives took to the streets outside Parliament demanding their men back. Less publicly, ambassadors from the conquered nations of Europe were arriving in London and urged the Prime Minister to negotiate a settlement that might restore their independence.

In October Britain and Germany came to terms, signing a non-aggression pact and creating the Council of New Europe (the CONE in diplomatic-speak). The occupied countries – France, Belgium, the Netherlands, Denmark and Norway – would be granted their autonomy under newly elected right-wing governments, taking their place alongside Italy, Spain, Portugal, Sweden and Finland. It was also agreed that the Wehrmacht should maintain its foreign bases to ensure the stability of this new community. In the east, Britain promised to remain impartial if ever

Germany needed to defend its borders against Soviet aggression. Most of the Dunkirk prisoners were home in time for Christmas. Hitler congratulated the British people on their common sense; sent them a Yuletide tree to stand in Trafalgar Square – a tradition that had continued in the years since.

Other peace accords followed, guaranteeing the two countries' neutrality towards each other and returning the African colonies Germany had been stripped of by the Versailles Treaty.

The culmination was the Casablanca Conference of 1943 when the continent was divided – Churchill said 'cleaved' – between the two powers. Britain would retain its interests in East Africa (the only concession being the former German colony of Tanganyika); Germany would take the west, subsuming the territory of its newly independent European neighbours – one of Hitler's founding principles for the Council of New Europe. Not all had gone quietly. War raged in Congo for over a year, while the Free French, under General de Gaulle, put up a final stand in Douala, Cameroon, before being driven into the Atlantic by the Afrika Korps.

Since then a decade of peace and prosperity.

When Burton got back to the jeeps Patrick was waiting for him. 'If Dolan says one more thing I'll gut him, I swear—'

'I need you up top. See if you can spot the plane.'

'I told you already: I'm too old to climb trees.'

'It's either you or Dolan.'

The American humphed. 'Time?' he asked.

Burton checked his watch again: '02:19.'

'We should be able to hear them by now,' Patrick said, clambering upwards.

'I know.'

Patrick disappeared into the foliage. 'I never did trust Ackerman,' he called back after him through the leaves. 'Now the job's done we're just an expense.'

Burton stood for a few seconds longer, ear cocked to the sky, then climbed back into the Ziege next to Lapinski.

'I heard Major Whaler,' said the driver. 'What if he's right?'

Burton sighed. His feet ached in his boots; at least he was wearing socks. *'Be not faithless, but believing.'*

'Eh?'

'John, Chapter 20. Forget it. Ackerman will play us straight.'

'But what if they don't show?'

'Then I'm lucky I've got you.'

Lapinski gave him a quizzical look.

'It's going to be a very long drive back home. Don't worry, five minutes from now you'll be bellyaching about the turbulence.'

They fell into silence, Burton listening for the faint hum of propellers to the south. The flight was a regular Central African Airways one that flew freight from Salisbury in Southern Rhodesia to Khartoum each week. No Nazi operator would give the blip on his radar screen a second glance. Or so Ackerman had reassured them.

Lapinksi spoke again. Burton guessed he was jittery. 'I'm going to teach Elizabeth to drive. Buy her a car. That will impress her folks, don't you think?'

'Especially if you buy British.'

'I wouldn't think of anything else. A little Austin.'

'I'm sure they'll welcome you to the family,' Burton said, trying not to sound insincere. He knew the driver had only taken the job for the money, trusting a fat wallet to sway the prejudices of his sweetheart's parents. Poland no longer existed, Warsaw razed to the ground. An ex-corporal from an ex-country wasn't exactly what they had in mind for their little girl.

'I hope so, Major. She's all I ever wanted.'

'I know what you mean,' said Burton, thinking of Madeleine. Next moment, he held his finger to his lips: 'You hear that?'

Lapinski listened, then shook his head.

Burton leaned out of the window, cupped his ear. He was sure he had caught the distant hum of propellers, but now all he could hear was the sound of insects. *Das Heimchenchor*, his father used to call it. Burton wondered what they were saying to each other, what songs they sang. In this part of the jungle they would be oecanthinae: tree crickets.

At the far end of the runway a fountain of red light erupted. Dolan had lit the first flare.

'Let's hope it doesn't guide the Krauts to us,' said Lapinski.

Burton didn't reply, his ears still sifting the soundtrack of the night. When he was a boy Hochburg used to tell him tales about the crickets. How they had citadels hidden in the undergrowth, waged wars like men, bred warriors and princesses. And how one day – if Burton was *sehr artig* and didn't disturb him when he was praying with his mother – he'd teach him the crickets' secret language. Like so many of Hochburg's promises it never came to anything, but sometimes he would make strange chirping noises; then laugh at him.

Hochburg and his stories.

Burton shifted on his seat, hotter than ever, the SS uniform cloying against his chest; all he wanted to do was rip it off. He thumped the dashboard. 'Where's that fucking plane?'

As if to answer him the burr of propellers was suddenly heavy in the sky. How had he missed it? It was coming in from the south-west. Growing louder and more welcome by the second.

Burton and Lapinski abandoned the jeep and ran to the tree line. Dolan was already waiting. There was another flare of light as Vacher lit the second beacon. Burton glimpsed the silhouette of the young soldier as he hurried back towards them. A decade ago a night-time pick-up would have been impossible – even with flares. But Ackerman had supplied the pilots with the same equipment as Patrick. It was cascade tube, state-of-the-art, German manufactured of course.

'There she is!' boomed Dolan. He began to sing in Welsh, '*Lord, lead me through the wilderness* . . .' For once Burton didn't tell him to keep it down.

The plane was already on its final approach: a Vickers Viscount, its four propellers a grey blur against the sky, wheels low enough to skim the canopy.

The tree above them swayed and rustled and Patrick jumped to the ground, his own night-vision gear still wrapped around his head.

Burton beamed reassurance at him.

'We got Lebbs,' said Patrick. His tone conveyed no expression. 'A whole convoy. At least a dozen vehicles, some with MG48s.'

Burton's grin vanished. Dolan scowled at Patrick like it was his fault.

'Are they on our track?' said Burton. 'How long?'

Behind them the plane touched down, its wheels groaning as they hit the compacted earth of the runway. Instantly the engines began to power down to give the aircraft enough room to stop.

'If they didn't know we were here before, they do now,' said Patrick. 'Two minutes tops.'

'What if they send up a patrol?' Lapinski had asked the same question a hundred times during the training. 'We'll never outrun a jet-fighter.'

'They can't shoot down a commercial flight,' replied Burton for the hundred and first. 'Not without proof it's us.' This time his voice carried less conviction. 'Two minutes is plenty.'

The Vickers had slowed to a running pace, its rear hatch open. An airman emerged, descending with all the enthusiasm of a swimmer entering crocodile-infested waters. The Vickers trundled on towards the far end of the runway to turn around. Burton could make out the blue CAA logo on its tailfin. The airman beckoned towards them.

'Let's go,' said Burton. Nobody needed telling twice. They left the cover of the trees, Vacher joining them as they crossed the runway. Dolan kept glancing behind, his machine gun ready. He seemed disappointed when no Nazis emerged.

Even though the wind from the propellers was too far away to be felt, the airman was hunched up against it. 'Nares,' he introduced himself. 'You all set?'

Burton nodded.

'Good. Cos I don't want to spend a second longer on the ground than I have to.'

'That's why I love flyboys,' said Patrick.

Nares asked, 'Is the area secure?'

'Not for much longer,' replied Burton.

The airman's mouth turned queasy.

At the opposite end of the runway the Vickers had completed its turn and was ready for take-off. The pilots revved the throttle. Nares led the group towards the plane, not bothering to check if they were following him. They had three hundred yards to go. If the Nazis were closing in, the roar of the propellers drowned out their approach.

Burton glanced backwards. The runway was empty. So were the trees.

Ahead, another airman emerged from the plane and encouraged them on. Every wave of his hand said one thing. Home.

A surge of jubilation flooded through Burton. He was going to keep his promise to Madeleine. Five plus five plus ten: they'd never have to worry about anything again. Next to him, Patrick was running with the vigour of a free man, sniper rifle slung over his shoulder, pistol in his hand; he seemed younger.

They were fifty yards from the Vickers.

'Told you so,' Burton mouthed to his old friend; all his fears had been unfounded. He tore off his swastika armband and threw it to the wind.

The plane exploded.

Chapter Four

THEY both had secrets to tell that evening.

Burton and Madeleine were sitting in an arbour at the back of the farmhouse. They had bought the place earlier in the year after finally admitting their affair was something deeper: they wanted to be together. Madeleine, with her pluck and inner quiet, had given Burton a contentment he hadn't felt since childhood. In front of them was a lawn dotted with weeds, beyond that sloping orchards. Although the sun was setting the air was still warm from the day's cloudless heat. Whenever they moved, the arbour creaked beneath them as though it might splinter.

Just as Burton was about to speak, Madeleine broke the silence. Although her English was flawless she still carried an accent that spoke of Vienna and persecution.

'I've decided,' she said. 'I'm going to tell him. When I get back.' She sighed before adding, 'I'm so happy here.'

When Burton made no response, Madeleine turned to face him. She was wearing tailored slacks and a jersey. Her dark hair was tied in a loose ponytail, smelt of honeysuckle and breezy sweat. 'You don't look very pleased. I thought that's what you wanted.'

'It is.'

'Then why the face?'

Burton reached out for her hand and took hold of it. She had beautiful fingers – long, delicate, with nails always in a French manicure. They looked so fragile compared to his, so unblemished; Burton's hands were pockmarked with scars. Instinctively their fingers curled into each other's. Burton squeezed gently but still didn't speak. He felt elation at her words but also trepidation at what he must tell.

'Promise me we'll always live here,' she said. 'This place is perfect. So quiet after London. Listen: you can actually hear the sun setting.'

Burton cocked his ear to the sky. 'All I can hear is old man Friar chugging away on his tractor somewhere.'

Madeleine gave him a playful dig in the ribs. '*Komiker*. You know what I mean.'

'Are you really going to leave him?' asked Burton.

'I have to.'

'You promise?'

'We can't keep sneaking about like this. Besides, Alice is getting to the age where she understands. What if she says something? Better I tell him than he finds out.' She raised his hand to her lips. 'I want to be with you.'

They sat in silence for several moments, Madeleine waiting for a response.

Finally he said, 'I've got to go away.'

Madeleine smiled – that wide-eyed, girlish smile she used when teasing him. 'Go where?'

'I can't tell you.'

She smiled again. 'Oh, you know how much I like your surprises! What is it this time? More cakes? Silk underwear?'

'It's not that kind of surprise. It will only be for a few weeks.'

Madeleine stiffened. 'What do you mean?'

'I'll be back by the end of September.'

She snatched her hand back and stood up. 'You promised, Burton. You promised!'

'You'll wake Alice.'

'No more, you said. You were giving up that life.'

'I have.'

'Then what are you doing?'

'This is different.'

'And you tell me this now. Just when I want to leave him.'

Neither of them ever mentioned her husband's name any more: it was too awkward, too unsettling. He was simply referred to as *him*.

'It's got nothing to do with that. Of course I want you to leave him. How many times have I asked you? Do it when you get back to London. Then come and live here.'

'On my own.'

'I've already told you,' he said in a defensive voice. 'I'll be home in a few weeks.'

'And if you're not?'

'I will be.'

'No, Burton. I'm not going to do it.' Her hands curled into fists. 'I'm not going to walk out to find myself alone. Not again.'

'Please. Will you listen to me? I'm not saying that.'

'I didn't have a choice when I left Vienna. This time I do. Besides, there's Alice.'

'We need the money.'

'That's the type of thing my father used to say. Look where it got him.' She sat down again and put her face in her hands. A curl of hair came loose from her scalp. Burton watched it bounce up and down before tucking it behind her ear.

Madeleine looked up. 'Burton, I'm pregnant.'

'What?'

'I've been looking for the right time to tell you all day. But there was Alice, there was the house . . .'

'You can't be.' Burton suddenly felt like a boy soldier again on that first Legion march. Unsteady in the sand, tripping on the crests of dunes, tumbling in a cloud of dust and confusion. 'You're just saying that.'

'Four months. I was going to tell you last time but wanted to make sure first.'

'Is it mine?'

A stab of such profound pain creased Madeleine's face that Burton felt it in his own heart.

'He hasn't touched me in months,' she replied.

'I'm sorry,' he said. 'I didn't mean that.'

The last time Madeleine visited they had gone for one of their strolls and ended up making love beneath an ancient oak. Burton could see the spot now. He remembered the roughness of the ground, the creamy, taut flesh of her thighs: she brought the world alive for him. As they lay there afterwards, semi-naked on the grass, Madeleine joked, 'I won't be doing this come January.' Burton had laughed and traced the meniscus of her belly, thinking it looked a little swollen. He had put it down to her insatiable sweet tooth, never once suspecting she might be carrying a child. His child.

'We'll definitely need the money,' Burton said.

'No, we won't.'

'How will we live? We're not going to get rich on quinces this year. Meantime the place is falling apart.'

'Do you think I care?'

'I've seen how you live, remember. The servants. Hot water. Furniture so expensive you could buy a racehorse with it.' Every time he pictured her house in Hampstead his thoughts turned to shards of the blackest glass. 'I want to give you all that.'

'How many times do I have to tell you? None of it matters. I'd sleep on the floor as long as I was next to you.'

Burton felt a pang go through him. 'What about my aunt? Do you have any idea how it felt to take that money from her?'

'It bought you the farm.'

'*Us* the farm.'

'It was only a loan. She wanted to give it to you.'

Yes, thought Burton. Blood money to make up for her sister. 'This job pays a fortune,' he said. 'I do it and everything is ours.

No debt, no loans. We won't have to worry about anyone. My aunt. Him. I'll be able to get you everything you want. And the baby.'

'But I don't want anything!' The words came out as a howl of exasperation. 'Just a future. If you go away, you might never come back.'

'Does he know? About you being pregnant.'

'That's why I have to leave. It was scandal enough when he married me. Can you imagine how he'll react to this?'

'And I thought it was because you were so happy here.'

Madeleine puckered her mouth to control the rising tears. 'Why are you doing this? What job could be so important?'

'I can't tell you. There's no time.'

'No time: when are you leaving?'

'Tomorrow morning.'

Her eyes began to blur. Burton reached out to touch her, but Madeleine brushed him away. An angry, hurt flick of the hand. 'You promised.'

'And I promise I'll be back.'

'And the next time? How many other promises will there be? You won't even tell me where you're going.'

Burton slid off the arbour and knelt before her. Her face was flushed, so beautiful he wanted to cup it and kiss her. Instead he took her hands. Madeleine resisted before allowing their fingers to entwine again.

'Africa,' he said. 'That's where I have to go.'

Madeleine tried to pull away but he held her fast. 'It's Angola, isn't it?' she said. 'I heard it on the wireless: the Nazis are going to invade.'

'No. German Africa. Kongo.'

'But you don't care about Africa any more. Nobody does. What is it they say? Let the Germans get on with it—'

'Because the alternative is worse, and at least there's peace and we kept the empire and it's all so far away . . . I know, I read the papers.'

'Then why?'

For an instant Burton saw Hochburg's face, laughing like a jackal. Then the smoking ruins of his childhood home: burned timbers, wawa trees, the indifferent flow of the Oti River. 'It's to do with the past. A score that needs to be settled.'

'You said it was for the money.'

Burton hesitated. 'It's both. I swear to you I'll be back in three weeks.'

'And I'll be in London. I can't do it, Burton. Leave if you must – but don't ask me to wait. It's too much.'

'After all we've been through? All those plans we made?'

'I don't remember mentioning Kongo in any of them.'

'What about the baby?'

'I want another girl. Want her to know her father.' Fear was rising in her voice. Fear, hysteria, a torrent of weeping. Madeleine rarely cried, even after her husband's outbursts.

'You're talking about me as if I'm already dead.'

'You won't even tell me why.'

Burton hesitated. 'To kill a man. A Nazi.'

'A Nazi?'

'One of the SS leadership. Someone who stands for everything you hate.'

'I don't need a lecture on the Schutzstaffel.'

'Everything that's wrong in Africa.'

'Kill him and you change nothing. Another will come in his place. And another. What is it Goebbels says? This is going to be the German millennium. It's not worth it.'

For a long moment Burton said nothing, just looked at her hands in his.

Then he told her.

Told her it all. A tale he had never breathed to a single soul, not even Patrick. And every time he mentioned Hochburg's name his resolve grew more bloodthirsty. Burton never imagined he'd be a father. The idea filled him with panic and pleasure equally. But even less did he think he'd be an absent parent. Not after what his mother had done. He sometimes wondered if he was still that fourteen-year-old boy watching the tree line, hoping that one day she might emerge again from the jungle.

Madeleine listened intently. She knew his parents had died when he was young. But not how. That part of his childhood had always been an omission to her, something he was ashamed to admit. Maddie had learned to accept the cruelties of life, why couldn't he? At first she was intrigued, then tears fell from her eyes. Finally her face became as cold and impassive as a mountain god. It was as if she were seeing Burton anew.

By the time he finished a thin, chilly mist was curling off the fields. For a while neither of them spoke. Close by, Burton heard the wind-chime that hung over the back door. It had been his mother's, was one of the few possessions of hers he still had. When he was a boy she had taken to decking their home with them, much to Father's disapproval. At night Burton would fall asleep to their shimmering.

'I'm hungry,' said Madeleine eventually.

'You want me to make you something? How about a jam sandwich?' She loved jam sandwiches, especially with bread dipped in milk, eaten off one of their chipped plates with a knife and fork.

She shook her head. 'You know, I sometimes wonder what would have happened if things were different. Would I still be in Austria? Or shipped off to Madagaskar? What about my parents? My brothers, sister?' Her voice trailed off.

'We wouldn't have met.'

'Papa used to say, let them have their fun. They'll soon get bored and leave us alone. I think he believed it, even as they made him scrub the streets. Even when they spat in his face.'

Every time Burton heard this story he wanted to pull Maddie into his chest and never let go.

'But if I could get my hands on those fuckers,' she continued, 'if I could make them feel all this—' she thumped her breast '—I'd do it without a care.'

Burton felt the tension in his gut slacken: she was going to give her blessing. He didn't think he could have left without it.

'But you, Burton, you should forget it. You've kept this buried in you so long, it should stay in the ground. There's nothing for you in Africa.' She looked him full in the eye, pleading and defiant. 'Hochburg's a ghost. *Don't bring him back to life*.' She spoke those last words in German.

'I love you, Madeleine,' said Burton. 'You've given me so much. But I need to do this, need to know the truth about my mother.'

'And what will it bring you?'

He traced the lines on his palm. Before they had met his life had been brutal, incessant. *We're hollow men*, he remembered a fellow legionnaire once saying, *lost violent souls*. That's why he had signed up to begin with: the Legion's hard days and short nights left little time for dwelling on the past. That's why he had returned to Africa when the rest of Europe was celebrating peace. He needed something to slake his rage, to blot out the past. Except somehow the past always managed to bore through. The same unanswered questions taunting him. Now he had a chance to exorcise them for good.

'A future,' he replied. 'No more looking back, always wondering what happened. I'm so tired of it. Once I know the truth, once Hochburg is dead, I'll never leave you or the baby or Alice again.' He turned his eye to the orchards, the dilapidated farm buildings around them. 'Everything I want is here.'

For a long moment Madeleine was silent again. 'Three weeks?'

'There's a flight back from Egypt on the 18th. In plenty of time for the harvest. We'll have a huge tagine to celebrate.' Burton forced a laugh. 'I'll cook. Lamb with quinces, like in the Legion, you never tasted anything so good.'

'Lamb's not in season, silly.' Her voice ached with misery.

'Then mutton. Or beef. All washed down with champagne. Something to toast our future.'

A long pause, then Madeleine spoke. 'I'll be waiting for you, but don't you dare – *don't you dare* – get yourself hurt. Or killed.'

He took her in his arms, cupped the back of her head with his hand. It felt as if he were holding the entire weight of her. 'You have my word, Madeleine. I promise you.'

And he had meant it.

The burning plane was to have taken him to Khartoum; then to Cairo, London and finally back to that potholed driveway and home.

Chapter Five

𝔄 screaming sound. A second rocket slammed into the plane. Then a third.

Burton hit the deck, the stench of kerosene and fire in his mouth. Another missile screamed past. Hidden among the trees he could see a *Nebelwerfer*, a rocket-lorry.

Burning debris rained down on them. Dolan was rolling around, the whole of his left arm in flames. Patrick tore off his smock and threw it over the Welshman, smothered the fire. Bullets were whipping round them like hailstones.

For several seconds Burton was overcome with disbelief . . . then he was on his feet yanking Lapinksi up next to him. 'Back to the jeeps. Everyone: move!'

They sprinted to the vehicles. From all round the perimeter of the airfield soldiers were appearing. Burton recognised the black uniform of the Waffen-SS, the grinning skull badges.

'What about him?' said Lapinski as he started the Ziege.

Nares was still standing where they left him, eyes clenched shut, his body shaking violently. Somehow not a single bullet had struck him. 'Nares!' Burton called. 'Move yourself!'

The airman remained dumbfounded.

'Leave him,' said Patrick.

Burton darted back, willing himself not to get hit. He grabbed

Nares and dragged him to the jeep. They were off before he even closed the door.

Gunfire raked the windscreen, shattered part of it. Burton got a face full of glass: a thousand burning stings. Troops appeared in front of them. Lapinski floored the accelerator, knocking through them like skittles. Burton snatched a glimpse of a startled white face. Next moment it was gone. Somewhere there was another blast.

'Stop the jeep,' said Patrick from the rear.

'Faster!' yelled Burton. 'Faster!'

'I said stop.'

Lapinski ignored him. Suddenly Patrick was between them, his pistol hard against the driver's head. 'Stop it now!'

Lapinski stamped on the brakes. They all lurched forward as the jeep skidded to a halt. The engine stalled. Behind them the second vehicle, driven by Vacher, also tried to stop. There was a crunch of metal and glass as the two collided.

'Are you fucking crazy?' said Burton.

The driver was struggling with the ignition.

'The road,' said Patrick; he was still wearing his night-vision equipment. 'I'll cover you.'

Burton was out of the Ziege in an instant. Behind them headlights were beginning to appear like the eyes of monsters. Stretched out in front was a chain of steel spikes, enough to shred the tyres of any vehicle. Burton prised the chain off the ground and hurled it into the jungle.

'Major?' Dolan was also out of his vehicle. In his fist was a bundle of dynamite.

'Twenty seconds,' Burton shouted back.

Dolan flicked a timer and wedged the explosives at the base of a tree then clambered back into the Ziege. Vacher hit reverse, manoeuvred round the lead vehicle and throttled away.

Lapinski had restarted the engine, was revving it wildly.

Burton got in beside him. 'Go!'

Before he could press the accelerator again they were surrounded by soldiers. There was a burst of gunfire, close enough to taste. The remainder of the windscreen vanished. The jeep's cab exploded in sparks and smoke, somebody screamed.

Burton pulled his Browning and fired it blindly out of the window.

The jeep lurched forward in first gear, the revs biting red. They were heading off the road, into the trees.

'Lapinski. Watch out,' cried Burton, turning to the driver. He was slumped over, foot jammed on the throttle. Half his face was missing.

Burton grabbed the wheel and pulled hard to avoid the trees. The jeep bashed a trunk, buckling the bonnet, but skidded back on to the road.

In the rear Nares was bawling.

Burton reached for the handbrake, yanked it with such force he felt it would rip off. The jeep ground to a halt. Nearby he heard German voices. And the silenced retort of Patrick's rifle.

He hauled Lapinski back and stared at him for a moment that seemed to last for ever. His skull was caved in, the blood turning black as it gushed out. The one remaining eye looked accusingly at him for what would happen next.

Burton opened the driver door. Shoved Lapinski's body out. Climbed over and took the wheel.

There was an explosion as Dolan's dynamite detonated, then a terrible cracking sound as the base of the tree gave way and the trunk crashed down across the road. Burton stamped on the throttle. The jeep bucked up and down. 'I need the lights on,' he shouted back at Patrick.

'You want more of them shooting us?'

'I can't fucking see! Kill the rear ones.'

Burton flicked the main beams as Patrick leaned over the side and smashed his rifle butt into the red glass below. Ahead the road was bathed in silver light, Dolan already disappearing beyond its glow. The road was bumpy but straight. Burton watched the speedo rise to 30 kph. Then 40, 45, 50. Behind them the flash of gunfire began to diminish till it was swallowed by the jungle. Burton let out a sigh of strangled relief.

In the rear-view mirror Patrick scowled at him.

They drove through the night, always sticking to the old dirt roads. To the west were the vast rubber plantations of Volkswagen, producing cheap tyres for their ubiquitous People's Car; the coffee and cocoa fields that kept Europe happy at breakfast. But this region, deep in the interior, had largely been ignored since Deutsch Kongo became the official name of the country. Burton was astounded at how much the jungle had swallowed Belgian efforts to master it. There's a lesson for the Nazis here, he thought. No matter how high they fly the swastika, sooner or later the vines will reach it.

At some point the road widened and Burton had overtaken the front vehicle. After that he stayed in the lead. Eventually the adrenaline subsided, his limbs grew stiff, the tiny cuts in his face began to sting. In the back Patrick had removed the night-goggles. His eyes were shut though Burton guessed he wasn't asleep – it was an old habit of his. He nestled his rifle close to him, tracing the words carved on the stock. Nares was as sweaty and pale as a man about to have his leg amputated.

An hour after sunrise, with the morning mists reducing visibility, Burton decided to stop. He slowed to 20 kph and when he spied a gap in the jungle turned off. Vacher followed. They reversed the vehicles under the trees, moving far enough beneath the canopy to be hidden from the road. Around them were the remnants of a native village. From the state of the rotting huts it was clear no one had lived there for a long time; not since the Windhuk Decree, thought Burton.

Windhuk, the capital of DSWA, Deutsch Südwest Afrika. In 1949 it had been the location of a conference chaired by Himmler to discuss 'the racial security of German Africa'. The details remained shrouded in secrecy, but in the months that followed the resettlement of the blacks to the Sahara – 'Muspel' – had begun. 'Ethnic reallocation and consolidation' was the official description, though exactly what this meant was a question most preferred not to ask.

Burton turned off the ignition. Silence except for the brittle pinging of the engines. After the constant roar of driving the sound seemed supernaturally loud, as if it might give away their position. The trees dripped above them.

Burton faced Patrick. Earlier in the night he'd put atropine drops in his eyes to dilate the pupils, a common practice among snipers to maximise the effect of night-vision equipment. His eyes were still wide: he looked manic and startled. 'You good, *Chef*?' Burton asked. *Chef*, his Legion title: boss.

'Nares has been hit.'

'Is it serious?' he said, turning to the airman. He was older than Burton, with a tuft of Stan Laurel hair, but somehow seemed younger. His lips were like strips of raw liver.

'Flesh wound,' replied Patrick. 'I already bandaged it.'

They got out of the Ziege and headed towards the others. As they approached, Dolan whispered something to Vacher. They exchanged knowing looks, then half stood to attention. Their eyes were bleary but expectant. Poor bastards, thought Burton, this was still some sort of adventure to them.

'Where's Lapinski?' asked Vacher.

Burton shook his head. 'Gone for six.'

'Oh.' The Rhodesian's face turned grey, his shoulders sagged. 'He was . . . a good bloke.'

'For a Pole,' added Dolan.

Vacher continued, 'Who gets to tell his fiancée when we get back?'

'We have to get there first,' said Burton. 'Anyone climb trees?'

Nobody answered.

'I need someone to get above the mist. See what's going on.'

'I already had enough tree climbing for one night,' said Patrick.

'I'll do it,' said Dolan, flashing the older man a toothy sneer.

'What about your arm?' said Burton. It was wrapped in moist

bandages, the hand that emerged from the end of the dressing livid.

'It's nothing.' He laid down his BK44 and shinned up the nearest trunk.

While they waited Burton reached for his canteen. He washed the blood – Hochburg's blood – from his hands, splashed his face. Then he raised it to his lips. 'The Kaiser!' he said to Patrick, an old Legion joke of theirs.

His friend ignored him.

Burton took a deep swig and handed the bottle round. 'Anybody have some food? I'm famished.'

'I got some oranges,' said Vacher. He retrieved them from the jeep. 'They remind me of home.' Vacher was the pup of the team with the alert eyes of a hunter and an expression that always seemed ashamed or apologetic. Physically he was as broad as Dolan, could almost be mistaken for his kid brother. Gorilla Dum and Gorilla Dee, Patrick called them; Vacher was Dee.

The oranges were doled out, Patrick taking a single segment and nibbling it slowly. When he finished he reached into his tunic for his pipe – his 'lucky pipe' – and flicked his lighter. Patrick had owned it since the Great War, believed that as long as it was safe, so would he be. The familiar smell of the smoke buoyed Burton.

Dolan rejoined them, his trousers smeared wet and green. Vacher handed him his share of the oranges. He wolfed them down. 'There's a chopper buzzing around way over to the south-east,' he said, spitting pips. 'Apart from that, nothing.'

'So we're safe?' asked Nares. His voice carried that distinctive Rhodesian twang.

'For now,' replied Burton.

They continued eating and drinking for a few minutes, everyone arching their backs. Vacher removed the magazine from his BK44 and checked the firing mechanism. The BK was the favoured weapon of the Nazis in Africa, manufactured in their millions in the SS factories of Muspel. It had been designed in the months following the invasion of Belgian Congo (as it was then still named) when soldiers found their traditional rifles jamming in the humidity. The BK44 had only seven moving parts, derived its name from its distinctively shaped magazine: *Bananen Kanone*. Banana-gun.

Burton reached for his map. He had to find a way out of Africa, back to Madeleine. That last night they had decided she should return to London, continue a pretence of normal life. Then back to the farm for Burton's homecoming on the 18th. She would tell her husband everything after that.

He spread the map over the bonnet of his jeep and began studying it. The others soon crowded around him. It was an old Naval Intelligence chart from 1943 with the original Belgian roads marked on it. Burton had added the new German highways in black; there was a mass of thick lines. He traced his finger along the paper until he tapped a point. 'I say we're here. Give or take a few miles.'

Dolan leaned over and nodded. Then he ran his finger a few inches north-east to a spot marked Doruma. 'I say we head for Sudan.' Nares stared at the map. 'It's got to be less than a hundred and fifty miles. We can be there by dusk. Across the border and safe by midnight.' He looked up expectantly at everyone.

Nares and Vacher nodded.

'I say British Nigeria,' said Burton.

A sharp intake of breath. 'With respect, Major,' said Dolan, 'are you fucking crazy? It's got to be—'

'Twelve hundred miles. I know. Straight through Aquatoriana.' Aquatoriana: formerly French Equatorial Africa, now the Nazis' central-west province.

'We'll never make it. What about fuel? I don't know if there's enough even to get to Sudan.'

'Fuel is a problem,' admitted Burton. 'But think about it: Doruma is the nearest crossing point. And with the Yu-Ba Minefield blocking the rest of the border – the most obvious. If you were the Lebbs where would you concentrate your efforts? It'll be like stepping into the lions' den.'

'He's right,' said Patrick reluctantly.

'What about Rougier?' asked Vacher. Lazlo Rougier was Ackerman's contact in Stanleystadt, the man who had provided them with the jeeps and weapons. They had all memorised the address of his safe house in case of disaster. 'Maybe he could help. Smuggle us down river somehow.'

Patrick shook his head. 'The Lebbs were waiting for us back there.'

'No,' said Burton in a rush. 'They chased us. You saw it yourself.' He didn't want to admit the alternative to himself.

'Screaming Minnies? Spikes on the road? I tell you, boy, it was an ambush. Ackerman double-crossed us.'

'So?' said Vacher.

'So if they knew about us, they know about Rougier. He's probably had his nuts cut off and mailed to Himmler already.'

Dolan said, 'He'd be a fool to talk.'

'Pain makes a fool of every man.'

'Me and Vacher have worked for Ackerman before. He's always played us straight. Paid well. You're talking shit, old man.'

'He checked out,' agreed Burton, intervening to head off a brawl. 'Everyone I asked agreed he was legitimate.'

'Maybe everyone was wrong,' replied Patrick.

Dolan ignored the comment. 'Who cares if we were set up, all that matters is getting out of here. I say we head for Sudan.' In 'we' he seemed to include Vacher; the Rhodesian offered no dissent.

Burton could see there was little point arguing. 'It will be crawling with Germans.'

'Then we fight our way out!' boomed Dolan. His eyes glinted at the thought, as if killing a few Nazis could change the world.

'Jesus H. Christ,' said Patrick, shaking his head.

'You got a problem, old man?'

'You want to get yourself killed?' Patrick sucked on his pipe. 'No problem at all.'

'Typical Yank: too scared to fight.'

A sigh. 'We're not all isolationists, you know.'

'Enough of you are. If you hadn't been such a chickenshit country, we could have taken on the Krauts. Given Adolf a good hiding.'

During his brief premiership, Churchill had repeatedly tried to coax the United States into the war. President Roosevelt was sympathetic to the British cause – but there was no popular support for it. The America First Committee urged the nation not to fight. There were enough problems at home, fixing the country's ruined economy, without embarking on European adventures. Congress agreed, ratifying the 1940 Neutrality Act. It had defined American foreign policy ever since.

'And where were you at Dunkirk?' asked Patrick. 'Still at school, mommy wiping your ass.'

'Where are you now?' Dolan's cheeks burned. 'Ready to piss yourself. I always said we didn't need you. You're too old. Too old and a coward.'

He's going to kill him, thought Burton. What would Patrick care now? One snap of the neck and Dolan would be dead.

Instead Patrick laughed – a short rumble of mirth – and said nothing. Next time Burton glanced at him he was gazing upwards, letting the misty sun warm his face.

'Okay,' said Burton, keen to move the subject on. 'We split into groups. You two head for Sudan. Me, Patrick and Nares for Nigeria.'

'I want to go with them.' Nares was pointing at Dolan and Vacher as if they were the only sane men in a tribe of lunatics. 'Sudan is closer.'

'Trust me: you don't.'

'Trust me, I bloody well do!' Nares had already moved towards the others.

'Listen, we need you. Nigeria is too far for us to drive alone, especially if—' he hesitated '—especially if one of us gets wounded. We need a team of three. Rotate the driving.'

'I'm sorry but it's not my problem.'

'You weren't so sorry when I saved your neck on the airfield.'

'I shouldn't have even got out of the plane.'

Dolan said, 'I'd think about that statement if I were you. Think about it very carefully.' He took a step away from the airman. Burton guessed what was going through his mind: liability.

Burton continued, 'Nares, this is a military operation. Which gives me senior rank. I'm not asking for you to come with us. I'm telling you.'

Nares looked at Dolan for support.

'The major's right. You'd probably be better off with him.'

The airman's fate was sealed.

'That's it then,' said Dolan. He seemed eager to be on the road again. 'See you back in Blighty.'

'Wait,' said Patrick. 'We need cover stories. In case we're captured.' It was standard escape and evasion procedure. 'If they catch the muzzle-monkey here—' he jerked his head towards Dolan '—I don't want him ratting us out.'

'What the fuck does that mean?'

'First click of the cell door and I guarantee you'll tell them everything. Right down to our boot sizes.'

Dolan went for his pistol – but Burton was faster. He stepped in between the two men.

'If it comes to it, you can lie about our foot sizes. But Patrick's right. We do need a cover story.'

Dolan's hand retreated from his gun, though he gave the older man a punch-in-the-teeth glare.

'Sudan and Aquatoriana are out,' said Burton. 'So that leaves east or south.'

Vacher chewed on his thumbnail. 'East doesn't make much sense, unless we want to go swimming. I reckon south.'

'Agreed,' replied Burton. 'To Stanleystadt. If they know about Rougier it will make sense.'

There were nods all around, everyone except Nares who hung his head.

Then they stood watching each other. No one spoke. The mist had thinned; in its place the morning heat pressed upon them.

It was like a physical presence emerging from the forest, determined to squeeze every last drop of sweat out of them. Somewhere a monkey screamed.

Patrick nodded to Vacher, gave Dolan the sweetest effluent smile, and headed behind one of the huts to urinate. Burton followed the other two to their Ziege, closed the door behind Dolan as he climbed in behind the wheel; his burned hand was turning a whitish-pink. Would they get through? Maybe. They might be stepping foot on British soil by the end of the week while he was lost and fuelless a thousand miles from sanctuary. For a moment he was tempted to give them a message for Maddie.

Dolan started the engine.

'Will we still get paid?' asked Vacher.

'I think things have rather moved on from that, Pieter. Remember, if you get caught: Stanleystadt.' He hesitated, searching for some parting words. 'I feel as if I should say something.'

'Save it, Major,' said Dolan. 'You've got a long drive.'

'Good luck,' said Burton. He didn't offer his hand.

'You too.'

Burton stepped away as the jeep rolled forward and joined the road. Moments later, with Patrick up front and Nares in the back, Burton's own vehicle followed. They drove in tandem for twenty minutes till the road forked. Dolan headed north, Burton turned the wheel west towards Aquatoriana.

And twelve hundred miles of unbroken Nazi territory.

Chapter Six

'WHAT shall we do with him?' asked the two SS troopers.

Gruppenführer Derbus Kepplar stared at the corpse they were holding. They had found it by the side of the road. Half its face was missing, the other half a trough for hungry insects. From the structure of its skull it looked like a Category Four: a fucking Polack.

'Was there any identification on him? Papers?'

'Just this. We found it in his pocket.'

One of the men handed over a photograph. Kepplar studied it: a young woman, northern European, a Two/Three. Good cheek-bones, adequate teeth. A wife or sweetheart no doubt. If the British tolerated such couplings no wonder their empire was rotting from within.

Kepplar tore the photo in quarters and tossed it aside. He looked back at the corpse's mangled face, then its black clothing and felt his stomach convulse.

'Strip him,' said Kepplar. 'No Slav deserves to wear our uniform. Then hang him out for the vultures. Let this be a warning to all our enemies.'

The SS men dumped the body and gleefully went to find some rope.

59

Kepplar's first reaction to the news about Hochburg was relief. Relief that his leave would be cancelled. For over a year he had been finding excuses not to return home till finally there were none left. Even Hochburg considered it was time for him to see his family again. A three-week stint in Germania seemed inevitable. Three weeks in his beautiful apartment on Tiergartenstrasse with his beautiful wife and their three beautiful children. Devoted blue eyes marvelling at his every move. At night he would dream of torching the building with his family in it. The only joy he ever took back home was watching Reichminister Speer's new metropolis rise towards the heavens or strolling down the Avenue of Victory.

Now events had saved him.

Kepplar was a One/Two, muscular with shaved blond hair and had been the genetic propagator of his children's eyes. Half his right ear was missing.

He had made the Mupe airfield his temporary command centre. On the roof technicians were establishing radio links; in the control room below, a map of Kongo was spread out over two tables, the positions of the roadblocks marked with black pins. Pursuit vehicles were already tearing through the jungle in all directions. Kepplar had to admit, however, that securing an area the size of Ostland was an impossibility, no matter what Germania was demanding. His best hope was that the assassins would try to cross into Sudan. That's where he would concentrate his efforts, east of the Yuba-Bangalia Minefield. Three truckloads of his finest troops were preparing to leave for the border, along with his own Ziege and motorcycle outriders.

An adjutant hurried into the room and addressed Kepplar. 'Herr Gruppenführer, the Spanish consul has arrived from Stanleystadt.'

'Good,' said Kepplar. 'Now get me a line through to Sudan. It's imperative I speak to the British.' He left the control room and went to greet Señor Aguilar, the Spanish consul. Aguilar was leaning against the bodywork of his Mercedes. He was as fat as Göring, with a carrot-juice complexion.

'Heil Hitler!' said Kepplar, giving him a rigid salute.

'Heil! Kepplar, my old friend, what is it that brings me from my bed to the middle of the fucking jungle at this hour in the morning?'

They both spoke in German, the lingua franca in this part of Africa.

'Haven't you heard? The Governor General has been assassinated.'

Aguilar's face turned to the colour of sour milk. Kepplar guessed what he was thinking: who's going to pay for all my whores and silk suits now? The Mercedes had been a gift from Hochburg.

'That's why I've asked you here,' continued Kepplar. 'Germania wants independent verification of the facts. What's happened is an act of war. Did you bring a photographer?'

'Of course.' Aguilar clicked his fingers and a man with a Hasselblad and camera bag appeared.

'Please, come with me,' said Kepplar and he led the men towards the burned-out remains of the plane.

The morning air was already hot enough to soften leather. Kepplar felt his face prickle; it was covered in constellations of scarlet spots. The heat and humidity of the jungle wreaked continual havoc with his skin, no matter how much peppermint oil he rubbed into it.

A fire crew had doused the flames of the explosion but there was still an intense heat radiating from the centre of the wreckage. Kepplar led Aguilar and the photographer to the rear of the plane where the tailfin was still visible.

'As if I don't have enough to deal with,' lamented the Gruppenführer. 'Insurgents in the west, labour shortages – and now this!'

Aguilar looked at the charred CAA livery. 'Rhodesians? Are these your assassins?'

'Get your man to photograph everything,' replied Kepplar. 'From every last angle.' The photographer set to work. 'As far as we can tell,' continued Kepplar, 'there were two teams. A single assassin who posed as an officer of the SS and flew into Kondolele last night. And a support squad, four men, waiting for him in the jungle. They destroyed half of the Schädelplatz in the process.'

'Tut-tut. I always said the Führer should have pressed for Rhodesia when they re-drew the map. Or at least the north. It's good mining country, would have kept the British at arm's length.'

The photographer's flash popped.

'It's our belief that the British are behind this.'

Aguilar raised his eyebrows.

'The plane's Rhodesian.' Kepplar consulted his notebook. 'A commercial flight from Salisbury. But the killers themselves were mercenaries in the pay of London.'

'They wouldn't dare! I know Hochburg feared they'd try something like this. But I never once believed him. The British are too weak, haven't got the belly to fight any more. All they want is peace.'

Kepplar handed Aguilar a document wallet. 'I suggest you look at this.'

Aguilar opened the wallet and took out three ID cards. 'Dolan,' he said, reading the first card. 'Lieutenant, Welsh Guards. Born, 1928. Vacher – a Rhodesian. Lapinski—'

'A fucking Slav,' said Kepplar as if there were shit on his tongue. 'My men took him out. We have nothing on the other two. But we suspect they are also British.'

'Where did you get these?' demanded Aguilar.

'One of my blackshirts was brave enough to recover them from the plane,' said Kepplar.

Aguilar looked at the smouldering wreckage, then back at the pristine document cards. Spain had never fought in the war. Later, its long-standing neutrality made it a helpful arbitrator. As Hochburg used to tell Kepplar, the Spaniards offer the right kind of impartiality. The Führer was in agreement – making them the host nation at the Casablanca Conference; henceforth Morocco was a Spanish colony.

'I understand, my old friend,' said Aguilar. 'Understand perfectly.'

'Thank you, Señor. I know the Governor would have appreciated your loyalty.'

Aguilar licked his lips. 'You don't know who will replace him yet, do you? Perhaps yourself?'

'It is a job I would be unworthy of. But these are still early days. The German people, Africa, are in mourning.'

'Of course.'

The photographer had finished his work. They walked back to the Mercedes. 'I will write a report for Madrid at once,' said Aguilar. 'One they can pass on to the Council of New Europe, along with the documents and photographs. London should not be allowed to get away with this outrage.'

'If the British want fire,' said Kepplar, 'we shall burn them to the ground, just like Dunkirk. Thank you for your time, Señor Aguilar.'

He helped him into his car and watched as it disappeared towards Stanleystadt.

Kepplar strode back to the control room. An adjutant held out a field-phone as he entered. 'Herr Gruppenführer, I have the British for you. The OIC of the Muzunga garrison.'

Kepplar snatched the phone and placed it to his left ear. He could still hear with the other one but it was uncomfortable to rest a receiver against the stump. 'This is Gruppenführer Derbus Kepplar.' He spoke in English. 'I am the deputy to Governor General Hochburg. *Was* the deputy. The Governor has been assassinated.'

A hesitation at the other end of the line, then: 'I understand, Herr Kepplar. On behalf of Her Majesty's Government may I offer—'

'We have reason to believe the criminals responsible are heading towards Doruma. Our plan is to apprehend them before they reach it. But as a safeguard I want you to close your side of the border.'

'How can you be so sure they're heading here?'

'It's the only place to cross.'

Another hesitation. The line crackled. 'Herr Kepplar, I feel this is a diplomatic issue and should really be raised with Khartoum. I don't have the authority to close an international border—'

'The assassins are British.'

'Surely not, sir.'

'Germania will be making an official complaint to London later today, as soon as we have independent verification of the facts. In the meantime it would reflect badly on you if you were to let the murderers escape. One might see it as an admission of guilt.'

'Let me reassure you that no British soldier would ever be involved in such an act.'

'The only reassurance I want is that you will close the border. Immediately.'

The voice at the other end hesitated again. 'One moment, please.'

The line went silent. Outside SS soldiers were loading up the trucks with MG48s, their faces robotic and grim. Kepplar turned his eye to the portrait of Leopold III on the wall and studied his graffitoed cock. The king's great-grandfather had known how to run Kongo; pity the younger. He'd met the Führer in the autumn of 1940 and signed away his colony to guarantee Belgium a place in the Council of New Europe. The most expensive 'cone' in history went the joke at the time – one not shared by Belgium's colonists.

The phone came to life again. 'Herr Kepplar, the border will be closed straight away. No one will be allowed to cross over from Kongo until we get word from you.'

'Good.'

'If there is anything else we can do to assist—'

Kepplar terminated the call.

He beckoned the adjutant over. 'Send a signal to the Schädelplatz that the border has been closed. Let them know I leave for Doruma immediately. The British won't escape. I'll string them up for what they've done, do it with my own hands.'

Chapter Seven

Aquatoriana
14 September, 17:30

BURTON slammed on the brakes, bringing the jeep to a complete standstill; he couldn't take any more. It was late afternoon, the sun preparing for its nosedive towards the night.

In the back, Nares, who had been dozing, was suddenly wide-eyed and awake. 'What's happened?' he demanded.

After separating from Dolan they had driven till noon, crossing the Bomu River (the natural boundary between Kongo and Aquatoriana) before stopping to hide up and rest. By then the fog had withered away; in its place a festering, moist heat. While Patrick and Nares slept, Burton took the first guard duty, dripping sweat and trying to think himself cold. As he watched the jungle, he daydreamed of his first Christmas with Madeleine, the memory playing over and over.

It was an icy evening, not long after they'd got together, and they were supposed to meet under the tree in Trafalgar Square. Burton was late and as he rushed through London he convinced himself she would have long since left. They always did. But when he arrived Madeleine was still there. She'd spent an hour in the frost, stamping her feet, her nose an icicle. Burton had wrapped his arms around her in surprise and delight, felt the rosy chill of her cheek seep into him. She'd stayed!

Later, when Patrick took over the watch and Burton was unable to sleep, there were no more thoughts of Madeleine. Only Hochburg visited his weary mind. He'd risked so much to discover the truth about his mother – and had left the Schädelplatz with no answers. Just more blood on his hands.

At some point a jet-fighter streaked over the horizon but apart from that they saw no one. It was hard to believe they were being pursued. Indeed it was hard to believe that anything – beyond the legions of insects and howling monkeys – inhabited the continent at all. The lack of chase was disquieting; Burton hoped it didn't spell trouble for Dolan and Vacher. At 15:00 he started the engine again. For the last hour his eye had been fixed on the fuel gauge.

'What's happened?' repeated Nares.

'You get back to sleep,' said Burton. 'You're going to need it tonight. Me and the major need to talk.'

He turned to Patrick. He had spoken barely a word since they had been on the road. Simply sat there cradling his rifle, face impassive. Even his pipe failed to console him.

'Go on,' said Burton, 'say it.'

Patrick loosened the grip on his weapon. 'Say what?'

'You know exactly what.'

Patrick shook his head.

'"Told you so,"' said Burton.

'I'm not going to say that.'

'But you're thinking it.'

Patrick turned to stare at him; the skin around his eyes was a mass of crow's feet. 'Right now, Burton, in fact for the past hundred miles the only thing I've been thinking is how we – *how I* – get out of this.'

He had said the same thing three weeks earlier, in prison.

Patrick had been arrested on the Night of the Red Flag. With Hitler's victory over the Soviet Union in 1943, Britain found itself flooded with Communist refugees. They would arrive in lice-ridden ships having made the long journey from Krasnoyarsk, the Red Army's last fisthold of resistance. For a while their presence was tolerated, as long as they kept to the tenements of Tyneside and Aberdeen, but when newsrags began appearing in Cyrillic to demand better conditions, when Geordie and Scots were drowned out by Russian dialects, public opinion swayed. There were demonstrations and riots; banners demanding: *immigrants out!* The government acted. The lucky few were allowed to continue westwards; the rest were shipped back east, to a Greater Germany that now stretched beyond the Urals.

Soon the merest whiff of Communist sympathy – past or present – was like reeking of the plague. Stalin and his warmongers had almost brought catastrophe to Europe, what might their ilk do if allowed to poison Britain? Patrick was interned along with thirty thousand others on May Day 1950. 'Crazy thing is,' he told Burton, 'I was never a Commie, not a proper one. And definitely not after Spain or the Red Terror. How could anybody be?' All his requests to be repatriated to America were denied, his homeland refusing him back. Anyone against isolationism was deemed too subversive, old war heroes in particular.

At the beginning of Patrick's incarceration, Burton visited several times. Then his affair with Madeleine took a more serious turn and the visits became less frequent till they stopped altogether. Burton liked to fool himself this was because he'd rather be in Maddie's bed than reminiscing about best forgotten battles. The real reason, however, was embarrassment. Embarrassment that he could do nothing to help his friend.

Then Ackerman had come jangling his diamonds. Burton was at the internment camp two days later.

It was one of a series on the Norfolk coast: a defunct, windbattered army base. Burton was ushered into a Nissen hut with a row of tables, chairs on either side. There were a few other visitors, mostly wives in shabby coats. The air smelt of sour mops. It was more depressing than he remembered. Burton hadn't seen Patrick in over a year but did not expect the time to have changed him; he'd seen plenty worse. The prisoner who was led in, however, had a slight stoop, looked as if the smell of potato soup had seeped into his veins, whittled his muscles. His hair was thinner and grey. For the first time he looked like a man in his late fifties.

They stood separated by the table, appraising each other. If Patrick was self-conscious about his decline he made no show. Burton offered his hand.

Patrick brushed it aside. 'For chrissake, boy,' he said and reached across to hug him; their embrace was brief but warm. Patrick's body felt bony. 'It's been a long time. Too long.'

'I'm sorry I stopped coming,' said Burton ruefully.

'No, you're not.'

Burton grinned, this was more like the Patrick Whaler he knew.

'I guess it was that dame of yours,' continued Patrick.

Burton nodded.

'Don't blame you. Given a choice between this dump and some Sheba I know which I'd choose.' There was no bitterness in his voice; he seemed glad that Burton had finally found someone. 'I bet she's a brunette, right? Real tough cookie.'

'How d'you figure that out?'

'After all those helpless blondes it makes sense. Got a ring on her finger yet?'

'No.'

'Smart. Kids?'

Burton allowed himself a secret moment of pleasure. 'No. But we do own a farm. Quinces and apples mostly. It's a beautiful place.'

Patrick looked at Burton for a moment, then shook with laughter. 'Burton the farmer. Never thought I'd see that.'

'That's Maddie for you – she found the decent side of me.'

They sat and Burton produced a tin of baccy from his pocket. 'It's your favourite, Brindley's.'

Patrick's eyes danced. He reached for his pipe, stuffed the bowl till it was brimming and lit up. A billow of molasses smoke drifted between them. It was the smell Burton always associated with his old commanding officer.

'I got news of my own,' said Patrick tonelessly. 'Ruth's dead. Pancreatic cancer.'

'Who's Ruth?'

'My wife.'

Burton looked away, he always forgot that Patrick was married. He'd abandoned his family a decade before, rarely mentioned them. 'I'm sorry. How did you find out?'

'My daughter wrote me. She's fourteen now.' He reached inside the pocket of his prison uniform and withdrew an envelope. It looked worn as if the heat from Patrick's body was eroding it. From the envelope he took a black and white photo. A portrait.

'Her name's Hannah. She wants me home.'

'I thought she never—'

'It's was her mom's dying wish. She's living with Ruth's sister now. In Baltimore. Hates it.'

Burton took a closer look at the picture. He saw a girl with slightly malnourished features, blonde hair in pigtails. There was an emptiness to her smile. He could see nothing of Patrick in her. 'She's beautiful.'

He slid back the photo. A silence descended between them again, disturbed only by the murmur of the other prisoners and their visitors. One man occasionally erupted into bitter laughter.

The movement was so fast Burton didn't see it coming.

Patrick lurched over the table and grabbed his cuff. Across the room, a guard hurried towards them; Burton waved him off. Patrick's grip could have crushed steel.

'You have to help me. You're the only friend I got. I need out of here. Need to get back home. To America.' He let go, all the strength sagging out of him, and sat slumped in the chair.

Burton leaned forward, his voice dropping. He felt the tingle of conspirators. 'You're in luck, old friend. Remember that retire-for-good job we used to talk about? It found me.'

'North Angola,' said Patrick with excitement. 'The warders keep saying how the Lebbs are going to invade.'

'Not Angola. Kongo.' Burton explained about meeting with

Ackerman. His plan to kill Hochburg. Their escape. The team: Lapinski, Dolan, Vacher. 'He's C Squadron, SAS; you'll like him.' Ten days of training in the Rhodesian bush. 'I've got transport,' he said, 'munitions, firepower. Everyone speaks German. What I don't have is someone salty. Someone to watch my back. What do you say?'

Patrick had listened intently to everything, sucking on his pipe. When Burton finished he rolled his head and looked out of the window at the far end of the Nissen hut. Burton followed his eye, waiting for him to say, 'How much?' After Dunkirk the only thing that mattered to Patrick was the money; if governments no longer cared about rights and wrongs, if the man on the street didn't, why should he? Through the window Burton glimpsed grey barracks and an even greyer sky. Sidi Bel Abbès hadn't offered much more, but at least it had a vigour, that contrast between the mustard-coloured rocks and endless blue sky. He remembered how much he wanted to bludgeon Patrick back then. But that was the *esprit* of the Legion, its baptism of sand and blood: you had to hate your superiors before you could learn from them.

'I have full authority to get you out of this place,' continued Burton. 'Ackerman's got more contacts than we've had cold, miserable dinners.'

'No.'

'You can leave straight away. Tonight. Then we fly to Lusaka to meet the others.'

'Burton, you're not catching me. No.'

'Once the job is done you'll be free to return to America—' Burton stopped as if he were hearing Patrick's response for the first time. 'What do you mean, no? You can't possibly want to stay here?'

Patrick shook his head. 'All you're giving me is *la main en bois*.' *La main en bois*, an old Legion expression: the wooden hand. A suicide mission.

'You said the same about Dunkirk.'

'And I was right. We just got lucky that day.'

'That was more than luck.'

'Tell that to the poor sonsofbitches who didn't make it. You remember afterwards? I never saw the sea so red.'

Burton watched Patrick's hand drift towards his stomach. Beneath his prison uniform was a poorly stitched, half-moon scar. His Dunkirk scar.

'Sounds like prison's given you too much time to think,' said Burton.

'Maybe you're right. Or maybe I figured out that's all war is. Luck. And you only got so much.'

'Trust me. Kongo will be a pip. Quick and safe.'

'Safe?' Patrick snorted. The gesture could have signified amusement or derision.

'What we did ten years ago, saving all those fat Frenchmen and their mistresses, that was much worse.'

'And the poodles,' said Patrick, laughing suddenly. 'You remember the guy with the poodle?'

Burton joined him. 'Ten thousand francs for a dog. Fat days for mercenaries. I never did know what you did with that money.'

'Same as you: wasted it.'

'Not me. I kept enough to buy the farm – or at least half of it.'

'I used to have a mattress stuffed with cash . . .' Patrick's mood plummeted again. 'And I never sent anything to Ruth or Hannah. Not a single dime.'

'Now's your chance to give some back.'

'Don't twist this, Burton. There's nothing I want more than to see my girl again. She was five last time we met. But you're talking a one-way job.'

'Ground time will be less than four hours,' said Burton. 'You'll fly commercial to Stanleystadt, pick up the jeeps from Ackerman's man there, drive to the RV. I do my bit. And we're home. What can go wrong?'

'When was the last time you were in Africa?'

Burton shrugged. 'Not since Madeleine.'

'It's a whole new ball game. The Afrika Korps have been dumped. The SS are in charge now and they're . . .' He raised his fist and squeezed it till his knuckles cracked. 'Life don't mean shit to them.'

'Since when did you care about what they were doing?'

'I don't. I don't want to die there either.'

'You can't tell me this place is preferable.'

'They'll let me out in the end. They have to. For chrissake I was a Communist twenty years ago, when it still mattered. Before we all shacked up with the Nazis and convinced ourselves we were saving the world.'

He's getting old, thought Burton, old and scared. That's what this was really about. 'You're still a soldier, Patrick. The best shot I ever knew.'

'Don't give me all that baloney. You're twisting things again.'

'Then help me.'

'Since when did you play the dice? You were always the cautious one. Not me. Can't you see what this job is?'

Burton leaned forward. 'Patrick – *Chef* – I need you on this. What do I have to say to convince you? You can spend the next ten years in here. Or you can be out tonight. A month from now you'll be on a flight to New York.'

'You know I hate planes.'

'Boat then, the *Queen Mary*. Luxury all the way.'

'It's easy to make promises to dead men.' But his voice gave him away, something was shifting.

Burton pushed on, dredging every memory he could. 'You'll be able to buy that house. You know that one you always used to talk about. In New Mexico.'

'In Las Cruces? You remember that?' Patrick seemed touched. 'I still think about it every day, walk the rooms in my head.'

'That's your toss-up. Another fifteen years of this or you and Hannah on the terrace, sipping cool drinks. Watching the sun go down over the mountains. Besides—' Burton shifted awkwardly '—you still owe me.'

'I wondered when you'd bring that up.'

'I never called in that favour. Never. You know that.'

'Just feels as if you did,' said Patrick. 'Every time you need something.' He put down his pipe, linked his fingers behind his head and looked down at his uniform. It was a size too big – or maybe he'd become a size too small – and threadbare, nothing like the perfectly fitting legionnaire's capote and kepi he used to wear with such pride. His boots were all spit, no polish. 'Jesus H. Christ,' he said. 'Guess I don't have a choice.'

'Of course you got a choice. You can stay here and rot.'

'If I leave with you tonight, what's to stop me from disappearing?'

'Twenty years of friendship?'

Patrick snorted again.

'We'll have your passport,' Burton said.

'Like that's going to stop me.'

'You'll have no money. No papers. Besides, I know where you'll be headed.'

'That a threat?'

Burton shook his head sadly. 'Kongo will be safe, you have my word. I've figured it all out. By the time the Lebbs know what's happened we'll be homeward bound.' Later he thought about that vow. And the one he made to Madeleine. It seemed the whole mission was founded on broken promises. A chain of them running through him, Ackerman, right back to his mother.

Patrick leaned forward in his chair, teetering on a decision but still unsure. He rubbed his hand over his chin. Burton saw patches of white stubble on it: too much shaving with blunt razors. The laughing prisoner was at it again, chortling like a man who inherits a million on the same day he is sentenced to death.

Burton stood and prepared to leave. 'I have a flight to catch. I'll give you thirty minutes to think about it. Then I'm gone. I'll try and make sure you get regular tobacco.'

'Wait,' said Patrick. 'You bought yourself an American.'

Burton felt a surge of relief. 'Thank you. Thank you, old friend.'

'But, remember, this is to get back home. This is for my daughter, not you. Things fuck up, boy, and you're on your own. I'll leave you without a second thought. Every man for himself.'

'Like I did at Dunkirk?'

'That was different.' There was a snarl behind Patrick's lips. 'You get hurt I won't be hauling your ass home.'

Burton forced a smile. 'Too heavy for you?'

'No. Twenty years or not, I'll put a bullet in your head.'

'So I was wrong.' Back in the jeep, the sun starting its rapid decline. This close to the equator it went from daylight to pitch black in less than thirty minutes.

'No more bullshit,' said Patrick. He inverted his pipe to make sure the glow of the tobacco didn't give away their position as it grew darker. 'What aren't you telling me, Burton? Why did you want this job? I never saw you so sand-happy for anything.'

For a second Burton was tempted to tell him it all – Hochburg, his parents, all the secrets between them – but now wasn't the time. Not with Nares pretending to sleep in the back, ears twitching. 'I told you. The money. I was desperate. It was the only way I was going to get Maddie.'

'She must be some woman.'

'You're getting paid for this?' Nares had moved up from the back. 'What are you? Mercenaries?'

'No,' said Patrick. 'We're on fucking safari.'

Burton spoke: 'Didn't Ackerman brief you?'

'Who?'

'Ackerman. Our paymaster, from LMC.'

'Never heard of him. We fly in diamonds once a month. That's all.'

'Smuggling?'

'Of course smuggling, for the Nazis. I'm not stupid. But we're a commercial flight. We get a little extra for the detour and no questions. We've never picked anyone up before though. Never had anything like this.' His voice stumbled. 'I flew with those blokes for three years.'

'I tell you,' said Patrick, 'it was a set-up. The Lebbs were waiting for us.'

'We don't know that,' replied Burton.

'You saw the firepower.'

'And you saw them on the road chasing us.'

'That's my point. We left the Schädelplatz in a mess. There's no way they could have gotten to the airstrip so quick.'

Nares said, 'What did you do? That was a small army we escaped from.'

'We killed someone. *I* killed someone.'

'Who?'

'You really don't know?'

Nares shook his head.

'A man called Hochburg. A Nazi—'

'The Governor General?' The airman turned white. 'We're dead. We're fucking dead!' Suddenly there was venom in his voice. 'Why?'

'Diamonds,' said Burton.

'But we were already flying in diamonds.'

'I'm not talking the rocks themselves, I mean mining. The Kassai fields.'

'But they're in Kongo, belong to the Germans.'

'Yes, but they're mined by LMC. Have been since Belgian times. It was one of the conditions of Britain not getting involved when the Germans invaded in '44.' Burton shook his head in dismay. 'All standing mineral concessions would be honoured.'

'So why the smuggling?'

'The concessions were only guaranteed till 1950. After that they were up for renewal. For the past two years LMC has been paying Hochburg a "fee" to make sure they kept the mines. Twenty per cent of all production.'

'But that's more than any man could spend! Hochburg would be a king.'

'He wasn't spending the money on himself. He wasn't corrupt.' Burton almost felt like defending him: greed had never been one of his vices. 'He was buying workers from Russia.'

'Shitloads,' added Patrick. 'On the QT, so nobody knew. And that type of quiet don't come cheap.'

Nares shook his head as if none of this made any sense to him.

'There's a labour shortage,' explained Burton. 'Here in Kongo, in all of Nazi Africa. Nobody to build the roads, dig the sewers, work the plantations.'

'Get the *kaffirs* to do it.'

Burton flinched at the word. The one time he'd used the word as a child his father boxed his ears. 'Except there aren't any. All the blacks have been shipped to Muspel. You must know the rumours – the ones we all pretend to ignore.'

'You mean the Windhuk Decree?'

Burton nodded. 'So now they've all gone, Hochburg needs five thousand new workers a month.'

'But why kill him?'

'Ackerman got word he was going to change their arrangement. Put the mines under Nazi control. That way Hochburg would get all the loot, not just a percentage.'

'And what about Hochburg's replacement?'

'New man, new deal.'

'But what if the next Governor didn't want to cut a deal?'

'I been thinking about that too,' said Patrick. 'Nares is right. Ackerman had no guarantee of what would happen next ... unless he already knew.'

'What are you saying?'

'I think Ackerman was deeper into this than he let on. He knew exactly who was going to replace Hochburg. Somebody who would continue their deal on the same terms. Maybe that was the price for getting rid of Hochburg in the first place.'

'But a decision like that could only come from Germania,' said Burton. 'From high up. Maybe Himmler himself.'

The statement settled between them like an unwelcome guest.

'We're dead,' repeated Nares, 'we're fucking dead.'

'They haven't managed it yet,' said Patrick grimly.

'I can't believe it,' said Burton in a rush. 'Ackerman's too small fry. How could he ever get Germania's ear? They don't care about Africa.'

'What did he tell us about Kassai?' replied Patrick. 'Seventy per cent of the world's diamond production! Twenty million carats a year! That talks plenty loud.'

'You think he set us up?'

'If he did, he better pray I never catch him. But there's something else. Something that's been on my mind.' He turned to eyeball Burton. 'Why you?'

Since that first morning on the farm Burton had been asking himself the same question. It was a thought quickly stifled. The desire to see Hochburg again, to learn the truth then plunge a knife deep in his heart had been too consuming.

'Ackerman could have chosen anybody for this job,' continued Patrick. 'In fact he did. He chose Dolan. Then at the last minute comes knocking on your door. Why?'

'He said I was the best.'

'And you believed him?'

'Shhh!' said Nares. 'I can hear something.'

Burton and Patrick stopped speaking. Outside the jeep came the relentless shriek and throb of the jungle. Patrick turned irritably to the airman. 'I don't hear anything.'

'Listen.'

Over the insects a sound was swelling through the trees. Indistinct at first, but getting louder, the cry of a wolf cub at the bottom of a well. For an instant Burton couldn't identify it . . . then he slammed the jeep in gear, the tyres spitting earth as they tore away.

Patrick craned his head out of the window. 'It's right on us. Foot on the gas, boy! Hard as you can.'

'It's no good,' wailed Nares. His eyes were stretched wide again. 'We'll never outrun it. We'll—'

But before he could finish a black shape screamed overhead.

Chapter Eight

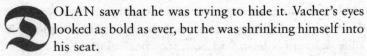OLAN saw that he was trying to hide it. Vacher's eyes looked as bold as ever, but he was shrinking himself into his seat.

'Maybe the major was right,' he said.

'Bah! Too late for that now,' replied Dolan as he slowed down the Ziege. 'We haven't got the juice to turn back. Unless you want to ask the Krauts for some.'

Vacher chewed on his thumbnail, remained silent.

'Don't worry,' continued Dolan, struggling to sound chummy. 'You see that—' he pointed past the walls of razor-wire to the lights blinking in the distance '—that's Sudan. We're less than a mile from home.'

'I'm from Salisbury,' said Vacher.

They had arrived at Doruma, one of the few crossing points where the British Empire and Third Reich met in Africa. A place to kiss the devil, Dolan joked on the drive there – or kick his arse. The place had the feel of a desert outpost even though it was surrounded by patchy jungle and bush. Dust blew through the streets. The buildings were a mixture of whitewashed prefabs and mock Bavarian. There were Arab traders on every corner (only tolerated because of the proximity to the border) selling an array of wares: watermelons, sunglasses, copper batteries, cheap copies of the Nazi national football strip. The occasional camel padded past. There were also Waffen-SS soldiers.

Lots of Waffen-SS soldiers.

Vacher said, 'Do you think they're looking for us?'

'It's a garrison town. There're bound to be a few squaddies. No one will give us a second thought.'

'The jeep's pretty bashed up.'

'We'll say I got hammered. Went for a race.' Dolan was finding the Rhodesian's worry unexpected and worse – contagious. 'Besides, I thought you were up for a fight.'

That was the reason Dolan had selected him for the mission in the first place. He may have been quiet but he was also ballsy. Eager to taste the spit and smoke of battle. They were from that generation of soldiers who were too young to have served in France or the Far East but wanted their own gulp of glory. To fight and win, not cower behind peace treaties. He knew Vacher's old man had been bagged by the Japs during the Nagasaki landings in '46.

'I am,' said Vacher, lifting his rifle. 'I am.' He seemed to reach back inside himself for something. 'Kraut bastards.'

'Good. I can't stand cowards.'

They were approaching the checkpoint. Dolan rested his arm on the window, trying to appear casual; he'd rolled his sleeve down to hide the burnmarks. His other hand gripped the steering wheel more tightly. There was traffic ahead of them and they slowed to a crawl. He scrutinised the crossing: sentry huts, a stop-barrier, then the gates themselves, twenty feet high, steel. Closed tight. Beyond that a kilometre of de-militarised road before the British outpost of Muzunga. There were a dozen guards, some type of commotion going on. Towering above them was a billboard that showed two men shaking hands over the outline of Africa: a member of the SS clad in black and a British Tommy. Both wore cartoon grins. The shame of a nation made reassuring, thought Dolan, something to be cheery about. All to keep an empire.

Throughout the 1930s and 40s Britain's control over its colonies had been slackening. There was widespread civil disobedience in India, the railways sabotaged, government buildings bombed, with officials admitting it was only a matter of time till the country won its independence. Similar movements were fermenting in Ceylon, Palestine, Gold Coast, Honduras. The fall of Singapore to the Japanese in 1942 was a disaster to rival Dunkirk. It seemed as if the sun was at last setting over the British Empire, as Halifax deplored.

In Africa the Nazis launched Operation Banane and knew nothing but victory. First Rommel, then his successor Field Marshal Arnim, swept across the Sahara like a sandstorm of shells and screaming metal before the Afrika Korps seized the port of Dakar (in what had been French West Africa).

Next came Operation Sisal, the conquest of the equatorial regions. Despite assurances that British interests would be respected, Churchill spoke up from the backbenches, arguing that the Nazis must not be allowed to dominate the continent. General de Gaulle, who had never recognised the European peace and decamped to Africa to continue the resistance, begged London to intervene to save his men. Each new battle saw the swastika hoisted above shattered cities.

Finally Halifax addressed the nation.

Dunkirk had shown they were no longer invincible. Peace with Herr Hitler may not have been the country's finest hour, but it had preserved their way of life. Brought security for their neighbours under the Council of New Europe. If they clashed with the Germans over Africa war might erupt again. Homes bombed, thousands slaughtered. And for what? To preserve the French colonial legacy?

British forces were already engaged in the Far East; with God's grace they would triumph – but it might take years, especially with the Americans' lack of help. To fight a second war could only weaken Britain's position further, perhaps beyond repair. It was too late to save India; now the rest of their possessions were watching. Colonies that had taken centuries of British toil to build were like restive children, might be lost in months . . . *if* they fought the Germans. *Our prosperity, our influence and power, has been built on Empire*, he declared. *So will our future. I say: Peace for Empire.*

The public heeded his call. Halifax was swept back into power in October 1943 with a landslide victory and a mandate for Africa.

He met Hitler at Casablanca, Morocco, two figures on the steps of the Anfa Hotel. The Führer in his tropical uniform, sweating and steely; Halifax's gangly figure towering over him. What followed was the most significant re-drawing of the map since the 'Scramble for Africa' had carved up the continent in the 1880s.

First the east-west divide between Britain and Germany. Then what Hitler dismissed as *Einzelheiten*. Details. The island of Madagaskar, in the Indian Ocean, was to come under the jurisdiction of the SS; be a homeland for the Jews deported from Europe. Mussolini would have his longed-for African empire: Libya, Abyssinia and Somaliland (known by Italians as 'il Corno'). Vichy France, under President Laval, Algeria. South Africa pledged to remain neutral. Portugal would retain its two African colonies: Mozambique on the east coast, and Angola in the west, nestled between Kongo and Deutsch Südwest Afrika.

Everyone smiled for the group photograph: diplomats and statesmen with a blooming pergola background. Hitler flew back from the conference to a torchlight procession along the half-built Avenue of Victory and a million cries hailing his triumph.

'Now?' said Vacher.

Dolan put the jeep into second, his foot hovering above the accelerator.

An Arab, leading a camel laden with packs, was trying to cross the border back to Sudan. The Germans had refused him and now he was arguing with the guards. Other soldiers had gathered round, laughing and jeering.

'Now?' repeated Vacher. He slipped a new magazine into his rifle.

Dolan throttled the vehicle . . . and took them past the checkpoint. 'We're going to need more than a camel to distract them.'

They headed towards the town centre, past rowdy taverns and DSHs. *Deutsches SoldatenHauses*: German Soldiers' Houses – the official euphemism for brothels. Girls as pale as Russian snow hung out over the balconies looking exhausted. Dolan saw Vacher give them a wistful glance. He's never had the ride, he thought.

Soon they entered a quieter part of town. Here were industrial units and compounds separated from the road by mesh fencing: SS workshops that did everything from engine repairs to manufacturing porcelain.

'Where are you?' said Dolan to himself. He took a left turn. 'Where are you?'

'What are we looking for?' asked Vacher.

'There!' boomed Dolan. He took the jeep past a site with a sentry box outside. On the fence was a sign that read, BRAND-GEFÄHRLICH. This was one of the first German expressions Dolan had ever learned: highly flammable. Two guards patrolled the exterior. Under the Belgians this place had been a gin factory, but now that schnapps was Africa's preferred liquor (shipped across the continent from the SS distilleries of Kamerun) it had a different use – the yard was stacked high with oil drums.

'We going to steal some petrol?' said Vacher. 'Follow the major after all?'

'Not likely.'

'So what we doing?'

'All towns have these places. Fuel dumps, until the Krauts can finish that pipeline from Persia. This is how we get across the border.'

Dolan rolled the jeep round a corner and parked by some industrial-sized bins at the back of a factory. The air stank of rubber.

He got out, left the engine running, and spoke to Vacher. 'Keep watch. Anybody comes sniffing around you whistle three times like this.' He made an owl-like sound.

'What are you going to do?'

Dolan grinned. 'My box of tricks.'

He pulled out his metal case and disappeared in the direction of the bins. They were full of tyre trimmings. He moved them, making a barricade so that he couldn't be seen from the road, then set to work.

He took out a stand and set it on the ground, using a stray piece of timber to keep it level. Next he connected four firing tubes and, glancing back towards the storage depot, adjusted their positions past the seventy degree mark so that each was at a slightly different angle. Ideally he would have taken a proper measurement but he didn't want to risk it. Loitering round the back streets was one thing, standing outside a fuel dump with a sextant and notepad quite another. His guess would be good enough. Finally he took out four cylinders. Each was packed with phosphorous connected to a C2 detonator and would—

From the darkness, Vacher's whistle.

Dolan reached for his pistol. He listened carefully. One whistle, two—

Nothing.

He strained to hear the sound of a struggle. In the distance accordion music and laughter drifted towards him; nearby, the Ziege's engine as it ticked over. He peered through the bins but couldn't see anything.

'Vacher?' he hissed. 'Vacher?'

'Hurry up,' came the reply.

'What's happened?'

'Just hurry!'

Dolan returned to the explosives. The cylinders had a timing mechanism operated by twisting it. A full twist meant twenty-eight minutes. He did a half turn on each one then placed them individually into the tubes. This type of set-up was called a 'daisy chain'. One after the other the cylinders would fire and fall. If he had guessed the angle of the pipes right at least one should land in the fuel dump. When it did the phosphorous would bite into the barrels like acid through blancmange. Pity any poor bastard within two hundred yards of the blast.

He squeezed out from behind the bins and made sure the device wasn't visible from the road. Then he went back to the jeep. Vacher was waiting for him, the front of his shirt soaked in blood. He clasped a dagger.

'Jesus,' said Dolan.

The Rhodesian motioned to the back of the jeep. Dolan turned to see a body on the ground. He was wearing a guard's uniform.

'I think he came for a piss,' said Vacher. 'I couldn't move him on my own. Not without making it too obvious.'

Further down the street there was now only one guard outside the fuel depot. Dolan didn't say another word. With Vacher's help he hauled the corpse up and shoved it in the back of the jeep. His hands turned crimson as he worked.

'We need something to cover the body,' said Dolan.

'I think there's a tarpaulin in the front.' Vacher went to retrieve it.

At that moment there was a scream of sirens.

Motorcycle outriders flew past. Seconds later a convoy of vehicles: a Ziege, three lorries laden with troops and, finally, an armoured Mercedes limousine, swastika flying from the front grille, windows blacked out, two more motorcycles protecting it at the rear.

The air turned to dust as the vehicles passed. Dolan followed the wail of the siren; it sounded as if it were heading towards the border crossing. He looked over at Vacher. Neither of them said what they were thinking.

They covered the body with the tarpaulin and climbed back into the jeep. Over by the fuel dump the solitary guard had come to a halt. Dolan could just make out his face. It was a mixture of irritation, curiosity and alarm.

'We haven't much time,' said Dolan, putting the jeep in gear. He did a U-turn and headed back towards the border.

'We'll get across, won't we?' asked Vacher, his voice sounded uncertain again.

'Trust me, soldier,' replied Dolan. 'Against us, the Krauts don't have a chance.' He had no idea why Ackerman had suddenly demoted him in favour of Cole, but it was good to be in command again. He'd show the old-timers how it was done.

In the rear of the vehicle, the smell of death began to fill the air.

Chapter Nine

NIGHT had fallen. Patrick was flat on his belly, looking through the scope of his rifle.

'What can you see?' asked Burton, who lay next to him.

They were on a ridge overlooking a valley. Jungle, like a tumbling black ocean, stretched endlessly round them. In the hours after sundown it had rained heavily, an Old Testament cloud burst, now everything was drenched. The insects were caterwauling again.

'Not much,' replied Patrick. 'This thing must have gotten knocked.' He removed the night-vision helmet from his head, rattled it harder than was necessary, then jammed it on again. 'Better.'

'What now?'

'Definitely an airfield: control tower, hangar, runway.' He whistled. 'Big runway. Couple of thousand feet at the least.'

'So that's where the Messerschmitt landed?'

'You tell me.'

The plane that screamed over them earlier had been on a routine patrol. A seek-and-destroy sortie, guessed Burton, to find insurgent camps. Despite the Nazi occupation of Aquatoriana, soldiers of the former French colony continued to fight a guerrilla war:

attacking German bases, harrying newly built outposts. On the occasions when Halifax was asked to assist the French the Prime Minster always gave the same excuse: would we have tolerated Nazi intervention in India? No, it was an internal security matter for the Germans. The aircraft itself was a Messerschmitt Me-362, the Nazi's latest jet-fighter capable of thirteen hundred kilometres an hour; the fastest ever built. They watched it soar over the horizon – the sunset glinting on its wings – before the plane dipped beneath the tree line.

'Did it crash?' said Nares. There was something almost jubilant about his tone.

'We'd have seen the pilot eject,' replied Burton. 'There'd have been an explosion. No, it landed somewhere.'

'Then we should head the opposite way.'

Burton had glanced down at the jeep's fuel gauge and ignored him.

From their viewpoint on the ridge Patrick handed Burton the night goggles and rifle. Through the goggles the impenetrable blackness of the jungle was suddenly grey like the picture on a cheap television set. It took him a few moments to orientate himself – then he spied the airfield.

'I couldn't see any gas,' said Patrick.

Burton scanned the scene below him, ignored the dampness that was spreading through his clothes as he lay on the ground. 'Near the barracks. There's some kind of filling station.'

'It's got to be aviation fuel.'

'No. I can see a tanker and separate pumps for planes, opposite the hangar. Look for yourself.' He handed back the equipment.

Patrick squinted through the scope again. 'It's too risky. There might be a hundred men in those barracks.'

'It looks smalty enough,' said Burton.

'So did the last airstrip.'

'We're running on empty. We don't have a choice.'

Patrick said nothing but the air prickled around him.

'If we wait till the middle of the night,' continued Burton, trying to reassure, 'nobody will ever know we were there.'

'There's always one insomniac.'

Burton drew his finger across his throat.

'And when they find the body? When they see our tyre tracks heading west?'

'Ten years ago you would have—'

Patrick cut him short. 'Ten years ago everything didn't ache so much. Ten years ago I had nothing to get home for.'

There was a disturbance in the undergrowth. Both men spun round, weapons ready.

It was Nares.

'I told you to stay with the jeep,' said Burton.

'You were a long time, I got worried. What have you found?'

Patrick passed him the night-vision equipment.

'I don't see the 362,' said the airman, settling himself next to the others.

'It must have already refuelled and taken off again,' said Burton. 'It's probably halfway to Muspel by now.'

'I don't like the look of those barracks.'

'We've already had that conversation.' Burton stood up. 'Maybe you two should have stayed with Dolan. We either risk it or we walk home.'

'Jesus on Friday,' said Patrick, also standing. 'Guess we don't have a choice.'

'Interesting,' said Nares. 'Very interesting.'

Burton tried to keep the impatience from his voice. 'What?'

'Inside the hangar. A Gotha. Look.'

Burton took the scope again. Peeping out of the hangar was a stumpy plane with a single propeller. 'So?'

'I can fly a Gotha.'

Burton looked over at Patrick, then both men turned to Nares. 'You know how to fly?'

'A Gotha's a kite. Everyone can.'

'What range does it have?'

'I don't know. Maybe seven, eight hundred miles. We could be in Nigeria by morning.'

'Or blown from the sky,' said Patrick. 'One of them Messerschmitts sees us, we'll never outrun it.'

Nigeria by morning. Burton saw Madeleine, the farm and quince trees. He knew BOAC flew from Lagos to London.

'What about those barracks you were trembling over?' continued Patrick to Nares.

'It's got to be better than sitting in the back of that bloody jeep for the next week.'

'Stealing fuel is one thing. Stealing a fucking plane, that's another. They just gonna lend it to us?'

'Think about Hannah,' said Burton. 'You could be with her by the end of the month.'

'No thanks to you.' Patrick rubbed his knuckles. 'Quick and safe, you said.'

'I'll get you out of here, *Chef*. Just like I did at Dunkirk.'

Patrick's face remained impassive for a moment, then he sighed an affirmative. An old, tired sigh. Burton gave him a brief smile in the darkness, then squeezed his eye tight to the scope again. He traced every inch of the airfield. There was a single guard, patrolling the perimeter as if on a Sunday afternoon stroll. In the tower another figure sat with his jackboots up, chewing. The Gotha was unprotected.

'Now you're sure you can fly this thing?' he said to Nares.

The airman nodded.

'Okay, let's get down there. Take a closer look.'

They waited till after midnight, leaving the Ziege hidden in the undergrowth half a mile away as they trudged the final distance. For the first time Burton was glad still to be in his SS uniform – he was invisible, a black phantom in a black landscape. His feet ached in his boots.

By the time they made it to the airfield the moon had risen. The whole place looked asleep, even the perimeter guard Burton spied earlier had vanished. There were no lights anywhere except for a single lamp in the control tower. Burton guessed this would be an easy posting for the sons of Nazi bigwigs doing their national service. Vitamin B boys they called them. No counter-insurgency in western Kongo for these lads. Just a year in some far-flung outpost: stints on guard duty, illicit copies of *Stag Party* at night, boredom. The worst they'd face was a bout of dysentery.

Burton motioned for Patrick to check the barracks while he and Nares headed for the tower. When they reached it they had a better view of the Gotha; there were no guards or ground personnel.

'Is she flight-worthy?' whispered Burton.

'I can't tell from here. I think so.'

'Get over to her, get her ready for take-off. And, Nares, keep it quiet.'

The airman slunk away as Burton mounted the stairs to the tower. They were made of wood, each step creaking as he trod on them. At the top he peeked in through the window. There was a lone radio operator sat by a console, flicking through a magazine. Burton could see the sweat roll down his neck.

The radio crackled to life. 'Mendiao Control, do you read?'

The operator reached for the microphone to reply.

'Stop!' said Burton, entering the room.

The operator spun round and put his hand to his heart. 'Sturmbannführer. You startled me.' Then a crease of confusion as he recognised the uniform but not the face.

Goshi. The *dambe* side-blow to the head. Burton's fist connected with the operator's temple. He crumpled instantly. Burton raised his hand to strike again . . . and lowered it. The German was just a kid, his cheeks covered in blond fluff. He let the operator slide back in his chair.

'Mendiao, do you read? Requesting runway lights. Over.'

Burton wiped the sweat from his face, grabbed the microphone, spoke in German: 'This is . . . er . . . Men-di-ao. Runway lights . . . inoperable. Please do not attempt to land.'

'I'm starting my final approach.'

'Negative. Do not attempt to land.'

Static.

Burton pressed the broadcast button again. 'Are you receiving? Repeat: do *not* attempt to land.'

When he got static for a second time Burton flung down the radio and rushed to the stairs. At the bottom he ran into Patrick. 'The barracks?'

Patrick shook his head. 'Twenty to thirty men, all asleep, but it's too many. Maybe if we had cyanide gas. I barricaded the door but it won't hold them long.'

They darted towards the hangar and the Gotha. At the foot of the plane was a body. Burton bent down to examine it: it was an engineer, the back of his head sticky with blood. He was breathing deeply as though fast asleep.

'Maybe there's more to Nares after all,' said Patrick.

They hauled themselves up through the hatch in the fuselage of the aircraft. Nares was already in the cockpit, checking the instrument panel. His hands trembled.

'The only thing I could find was a wrench,' he said. 'I killed him.'

'You've given him a bad hangover,' said Burton. 'That's all.'

'You sure he's not dead?'

'Give me the wrench and I can make sure.'

Nares offered a weak smile and turned back to the controls. He checked a few more switches, then tapped a dial.

'What is it?' asked Burton.

The airman hesitated. 'Nothing. I'm ready.'

Burton leaned forward to check the panel himself. It meant as much to him as a wall of hieroglyphics.

Patrick shifted from foot to foot. 'Is he sure he knows what he's doing?' he said to Burton.

'*He* is,' said Nares. 'Ready when you are.'

There was only room for two in the cockpit. Burton strapped himself in next to the pilot while Patrick sat behind in the hold.

'Nigeria by morning,' said Burton.

Nares pressed the ignition switch. There was a rapid *tick-tick-tick* followed by a heaving sound, like a clockwork mule waking from its slumber. Then falling back to sleep once more.

Nares jabbed the switch again. Then a third time, more violently. *Tick-tick-tick*. Nothing.

Nares tapped the dial that had caused him concern. 'I thought so,' he said. 'No fuel.'

'Just the news I was hoping for,' said Patrick behind them.

'The tanker,' said Burton, already climbing out of his seat. 'The one opposite the hangar.' He turned to Nares. 'Me and Patrick will get it. You make sure the plane is ready to refuel.'

They jumped out of the Gotha.

Burton looked round the empty hangar: felt a pang of dismay.

'You should have hit him harder,' he called back to Nares. There was no sign of the unconscious engineer, just a trail of blood spots leading towards the door.

Burton and Patrick double-timed over to the tanker and started her up, the roar of the engine excruciatingly loud as it echoed round the sleeping aerodrome. They drove back towards the hangar and started to refuel the plane.

'How soon?' said Patrick as the kerosene pumped through the hoses.

'I don't know,' replied Nares.

'You're the pilot.'

'Am I a Kraut? It's a German plane.'

Burton watched the numbers on the counter churn over: 10 litres, 20, 30. It was like waiting for fruit to grow. He tried to calculate the fuel in gallons . . . but failed. The Germans had encouraged the British to convert to the metric system to simplify trade with the rest of Europe. But whereas the Dunkirk Fiasco had been borne with grim acceptance, the merest hint of metrification provoked outrage. Litres meant nothing to him – and that was how he preferred it.

50. 100. 150. 200. 250 . . .

'Come on!' said Patrick.

Suddenly bright light.

The huge Klieg lamps that illuminated the airfield burst into life. After so much gloom Burton felt as if his retinas were being squeezed between hot fingers. The world shimmered red, green, blue. Patrick and Nares were also shielding their eyes. Next, the runway lights were coming on.

Patrick grabbed his sniper rifle and moved to the hangar door. He took a shot at one of the lights above. It shattered in a cascade of sparks.

A trail of machine gun fire raked the ground nearby. Warning shots, thought Burton. The Lebbs don't want to hit the fuel tanker. He looked at the gauge: 300 litres.

'How much do we need?' he shouted at Nares.

'I don't know.'

'Guess!'

'Five hundred litres. But we could be free-falling the last bit.'

Another round of fire. Somewhere a vehicle was starting up and in the distance another sound. Something familiar, a far-away scream –

350 litres.

– the sound of a Messerschmitt coming in to land.

A harsh, metallic voice rang out. 'Put down your weapons. Come out with your hands raised.' Then, as an afterthought, 'You are surrounded.'

'Nares, inside the plane. Get her ready to go,' said Burton. 'Then wait for my command.'

Nares scrambled on board, quick as a squirrel. The tanker continued to pump fuel.

360 litres.

Above them Burton heard boots clanging on the roof. He ran to the hangar door. There were troops fanning out on the edge of the runway, a half-track with mounted MG48 gun. Patrick had taken out four more of the arc lights, leaving two-thirds of the field in darkness. Clouds of insects swarmed around the remaining lamps.

'Something's coming in from the left,' said Patrick. Far off on the horizon Burton saw flashing red pinpoints.

'Can we shut down the runway lights?'

'How?'

Tick-tick-tick. Nares was trying to start the plane.

Burton turned to the cockpit, gesturing for him to stop. 'The fuel's still running!' he shouted.

'Who's going to kill us first?' said Patrick. 'You, him, them?'

'Cover us till the plane's out. Then get on board.'

'What about you?'

'Age before chancers,' said Burton, already heading back to the Gotha. He checked the fuel: 420 litres. A portion of the roof caved in, jackboots appeared through the hole. 421, 422, 423, 424, 425—

It would have to do. Burton turned off the fuel pump, the hose still in his hand.

'Now, Nares!'

The tail-rudder flicked back and forth. Then, *tick-tick-tick*.

Nothing happened.

Burton felt his chest deflate.

Tick-tick-tick . . .

This time the engine roared to life!

Exhaust fumes billowed out. The sound of the engines was deafening inside the hangar. It dropped an octave and the aircraft jerked forward, rolled out of the building. Patrick signalled to Nares to turn right. There was a burst of gunfire as the plane emerged from the hangar. Patrick responded.

Burton turned the pump back on. Aviation fuel gushed out all over the floor, the vapour burning his eyes. He left it pumping and sprinted to Patrick. 'Go! Then cover me.'

Patrick raced after the Gotha.

At the far end of the field, in the direction the plane was headed, Burton could see a group of soldiers erecting some kind of barricade. It looked like a pyramid of tyres. They doused it in petrol and set it aflame.

Burton raised his banana-gun to his shoulder, taking out several men. Gunfire pelted him from the opposite direction. He turned and fired. Then back towards the plane. Patrick had made the door. He threw in his rifle and heaved himself in after it. Seconds later he reappeared, beckoning for Burton to follow.

Burton fired off a few more rounds – and ran, his legs pumping ferociously. Shots zipped past him. He felt a scorching slash across his neck, then hot liquid spread beneath his collar.

At the door of the aircraft Patrick urged him onwards, his face contorted with the effort. He was trying to say something. He ducked inside the cabin. Burton expected him to reappear at any moment. But he didn't.

Instead the plane's engines began to power up.

Burton chased after it, cursing Nares with what little breath he had left. He'd never catch it. His only hope was that Patrick would order the pilot to stop.

Things fuck up, boy, and you're on your own. I'll leave you without a second thought. Every man for himself. Patrick's words in prison. A bayonet driven through hope. The plane was picking up speed.

'Nares, you bastard! Wait! Patrick!'

Burton's cries were drowned out by the propellers as the Gotha pulled away.

Chapter Ten

FOR *the hope of the ungodly passeth, as the remembrance of a guest that tarrieth but a day* ... Burton had tried to forget everything his parents taught him, but sometimes fragments would return, appearing like unbidden phantoms when his heart reeled.

The hope of the ungodly ...

He stumbled and came to a halt, blood weeping from his neck, rifle limp at his side. He should have been honest with Patrick, told him about Hochburg, the fruitless revenge he had taken. If his friend had understood, maybe he wouldn't have abandoned him.

Burton began to churn over what-next: get back to the jeep, keep heading west. He'd be faster on his own anyway. The Gotha was never going to clear the barricade – it hadn't picked up enough speed – maybe he could escape in the confusion as it hit the flaming tyres.

A fresh volley of bullets chewed the ground near him.

Burton was on the move again, heading for the jungle. Its tangled darkness offered the best hope of escape. More gunfire. It chased him across the runway till he dived behind some rusty oil drums for cover. Shells slammed into steel inches above his head, each hollow thud making him flinch. The urge to curl up and never move again was almost irresistible. Burton glanced over to see if the Gotha had made it. He hoped it had already careered into the barrier.

It was slowing.

Patrick was hanging out of the door scanning the runway for him. Burton shot to his feet and waved euphorically. He was met by a torrent of bullets and tracer fire and ducked out of sight again. But Patrick had seen him. He made a swivelling motion with his hand: we're turning round.

Burton laughed, all teeth and spit.

He got to his knees, forced his breathing steady and began to fire at the soldiers on the other side of the runway. Aimed, deliberate shots. Now the lights were in his favour. One kill, two kill; steady and relentless to give the plane time to manoeuvre.

The Gotha completed its turn. It began to throttle up once more and moved down the airstrip – away from the barricade. In the opposite direction the landing lights of the Me-362 were burning brighter in the sky.

Burton waited till the Gotha was parallel with him, then he broke cover. Ran with all the blood in his body. The force of the propellers whipped grit into his mouth.

'Move!' shouted Patrick, his voice as insistent as any drill instructor. 'Move!' He had his hand out, straining for Burton's.

Burton had a sudden moment of horror – of a bullet splitting his ankle, forcing him to the dirt, the plane leaving, no second chance. Madeleine waiting for him on the porch for ever, Alice and his own orphaned child at her knee.

Patrick grasped hold of his hand. Abruptly, Burton was inside the fuselage. Patrick shoved him out of the way and resumed his position by the door, his rifle hungry for more targets. In the cockpit Nares was yelling. Burton made his way up to him, checked the wound on his neck: it was a scratch, nothing more. Bullets ricocheted either side of them, the skin of the aircraft already punctured with holes.

'There's another plane,' screamed Nares. 'Coming straight for us.'

The Messerschmitt's lights were growing in the cockpit.

Burton strapped himself into the co-pilot's seat. 'We can make it.' His voice was coarse.

Nares throttled harder. He kept glancing down at the control panel. Both his hands were on the stick, ready to yank back as soon as they had enough lift. He was trying to guide the Gotha to the right of the runway to avoid the other plane.

The Gotha tore past the hangar and control tower. Burton could feel the air swelling beneath the wings. There was a blast of gunfire, bullets zinging through the cockpit. It was a miracle that neither of them was hit. He heard his father's bitter voice: *there are no more miracles, son.* Then a second burst. Another miracle, except this time something hot splattered Burton's arms.

'Sorry,' said Nares. He spoke as if straining his bowels. Burton looked at him. A dark patch was spreading across the airman's stomach, blood pumped from his thigh. His face was sweaty and lolling.

The nose of the aircraft was fighting to take off.

'What do I do?' said Burton.

'I can manage the stick. You do the pedals. Push hard when I say so.'

Burton put his feet on them. In the back he heard Patrick slam the fuselage door shut. The Me-362 was almost upon them.

'Now!' said Nares, it sounded as if all the breath in him had escaped his lungs. He pulled on the control column, grimacing as he did so. Burton depressed the pedals. The only thing he could see was the fighter plane in front. It was so close it blocked out the night. The engines were screaming.

The Messerschmitt touched down – flashed past them – and clipped the Gotha's wing.

For an instant nothing happened. There was no explosion, no fire, just a muffled clap. Burton felt them escaping the ground. Then a bump so hard it was like a brick had been broken into his chest. The Gotha spun violently to the right. Through the cockpit he was aware of the jungle. Then runway.

Jungle. Runway. Jungle.

The tendons in his neck were straining as if they would snap. The plane surged into the trees. There was the sound of screaming metal and something – a wing, an engine – was ripped off. He glimpsed Nares struggle to control the stick but his hands were jelly.

The Gotha continued forward, cutting into the jungle like a corkscrew. Finally it shuddered to a halt.

Burton's vision was blurred. On the periphery he sensed the burning wreckage of the Me-362. Or maybe it was just the tyres at the end of the runway. His stomach felt jolted loose, arms limp, fingers teeming with pins and needles. He attempted to move but couldn't. He knew nothing was broken but it was as if part of him had been left behind and needed to catch up.

Burton lifted his head. Nares's mouth was opening and closing like a fish tossed on the quayside. Great belches of blood oozed from it. Burton saw Hochburg again.

'Can . . . you . . . move?' He didn't know who had spoken. Then he realised it was himself. 'Nares . . . can you move?'

The airman didn't speak but feebly struggled to unstrap himself.

Movement was coming back to Burton's body. He shrugged off the seat harness and stood. The world was lopsided, reeked of kerosene and blood. He reached to unbuckle the pilot, tried to swivel him round. Nares screamed. Burton's hands came away like a butcher's.

'Patrick! I need your help!'

His old friend emerged from the fuselage. There was a vicious gash across his nose, the blood tracing his wrinkles. His eyes look focused.

'I can't move Nares,' explained Burton.

'Leave him. We have to go. The Lebbs are coming.'

Nares opened his mouth to complain. Nothing but a gurgle of blood came out.

The fuzziness was clearing from Burton's thoughts. He could hear a *drip-drip-drip* from Nares.

'There's nothing we can do for him,' said Patrick.

'We have to try.' He struggled to move the airman's legs again.

Patrick reached for his pistol and aimed it at Nares's head.

'What are you doing?' said Burton. 'We—'

A single shot. The cockpit window was misted in blood and brain. Nares's body jerked several times. Then was still.

Burton looked on in frozen horror.

In the distance came the sound of men breaking through the undergrowth.

Patrick pulled at Burton's shoulder. 'Move!'

Burton stood fast.

'Move yourself, Cole!' said Patrick again, pulling more roughly this time. 'Or I swear I'll leave you.'

Burton did as directed but it was as if he were in a dream. At the fuselage door he stole a look backwards, hoping to convince himself Nares was still alive. The cockpit window was smeared red. Patrick shoved him out of the door, and they disappeared into the jungle.

Chapter Eleven

Doruma, Kongo-Sudan border
14 September, 21:15

'HOW much longer?' asked Vacher.

'Couple of minutes. No more,' replied Dolan, even though he calculated the charges should have already fired. He kept replaying the moment when he twisted the timer on the explosive, wondered if he had turned it too far.

They were sitting in the Ziege, engine purring, a hundred yards from the border crossing. The windows were up, doors locked. With every passing second there were more Waffen-SS troops; the town like a basin filling with black ink.

'What if they don't explode?' asked Vacher.

'In three years that's never happened,' said Dolan. He decided it was best not to mention year four at that precise moment.

'But what if they don't? The major was right, this place is crawling with Krauts.'

'You're starting to sound like Lapinski.'

'Poor bloke,' said Vacher. 'If we get back I'm going to see his popsey—'

'*When* we get back.'

There was a knock at the window.

Dolan saw a leather-gloved hand rapping on the glass. He wound down the window and an SS officer peered in. He had pale acned skin, reeked of peppermint; one of his ears was missing.

There was another officer behind him examining the bodywork of the jeep.

'What are you doing here?' asked the one-eared officer.

From the tinsel on his sleeve Dolan could see that he was a Gruppenführer. Since when were fucking major generals on traffic patrol? He kept his voice jaunty but respectful. 'Waiting for a friend of ours,' he said in German. 'Then back off to barracks. We're on leave tonight.'

'All leave has been cancelled,' said the Gruppenführer. 'Surely you know that?'

Vacher leaned over. 'What's going on?'

The Gruppenführer raised an eyebrow. It made him look like a puppet. 'Where have you two been? The Governor General has been assassinated.'

'Who by?'

'Take your pick. Insurgents from the west. Angolan rebels. The British.' He looked at Vacher. 'Rhodesians. Our enemies are everywhere.'

'Fuckers,' said Dolan.

'They won't escape,' said the Gruppenführer. He leaned in closer. 'Now this friend of yours. Where did you say he is?'

Dolan found his most lascivious grin. 'At a whorehouse. He was supposed to be done ten minutes ago. Guess he wants his money's worth. You know what these Polish girls are like.'

'Polluters of our German blood. Your papers. You too,' he said, motioning at Vacher. His face was expressionless.

Vacher reached into his tunic. For a split-second, Dolan thought he was going to draw his pistol and shoot the SS officer dead, but the Rhodesian simply handed over his documents. Dolan hesitated, then did the same. Ackerman had assured them they were as good as the real thing. He'd also assured them they would be home by now, rolling diamonds in their hands.

The Gruppenführer flicked through them. Further up the road another officer was briefing the border guards. Their number had doubled in the last half hour. There were other troops patrolling the streets. Eyes everywhere. On the billboard above them, the SS soldier's grin suddenly seemed demonic.

The one-eared officer continued flicking through their papers; he seemed to be weighing up something.

'Is there a problem?' said Vacher.

Dolan gestured at him to shut up.

The Gruppenführer snapped the documents shut and handed them back over. 'Everything is in order.'

Inside, Dolan felt like a knot had been loosened.

Then another question: 'What's in the back of your vehicle?'

'Just some tarpaulins.' Dolan struggled to keep his voice calm. 'Maybe a few bottles of Primus if we have any left. You and your colleague want one?'

The Gruppenführer clicked his finger. The other SS officer moved to the back and opened the jeep.

Dolan shifted his foot to the clutch and depressed it. Very slowly his hand drifted to the gear stick. He put the engine in first. Once again he replayed turning the timer on the charges. Surely it was fourteen minutes by now? Next to him Vacher gripped his weapon.

The officer at the back was riffling through the tarpaulin. He called his superior over.

'Let's go!' hissed Vacher.

With his free hand Dolan gripped the wheel. He began dipping the accelerator.

The doors slammed shut.

'I hope your friend doesn't catch anything. Those Polack sluts are worse than sewer rats,' said the Gruppenführer, striding away. 'If you see anything suspicious, report it immediately. Goodnight to you both.'

Dolan released the clutch.

The Gruppenführer stopped and turned back to them. 'One last thing.' Dolan's feet shot back to the pedals. 'Turn off your engine. There's a fuel shortage, remember.'

Dolan killed the engine. A second later it was as if his lungs had popped.

'Mary, Mother of God,' said Vacher, crossing himself.

'I didn't know you were religious.'

'I'm not.'

They both laughed, like raw recruits who'd outfoxed the colour-sergeant.

'We've got to get out of here,' said Vacher. 'Sudan, Nigeria. Who cares.'

There was a loud fizzing sound.

On the other side of the town a blob of pink phosphorous rocketed into the heavens. Everyone – the border guards, soldiers on the street, Dolan and Vacher – stopped to stare. It rose in an elegant arc before tumbling to the ground and reminded Dolan of the first fireworks he'd seen as a boy. That had been in Newport on the day Halifax announced peace between Britain and Germany. His mam wept as the heavens exploded above them, though whether through shame or grief he never asked. Dolan simply walked off in wordless dismay. The war had been short but still left plenty of families with graves to tend; his elder brother hadn't made it back from France.

'Isn't something supposed to happen?' There was a clawing to Vacher's voice.

'It missed the fuel dump. I couldn't measure the trajectory. I had to guess.' Dolan started the engine again. 'There are three more, each at different angles—'

Two lorries skidded to a halt in front of them. Troops were disgorging like a torrent of black water. Leading them was the one-eared Gruppenführer.

The second phosphorous shell blasted into the sky.

Dolan drove, smashing through the soldiers. He aimed between the two lorries but the gap wasn't big enough. The screech of tearing metal. The jeep's front lights shattered. The lorries jerked out of position . . . And they were through.

The phosphorous landed harmlessly.

Vacher fired his BK44 out of the window.

'Get down! Get down!' shouted Dolan as he steered towards

the border gates. A tide of bullets smacked into the jeep. He saw sparks ping and flash off the bonnet. The windscreen disintegrated. They were almost there.

Above them, another blast of phosphorous. And another.

The jeep hit something, throwing them violently forward. Then back. They were past the barrier. Now the gates. They crashed through them. More screaming metal, like a steel animal being disembowelled. Gunshots. The back of the vehicle imploded.

The phosphorous dropped, found its target. The night turned yellow, orange, scarlet. Soldiers were whipped off their feet. For a few brief moments the firing stopped.

'Drive!' yelled Vacher. He positioned himself between the seats and fired backwards, out of the vehicle.

Already the SS troops were gathering themselves. There were fresh muzzle flashes. They were firing low.

There was a blast and one of the back tyres blew. Rubber shrapnel whipped the side of Dolan's face. He fought to control the jeep, as the chassis grated along the ground. It dragged and careered, left to right.

Ahead he could already see the fence that marked the British side. A Union Jack hung limply from a flagpole. Beneath it a group of soldiers seemed to be encouraging them on. They were no more than two hundred yards away. I'll buy them all a pint, thought Dolan, tonight back at barracks. He could almost taste it.

Vacher threw down his rifle. Hunkered himself into a ball.

'Brace yourself!'

A bazooka slammed into the back of the jeep, lifted it into the air. The Ziege landed on its roof, spinning crazily. A molten spike of pain rammed into Dolan's body. His vision whirled.

Everything became still and peaceful.

Next moment Vacher was screaming in his ear. 'You got to help me! I can't do it alone.'

Dolan's mouth was raw with smoke and blood. It felt as if someone were slapping their hand against his ear. He was crunched up inside the jeep, Vacher on the outside trying to drag him free. Dolan heaved with all his strength, managed to slide out. Vacher helped him stand. He almost collapsed again: his right leg felt useless, the material of his trouser soaked. He was in agony.

'Can you walk?' Vacher was shouting into his ear again.

Dolan struggled forward a few paces, tried to breathe deeply. His head was clearing. He snatched a look backwards – swarms of troops, revving engines – and threw his arm around Vacher's shoulder. If only there'd been time to set his box of tricks: that would have given the Krauts something to chew on. They half ran, half limped, the Rhodesian taking most of his weight.

Ahead a wall of steel and barbed wire stretched as far as the eye could see. The border gates were still closed. With every wincing step, Dolan expected them to swing wide open. Any second now.

Gunshots rang out behind them.

Finally, they collapsed into the barrier. On the other side stood a dozen British soldiers – members of the Equatorial Corps from their berets – all in immaculate, sweaty uniforms. Their .303s looked as if they had never been fired. Above them a wooden sign: WELCOME TO ANGLO-EGYPTIAN SUDAN.

Dolan buckled to his knees, rattled the gate. 'Let us through!'

The soldiers did nothing.

'Open it!' Dolan stole a look behind him. 'Please.' The Germans would be on them in seconds. They were no longer shooting. Instead they were leisurely marching forward, their weapons held out in front. Behind them were the headlights of countless vehicles.

'Open it!' shouted Dolan again.

'Open it!' Vacher joined in with his pleas.

Still the soldiers did nothing. An officer emerged from a pill box and strode towards them. Dolan noticed a George Cross pinned to his breast. 'I'm sorry, gentlemen. I'm under strict orders not to allow anyone to cross the border.'

'Fuck orders. Let us through. We're British soldiers. The Krauts will string us up if they catch us.'

The officer looked at Vacher. 'He sounds Rhodesian.'

'We're all on the same side, man.'

'Tell that to our cricket team.'

Dolan checked over his shoulder again, then turned back to the officer. He shook the fence wildly, spit bursting from his mouth. 'Come on!'

The officer tugged down on his tunic and looked straight ahead of him. 'I have my orders. Now I'm going to ask you to step back from the fence, please.'

'Fuck you!'

Behind them the stomp of boots. Vacher strapped his rifle to his chest, eyes darting around for a means of escape.

The officer signalled to his men and they drew their weapons.

'Please,' begged Dolan. 'Please.' His face was a mask of rage and teeth; the pain in his leg like a jackal gnawing the bone.

Vacher looked down at him. 'Can you climb?'

Dolan shook his head. 'Save yourself, Pieter.' He slumped to the ground, and twisted over to face the Germans. 'I'll cover you,' he said, letting go a few rounds. His hands were so wet with blood he couldn't hold the gun straight. The bullets vanished harmlessly into the darkness. In the distance he could see the fuel dump billowing flames. It looked beautiful.

Vacher darted further along the border and began to scale the fence. The chain-links sagged under his weight.

The British officer said, 'Please let go of the barrier and step back.'

The Germans fired some warning shots.

Dolan fired back. He might as well have been shooting peas. Through the fence a rifle butt prodded him in the neck. 'Put down your weapon,' hissed a voice. 'Don't make it worse for yourself.'

Dolan was too weak to disagree. The gun slipped from his grip. Numbness was spreading up his right side. He remembered Ackerman

offering them suicide pills before they left Lusaka, *just in case of
. . . "the worst"*. Had he set them up like Patrick said? Perhaps
Ackerman knew it would end in disaster and wanted to give them
an easy way out. Dolan refused the pill – all the team did. Now he
wished he had some bitter capsule to crunch down on.

Vacher was almost at the top of the fence. Dolan watched him,
willing him on. He swung his leg over and then was on the other
side. Thirty feet up, but back in civilisation. Back in the British
Empire.

A single shot rang out.

Vacher lurched forward, seemed to hover for an instant, then
tumbled to the ground. His body landed with the thud of a
sandbag hitting slate.

'You Kraut bastards . . .' began Dolan but his voice failed. The
shot had come from the British side.

He struggled to turn round and see. The British officer was
ordering his men to lift up the body.

'Vacher?' said Dolan. 'Vacher?'

The officer shook his head: 'Like I said: orders. If someone
can do the paperwork we'll ship him back home. If not, it's a
grave in Sudan.' A curt nod and he and his men were gone.

Dolan had never felt so alone.

Headlights shone in his eyes. The legs of a hundred German
troops in silhouette.

The Nazi officer in command stepped forward. Dolan struggled to look up at him, the muscles in his neck were feeble. It
was the one-eared Gruppenführer. He gave a signal to his men.
Weapons were cocked.

Dolan waited to die.

Then another sound: an engine.

A black Mercedes rolled up, the limousine Dolan had seen
earlier that night. The door opened and a huge dog clambered
out. The animal was followed by another officer – someone very
senior to judge from all the braiding and silver on his uniform.
His jackboots rang out as he approached.

The dog reached Dolan first. It sniffed him, then ran a slobbering tongue over his face. Its breath stank of flesh. Dolan tried not to retch.

'Fenris, heel!' The dog padded back to its master. Then the Nazi spoke. In English. His voice was deep and raw. 'Fee-fi-fo-fum, I smell the blood of an Englishman . . .'

Dolan grimaced. 'I'm Welsh.'

The Nazi chuckled. 'Be that as it may, I'll still grind your bones to make my bread.'

The Gruppenführer stepped forward. 'Is it him? Is it Cole?'

'No,' said his superior, squatting down on his haunches. He reached out for Dolan's face. His hands were massive, like the paws of a bear. He pinched Dolan's chin, forced his head up till their gazes met.

Dolan stared into the blackest eyes he had ever seen. It was only then that he realised who he was looking at.

Before him was Walter Hochburg.

Part Two

STANLEYSTADT AND THE P.A.A.

The construction of at least one thousand miles of autobahn is required each year . . . for unless we have exceptional roads at our disposal we will not be able to mop up militarily or make our new territories secure

ADOLF HITLER
27 June 1942

Chapter Twelve

Terras de Chisengue, North Angola
15 September, 10:30

ON the second evening of the Casablanca Conference –
as bureaucrats continued to re-draw the map – President
Salazar of Portugal requested an audience with the
Führer. He was passed off to Ribbentrop, Hitler's Foreign
Minister. Salazar wanted guarantees about Portugal's colonies in
Africa, especially mineral-rich Angola which was now bordered
by Kongo and the Nazis' south-western province, DSWA.
Ribbentrop put another glass of champagne in his hand, told
him not to fret. *My dear Antonio, we're all friends here.*
Europeans together. You've nothing to fear from us. Halifax offered
a smile and similar reassurance.

The true fate of Angola, however, was not decided by Halifax
or Ribbentrop; it was decided by Hitler's architect, Albert Speer.

The incessant rebuilding of the Reich's cities after the war (a
project known as *Die Fünf-und-zwanzig*, 'The Twenty-Five') had
left a world shortage of marble. As prices soared, the quarries
of southern Angola – abundant in the black anorthosite so prized
by Speer's designs – were suddenly rich. Seeing an opportunity
to fill Portugal's coffers, President Salazar decided to levy extra
tariffs on all mineral exports: a breach of the Council of New
Europe's trade policy. Hitler demanded concessions. When none
was forthcoming panzers began massing on the border; it looked

as if all of southern Africa might be plunged into war. Finally, Halifax intervened to negotiate a peace settlement and secure the Casablanca Treaty. Calling an emergency meeting of the CONE, he cited Lloyd George's famous observation that 'Portugal had far too much African territory for a country of her size'.

Salazar was forced to see sense. There were no smiles or champagne this time.

In November 1949, all Angola's provinces south of the Benguela Railway were subsumed into DSWA (which led Göring to point out that the country was the first ever to be divided 'along railway lines'). Northern Angola would remain under Portuguese control on the condition that it didn't foment rebellion in the south. Speer could continue his work. A resistance movement formed, with clandestine backing from Portugal, but officially peace had returned to the continent.

Neliah Tavares knew that peace well. It came dressed in black with silver skulls and machine guns. A peace that had murdered her parents.

She was in the kitchens when the *comandante* returned to camp. He was carrying orders. The whites cheered, fired their guns into the air. A few hours later, a boy-lieutenant – a stranger – arrived. He had travelled from Loanda, Angola's capital.

Neliah had lost count of the weeks – the months – they had waited. Every day there was new talk of the *Nazistas* invading the north, and every day they did nothing but sit and sweat and wait, slowly going crazy in the *ndeera*-grass. And never a mouthful of revenge. Some of the soldiers poured *caporotto* down their throats and beat each other till their faces ran. The officers said nothing, even allowed gambles on it: anything to keep whispers of revolt at bay. Finally, sick of waiting, the *comandante* himself went to Loanda to get some orders. He had come back that morning.

Then the boy-officer – and different orders.

When Neliah heard she ran to the *octógono* at once. She was as tall as most of the men, athletic, with chopped hair and skin the colour of river mud, much darker than her sister's. Her eyes gleamed bright and wild like those of a mongoose. She was seventeen years old.

The *octógono* was at the heart of the rebel camp and like all the buildings for the whites was built on legs to keep it safe from mambas and flash floods. Neliah climbed the steps, the nerves rising in her. Inside it was crowded with the Portuguese officers and white Angolan soldiers of the *Resistencia*. None paid her any attention except *Comandante* Penhor who frowned but said nothing. Every time orders arrived she would come to fight, every time Penhor would pat her rump and send her back to cook. She flinched when he touched her.

Penhor was addressing the crowd: 'This morning we have two sets of orders,' he said. 'Both from Carvalho himself.' José Agapito de Silva Carvalho: the Governor of Angola. Neliah watched the soldiers whisper excitedly to each other.

'The second set of orders says that there has been some kind of "incident" in Kongo, they don't specify what. Tanks are gathering on the autobahn at Manloga. It appears the Germans intend to invade Northern Rhodesia. To protect their borders. We are to stop them at all costs.

'The first set, the ones I got from the Governador's Palace myself, also says that German tanks are gathering. But on the Kongolese-Angolan border. The whole of 90 Light Division.' He paused for effect. 'At the Matadi Bridge.'

There was uproar.

'I needn't tell you the full consequences of this,' shouted Penhor, struggling to be heard over the crowd. 'From Matadi the *Nazistas* could be on the outskirts of Loanda in three days. Our orders are to return to the capital at once.'

A thrill of excitement ran through Neliah. This time they'd have to let her fight!

'But why?' shouted one of the soldiers. 'They already have the south. We signed a peace agreement.'

'The Germans are claiming it's to destroy the *Resistencia*, camps like ours.'

'That's just a ruse,' called another voice. 'They want the whole country. Want to turn Angola into a German colony.'

There was a clamour of agreement.

Penhor waited for the hubbub to die down before continuing. He was wearing the blue uniform of the Portuguese Army with a red ceremonial sash around his chest, the creases in trousers and tunic sharp as knives. His skin was like bricks, hair painted black. Neliah never understood why he coloured it.

'Back to our orders,' said Penhor. 'They come with no precedence. However, given the imminent threat to the colony, I say we make all haste to Loanda.'

A voice spoke out among the soldiers. Neliah knew its rough tone at once, felt her belly tighten.

'The second set, about Rhodesia. Did they say anything else?'

Penhor stopped, ran his tongue between his teeth and top lip. 'Nothing.'

'How were we supposed to stop the Boche? We'd be forty men against an entire army. Carvalho must have said something.'

'Remind me of your name, soldier.'

'Gonsalves, sir.'

'Well, Gon-sal-ves, I assume the Governador's intention was sabotage. That we destroy one of the tunnels heading south on the autobahn.'

'Let me do it.'

Penhor snorted. 'Denied. Our orders are to return forthwith.'

'But you said there was no precedence.'

'What's your point, soldier?'

Gonsalves moved so he could address Penhor and the rest of the soldiers at the same time. Neliah had known men like him before. He was a newcomer to the *Resistencia*, a one-time convict from when Angola was still a penal colony. His skin was as white as zebu milk with curly black hair that sprouted from his collar and cuffs. Whenever she served him in the kitchen he took the food as if it were swimming in spit.

'Governador Carvalho wouldn't have sent orders to destroy

the tunnel unless he thought it important,' said Gonsalves, 'at least as important as defending Loanda.'

'Maybe they were meant for another of the *Resistencia* groups,' suggested one of the soldiers. 'You know how bad communications are.'

'Or maybe he found out about Manloga after the *comandante* had left. Realised just how important it was to stop the Boche getting to Rhodesia and that's why he sent the second set. Think on it. If the *Nazistas* invade Loanda who're the only people that can help us? The Brits. Unless they're fighting their own war.'

'They signed away half our country last time.'

'This is different. We've all heard the talk. There are secret agreements between Portugal and Britain.' He looked to Penhor for support. 'I'm right, aren't I, *Comandante*?'

Neliah watched Penhor brush an invisible speck from his uniform. He kept his lips tight.

'And the Brits are the ones supplying us with weapons.'

Penhor looked at him sharply. 'Where did you hear that?'

'Everyone knows it.'

The *comandante* hesitated. 'The British are—' he chose his words carefully '—facilitating our struggle. There are those who believe in our cause at their embassy in Loanda.'

'You see!' said Gonsalves. 'If the *Nazistas* invade us the Brits will come to our defence. Unless they're fighting the Germans elsewhere – like in Rhodesia.' He faced the gathered soldiers, appealing to the Angolan fighters. 'That's when they'll turn their backs on us. Or barter us away at the negotiating table. And that's why we have to destroy the tunnel.'

Neliah saw several of the soldiers nodding in agreement.

Penhor asked, 'What rank are you, Gonsalves?'

'No rank, sir. I'm new to the *Resistencia*. Just volunteered.'

'And already the master tactician.'

Neliah covered her mouth. Smiled.

'But . . . the orders were from Carvalho.'

'Blowing up a tunnel won't be enough to beat the Germans.'

'But it will delay them. Give the Brits a chance to ready themselves.'

'He's got a point,' said one of the Portuguese officers.

'I say tunnel first,' replied Gonsalves. 'Then Loanda.'

Penhor bristled. 'I think you forget yourself, no-rank Gonsalves. This may be an irregular unit but I am still the commanding officer. We don't have enough soldiers as it is: can't afford to split our number. The defence of the capital outweighs any other considerations or orders.'

'I'll do it. I'll blow up the tunnel.'

Everyone turned to the back of the room – and stared at Neliah.

'You?' said Gonsalves, his mouth shrivelled with scorn.

'I know explosives. Know how to fight.'

'Neliah,' said the *comandante* to himself.

She didn't dare look at him: she was fearful he would refuse her. She couldn't bear another day stirring pots.

'Yes . . . yes, Neliah could do it. Take some other Herero girls with her.'

'And who'll cook us dinner?' said Gonsalves.

Some of the soldiers laughed.

Neliah ignored them. 'I want to fight,' she said more loudly. 'Want to kill Germans.'

'But she's a *negra*,' said Gonsalves, appealing to Penhor. 'Send her out into the jungle and she'll run away. All of them will.'

Neliah felt the fury beat in her throat – stilled it. The *comandante* might change his mind if she lashed out.

'Or she'll fuck it up. The explosives will be too complicated for her.'

Penhor held up his hand to silence Gonsalves and the other soldiers baying with him. Neliah watched him suspiciously. 'It's decided,' he said. 'Neliah will go to the tunnel. The rest of us will leave for Loanda. We can be there the day after tomorrow.'

'You can't leave something so important to a girl.'

'That's enough.'

'A nig-girl.'

'I said, that's enough. One more word and I'll have *you* in the kitchens, Gonsalves.'

Sniggers.

The skin round Gonsalves's jaw flushed red.

Penhor turned to one of his officers. 'Send word to Quimbundo to prepare the train. Neliah, come with me. The rest of you get ready to move. We leave tomorrow. Dismissed!'

Neliah waited for the soldiers to file out. As Gonsalves passed he flashed her a look. A look that spoke murder.

Neliah had always been forbidden here before. She followed the *comandante* to the strongroom. It was the only stone building in the camp, had originally been built to store diamonds from the nearby mines. Now its cellar served as the *Resistencia's* armoury. She looked around the racks of rifles as breathlessly as that one time she had kissed a boy.

'Will you give us guns?' she asked.

'I thought you Herero had your own weapons.'

'We do, but no guns.'

Penhor considered it a moment. 'I'll give you this, girl,' he said, reaching for a leather sheath.

Neliah took it and withdrew the blade inside. Her eyes shone. It was a panga-machete, two feet long, the edge rough with rust.

'It will need sharpening,' said Penhor.

'No. Blunt is good,' breathed Neliah. 'It cuts worse. But what about a gun?'

'We'll need them for Loanda.'

'Grenades?'

'They're too noisy. You'll need to be as silent as possible.'

'Will there be many Germans to kill?'

'I don't know, maybe none.'

Neliah's face dropped.

'But you'll be doing much worse,' said Penhor, seeing her expression. 'Destroying the enemy's transport links, their bricks and tarmac, that hurts them much more.'

'There's an old Herero saying: *only what bleeds hurts*.'

Penhor reached for a crowbar and prised open a wooden case. Inside were bundles of dynamite and detonators. 'There are two types,' explained Penhor. 'Radio-triggered or on timer.'

Neliah picked up one of the bundles. The dynamite looked as old and white as bone. She put her face to it: it smelt of nothing, certainly not revenge. 'Was it true what Gonsalves said about the British?' she asked.

'Yes, I visit their embassy. They are our allies, supplied all of this.'

'But they let the *Nazistas* take the south. My parents died because of what they did. Murdered.'

'I know,' he said, his voice flat, 'Zuri told me.' He eased the dynamite from her hand, patted her. Neliah pulled away. 'The radio ones will be too complicated. Better you take the timers.'

'I understand the radios,' Neliah replied. 'My father used similar on the quarries.'

'Nevertheless, that's what I'm giving you. I assume you know how they work too?'

She nodded.

'I'll show you anyway. Watch carefully.'

When he was finished Penhor stuffed the explosives into a haversack. 'The men will still need food. You can take five others with you, but not Zuri.'

Neliah secretly hoped he would say this. 'My sister wants to fight also.'

'I don't care what she wants. It's safer here.'

He pulled the haversack away from her.

'She will be angry if I go alone.'

'I can always send Gonsalves instead.'

'No! Five others is enough – Zuri can stay.'

'Good girl.' Penhor handed back the explosives, squeezed them against her breasts. 'Now, Neliah, I can't stress how important this task is. Gonsalves was right: if the Germans manage to invade Rhodesia, we're done for.'

Neliah frowned. 'Then why not give it to him?'

'Because you're braver than he is.'

'How do you know?'

He looked at her bare arms, the dark skin. 'You've got more to lose.'

Chapter Thirteen

HIS father's voice was urgent. 'Burton! Get up.'

It was Mama, she'd come back to them. Hochburg was dead and Mama was home. It had to be. Only her return could have roused such fervour. He'd missed her so much . . .

'Burton!'

Someone was shaking him.

Burton's eyes opened with a start – but his bedroom was different. Where were the etchings of Noah, of David and Goliath? Where was the painting he'd done of the beanstalk with Onkel Walter?

Where was his mother?

Patrick was leaning over him. 'We got trouble.' The air reeked of his pipe smoke.

Burton pushed himself up, positive he could still hear the echo of his father's voice. He was lying on a mattress in a squalid room; his ankles itched from bed bugs despite sleeping with his boots on. They were in a dosshouse by the old docks, the type of place where labourers could get a bed for a few marks and no questions. Nearby, Burton heard the sound of an engine. A lorry – no, two – approaching at speed.

Burton pushed past Patrick to the window, Browning clutched

122

tight; he had slept with it in his hand. He looked outside then squatted below the sill and flicked off the safety.

Patrick grabbed his own pistol, a Mauser, and made for the door.

'Wait,' said Burton.

'And have them storm the fucking place?'

'They can't know we're here. Run, and you'll bring them down on us.' Burton peered over the window ledge again. The lorries had come to a halt; troops clambered out of the back. An officer was issuing commands. He pointed at the building opposite, another dosshouse.

'See,' said Burton.

Patrick's hand hovered above the handle.

'See.'

He relented, joined Burton by the window.

The officer was knocking on the door of the other building. Several moments passed before a woman opened it. The officer flashed some ID and stood aside to allow his troops to enter. They were all armed with banana-guns.

'They're Unterjocher,' said Burton. He could see two Gothic letters on the officer's lapels: UJ.

There was the sound of crockery breaking, a muffled shout, then the troops began to lead men out of the house. Most were wearing nothing more than shorts and vests, hair rough with sleep. One man approached the officer and began an elaborate display of his documents. The Unterjocher were only supposed to remove illegal workers, those without the correct papers; this part of the city was an ideal hunting ground. The man was slapped away and dragged to the lorry.

Burton shook his head. 'Poor bastards.'

'Better them than us,' replied Patrick.

The troops escorted a dozen or so men to the waiting lorries before the officer directed them to another house. There seemed no method in his choosing, he simply pointed at a building and let his troops loose. Suddenly he was looking in their direction. Burton ducked below the sill.

'We got to move,' hissed Patrick.

Burton's grip tightened around the Browning. He shook his head.

Patrick crawled from the window to the door, reached for the handle and turned it. The door opened silently.

From below: shouting. Then engines as they started up.

Burton risked a peek outside. The lorries were pulling away. Soon the road was silent again except for the clanking of cranes by the docks.

Burton let his head loll against the wall. 'Jesus.' His limbs ached from the long drive from Aquatoriana. His eyes were raw, mouth dry and full of yawns. He rubbed his face to force some vigour into himself. He had a strong urge to crawl back into bed. 'So now what?' he asked Patrick.

Stanleystadt had been his idea. *We can't continue to Nigeria,* Patrick said after the airfield, *every Lebb in Aquatoriana will be on our trail now. Better get to the city, we can disappear there. They'll never find us. Then downriver, like we did in '44 . . .* What if the others are captured? asked Burton. The cover story: we said Stanleystadt, remember? *Dolan seemed pretty cocksure he'd get out. Let's hope he was right.*

Patrick joined him beneath the window; there was a scab across the bridge of his nose from the plane crash. He stuffed his pipe back in his mouth, flicked his Zippo lighter.

'Do you have to smoke that thing?' said Burton.

'It's my lucky pipe.'

'Well, it's starting to stink.' Patrick had puffed away throughout his watch: there was a bitter fug to the room.

The flame in Patrick's hand hovered over the bowl before he extinguished it. The pipe stayed in his mouth. 'We head for the docks,' he said, 'see if we can get a ship to Neu Berlin. Then the Atlantic, and home.'

Home. The word had never sounded so sweet to Burton.

'What about the right papers? Work permits?'

'They won't care in the old port. Besides—' Patrick rubbed

his thumb and forefingers together '—bank notes are the best papers.' As part of their contingency equipment each member of the team had been given two hundred Reichmarks and some solid gold coins.

'It's not enough.'

'We'll offer it as a down payment. Promise more.'

'And if we bribe the wrong person?'

'You got a smarter idea?'

'Rougier. He's the other side of town.'

Patrick snorted. Counted off on his fingers: 'He's either captured. Dead. Or is in it with Ackerman, helped set us up.'

'We still don't know it was Ackerman.'

'Who else then?'

'Rougier might be the only friend we have.'

'Suppose you're right, what we going to do?' said Patrick. 'Knock on his door and say hi, maybe bring him a bunch of roses?'

'He could get us the right documents, help us get down river.'

'Or get us shot.'

Burton stood up. 'What? Like Nares?'

Patrick had avoided all Burton's previous comments about the airman. For a moment it seemed as if he would again ignore him. Then he seemed to deflate. 'There's nothing we could've done,' he said, almost a whisper. 'You saw his injuries. If we'd stayed the Lebbs would have gotten us. And that's not going to happen. Not to me.'

'But—'

'I made it clear, remember, back in prison.'

Burton hated him for being right. 'And if it had been me?'

'Nares was as good as dead. I didn't want to do it but it was the only thing.'

'And if it had been me? Could you have looked me in the eye and pulled the trigger?'

Patrick made no reply.

The American stood, his joints creaking, and put his pipe into his pocket. Like Burton he was wearing canvas trousers and a Wehrmacht surplus shirt. With so many itinerant workers in Stanleystadt they wouldn't get a second glance dressed as navvies. They'd stolen the clothes on the outskirts of the city before ditching their SS uniforms (a blessed relief), documents and rifles. Burton had noticed Patrick rub his thumb over the words carved into the stock – *für Hannah* – before breaking the weapon and tossing it into the river. They kept their jackboots and pistols.

Burton looked him straight in the eye. 'Could you have done it?'

Patrick stepped towards the door, opened it and only then turned round. His voice was halting, conciliatory. 'Okay, let's find Rougier. But you buy the roses.'

Burton faked a smile. 'And breakfast: I'm famished.'

'We can eat when we're safe.'

The flophouse they had spent the night in was on the north bank of the Kongo, the old Belgian part of the city called Otraco dominated by its decaying cathedral. Here, you could still find bomb craters and piles of rubble from the invasion, buildings pockmarked with bullets. Beyond the patchwork of streets there were warehouses riddled with rain and rats. Tanneries belched clouds of sulphur into the air. The Nazis were waiting for Otraco to sink back into the mud before rebuilding: a physical demonstration of Belgium's deluded colonial ambitions.

In the meantime WVHA, the Economic Department of the SS, had concentrated its efforts on the other side of the river – the Salumu district – with a challenge from Hochburg 'to create a lustrous white pearl: a city that would be the envy of Africa'. A new river port had been constructed to encourage trade; a stock exchange, known as the Mittelafrika Börse; state-of-the-art hospital; and two universities, one that specialised in agronomy, the other in tropical medicine and racial hygiene. There were gleaming avenues that flowed with Volkswagens and BMWs, high-rise blocks to rival the cathedral's spire. For Stanleystadt's citizens: townhouses and air-conditioned villas filled with Polish

126

maidservants. Water as sweet as any Alpine brook from new treatment plants. A cornucopia of boutiques. Sports facilities. Lush communal parks. All built on black slave labour in the years before Windhuk.

It was reached by a bridge designed by Hermann Giesler. Brutal pillars of concrete in the shape of an eagle's wings – seventeen of them – spanning the width of the Kongo. Burton watched the muddy water flow beneath them as they crossed it. When he was younger, Hochburg told him how he had navigated the river's length, retraced Stanley's journey. Another of his stories.

By the time Burton and Patrick were on the Salumu side a muggy grey heat had risen. Burton's shirt was plastered to him, sweat pooling around the small of his back where his Browning was hidden. They had memorised the route to Rougier's safe house during their training: followed a course through a canyon of steel and stone where a few years earlier there had been nothing but trees. Burton didn't want to imagine the suffering that had raised a new city so quickly. He heard his father's voice again, the Book of Exodus, words spoken in disgust: *and they made their lives bitter with hard bondage, in mortar and in brick* . . . It was only then that it struck him.

'There's something wrong.'

They were walking down 25 Mai Strasse. On either side of them was Belgian artillery: captured guns displayed on low plinths.

'You just figured that out?' said Patrick.

'I mean about this place.'

The last time they'd been here was in September 1944, during Operation Sisal, and those final days before the Afrika Korps's assault on the city. With the Belgian administration in chaos and unable to evacuate its citizens, the job fell to mercenaries. The streets thronged with people desperate to escape, but only those with enough 'portable' – gold, jewels – had been saved. Everyone else was left to their fate. Burton felt a stirring of long-suppressed guilt. He could still remember them, the sweat, the panic, wide eyes set in beseeching faces . . .

'There are no blacks.'

'Say what?' said Patrick.

'Look at the faces.'

Apart from the heat, the palms and baobab trees, they might have been in Hamburg.

'Of course not. The Windhuk Decree.'

'But the blacks built this city.'

'Then got shipped north.'

'God only knows what they went through. How many died.'

'Keep your voice down,' hissed Patrick and picked up the pace.

They passed offices – IG Farben, Siemens, Lufthansa – a cinema showing *Das Wunder von Rio*, Leni Riefenstahl's film about the World Cup earlier that summer in Brazil. Somewhere Burton smelt freshly baked bread; his stomach growled. The traffic was getting heavier. Finally they reached Eiskeller Strasse.

'Ackerman said it was on the corner with Lubeku Strasse. Number 131.'

'Is this right?' said Patrick. 'Doesn't look residential.'

'We'll soon see.' They continued walking, Burton counting off the numbers: 91, 93, 95, 97 . . . There seemed to be a lot of black uniforms on the street. Burton and Patrick kept their eyes averted. A lorry laden with troops drove past.

119, 121, 123, 125 . . .

'There it is,' said Burton, coming to a halt. 'On the other side of the road. Seems discreet enough.'

Patrick wasn't paying any attention. He was staring at the building opposite. 'You got to be kidding.' He looked as if he were about to run.

Burton turned round and gazed up. It was built in the new imperial style: seven storeys tall, angular, with windows like a prison. The construction was white granite with Doric columns marking the entrance. On top of the columns was a huge eagle and swastika.

They were outside the headquarters of the SS.

*

'He's not expecting us,' said Burton, 'so we should go one at a time. I'll take point.'

'No,' replied Patrick. 'I'll go first. He knows me, remember. From picking up the jeeps.' He glanced at the building looming over them. There were two sentries on the gate, BKs slung over their shoulders; one was already looking in their direction. 'More important, I don't want to spend a second longer out here than I have to.'

'And if it is a set-up?'

Patrick ignored the question. 'You can't hang around here. Keep going round the block. Once I'm in we'll look for you.' Patrick headed towards the house without another word.

Burton began walking again. When SS HQ was behind him he risked a glance over his shoulder: Patrick had vanished. He went round the block anti-clockwise. The streets were crowded: foreign businessmen, settlers in town for the day, a gaggle of Pfadfinders, the African Hitler Youth, on a school outing. For some reason 'The Sambo March' was back in his head. He remembered raucous renditions of it in the streets before the Peace for Empire election, had always hated the song:

> . . .*What for Winston?*
> *Dead chums and kingdom come*
> *We ain't fighting for no blacks.*

Three minutes later he had returned to Eiskeller Strasse. He slowed as he approached number 131, expecting the door to open at any moment. For Patrick to beckon him over.

The door remained shut.

Burton slowed further before coming to a complete halt opposite Rougier's building. Next door he noticed Texaco's office, the US oil company. He'd heard they were prospecting in the east of the colony, a joint venture with the MittelafrikaÖl-SS: one of the benefits of neutrality. Burton leaned against a lamppost and tugged off his jackboot. To anyone observing him he was just some labourer with a stone in his shoe. He made a show of shaking it, peering in it, then trying to remove the offending rock, all the time glancing at Rougier's door. With his foot out in the air he felt strangely exposed.

Further up the road one of the sentries had spied him. He knocked his colleague's elbow. Next moment he was marching in his direction. The light glinted on his helmet. Even the briefest of interrogations would reveal Burton had no documents.

The door was still closed.

Burton yanked on his boot. Momentarily he was back home on that pink August morning, pulling on his boots to intercept Ackerman. What would he have done if he'd known the fate that awaited him in Africa? Would he have still stridden out to meet the Rhodesian or would he have gone back to bed and waited for Maddie?

At least Hochburg was dead. That had to count for something – though he was no longer sure what.

The sentry was twenty feet away. Burton turned in the opposite direction, heart thudding, and began to walk.

Suddenly the door was open. A man was beckoning to him.

Rougier? The rest of the team had met him two nights earlier when they arrived in Kongo but Burton had no idea what he looked like. The man looked furtively at the SS headquarters, saw the sentry heading towards them.

His gesturing became more insistent.

Burton felt his instincts prickle. Something was wrong here. He had an instant to decide whether to bolt or not.

He strode towards the man. 'Rougier?' he asked.

'*Vite, vite!*' came the reply in French.

'Where's Patrick?'

The Frenchman didn't respond, just pulled Burton into the building. The door snapped shut behind him.

Chapter Fourteen

Schädelplatz, Kongo
16 September, 07:10

ALL he could taste was blood and snot. Several of his teeth were missing.

Dolan lay on the floor, hands cuffed, his body curled up tight. In his head he kept hearing Patrick's words: *First click of the cell door and you'll tell them everything. Right down to our boot sizes.* He wasn't going to give the old bollocksucker the satisfaction. Nor the Kraut bastards who were beating him.

There were four of them, three heavies and the Gruppenführer without an ear; Kepplar he called himself. He hadn't hit him once, merely instructed the others. Right now he nodded again. Dolan clasped his eyes shut.

Another kick, then another. Both to the ribs. They had to be broken by now. Then a thwack to the head. And the same questions over and over:

'Who are you working for? Who are your comrades? I want their names. Where are they headed?' That last question obsessed Kepplar the most.

And always the same response, panted between gulps of bloody air. 'Dolan . . . Lieutenant . . . 2200118.'

Kepplar sighed. 'This is getting us nowhere. Get him off the floor.' Dolan was lifted up and shoved into a chair. The Nazi leaned in close, so close Dolan smelt the peppermint oil on his skin. It stung his nostrils.

'Maybe it's time to use more persuasive methods,' said Kepplar. 'I ask again: where are they headed?'

Dolan remained silent.

Kepplar nodded at one of the guards. Behind him Dolan heard a sound – metal rattling against metal – but couldn't identify it. He coughed blood, tried to shrink himself in the seat like Vacher had done in the jeep when they arrived at Doruma. He still couldn't believe the Rhodesian had been shot by their own. The world had gone crazy. Poor Pieter . . .

'Tell me where,' said Kepplar.

They had taken Dolan from the border crossing and driven him through the night. His boots, belt and watch had been removed, no medical attention was offered. For the first hour his right leg had roared red-hot (he grimaced with every bump on the road) before subsiding into a grey fire; he guessed it was broken. When they arrived at the Schädelplatz, he was thrown into a cell and left for several hours, time enough to let his imagination fester in the darkness. The air stank of wet stone, blood and excrement. He thought of that time his brother had locked him in the coal cellar back home for borrowing his French magazines. Then Kepplar arrived. The beatings had continued ever since.

Who are you working for? Who are your comrades? Where are they headed?

Dolan took solace in those questions. If they were asking them, they hadn't captured Burton or the old man. He pictured them in their Ziege, driving west through the jungle. Nares cowering in the back. Pathetic. Dolan swore he'd rather die first. He doubted they'd make it to Nigeria but if they were captured it wouldn't be because of him. He reckoned he could hold out for a long time yet before offering the Stanleystadt cover story. Each kick, each punch had become a matter of professional pride.

The rattle of metal again.

Kepplar moved back and allowed the guards to step in front of Dolan. They were holding rusty chains.

Dolan was toppled out of the chair. He screamed as his leg crunched into the ground. Chains whipped down on him, thrashing his head, arms, kidneys. White stars shot up his spine.

'Who are you working for?'

Whip.

'Where are your comrades headed?'

Whip. Whip.

Kepplar squatted next to him, yanked up his head by the hair. 'Tell me.' He seemed ready to weep from his inability to extract any answers.

Dolan felt a surge of triumph. Laughed. 'Go fuck yourself,' he boomed.

'Tell me!'

'And your mother.'

Kepplar bounced his head on the floor and stood up. 'My mother is dead. Killed in a British bombing raid at the beginning of the war.'

Dolan stopped laughing. His lungs suddenly felt full of blood.

Kepplar gave a signal and the chains came lashing down again. More vicious this time. Again and again and again. Dolan howled, his body rigid with pain.

'Enough!'

The guards snapped to attention. Kepplar saluted: 'Heil Hitler.'

Next moment Dolan was back in the chair. He felt two immense hands settle themselves gently on his shoulders, the way his father used to when he was a boy. He was panting hard, felt a desperate urge to shit.

Kepplar spoke. 'I regret to inform the Herr Oberstgruppenführer that the prisoner has yet to talk.'

The hands on Dolan's shoulders squeezed tighter. 'That's because he's strong,' said Hochburg in English. 'We could do with more like him in our ranks.' He gave a final, pincer squeeze and walked round to face him.

133

Dolan cautiously met his gaze. 'I . . . I thought you were dead.'

'Then call me Lazarus.'

He was clad entirely in black, no tie, open shirt; three silver diamonds and the outline of Africa on his shoulder lapels. 'I'm sorry about your leg,' said Hochburg, casting his eyes over Dolan's injuries and wincing. 'Normally we would have treated it, but I hope you understand that analgesics are counter-productive to you talking. We're not savages though. Tell us what we want and I promise my very own physician will see to you.'

Dolan said nothing, probed the gaps in his teeth.

Kepplar stepped forward. 'I'm sure with more time, Herr Oberst—'

Hochburg held up his hand to silence him. 'Can you walk?' he asked Dolan.

Again he said nothing.

'It's not a state fucking secret,' said Hochburg. 'Can you walk?'

'I'm a soldier,' Dolan replied this time. 'An enemy combatant. If I'm to be questioned, sir, it should be by officers of the Wehrmacht under the rules of the Geneva Convention.'

'We Schutzstaffel are in charge of Africa, not the Wehrmacht. They're finished. And Geneva is only good for clocks and chocolate. Now I'm growing bored of asking this, so you'd better humour me. Can you walk?'

'I don't know. Yes.'

'On your feet.'

Dolan clamped his jaw shut and struggled to stand. For an instant he remained upright, then he crumpled.

'Help him up,' said Hochburg and left the cell. The three guards dragged him to his feet and followed. Dolan caught a final glimpse of Kepplar, standing in the gloom, head hung in dejection.

They walked along an underground passage to a lift, then upwards to another corridor and the open air. They were in the Schädelplatz. Dolan tried to raise his cuffed hands to shield his eyes from the steamy sunlight. High above, like two triangular smudges, he glimpsed a pair of Horten flying-wings and felt a terrible yearning.

They seemed so free: if only he could soar away on their jet trails. The Horten was a long-range bomber. From their bases in western Sahara they could strike New York, even Washington DC itself, and return without refuelling. Another justification for US neutrality – no American wanted to see the White House in flames.

They continued across the square to a small arch set in one of the quadrangle walls; Dolan didn't remember seeing it on the plans of the camp Ackerman had provided. The square was busy with engineers repairing the damage Dolan's box of tricks had wrought two nights previously. He noted with particular pleasure how one of the cranes at the front of the complex had come crashing down into the square just as he planned. Then his eyes fell on the skulls at his feet.

Inside him something rolled over. Rolled over and sank.

Hochburg led them through the archway and into a garden. It was screened on all sides by foliage and blended into the jungle beyond. Dolan heard monkeys chattering in the trees. The planting was regimented, lots of red and white flowers. At one end of the garden was a stone table and chairs; the table was laid for breakfast. Fresh bread, fruit, a pitcher of juice. Despite the throbbing in his abdomen, Dolan's stomach gurgled. He had been offered no food or water since his capture. Tied to one of the chairs was Hochburg's dog. It looked bigger and more vicious than Dolan remembered even though it was currently dozing in the heat.

'I always start my day here,' said Hochburg, spreading his arms around the garden. 'It's my great pride, my very own Eden.' Dolan was forced into one of the chairs, pain jarring through his leg. 'You know the negroid never cultivates,' continued Hochburg. 'All this fecundity and they struggle to scratch an existence. And the so-called intellectuals puzzle over why they never built cities, have no culture. Our Aryan ancestors were growing wheat ten thousand years before Christ.'

The dog woke at Hochburg's voice, yawned to show a mouthful of teeth.

Hochburg was wandering about the garden pointing out

135

flowers and shrubs. 'This is *Cleome Eleanora*, my own propagation, and *Disa Stairsii*, and *Impatiens Niamensis*. This here is a mango tree. Brazilian. I don't like the native ones, the fruit's too stringy, so I had it imported.'

He turned back to face Dolan. In his hand was a knife. Dolan recognised it at once: it was the one Burton had carried during their training, the one that looked like a table knife. Hochburg took a step closer.

'Have you ever tried mango?'

Dolan hesitated. Shook his head.

'Not many in Wales I imagine.' Hochburg reached over for a branch and plucked a fruit. He peeled it expertly, cut off a slice and popped it in Dolan's mouth.

Dolan slurped it down.

'Good?'

Dolan's taste buds had been beaten senseless. All he got was the texture of the fruit and something coppery: the open cuts in his mouth. The juice was refreshing though. He nodded.

Hochburg cut off a slice for himself and ate it. Then another for Dolan. The dog was staring at him.

'Now, Lieutenant,' said Hochburg, 'I'm sure you appreciate we need information from you. The names of your colleagues. Who you are working for.' He cut a final slice of mango for Dolan, sucked on the stone before tossing it into the trees. 'Where the others are going.'

'Dolan, Lieutenant, 2200118.'

Hochburg took a napkin off the table and studiously wiped his hands clean. 'Let me put it another way. I know all about you, Lieutenant; you, Vacher, Lapinski. As for Burton Cole . . . we're old friends.'

'You know the major?'

'*Major* Cole, is it?'

Dolan cursed himself.

'I've known young Burtchen since he was a boy. Knew his father – a geriatric missionary, hell-bent on saving the niggers. And of course his mother. She had the same blue eyes . . .' Hochburg's voice trailed off. He looked into the trees as if searching for something. Then abruptly: 'My spies also tell me that you were hired by Donald Ackerman, that you trained in Northern Rhodesia, that it was you who were supposed to lead the mission until a last-moment change of plan.'

And that none of this would have happened, thought Dolan, if I'd been left in charge. I'd have got the team out safe.

'So you see, I know everything about you. Everything except where young Burtchen is headed.' Hochburg leaned forward until their faces were inches apart. 'I have to find him.'

This close Dolan could see that there wasn't a drop of sweat on him. His eyes were so black that he had to look away.

Hochburg tapped his boot softly against Dolan's leg. Pain, like an electric shock, flared up his shin to the kneecap. 'Where?'

'Dolan, Lieutenant, 2200118.'

Hochburg straightened himself and reached for the knife again. 'You know, the negroid doesn't understand pain, at least not in the same sense as you and I do. You could never interrogate one because their brains are too crude to understand the cause and effect. I've conducted experiments to prove it. But you, Lieutenant 220, you're a white man. The effects can be . . . devastating.'

Dolan could feel his heart crawling upwards, as if it were caught in his chest and desperate to escape. He could hear Patrick taunting him again, that croaky Yank accent. I'm not going to tell, thought Dolan. *Not going to tell.* His breathing was ragged.

'I don't want to hurt you,' continued Hochburg, staring at him. He was still tapping Dolan's leg. 'The thought distresses me. My battle is out there, with the black races, so tell me what I want and this will all be over.'

'We split up.'

'Yes.'

'After the airfield at Mupe. I don't know where he went. We didn't tell each other. We thought it would be safer.'

'That makes sense, but doesn't help me. Or you.'

Hochburg toyed with the knife in his hand. The point glinted. He walked into the garden and took another cutting. 'Do you know what this is?' He held up a small red fruit.

Dolan shook his head.

Hochburg placed the fruit on the table and began cutting it into thin strips. 'Hold him fast.'

The guards clamped him down, one either side; the third grabbed his hair, held his head straight.

Hochburg turned back to face him, a piece of the fruit in his palm. 'This, Lieutenant, is *Capsicum Chinese Habanero*. Another Brazilian import. More commonly known as the chilli.' He took the fruit and began rubbing it between his fingers and thumbs. The tips turned livid. 'Where is Burton headed?'

'I don't know, I swear. I—'

Hochburg gouged his thumbs into Dolan's eyes.

Dolan felt the chilli crush into the sockets.

'Where?'

He screamed.

A scream so loud he felt his throat would burst. He writhed around, tried to escape. But the guards were too strong. And all the time Hochburg kept pressing down. Heat, like a living entity, burrowed through his eyeballs. The dog was barking.

'Stanleystadt!'

Hochburg gave one last dig, then removed his thumbs. 'You see. Do the same to the nigger and all you get is bawling.'

The guards released their grip.

Dolan tumbled to the ground. Writhing, blind. Tears cascaded down his face; his nose was a fountain of mucus.

'It's a city of a hundred thousand,' said Hochburg. 'I need more. Who's protecting him? Does he have a safe house?'

'I don't know . . . I don't know.'

The thumbs in his eyes again. 'A name. An address.'

Dolan screamed and screamed. The monkeys in the jungle had fallen silent.

'*I don't know!*'

The thumbs were gone.

'Put him there,' said Hochburg.

Dolan was dimly aware of movement around him. The breakfast things being swiped off the table; the dog unleashed. He was grabbed by the wrists and ankles. Was hoisted up. Dolan tried to open his eyes: they were soldered together.

Hochburg was chopping again.

Next moment the table was against Dolan's back. Hands pinned him down. He tried to struggle but was too weak. His face felt as if it had been dipped in phosphorous.

'Trousers,' said Hochburg.

Dolan's trousers were yanked down, then his smalls; they caught around his ankles. He could feel the air on his skin. Felt utterly exposed. He tried to move to cover himself but the hands wouldn't let him. His genitals were shrivelled in fear.

The dog, he thought hysterically, *he's going to feed my bollocks to the dog*.

Then a hand – Hochburg's huge hand – on his penis, as gentle as a virgin bride. He felt his foreskin being pulled back. His heart was ready to explode.

Something was inserted into his urethra.

Pain.

Pain like he had never known. A searing red-white agony as a sliver of chilli spread its fire.

This time Dolan screamed so loud his mam might have heard him. In the haze of his mind he pictured her: wearing her pinny, scrubbing dishes at the sink, looking up and muttering under her breath about all the racket.

'Rougier!' yelled Dolan. It was the only thing he could think of. '*Rougier!*'

Next moment he was free.

Dolan rolled off the table, crashed on to the ground. His leg roared. Crockery broke beneath him as he shrank himself up into a foetal ball. His groin was ablaze. He hoped he had held off long enough. Hoped it would allow Patrick and the major to escape.

But most of all he hoped the agony would end.

Chapter Fifteen

Stanleystadt, Kongo
16 September, 08:00

ROUGIER closed the door behind Burton and put his finger to his lips. The Frenchman had a face that looked as if it had been battered into shape by truncheons, bulbous nose, inscrutable eyes. He was wearing a cheap safari suit.

'You know the rules,' came a voice. 'Guests forbidden.'

Burton quickly took in the surroundings. They were in a vestibule of a lodging house. On the wall hung a copy of Lanzinger's ridiculous portrait of the Führer clad in armour, gripping the banner of National Socialism; Hitler as Sir Lancelot! Standing beneath the picture was a tiny wizened lady, her arms crossed.

There was no sign of Patrick.

'Frau Gift,' Rougier said to the woman, 'this is a business colleague of mine, come to discuss mineral rights.'

Frau Gift was unimpressed. 'Mineral rights. Looks more like he's been down a mine.'

Burton straightened his shirt, aware of the stains on it.

'We shall be no more than half an hour.'

'If you want to talk business, go to your office. I'm trying to have my breakfast. *In peace.*'

'Please, Frau Gift. Our negotiations are at a crucial stage, will be of great benefit to your Fatherland. Unless you'd rather the rights go to the British. Or maybe Americans . . .'

The old woman scowled. Opposite the Führer's portrait was a cuckoo clock, its hands just after eight. Frau Gift pointed at it. 'Thirty minutes, no more. If he's not gone by then, I'll double your rent for the month. And keep it quiet!'

Rougier made a curt bow and led Burton away. 'Bitch,' he muttered when they were out of earshot. They began climbing a steep staircase.

There was a rap at the front door.

'The sentry,' hissed Burton. 'From outside.'

They hurried up to the first floor, leaned over the balustrade to listen. Burton reached for his Browning. Rougier's eyes blinked with alarm.

'Now what?' sighed Frau Gift as she answered the door. Hushed voices. Burton couldn't see who was standing there.

Moments later the old woman stalked back across the vestibule. Alone.

'Keep going,' said Rougier.

They went up three more flights to a landing at the top of the building. The place was cool, utilitarian, soulless; smelt of nylon carpets and vinegar. Rougier ushered Burton through a door and bolted it after them. They were in a bathroom. Standing in the corner, gun in hand, was Patrick. When he realised it was them he lowered the Mauser but didn't put it away.

Burton began to speak, 'This is some—'

Once more Rougier put his finger to his lips. He bent over the bath and turned on the taps. Water came gushing out. 'The Nazis want as many foreign businessmen in the city as possible, but they don't trust us,' he said over the hiss of the taps. 'I check my room for bugs every week, never find anything. But better safe than sorry.' He settled himself on the toilet and gestured for Burton and Patrick to sit. His hands reminded Burton of Hochburg's: big, murderous.

'This is some place you chose,' resumed Burton, perching

himself next to Patrick on the edge of the bath. Opposite them was a mirror.

'They'd never think of looking on their own doorstep,' replied Rougier. 'The SS aren't half as smart as they imagine. You must be Major Cole.'

Burton nodded.

'Lazlo Rougier.' Neither of them offered hands. 'What about the others?'

'We split up. Lapinksi's dead. Dolan and Vacher were heading for—'

'The others aren't important now,' said Patrick. 'What matters is whether you can help us.'

Burton spoke. 'We need you to contact Ackerman, get us out of here.'

'Ackerman's gone.'

Patrick flashed Burton a look.

'Back to Rhodesia?'

'Angola. It will take at least twenty-four hours for me to get a message to him. Same again for a reply.'

'Two days?' said Patrick. 'We could be dead in two days.'

'What's he doing in Angola?' asked Burton.

Rougier looked at him, a puzzled expression on his battered face. 'You don't know?' When he got no response, Rougier stood and turned to look out of the window at the city below. From his angle on the bath all Burton could see was sky.

Rougier moved back to face them, his eyes serious. 'You'd better tell me what happened.'

'We were double-crossed,' said Patrick. His voice was a growl. 'We got to the RV and the Nazis were waiting for us. *Nebelwerfers*, Waffen-SS troops—'

'You were followed?'

Patrick shook his head. 'Somebody betrayed us. I say it was Ackerman. To keep from paying us.'

'That makes no sense.'

'If not Ackerman, then who? One of us? Impossible. The

142

aircrew? Blown to bits. The Negroes at the training camp? Hardly closet Nazis.'

'The Germans have spies everywhere.'

Patrick skewered him with a dangerous look. 'What about *you*?'

Burton went to speak but Patrick held up his hand.

'If Ackerman wanted to get rid of us, why not you too? You supplied the jeeps, the weapons – that must have cost. Unless the two of you were in it together. Or Ackerman is innocent and you're the rat.'

Rougier shifted uncomfortably. Dug his hands into his pockets.

'You sure seem safe enough here,' continued Patrick, 'next door to your SS buddies.'

The movement was so fast Burton didn't have time to stop him.

Patrick leapt up, drove his fist hard into the Frenchman's sternum. Rougier doubled over, collapsed to his knees. Patrick grabbed him by the hair, forced his head into the toilet bowl and pulled the chain. *La leçon de la cuvette.* A favourite punishment of the Legion.

'Patrick!' said Burton. 'This isn't going to help.'

Rougier struggled wildly as his face was engulfed in swirling water. There was a smell of carbolic acid.

Patrick's eyes were white. He held fast, plunged Rougier's face deeper. 'I was supposed to be with my daughter!'

The cistern emptied. Patrick let go of the chain, snapped Rougier's head back until his Adam's apple was bulging.

'Why did you do it?'

Rougier was struggling to speak, his mouth foaming with water. 'Not . . . spy . . . Angolan . . . camp . . .'

Patrick shoved his head back into the bowl.

'Quiet!' said Burton. Over the water and Rougier's choking he thought he heard something.

Patrick pulled Rougier back out, clamped his hand over his mouth. The Frenchman bit hard but Patrick ignored it, a trickle of blood oozing between his fingers. Burton pulled out his Browning and opened the door. How much noise had they been making?

He looked down the landing – nothing – then crept to the stairs. He could see right down to the vestibule: it too was empty. The building creaked around him. Outside he could hear the hum of traffic.

He moved silently back to the bathroom. 'Nothing,' he said, locking the door behind him. The taps were still running.

Patrick sat slumped on the bath staring at the floor, his fury spent as fast as it had erupted. The lines on his face seemed deeper. Rougier watched him warily from the corner. 'I had nothing to do with it,' he said coughing, slicking back his hair. 'I swear it, on my kids' lives. And I can't believe it was Ackerman either.'

'How are you so sure?'

'It's like you said: if it was him I'd already be face down in the river. He's more ruthless than he seems.'

Burton's head was throbbing. 'Can you help us?' he asked.

Rougier threw a look at Patrick. 'Why should I?'

'Because if we're captured, the only thing we've got is your name.'

'I don't even know what you did.' He sounded resentful. 'Ackerman never tells me.'

'Bullshit.'

'There are rumours going round the city. An attack on the Schädelplatz. Tell me.' When Burton said nothing he continued, 'My job was to organise the Zieges and weapons. That's all. It wasn't safe for me to know anything else.'

'You know our names.'

'I'm just a businessman. I help Ackerman out from time to time – but that's all.'

'Why?'

'It must be his Rhodesian charm,' said Patrick, still looking at the ground.

Rougier ignored him. 'My family never signed up to Vichy. We lost everything, had to flee France. I hate the Nazis. So my motives are . . . ideological.' His voice became bitter. 'I guess I was ripe for Ackerman's picking. I haven't even been paid yet.'

'You mentioned an Angolan camp,' said Burton. 'What did you mean?'

'If anyone betrayed you it's them.'

'Why? We're nothing to do with them,' said Burton. He sat down next to Patrick and glanced at himself in the mirror. With their shabby clothes and filthy matted hair they looked like a pair of tramps. At least he was free of the SS uniform. The thought of Madeleine seeing him like that had made his stomach retch. Now he felt human again. The stubble on his chin was also a relief.

'Of course you are! They're the ones that hired you.'

This time even Patrick looked up.

'We work for Ackerman,' said Burton.

'And he works with the Angolans. The *Resistencia*. Is their middle man.'

'Middle man for who?'

'You don't know?'

Burton studied the Frenchman's face: despite his dripping hair he appeared to be enjoying himself. For once he held the secrets. 'LMC,' said Burton. 'The mining syndicate in Lusaka.'

'You've been misled,' replied Rougier.

'I checked him out.'

'You didn't look hard enough.'

'Who is he then?'

'Oh no, Major. You want to know who Ackerman is, I want to know what you did. If I'm going to help it's the least you can offer.'

Burton turned to Patrick. 'What do you say?'

'I can't see it matters any more,' replied the older man. He sighed. 'We're assassins.'

Rougier nodded.

'Our mission was to remove the Governor General,' said Burton, leaning in closer.

'Remove . . . remove how?'

'With extreme prejudice. I killed Hochburg with my own hands.'

'You strangled him?'

Burton saw a flash of silver. 'Knife. He was taking a percentage of Ackerman's diamonds, wanted the lot.'

'What on earth would Hochburg need diamonds for? I hear the man lives like a monk.'

'To pay for slaves.'

Rougier looked at him for a moment, then guffawed. 'Pay for slaves!'

'There's a labour shortage.'

'Of course there's a labour shortage. Has been since Windhuk; deporting the blacks was a stupid idea. But you don't declare yourself master of Africa, then fork out for slaves on the sly. What do you think the Unterjocher is for? Or POWs? I hear they're even shipping in Jews now, from Madagaskar. Anyone to work the fields.'

'Why does he need the diamonds then?'

'How the hell am I supposed to know?'

'But you do know who Ackerman is,' said Patrick.

'He's nothing as grand as LMC, that's for sure.'

'Who is he?'

'You really don't know?' Rougier paused, relishing his moment. 'Ackerman is British intelligence.'

Silence except for the rush of the taps.

Burton and Patrick looked at each other.

'British intelligence . . .' said Burton. His throat felt slack. 'Why didn't he tell us?'

'Most intelligence officers prefer to keep it quiet,' replied Rougier. 'He works out of Loanda. The British have a consulate there.'

'Yes,' said Burton absently, 'I know it.' He'd been there once before on a trip back from DSWA. It was in the old part of the city, a white building with green shutters and a view of the bay.

He tried to picture Ackerman there with his sombre suit and Rhodesian accent but the image kept slipping. All he could see was him standing in the orchard back home laughing at him. *What about your quinces . . .*

'You see,' said Patrick. 'He didn't play us straight from the start.'

'That doesn't prove he set us up.'

'No,' agreed Rougier. 'Whatever his reason for lying, I still can't see why he'd betray you. It must have been the Angolans. The *Resistencia* is riddled with spies. Ackerman knew as much.'

'Then why trust them?' demanded Patrick. 'Why set up the mission? Why come all the way to England to find Burton?'

Rougier stepped back into the corner, raised his hands. 'I don't know.'

'And why, for fuck's sake, would British intelligence want to kill Hochburg?'

'I don't know! You'd have to go to Loanda, ask him yourself. You'd—'

The sound of wood splitting.

An axe crashed through the door.

It was prised out, came crashing down again, breaking open a hole. Through the gap Burton saw a swarm of black uniforms and BK44s. Heard Frau Gift screeching: 'I told you they were in there! I told you!'

Burton pulled his Browning and fired at the door. In the enclosed space of the bathroom the sound was ear-bursting. The lead blackshirt tumbled back, blood spraying the tiles. The old woman screamed.

Patrick tugged at the window. 'It's locked.' He got out his own pistol and aimed at the glass. Another deafening retort. Glass flew everywhere.

Beyond the door Burton heard breeches being pulled on machine guns.

'No,' came a voice. 'We need them alive.'

Patrick flipped his gun in his hand, used the handle to smash

147

out the jagged teeth of glass still left in the frame. Then he was pulling himself up and out.

The axe smashed into the door again.

Burton turned to Rougier. All the blood had drained from his face. 'Move!'

'I'll hold them off.'

'Don't be stupid,' said Burton, shoving him towards the window.

The Frenchman gingerly stood on the toilet and began to heave himself out.

The axe came down again. A few more blows and they'd be through. 'Quickly!'

Rougier's legs disappeared upwards.

Burton leapt to the window, moved himself into position. He looked down: a three-storey fall on to concrete. Below, a brown-shirt stared up, gawping.

The door burst inwards.

Burton aimed the Browning again. Pulled the trigger: once, twice. Another two soldiers dropped in an explosion of blood. A spurt of gunfire came back, bullets ricocheting off the tiles and enamel bath.

Burton fired one more round and hauled himself out of the window.

Chapter Sixteen

THEY were on the roof.

It was terracotta tiled, led to the next building and the one after that. To the east and west the city sprawled towards the jungle; north was the river. Looming behind them was SS headquarters. From this higher elevation Burton could see the top of it: there was a landing pad and Flettner helicopter. It was armed with twin MK108 cannon.

Rougier looked as if he were about to be sick. 'I hate heights.'

'Which way?' said Patrick.

'Towards the river,' replied the Frenchman. 'If we can make it to the Börse we'll be able to get back down. Disappear.'

'Go!' said Burton. He was still perched on the edge above the bathroom window. 'I'll catch up.'

Patrick and Rougier began running along the spine of the roof, their arms held out like tightrope walkers.

Beneath him Burton heard someone climbing out of the window. A hand appeared on the eaves, then another. The type of hand that had shoved and slapped Madeleine before she fled Austria. Next moment an SS trooper heaved himself on to the roof.

Burton kicked him hard in the face.

The trooper tumbled backwards, screaming. Seconds later there was a thud on the street below. A car braked sharply.

Patrick and Rougier had already leapt on to the next building. Burton raced after them, willing himself not to slip. He couldn't see the ground from here – just the pitch of the roof and a drop into nothing. The soles of his boots felt as if they had been sheened. What he wouldn't give for his ones back home: they gripped like glue.

He heard shouts from behind. Two other blackshirts had managed to scale the roof. A volley of bullets sparked around him.

Burton approached the edge at full speed. He jumped and came crashing down on the next building. His ankle buckled, almost toppling him, but he regained his balance. Patrick and Rougier were just ahead. Burton spun round, pulled his Browning and fired twice. Both shots missed, the troopers ducked down.

Opposite them, several black figures had appeared on the roof of SS HQ. One of the troopers was spinning his hand at them. '*Los!*' he shouted. '*Fahren Sie Los!*'

Burton saw Rougier struggling to keep pace with Patrick. He caught up with him. They jumped to the next building. And the next. And the one after that. Then the one sound Burton had dreaded.

Rougier looked behind them, almost lost his balance. His eyes were giddy.

The whirr of rotor blades. Getting faster and faster.

The helicopter was preparing to take off.

Burton grabbed Rougier's arm, steadied him. 'Keep moving!'

'We have to get over there,' said Rougier, motioning to the roofs on the other side of the street. Otherwise we'll hit 25 Mai. It's too big to jump.'

'Patrick!' Burton pointed left before risking another look behind them. There were a dozen troopers, maybe more, scuttling over the skyline like black beetles. The helicopter took off, its nose dipping as it climbed, and rose rapidly towards the river. It turned over the water and headed back towards them.

They had thirty seconds at most.

Patrick followed Burton's directions, sprinted down the incline of the roof, leapt – arms swinging like a long jumper – and landed on the building opposite. He turned to see where the others were.

'Come on!' he shouted. Then he was up and running again.

Burton reached the apex of the roof, Rougier behind him. 'I can't do it,' Rougier panted. 'I can't.'

'You're dead if you don't.'

'I'll take my chances.'

The helicopter was bearing down on them, the thunder of its blades filling the air.

'Go!' said Burton, shoving the Frenchman.

He hurtled down the tiles and leapt.

Burton raced after him, took a deep breath as if the air in his lungs might carry him and launched himself across the gap. His arms swam in the air. His boots felt as if they were made of iron. He was descending, descending too fast . . .

The helicopter roared over them, its downdraught pummelling the air.

Burton crashed on to the roof, the impact so hard he felt his ribs crack. He swung his leg over to get a better purchase, pulled himself up.

'*Au secours!*'

Burton turned.

'*Major!*'

Rougier was grasping the edge of the roof. He had nothing but a handhold, the rest of him dangling over the edge. His face bulged with terror. Burton looked for Patrick but he had already reached the top of the next roof, was disappearing down the other side.

Burton lowered himself towards Rougier.

'*Vite!*' said the Frenchman.

The helicopter turned, preparing for another pass.

Burton moved as near as he dared. Any further and he would slide off. He held out his hand. Rougier reached for it. Their fingertips brushed.

Burton strained to get closer. The tiles felt slick beneath him. Just a couple more inches . . .

The roof erupted, fragments of tile exploding in a cloud of fire. The helicopter swooped low, cannon blazing.

Burton slipped. Managed to get a grip, dug his nails into the roof until it felt as if his fingers would pop.

Rougier held out his hand like a man in quicksand, face imploring. Burton reached for it. Missed. Reached for it again.

And grabbed him!

'Don't drop me,' begged Rougier. 'Don't drop me.'

'You've got to help.' Over the edge Burton could see the street below: people pointing upwards, a row of lime trees, exclusive boutiques with red canopies.

'Don't drop me.'

Burton heaved with all his strength. He could feel Rougier's huge, sweaty paw wrapped around his. Burton heaved again. He had no purchase. His arm felt as if it were being torn out of the socket.

And then his grip was slipping.

Rougier's eyes swelled with fear. He went to say something, mouth fluttering. Burton tried to grip harder . . .

Rougier's hand slipped through his.

He vanished from sight. Seconds later a ripping sound. A scream. Burton pressed his face against the roof, squeezed his eyes shut. His brow felt feverish.

He pulled himself back up the roof, struggled to his feet. Up the apex, down the other side. He heard the shouts of the soldiers. Bullets clattered all around him. Patrick was waiting for him at the end of the roof, staring at the office block opposite. Beyond that was the cinema they'd passed earlier in the morning.

'It's too far!' said the American. He was panting heavily, face dripping sweat. The gap between them and the next building was a gorge. 'We'll never make it.'

Burton snapped his head left, then right. 'We don't have a choice.'

The helicopter tore over them again. They ducked, the wind of its tail rotors tearing at their hair.

'Where's Rougier?' asked Patrick.

'We'll need a run up,' said Burton. They turned and sprinted back up to the top of the roof. Burton felt fire in his thigh muscles.

They reached the top. Ran straight into a trooper. *Kai-duka*. Burton headbutted him. The blackshirt sprawled backwards, dropped his weapon. He rolled down the roof, colliding with two of his comrades. They tumbled off the edge.

Others were climbing upwards. Patrick scooped up the fallen BK44. Raked the soldiers below with gunfire till the magazine was empty.

Burton and Patrick whirled round, facing the chasm between them and the next building, and ran.

Burton was pumping his arms, felt each breath as it penetrated deep into his lungs. He concentrated on the building opposite. It was as if nothing else in the world existed; like it hung in a void of smoggy, grey sky. It had a flat roof.

Two more strides and he'd be at the edge. The balls of his feet were throbbing. One last stride . . .

He leapt.

Earlier in the spring Madeleine had got it into her head to repair the weather vane on the farm; it was the type of escapade she thrilled at but her husband would never allow. Before Burton could stop her she scaled the roof, pointing out the holes and laughing as she went. He loved that fearlessness in her, it reassured him in a way that no other woman had made him feel. She was almost at the top before she slipped and fell. Later, as Burton bathed her bruises, he would remember that moment. How Madeleine seemed to plummet in slow motion, with him helpless to save her.

That's how he felt now as he soared through the air like some huge flightless bird.

Burton crashed on to the roof opposite, tumbling forward in

a ball of limbs. His head banged concrete. Then he was sprawled on his back looking at the overcast sky. It seemed a long, long way away.

Someone grabbed him. 'We got to keep moving.' It was Patrick.

Burton sat up. Across the chasm, the SS were preparing to follow. *Didn't these bastards ever quit?*

Burton was running again. The flat roof made it easier. He tried to remember where the Börse was. Ahead he could see the Giesler Bridge; the Börse was to the west of it: a squat, triangular building where everything from gold to palm oil was traded. It could be no more than two, three hundred yards.

They reached a wall, scaled it and dropped on to the next roof. There were air-conditioning units, a long skylight.

Cannon fire.

The helicopter was bearing down on them, swooping low. Too low. The pilot was insane. He'd crash the helicopter.

Burton sprinted away, Patrick in the lead. He could feel the air being bent around him. The ground erupted in spouts of dust and bullets.

Patrick veered towards the skylight. Tripped. The cannon strafed the glass. For an instant Patrick teetered on the edge of the skylight.

He plunged through it.

'Patrick!' yelled Burton.

The helicopter finished its pass, rising fast and high.

'Patrick!' Burton peered into the shattered skylight. Below him was a narrow loft, the walls hidden behind racks of canisters.

'Get your ass down here, Cole.' Patrick stood among them in a ragged pool of glass. Blood was gushing from the scab on his nose.

Burton jumped below. The floor was vibrating with the sound of cheers and triumphant music. In the corner of the room was a door. They ran through it to a staircase and began descending. Someone came up the stairs.

'What the fuck is going on here? Who are you—'

Burton kneed him in the balls, spun him round, slammed his head into the wall.

Above them gunfire. Boots crashing down into the canister room.

Burton and Patrick flew down the stairs, taking them three at a time. The cheering, the music was getting louder. At the bottom of the stairwell, another door. They burst through it, into a black-ened chamber. Sitting in front of them were hundreds of people, staring in rapt concentration. Above them a flickering beam of light.

Burton turned to look in the audience's direction. They were staring at a screen, on it black and white images of a football match, the Maracanã stadium in Rio de Janeiro.

The people in the nearest seats glared at them.

Burton and Patrick strode up the aisle. At the back of the cinema, illuminated in red letters, was the word ABTRETEN. They headed for it.

Behind them the door was flung open. Troops appeared, their banana-guns ready.

Burton pulled his Browning and fired a single shot into the air.

A woman screamed.

Next moment: pandemonium.

People were out of their seats, shouting, fighting their way to the aisles. Shoving limbs, trampling feet. Burton and Patrick joined the throng of bodies, let themselves be carried along in the panic. Vanished into the crowd.

On the screen behind them Germany scored with only seconds to spare before the final whistle. The World Cup was Hitler's.

Chapter Seventeen

Terras de Chisengue, North Angola
16 September 11:00

WHEN he saw it was her, the guard lowered his gun. 'Did you do it?' he asked. His face was white and expectant. 'Did you blow the tunnel?'

Neliah's nostrils flared with rage. 'Where's Penhor?'

'I don't know. Everyone's getting ready to move out to the train.'

Neliah stepped past him and continued through the trees. They were *eucaliptos*, had been planted to hide the camp because they grew fast. She trailed the panga in her hand.

'What about the tunnel?' he shouted after her. 'None of us thought you could do it. Neliah. Neliah!'

Neliah. It was an old Herero name. Her *ina*, her mother, had given it. *Strong of will* it meant. *Strong of will, vigorous of spirit, level of mind*. Heading to the camp she felt none of these. Only fury and a pebble of shame.

Her hunger for revenge an unfed beast.

Five seasons had passed since the *Nazistas* had stormed into Angola. When they arrived nothing, not even his white skin, could save her father. In those last moments of chaos he told Neliah and Zuri to hide – *go, my meninas, go!* Then he went to meet the skull-troops, opened-handed, full of willing just like the Portuguese and British told everyone to be. *Papai* was gunned

156

down, everything he had struggled for taken away: their home, the quarry, the excavation machines. The *Nazistas* painted the company diggers with their crooked-crosses, divided the miners into two groups. The whites would remain, toiling for their new masters. The blacks were forced to dig a pit and lie in it. None of them refused, none except *Ina*.

She always had fire in her belly, remembered the old stories of what the Germans had done to their people long before the *Nazistas*.

When *Ina* ran they caught her, bayoneted her again and again till the ground flowed black. Strung her up for the buzzards. After that the others did as they were told. Climbed into the trench, lay down like cattle and waited. The skull-troops flung in grenades. In her dreams Neliah could still hear that noise: the dull thud of earth and flesh. The screams. Afterwards, with moans still rising from the ground, the Germans fetched a digger. Filled the pit back up. The sisters saved themselves by hiding in the cesspit, noses deep in pigswill and shit. When night fell they escaped, ran and ran, blind with tears, and never went back.

At first the *Nazistas* slew her kindred wherever they found them. Later, when they no longer had time to dig pits, when the corpses piled up like mountains, they started transporting them. Herded like cattle in lorries and trains – always north, to a place beyond Angola, beyond Kongo and Aquatoriana, to where the deserts began. Muspel, the Germans called it. To her people it was a land of slavery and dying. A nightmare with no dawn to break it.

Neliah reached the camp as Penhor was marching his troops out. He was at the head of the column, a ceremonial sabre swinging in his hand. The scarlet sash around his chest had been tied tight. When he saw her he brought the men to a halt, told them to stand easy. They were all carrying backpacks and rifles. Neliah heard whispers behind hands as they stared at her.

She met their eyes without blinking, slid the panga back into its sheath and rubbed the scar above her brow. It was an old wound from a German bayonet. She hadn't bothered to sew it, wanted it left wide and ugly as a reminder. Her trousers, vest, boots were thick with mud.

Gonsalves stepped to the front. Put his fists on his hips. 'So, the great warrior returns.'

'That's enough,' said Penhor. 'I'm glad to see you back, girl.'

Neliah said nothing.

'And I know Zuri will be happy you're home.'

'Our home is in the south, where the *Nazistas* rule. Not here.'

'And will be again, I promise you.' He lowered the sabre he was carrying. 'Did you destroy the tunnel?'

Neliah was back in her hiding place above the Lulua River. Beneath its moonlit waters she could see the tunnel leading to Rhodesia. The road was empty, there were no guards. Her heart growled at that: she had wanted to kill as many Germans as possible. Neliah whispered a *kumbu* to her ancestors and counted down the timers. The night thundered, hurting her ears. There was a blast of fire and smoke. When it cleared she stood up, stared at the damage below. And hung her head.

Neliah lunged at Penhor. 'It didn't work!'

Soldiers crowded around her. She felt forked hands pulling her off.

'I told you she'd only fuck things up,' said Gonsalves.

'It was the dynamite,' replied Neliah, pushing away the soldiers. 'It was too old, didn't fire. Not all of it.'

Penhor flicked a speck of dust off his uniform. 'Impossible,' he said. 'It came from my contacts at the British embassy. In Loanda. They only give me the latest equipment.'

'The British handed this country to the *Nazistas* in a bowl,' said Neliah. 'How can you trust them?'

'The winds are changing. They're on our side now.'

Gonsalves spoke. 'I say there was nothing wrong with the explosives. It was her. She didn't know what she was doing.'

'It was the dynamite!' Neliah roared back, troubled that he might be speaking the truth. 'It wasn't right. Smelt like . . . old bones. The British are tricking us.'

'Old bones?' said Gonsalves. 'That explains everything!' He encouraged the other soldiers to laugh. 'I tell you, these things are too complicated for her kind. For a cook-girl. For a *negra*.'

Neliah hurled herself at him, held the panga to his throat. '*Omu-runde!*'

The soldiers crowded round again. She felt clawing, pinches. A hard punch to the low-back. Gonsalves was spitting.

Penhor dragged her off. 'Gonsalves, hold your tongue. Neliah, put the blade down.'

'Not till he eats his words—'

'Put it down!'

Reluctantly she lowered it. Her breathing was heavy. She'd fight them all: the *Nazistas*, the British, even the Angolans. White Angolans.

'Any more of this and I'll have you whipped. Both of you.' He fixed Neliah with his eyes. 'Now, tell us what happened.'

'I set the charges, just like you told me. Checked everything two times. But they didn't explode. Not enough of them.'

'And the tunnel?' Neliah thought his voice sounded tight, like wet cow hide left in the sun. 'Did you destroy the tunnel?'

Neliah glanced at the dirt, then looked up again. Stared Penhor in the face. 'The Germans will be able to repair the damage.'

Gonsalves turned to Penhor. '*Comandante*, give me three men,' he said. 'Three men and enough dynamite and I'll stop those Boche bastards in their tracks.'

Penhor ignored him. 'Where are the rest of your Herero?'

'Tungu and Bomani came back with me, are following behind. The others . . . ran.'

Gonsalves snorted as if a great truth had been proved.

Neliah tried to keep the begging from her voice. 'Let *me* go back. All I need is more dynamite.'

'You did your best, girl. Angola is proud of you. Now I need you to watch over Zuri—'

'Wait! There's something else,' said Neliah. She was searching for another reason to go back to the tunnel. 'Near the river we saw a camp.'

'What type of camp?'

'A German camp. A chimney-camp. There were lots of prisoners there.'

'White prisoners?'

Neliah couldn't still the savagery in her voice. 'Of course white.'

'There aren't enough of us as it is,' interrupted Gonsalves. 'You said so yourself, *Comandante*. Let me go. I'll release them, then bring that tunnel crashing down.'

'I can do it,' said Neliah. 'I can free them.'

Gonsalves laughed. 'The shame of it. I'd rather be a prisoner than rescued by a nig-girl.'

Neliah's eyes burned. She curled her fingers around the panga again.

'*Nobody* is going back to the tunnel,' said Penhor. 'Or this alleged camp.'

'But Angola,' said Gonsalves. 'We'll be left to burn if the Boche get through the tunnel to Rhodesia. There'll be no one to help us.'

'We have tried to do our duty by Carvalho, but now Loanda must be our priority.' Penhor turned to his soldiers, raised his voice. 'Men, fall back in.'

'Please,' said Neliah.

'You are to stay here, girl. With Zuri. Help guard the camp till we return, it's an important job.'

'Why won't you let me fight?'

'Fighting's for men.'

'You mean whites.'

'I mean men. If all goes well in Loanda, I'll send for you and your sister.' Neliah knew he was lying. 'If not, we'll fall back here. Regroup, try to get to Mozambique.'

'I'm sick of waiting,' said Neliah. 'I want blood, German blood. Me and Zuri deserve it. All I need is more dynamite.'

'There's none left, we've taken it all. For the battle ahead.'

'You can't stop me from going back to the tunnel.'

Penhor sighed, ran his tongue between his teeth and top lip.

'I'm leaving Lieutenant Ligio in charge of the camp. Ligio and a few other guards. They'll be under strict instructions to make sure you don't go wandering.'

'But—'

'I'll tell them to throw you in chains if they have to.' He patted her shoulder: Neliah pulled away. 'Look after Zuri for me.'

The soldiers were back in their ranks. Penhor straightened the sabre in his hand, took his position at the front again and marched them off. Neliah saw Gonsalves grumbling to the men nearest him. They were all nodding. She watched till they disappeared into the trees, bowed her shoulders. Above her, parrots chattered in the *eucaliptos*. She was exhausted, her body heavy like it was full of stones. If only she had taken more dynamite . . .

Neliah ran.

She darted through the camp, past the *octógono* to the strong-room. She wanted to be sure. There was a guard at the door, a white boy even younger than her.

'You're back,' he said, fumbling with his rifle. 'Did you blow up the tunnel?'

'No. I didn't have enough dynamite. *Comandante* Penhor sent me to get more.'

'I've got orders. No one is allowed in here except Lieutenant Ligio—'

She pushed past him before he could say another word, down the stairs into the cellar. It smelt of sun-baked straw. The gun racks were empty except for a few old rifles. Boxes and kitbags had been thrown to one side. Neliah rummaged through them, hoping that *gnambui* was smiling on her.

Gnambui was.

In the corner, hidden under some sacking, she found a wooden crate. Neliah felt a trill in her heart. She couldn't read the words on it but she understood the symbols. Explosives. She put her face to the box and breathed in. The smell of black powder like pepper and fire. It reminded her of *Papai*.

Behind her: footsteps.

161

Neliah quickly replaced the sacking, turned towards the stairs. It was Zuri, her sister.

She looked beautiful as always, was wearing a simple white dress the way Penhor – 'Alberto' – liked her to. Her skin was milky brown. She had inherited it from their father's side: it was Portuguese skin, not Herero. Her hair fell in a long, smooth plait that swished when she walked. It was her great joy. After they had fled home Zuri continued to keep her hair clean and adorned. Neliah chopped hers off.

'You're safe!' said Zuri standing on her toes to kiss her.

Neliah held her close, buried her face into her sister's hair. It smelt of the lemon-water Penhor splashed on his face. She pushed her away.

'Where have you been?' asked Zuri, looking at the mud on her clothes. 'I couldn't sleep last night. Alberto said you'd gone. I thought you'd left me.'

Neliah told her about the tunnel, everything that had happened.

'Next time you tell me,' said Zuri, grasping her sister's hands. 'We go together.'

'It was too dangerous,' replied Neliah. 'I already lost *Ina* and *Papai*. I'm not losing you.'

'I'm the older, I should be protecting you.'

Neliah withdrew her fingers. 'Penhor told me not to say. He didn't want you to go.'

'He said that?' She took a step back, her plait swishing. 'He worries what might happen if the *Nazistas* catch us.'

'Not us, *you*. I don't know how you let him touch you.'

Zuri folded her arms across her chest. 'It gives us a roof, keeps our bellies full.'

'But he's an old man,' said Neliah, crinkling her mouth. 'Has a wife!'

'In Portugal.'

'With his children.'

Zuri gave a bitter laugh. 'You sound like an old missionary.'

Penhor wasn't the first whose tastes Zuri had played. They

were always old, always white. Neliah huffed. 'What would *Papai* say?'

'*Si possis recte, si non, modo rem*,' replied Zuri.

Neliah hated it when her sister used the stupid Roman words their father had taught her – mostly because she hadn't been schooled in them herself. 'You know I don't understand.'

'If possible, be honest.' A sly grin. 'If not, do what's good for you.'

Neliah went to retort, stopped herself. She had bad teeth, preferred to keep her mouth straight, but she forced a smile for her sister. 'Do you really want to fight?'

'It was my mother they killed also.' Zuri's face hardened. 'My *papai*.'

'I'm going back to the tunnel. Will blow it all the way up to Mukuru this time.'

'How? I watched the soldiers. They took everything.'

Neliah smiled again. 'Look,' she said and went to the corner of the room. Pulled back the sacking.

'Is it enough?' asked Zuri. There was a spark in her eye.

Neliah nodded.

'What about Ligio? The other guards?'

'They're boys, they won't be able to stop us.'

'When will you go?'

'Tonight.'

'Together this time?' said Zuri.

Neliah held out her hand, it was still covered in mud. Her sister grasped it. '*Pamue*,' she said in Herero.

Pamue. As one, together.

Chapter Eighteen

Stanleystadt, Kongo
16 September, 12:45

'THE river,' said Patrick. 'It's our only hope now.'

From time immemorial it had been known as the Kongo. Then, in 1949, for the Führer's sixtieth birthday it was changed to the 'River Klara' – to honour his mother. Millennia of history rewritten with the stroke of a bureaucrat's pen. All except the zealots kept the old name. Along its waters flowed the goods that had made central Africa 'the warehouse of the Reich'. There were barges laden with cotton, timber, sugar and rice (Germany was now the world's largest producer of rice, even exported to Asia); tin and copper for the metalworks of the Ruhr; cobalt to make Messerschmitt jet engines. What the Fatherland didn't need – mostly second-rate materials – was traded with Europe and the United States. A system of exploit-siphon-sell that had helped finance Hitler's new empire and elevated the influence of Deutsch Kongo among the African colonies.

Burton and Patrick were trudging along the quaysides of Otraco. They had grown weary of discussing all that Rougier told them: it was leadening their spirits. They were no closer to discovering who'd betrayed them, or why Burton had been chosen to lead the mission. Worst, it seemed British intelligence was now their bankroller. All they wanted was a way out of the city. Burton's ribs ached from his fall on the roof. Every time he breathed in straps of pain squeezed around his chest.

Above them the sky oozed heat.

'Hey there!' called Patrick in German as they approached yet another vessel. 'Is the skipper on board?'

A man in a grubby cap leaned over the side. 'Who wants to know?'

'You hiring?'

He scowled. 'No.'

'You must have something,' said Patrick. Burton could hear the desperation in his voice.

'Nothing. Now fuck off.'

'We're hard workers,' said Burton.

'So?'

'And cheap,' added Patrick.

'Cheap?' The captain hawked and spat. 'How cheap?'

'Let us on and we can discuss it.'

He mulled it over, then: 'Gangplank's over there.'

Burton and Patrick climbed aboard the ship. Since escaping from the cinema they had scoured the docks for a boat heading to Neu Berlin. From there it was two hundred miles to the Atlantic and freedom. The new Salumu port, all regulations and paperwork, was too risky – so they had tried their luck on the Otraco side. Here were the one-man bands and occasional smugglers; owners willing to overlook formalities (documents, taxes) to maximise profits. But everyone they approached had given them the same gruff response: it was dry season, the river low, they had enough crew. Come back next month with the rains.

'So how cheap?' asked the captain. Up close he was much shorter than from the quayside, wore his cap at a jaunty angle. His cheeks were a mass of oily beard.

'Where you headed?' said Burton.

'I thought you said you were cheap.'

'Depends where you're going.'

The captain spat again and addressed his answer to Patrick.

'Downriver to Neu Berlin, leaving with the morning tide. I got a shipment of ivory. Now, how cheap?'

'We'll work for ten marks a day.'

Another gob of phlegm. Burton watched it land and glisten. 'I can get a Polack cheaper.'

'Five marks then.'

'Forget it.' He turned away. 'You know where the gangplank is.'

Patrick tugged at his sleeve. 'Give us a berth and one square meal and we'll work for free.'

The captain turned back and eyed them suspiciously. 'The black-shirts were here earlier, looking for spies. Anyone eager to leave the city.'

'That's nothing to do with us,' said Burton, sounding more defensive than he meant to.

'Working for free seems eager enough.'

'We are eager,' said Patrick, 'eager to get out of Kongo. I've had it with the heat and sweat and fucking mosquitoes. Another day here, I swear my nuts are gonna fry.'

The captain laughed. 'I know that feeling.'

Patrick breathed in. 'An ocean breeze, that's what I want.'

'One of my crew,' said the captain, 'he's fucking useless. I'm sure he's a vanilla-boy. You can have his bunk.'

'We'll take it,' said Burton.

The captain turned to Burton and grinned. His teeth were black. 'Only one bunk.'

'It's mine,' said Patrick. He spat on his hand and offered it to the skipper.

Burton's voice caught in his throat. 'What?'

'I'll expect you here at dusk,' replied the captain as they shook on it, 'ready for loading. Don't be late. And don't be drunk.'

'I'll be here.'

'Work hard and there'll be no grief. It's five days to NB.'

Patrick nodded and headed down the gangplank.

Burton strode after him, an emptying in his chest. 'Wait!'

Patrick ignored his cry.

'Wait! Where are you going?'

'I told you in the clink, Burton, this louses up: you're on your own.'

He stalked away.

Suddenly Burton was fourteen again. Opening the door to his mother's empty room, the curtains limp, bed stripped. He could still see the indent of her head on the pillow. When he placed his hand in the hollow it felt cold. Cold and damp. Everything else was gone – like she had never existed.

'You can't do this!' said Burton, trailing after him. 'I have to get back to Maddie. I promised her.'

'And I have to get back to Hannah.'

'We can make room on the boat, share the bunk. It wouldn't be the first time.'

'It's not about that. How many people saw you at the Schädelplatz? The soldiers, the Leibwache. The Schwarzflügel crew on the flight from Rhodesia.'

'What are you saying?'

'They know your face, Burton. Me, I'm nothing. A blank.'

Burton felt the hysteria rising in his chest. He knew Patrick was right, but wanted to disprove him. He dredged his mind. Nothing came, nothing except Patrick's words in Aquatoriana. *No more bullshit. Why did you want this job? I never saw you so sand-happy for anything.* Sand-happy, that's what they called legionnaires who had marched up too many dunes, whose brains had broiled in their skulls.

'I should have told you the truth, back in prison. Back on that first day in Bel Abbès.'

'For fuck's sake, man. *Auf Deutsch!*'

Without realising it, Burton had slipped into English. 'We have to do this together.'

'I said German!'

People on the docks were starting to stare at them.

Burton didn't care. 'You can't leave me.'

'Alone I got a chance. We stay together – I'm dead. I owe Hannah more than that.'

'Not for the last ten years.'

'You think that's going to make me stay?' replied Patrick in a warning tone.

'What about Dunkirk?' Burton tugged at Patrick's shirt, briefly exposed the half-moon scar. 'It would have been the easiest thing to have left you. When you were screaming—'

'I never screamed.'

'When the blood wouldn't stop. But I stayed. I held your hand, remember. Got you out of there.'

Their voices had risen. More curious eyes were turning in their direction. A passing brownshirt scrutinised them. Patrick freed himself from Burton's grip. 'I'm not going to die in Africa.'

'Neither am I,' said Burton.

They eyeballed each other. The sweat was trickling down Burton's back; all he wanted was to sit down. He could see Patrick was ashen.

Burton spoke in German. 'You know the Gospel of St Mark?'

'Just what I need. A fucking Sunday school lesson.'

'I spent most of my life trying to forget it. But right now it's the only thing I can think of.' He let out a dry laugh. 'Can even hear my father saying the words. *If a house be divided against itself, that house cannot stand.*'

'Jesus H. Christ.' Patrick sighed, rubbed the back of his neck, examined the sweat. People continued to look in their direction. 'You still hungry?'

'Famished.'

'Want a last supper?'

'Will it be safe?'

Patrick checked the faces staring at them. 'Safer than staying out here.'

They chose a booth hidden at the back. Ate sausage, sauerkraut and strudel – the only food on the menu. Burton tried to remember what Hochburg used to call them. That was it: 'the holy trinity of German cuisine'. Afterwards Burton ordered mango juice, Patrick a stein of Primus lager.

'The Kaiser,' said Burton lifting his glass. Patrick paused a moment before raising his beer, took a sullen gulp. He wiped the foam from his lips with the back of his hand.

They were in a dingy tavern near the quayside, the tables bustling with itinerant workers and a few brownshirts – thugs looking for cheap beer and the chance of a brawl. Before the invasion most of these places had been run by Indians, now it was the more racially acceptable Greeks.

Burton reached over for Patrick's half-finished strudel, began forking it into his mouth. The food had brought a surge of vigour to his aching muscles. He felt momentarily invincible: always a risky delusion. 'No nation that can make something so good can be all bad,' he said between mouthfuls.

'Spoken like Halifax,' replied Patrick. Every time the door opened his eyes darted to it. 'But try telling that to the Russians. Or the Negroes or Jews; I hear Madagaskar is a cesspit.'

'Point taken.' Burton continued to chew. 'You know Maddie makes the best apple strudel I ever tasted.'

'How come she wasn't shipped off to SS-Madagaskar?'

Burton grimaced. 'Her husband. He's some bigwig in the Colonial Office. Once she moved to London he was able to sort it out. It was the only good thing he did.'

'You didn't tell me she was married.'

'Unhappily. It was a mistake – on both their parts. He's very . . . overbearing.'

'This is perfect! You'll be telling me she's got kids next.'

'Alice, six years old. I don't think she likes me much.'

'I know the feeling.'

'It's worse. Maddie's pregnant. Can you imagine the scandal if her husband finds out?'

'So all this is because of her.' The conciliatory tone of dinner was slipping. 'I may never see my daughter again. Lapinski, Nares

169

dead. Who knows what with Gorilla Dum and Gorilla Dee . . . That's a helluva price to pay for a woman.'

'She gave me my life back. Saved me from becoming one of those old soldiers you see – no family, no roots; just scars and body counts.'

'Like me?'

'I didn't mean it that way.'

'It's still too much.'

Burton swallowed the last of the strudel. The pastry left a greasy trail on the roof of his mouth, the cinnamon suddenly bitter. They sat there staring at each other.

'Madeleine's not why I took the job.'

Patrick frowned, the wrinkles on his forehead deepening. 'What?'

'I never told you about it,' said Burton, 'when I first arrived at Bel Abbès.'

'That's the Legion way. Your past is your past and nobody's business.'

'Nobody's business,' repeated Burton softly.

Patrick leaned back in his chair, fished in his pocket for his pipe, kept looking around. At the bar a shout of laughter; someone playing an old Zarah Leander number on the accordion.

'It was after the war, that he came to us,' said Burton. 'The Great War. I was eleven, can still remember it like yesterday. See him emerging from the trees in his frock coat and hat, clasping his Bible. Wet and mud-stained, long black hair. Dashing, I suppose you'd call him. He'd been brought up from Lomé by a local guide.'

Patrick lit his pipe. 'Who? Ackerman?'

Burton gave a mirthless laugh. 'Not Ackerman. Hochburg.'

'Hochburg?'

'It started the first night, at the dinner table.'

Burton recalled it vividly. Father had just said grace; they were making polite conversation, Burton fiddling with the silverware, glancing at their strange new arrival. The first course arrived: a mulligatawny. For some reason that detail was etched on his mind. And then Hochburg began to weep. Tears streaming down his face, splashing into his soup. Burton had never seen a man cry before, certainly not his father. Later he heard Hochburg sobbing into his mother's breast: *There were bits of them everywhere. Limbs, intestines. They cut off their heads.* She stroked his hair. *I never saw so much blood, Eleanor, never saw so much blood . . .*

Burton looked at Patrick. 'He'd come to us to re-find his faith. Father told me his family had been killed by tribesmen in the Cameroons. His parents, brother, sister. He'd seen them all butchered.'

'Hochburg was a missionary too?'

Burton nodded. 'A true man of the cloth. I remember him saying, *How could God let this happen?* Sometimes he would cry, inconsolable. Other times there were rages. Rages like you never saw. Screaming to high heaven about "the niggers", vowing to burn them alive, every last one. When that happened I used to hide in bed. I was brought up to believe we're all God's children, no matter what our skin; still hold it true. Only my mother could comfort him.'

A silence descended between them. Patrick took a puff on his pipe, held the smoke in his lungs.

When Burton told Maddie about Hochburg it had been simple – a relief to unburden his secret after so long; the final barrier between them had been breached. But with Patrick he felt unsure. Exposed. He reached for his mango juice and took a sip. Wondered whether it was possible to make quince juice. You'd have to press it, need plenty of sugar. How far away the orchard seemed, like something from a picture book: close enough to touch, but unreal, someone else's image.

Patrick said, 'And your father accepted this?'

'He was always looking for lost souls. He and Hochburg were both nationalists, both felt betrayed by Versailles. Were Germans living in a colony that had become British. Walter would also have been the same age as my brothers—'

'I never knew you had brothers.'

'I forgot you had a wife and daughter. We served together for twenty years, Patrick, but sometimes I think we're strangers. What do we know – do we really know – about each other?'

'I know you're good in a fight, boy.'

'Two half-brothers, twins, from my father's first marriage. Livingstone and Stanley. That's where I get my name from.'

Patrick gave him a quizzical look.

'Richard Burton, the explorer. He went to find the source of the Nile. These men were my father's heroes.'

'And your brothers?'

'They volunteered in 1914. Fought in East Africa – for the Germans, for von Lettow. Never came home. That was before I was born.'

'So Hochburg became the stand-in son?'

'They talked, they prayed, built the orphanage together, tended the garden. Hochburg was good with the children, very kind. His "little black buttons" he used to call them.'

'When he didn't want to torch the poor bastards.'

'I don't know where the change came. Talk's one thing, murder another.'

Patrick chomped the end of his pipe. 'And you came all this way to kill him.'

'I wanted it more than anything. But it wasn't the only reason.'

'Which was?'

Burton hesitated. 'Are you really going to get on that boat?'

'I got to, it's my only way back to Hannah.' But there was an indecision in his voice, just like in prison.

That decided it.

'When I was fourteen years old,' said Burton, 'my mother walked out into the jungle. Hochburg disappeared the same day.' His voice was level, toneless. 'Why she did it, where she went, what happened: I don't know.'

Patrick seemed distracted, his eyes were roving outside. 'They were sweet on each other?'

Burton followed his gaze. A lorry was pulling up on the quayside. 'I don't know. She was much younger than my father, the same age as Hochburg.' A memory pounced on him: Hochburg in the river, the water rippling over his shoulders, Mama watching from behind her prayer book. His father snoring in the shade. 'He had some strange power over her.'

'So they were.'

Something in Burton squirmed. 'I never saw her again. Never said goodbye. Have you got any idea what that's like? The not knowing. It robbed me of something. A bit of my past, a bit of my future.' He screwed his thumb against his breastbone. 'It's been gnawing at me all my life. That's why I came to Kongo: to find . . .' He searched for an adequate word; failed. 'The truth.'

'Get up!' Patrick was on his feet. 'Quick, boy!'

Burton turned round, struggled to stand. He knocked the table. Mango juice spilled everywhere.

Outside, a second lorry pulled up. Its tailgate dropped. People were running.

Then a cry that sent panic through the tavern.

'*Der Unterjocher!*'

Chapter Nineteen

DER Unterjocher: the press gang.

The WVHA, the SS Economic Department, was divided into five sub-groups, or *Ämter*, of which Department W was the most infamous. It was Department W that ran the factories of Muspel; the concentration camps and slave labour programmes; administered Jewish Madagaskar under Governor Globocnik. The Unterjocher also came within its remit.

Burton pulled out his Browning, thumbed the safety.

Patrick shook his head. 'They'll be too many.' His eyes flitted round the tavern.

Outside Burton saw lorries, troops, the distinctive shape of banana-guns. They were heading to the building next door.

'If we get out fast, we're safe,' said Burton.

'Too late,' replied Patrick.

Guards were already positioned by the entrance. Two black sentinels.

There was a *drip-drip-drip* as the mango juice found the edge of the table.

Burton knew the reputation of the Unterjocher. Everyone did. With the blacks shipped north, and slaves from eastern Europe in demand for Speer's domestic rebuilding programme, the Nazis increasingly relied on the Unterjocher for labour in Africa:

mopping up economic migrants and former French and Belgian colonists, anyone without the correct papers. Few who were pressed survived more than six months. If sheer toil didn't destroy a man, malnutrition, disease and the guards' brutality would. Lord Halifax had attempted to raise the issue several times with Hitler. The Führer, all smiles-for-the-camera and barely suppressed rage, reassured the Prime Minister that the worst rumours were untrue. Vile propaganda spread by insurgents and the enemies of peace, those keen to stir up trouble between their two great empires, like the lurid falsehoods told about Muspel. Yes, conditions were sometimes harsh, but only criminals and undesirables made up the Unterjocher numbers. Surely the British operated something similar in their own colonies? All civilisations did. Perhaps if the Raj had been less lenient, India would still belong to them. Halifax would return home chastened.

'Put your piece away,' said Patrick. 'There's gotta be another exit.'

All around them people were scrambling for their documents. The tavern had fallen silent except for murmuring and the accordion player who had struck up 'Schweiss eines Weissen', the anthem of the SS in Africa. One man made a run for it. He burst through the front door, made it another two, three feet . . .

Was gunned down.

Roused by the shots, more troops headed towards the tavern. Orders were being shouted.

Burton tucked the Browning into his waistband and followed Patrick towards the rear of the building. The urge to bolt was almost irresistible, though nothing was more likely to get them arrested. He forced a measured pace as they weaved through the tables. Faces looked up at them: desperate, pleading, suspicious.

At the back, next to the bar, was a door. They pushed through it into a kitchen as hot as a Turkish bath. The air was heavy with sweat and sauerkraut. There were a couple of waitresses milling around. Beyond them another door – wide open. Through its frame Burton glimpsed an alleyway; it was unguarded.

'Come on,' he said, taking the lead.

They hurried towards it.

'Where you go?' A man stepped in front of them, barring their way. In his hand was a huge chef's knife. He had swarthy features and a walrus moustache drooping in the heat. He spoke German with a thick Greek accent.

Burton went to barge past him.

The Greek pointed the knife at his throat. 'Try it and I yell so noisy every soldier in city hear me. So do my girls.'

Patrick put a restraining hand on Burton's shoulder. 'We don't have the right papers,' he said to the Greek, adopting his comrade voice. 'If we don't get away it's the UJ for us.'

'You escape, they fine me. Take my place. Lock me up.'

'We'll go quietly. Quiet as gold.' Patrick produced one of the solid gold Reichmarks from their contingency packs. It winked in the dull light of the kitchen.

The Greek stood transfixed before reaching out to grab it.

Patrick snatched it away. 'Only if you let us through.'

'You got more?'

'Will you let us through?'

He made a hangman's gesture. 'They catch me, it rope.'

'It's a lot of money.'

'Money no good if I dead.'

Somewhere there was the sound of a struggle, a table being overturned.

Patrick took the Greek's hand and put the gold coin in his palm. Folded his fingers round it. 'You can let us through,' he soothed. 'The Germans will never know.'

The Greek hesitated a moment, then raised the coin to his mouth, tested it with his teeth.

He stood aside.

Patrick was first through the door. He took a few paces and came to a halt, looking in both directions. 'We're fucked.'

Burton followed his gaze. There were Unterjocher troops running down both ends of the alleyway, covering all the doors.

They stumbled back into the kitchen. 'You've got to help us,' said Burton.

There was a look of alarm on the tavern owner's face. He raised the knife again.

'There's got to be some place we can hide.'

'No,' said the Greek. 'Get out! Go!'

'We'll give you more gold.'

A hesitation. He tugged on his moustache. 'How much?'

'Two more coins.'

He held up his fingers. 'Five.'

'Three. It's all we have.'

The Greek held out his hand. Burton placed another gold coin in it. 'One now,' he said, 'the rest when we're safe.'

Next moment they were being led back into the kitchen. Past stoves and the waitresses, through a passage to another door. The Greek flung it open and herded Burton and Patrick through it, down a flight of rickety steps into darkness. Burton kept his hand on the wall to steady himself. At the bottom the Greek pulled a cord and a bare light bulb came on.

They were in a cellar, surrounded by barrels. The air smelt of damp and yeast.

'You help me. Quick!' At the far end of the cellar was some shelving. The Greek began removing boxes from it, then the planks themselves. Burton and Patrick joined him, lifting crates of Apollinaris mineral water and Reich-Kola; the SS was the largest producer of soft drinks in the world.

Once the shelving had been cleared a small cubby-hole was revealed. The Greek opened the door to cobwebs and crawling brickwork. 'In you go.'

'What is this?' said Patrick.

'Last owner. For contraband.'

Burton ducked and squeezed himself in. The space was no more than four feet by two, not high enough to stand upright. The mortar between the bricks was a hive of insects.

'Quick!'

Patrick was shoved into the hole. With both of them in it there was barely room to breathe. It was like that place in Dunkirk where they had hidden from the Lebbs, Patrick's blood soaking into Burton's skin.

They had survived that, thought Burton, they would survive today.

The Greek began closing the door, then pulled it open again. 'You promise you have rest of gold?'

Twisting his arm Burton managed to pull out his two remaining coins.

The Greek's eyes darted to them. 'You fuck me like dog, I tell blackshirts where you are.'

'You'll get your money,' replied Burton.

'When they gone, I wait half hour. Then come find you.'

The cupboard door closed, letting in only a splinter of light. There was a scraping sound as the shelves were put back in place, the barrels followed. The light pinged off. They heard the Greek climb the stairs, the door at the top being pulled to.

Silence.

Burton shut his eyes and realised it made no difference; open or closed everything was as black as the tomb. Stifling. He could hear Patrick's breathing: calm and controlled . . . something tight as he exhaled. Could smell the sweat on his body, the clinging scent of pipe smoke. Neither of them said a word.

Suddenly – from above them – a sound. The clomp of boots on floorboards, reverberating through the walls. Muffled shouts.

Silence once more. Burton counted the seconds.

More shouts. A crash. The indeterminate tremble of voices. Getting closer.

Burton became aware of something crawling up his neck. He tried to raise his hand to swat it but couldn't move far enough. Tiny legs burrowed into his hair. Behind him the whole wall felt alive with limbs and mandibles. His knees were already cramped at not being able to stand straight.

Next to him Patrick tried to shake something off.

The sound of shouting came again.

A bang that might have been a gunshot. They both breathed in.

One second, two, three, four, five, six . . .

Boots.

Fading away this time.

'Are they leaving?'

'Shhh!'

The minutes passed. Nothing. The darkness was solid around them, like deep water; the air turning acrid.

Burton's mind was full of Dunkirk. He'd volunteered for the British Expeditionary Force, gone AWOL from the Legion to fight for his mother's country. Africa might have been his birthplace but Mama had raised him to think of England as home.

He thought of the slaughter he'd seen, the charnel beaches; how he and Patrick had escaped to Calais then across the Channel in a motor launch, part of the flotilla Churchill had sent in a vain attempt to save the British forces. He still remembered the skipper's lamentations: how he'd lost all his mates at the Somme; that it was supposed to be the war to end all wars. Yet here they were again. Bloody fools!

Back home the look of defeat in everyone's face reminded him of his father. People avoided his gaze. He understood their need for peace but something about his own eyes gave him away – he wanted to keep fighting. Then came the October agreement, the Council of New Europe. The British Army stood down; returning to the Legion would have meant three years in a Vichy jail. That's why he went to Madagascar when the Waffen-SS invaded, why he had embraced the mercenary's call to arms.

Patrick shifted uncomfortably. 'You find it?' he whispered.

'What?'

'The truth. About your mother.'

Burton didn't reply.

'Did you?'

'No.'

'Then it's all been for nix.'

'Hochburg's dead.'

'Damn coincidence, isn't it?'

'What?'

'Of all the people Ackerman could have chosen. You.'

'I killed the bastard,' replied Burton, trying not to think about the tears he'd shed that night. 'That's enough.'

'I don't believe you.'

'I can go back to Maddie now. Have a future, the one we both deserve.' He forced a hushed laugh. 'Be a farmer.'

A pause. When Patrick spoke again his voice was ragged. 'When we get out of here, I'm on that boat.'

'But, *Chef*.'

'I'm sorry, Burton. I can't keep pushing my luck. I'm finished with Africa.'

'I should never have got you involved.'

'It's too late for that—'

Above them the cellar door opened with a creak.

Footsteps.

Something heavy-soled, thought Burton. Boots. He tried to count them, make sense of the different footfalls. Three pairs at least. Maybe more. They descended. Through the slit in the cupboard Burton glimpsed the beam of a torch. A hushed command.

The scrape of the barrels being moved.

Burton eased his Browning from his belt, tried to aim it at the door. In the enclosed space he couldn't straighten his elbow. The pounding of his heart was as loud as artillery in his ears.

Now the shelving was being lifted, the planks pulled off by strong hands.

Burton cocked the trigger.

The last of the shelves was moved out of the way. Someone reached for the cubby-hole.

Burton tensed himself. Squeezed the handle of his pistol as though he would crush it.

The door swung open.

Chapter Twenty

LOVE. Everything he had achieved was a monument to love. Walter Hochburg stood on the veranda of his office gazing pensively over the Schädelplatz. In his hand was the knife Burton had tried to slay him with. He ran his thumb over the blade. Pushed down till the skin broke.

A drop of blood – white blood – ran into his palm. He sucked the wound.

Below him the sunlight throbbed on the skulls. When the swastika first flew over Africa it was the Kolonialpolitisches Amt that had governed. But the KPA was ineffectual, bound by what Hochburg regarded as an indulgent, nineteenth-century colonialism. Along with Himmler he had fought to sideline them. Only when the SS took command did the continent's transformation truly begin. Hochburg's vision was of a racial utopia – one emanating from the Schädelplatz. He had overseen the laying of the square in person, had taken a trowel in his hand to embed the cranium at the centre. It was a specimen he had prized for a long time: a Category Five, the first negroid he ever killed, the bone still black with cleansing fire. That was twenty years ago but seemed, as the scriptures said, *only a few days for the love he had for her*. Genesis 29:20. He still remembered the man he had been before his true calling.

From his desk behind him came the buzz of the intercom.

Twenty years of conquest and frenzied activity to expunge her memory. Everything he had accomplished in Africa was because of Eleanor. She still haunted him: the slender, almost malnourished frame, tangles of golden hair, eyes possessed of such warmth and compassion and intelligence. The thought of her brought tears to his heart. The niggers had her blood on their hands.

The niggers and her son.

He was as much to blame. If it hadn't been for Burton his Eleanor would still be with him.

He thought the boy long dead, perished in the fire that gutted the family home in Togoland. Now that he knew he was alive, Hochburg had sworn to hunt him down. Another chapter and verse flared in his memory: Romans 12:19.

Vengeance is mine and I will repay.

The intercom buzzed again.

Hochburg wiped the blood from his hand, strode to his desk. 'I told you I didn't want to be disturbed,' he said, slipping the knife into a drawer.

'Apologies, Herr Oberstgruppenführer, but Field Marshal von Arnim has just arrived. He says he must speak to you. Urgently.'

'Let him wait.'

Hochburg flicked off the intercom and went back to the veranda. In the distance, coming from the direction of Stanleystadt, he could see a helicopter. It was his personal Flettner. He watched it land in the square, the blast from its rotor blades lashing the wind-chime above his head. Kepplar got out, crouched against the downdraught and hurried towards him.

'Do you have news?' Hochburg shouted.

'Yes, Herr Oberst.'

'Hurry then.'

Hochburg returned to his office and flopped down at his desk. Forewarned that an assassination attempt was going to be made, his precious books had been removed from their shelves; now they were back in place. His eyes flitted over various titles – *Mein*

Kampf, The Rising Tide of Colour, a leather-bound facsimile of Blumenbach's study of skulls, *Eugenica Afrika* – before coming to rest on Eleanor's battered copy of *Wuthering Heights*. He considered it for a pained moment before turning to the two portraits that dominated the room: Bismarck, his boyhood hero, and the Führer, re-kindler of his faith.

It was from the secret chamber behind the Führer's picture that he had watched Burton kill his double. At first he hadn't recognised the boy, then – when he declared his name – Hochburg was too overcome to move. That turn of the mouth, those same blue-grey eyes. Why hadn't it struck him immediately? He sat mesmerised as he watched the knife plunge into a throat that was meant to be his own.

Another buzz.

'Gruppenführer Kepplar is here.'

'Send him through.'

'And the field marshal is insisting—'

'Kepplar first.'

Hochburg pressed a button beneath the desk: the bolt on the door clicked. Seconds later it burst open.

'How dare you!' bellowed a starched, Prussian voice. 'Who do you think I am? Some lowly corporal waiting on your pleasure?'

In stormed Field Marshal Hans-Jürgen von Arnim, commander of the Afrika Korps.

He was as bald as Hochburg with a thin moustache and ears that caused his troops to dub him *'Der Elefant'*. It was a nickname he relished, presuming it meant he crushed everything in his path. He had succeeded Rommel's command in 1943 and led his men to victories in French West Africa, Congo and the Cameroons. General de Gaulle had surrendered to him personally at Douala. His uniform was dusty but perfectly tailored; around his neck was a cravat and Knight's Cross.

'Calm yourself, Field Marshal,' said Hochburg, standing. 'I thought you were in Angola, preparing for Operation Nelke.'

'I've just flown in from Matadi.'

Behind Arnim stood Kepplar; Hochburg motioned for him to disappear.

'On the eve of battle? How courageous of you, Herr Arnim. And what is it this time? Have you conjured up yet another excuse for the Führer not to invade?'

'Ninety Light Division is already on its way. Spearheading to Loanda.'

'For once you surprise me! And are my Einsatzgruppen ready to follow after your troops?' Einsatzgruppen: the SS's Special Action Groups that resettled the blacks to Muspel.

Arnim's face soured. 'They are chomping at the bit as always.'

'They are very dedicated,' said Hochburg with a carefully calibrated smile, 'have much work to do. And you came all this way to give me the news, how thoughtful of you.'

'Northern Rhodesia.'

'What of it?'

'I've learned that you intend to invade.'

'A team of British and Rhodesian assassins tried to kill me; the trail leads back to Lusaka. What would you have me do?'

'I have barely enough divisions for Angola, and now this!'

'Rhodesia will be a matter solely for the Waffen-SS. The Afrika Korps need not be involved.'

'And who will lead this invasion?' Arnim sneered. 'You?'

Hochburg swelled his chest. 'May I remind the field marshal that it was the SS who took southern Angola.'

'To my great regret.'

'Who took Madagaskar. Tana. Conquered it in a matter of weeks when you and Rommel said it couldn't even be done.'

'A city is one thing, a whole country another. But you misread the British: the mood in London is changing, becoming more belligerent. Invade and they'll fight. Fight to the last man.'

'As will my Waffen troops.'

'What about the Casablanca Treaty?' asked Arnim.

'That prized document of peace!' snorted Hochburg. 'In tatters, shredded by an assassin's knife.'

'And if your invasion fails?'

'Impossible. The British are weak, will be wiped out – just like Dunkirk.'

Arnim took a step closer, lowered his voice. 'But the Lulua River won't be.' Hochburg caught his breath: it stank of cigars.

'What do you mean by that?'

'I heard what happened to your tunnel.'

'You heard nothing. Nothing! The autobahn is already being cleared, ready for my tanks.'

Arnim took another step forward, till their faces were almost touching; he was taller than Hochburg. 'You can't control your current territory, are losing the insurgencies in the Aquatoriana and the western districts. How do you intend to conquer more?'

'The tunnel was attacked by Angolan terrorists. Do you hear me, Field Marshal: *Angolans*. If the Afrika Korps had done their job, secured the rest of the country and destroyed the rebel camps, this would never have happened. Instead all you do is delay. Loanda should have been ours six months ago. We've suffered enough provocations.'

'It will stretch us too far.'

'Always the same excuses.' Hochburg leaned over his desk, forcing Arnim to take a semi-step backwards. 'If we'd listened to milksops like you Versailles would never have been avenged, German Africa little more than a strip of Togoland.'

'We don't have the troops, the resources.'

'What is Angola? A country – a half country – of fat Portuguese, convicts and niggers. A troop of Pfadfinders could take it.'

'How dare you insult my men—'

'Your soldiers are among the bravest. True white men. It's their leaders who are cowards. It's a wonder you haven't been recalled to Germania.'

Arnim's face turned black.

He adopted his most affected Prussian accent. 'You talk easily of conquest, Herr Oberstgruppenführer, but it's my soldiers who die for your dreams.'

'You should learn a little Latin,' replied Hochburg, pointing at a volume on his bookshelves. 'Caesar's advice to the Legions: *amat victoria curam*. "Victory favours those who bleed for it." Besides, they are not just my dreams—' his finger turned to the picture of Bismarck '—they are Germany's. It is our destiny to rule middle Africa. Which is why the SS will storm Rhodesia.'

Arnim gave a flippant laugh. 'Destiny!'

'If you have no sense of the profound, then at least consider the bounty. The copper mines, tobacco fields—'

'It's a folly, like Angola.'

'I have the Führer's wholehearted blessing.'

'His mind has been turned, turned by people like you and Himmler.'

'The SS is the future now, not the army. You will see in Northern Rhodesia.'

Arnim straightened himself, adjusted the Knight's Cross at his throat. 'The Afrika Korps will take North Angola. But when the British grind you into the ground, when you and the SS choke on the dirt of Rhodesia . . . we will not support you.'

'I shall remind you of this conversation, Herr Field Marshal, on that garlanded day I enter Lusaka.'

Arnim turned and left.

'*Sieg Heil!*' Hochburg called mockingly after him. Hail Victory.

He sat down, a cold euphoria coursing through his veins. Moments later Kepplar entered the room. He offered a rigid Nazi salute – a waft of peppermint oil – then remained at attention.

'What news?' asked Hochburg.

Kepplar slipped his hands from his sides to behind his back, hesitated before he spoke. 'With respect, Oberstgruppenführer, I heard the field marshal. What if he's right? What if the British do beat us back?'

Hochburg looked up as if he wanted to drink blood. 'Do you doubt the uniform you wear, Gruppenführer? Doubt our mission in Africa?'

'No, Herr Oberst.'

'Maybe you doubt me.'

'Of course not. But . . .'

'But what?'

'Burton Cole. He's one man and yet . . .' Kepplar hesitated again. 'I'm loath to say this but I feel that the Herr Oberstgruppenführer has been distracted by his capture when his mind should be on Rhodesia.'

Hochburg fixed his subordinate with his black eyes. His voice came from the depths of his throat: 'And who was it that let him escape from the Mupe airfield?'

Kepplar bowed his head.

'The invasion has been planned to the last detail, Gruppenführer. The British won't know what's hit them. It's not your concern. Now, what news from Stanleystadt?'

'Dolan was telling the truth. We found Rougier.'

'And Burton?'

'The local SS got there before us, raided Rougier's home earlier this morning. A tip-off from his landlady.' He consulted his notebook. 'Two men were seen escaping the scene, I presume Cole and the American. Rougier himself was injured during the raid but is still alive. He will be ready to speak shortly.'

Hochburg let out a long, stony sigh. 'So you lost him?'

'With your permission, Herr Oberst, I would like to interrogate the prisoner Dolan again. He may still have information that—'

'Whatever he knows will be of little help now. He is, however, part of the team that tried to assassinate me, an act of war if ever there were one. Convene an emergency court martial and try him. Get RFA to broadcast it. Long-wave: so the whole continent can hear. In translation too. English, Portuguese, French.'

'At once, Oberstgruppenführer.'

'It will strengthen our position for the invasion, give Germania something extra against the British. In the meantime, return to Stanleystadt. Raise every SS man, every brownshirt, every flatfoot you can. Check the quays, the dosshouses, brothels, taverns.

187

Tear the city apart if you have to. Everything until you find me Burton Cole.'

'Alive or dead?'

For an instant Hochburg was back in the secret chamber behind the portrait, watching Burton press the knife against his decoy: *My mother. I want to know*. 'Alive of course!' he roared. 'The truth awaits him.'

'Herr Oberst?'

Hochburg gave a dismissive wave of his hand.

Kepplar lingered a moment longer, then headed for the door.

'Wait,' said Hochburg. 'Is the Unterjocher still at work in the city?'

'Yes. They are raising an extra workforce to clear the tunnel. We are short of strong backs as usual.'

'I doubt Burton has the proper papers. Check the Unterjocher too.'

'I will make it a priority.' Kepplar turned back to the door.

'And Derbus . . .'

Kepplar's face lit up.

'You have been my deputy for five years now, seen our achievements grow together.' Hochburg slid his hand over his bald head. 'Be warned: it counts for nothing. You failed me at the airfield. You also failed me with Dolan, and now Rougier.'

Kepplar's smile collapsed. 'Yes, Herr Oberstgruppenführer. Apologies.'

'Don't do it again. Now get to Stanleystadt.'

Chapter Twenty-One

Stanleystadt, Kongo
16 September, 13:40

THE door was opened by the Greek. He was holding a torch; behind him the cellar was hidden in darkness. He beckoned them out.

'Is it safe?' asked Burton.

'Germans gone.'

'Are you sure?'

'Now you give me gold.'

Burton relaxed his grip on the Browning, turned to Patrick and forced a smile. 'Age before chancers.'

Patrick didn't move. There was a cockroach crawling along his ear. 'I'm still on that boat.'

Burton flicked the safety catch back on and ducked out of the cubby-hole.

Next moment the muzzle of a BK44 was hard against his cheek. Someone tugged the light switch.

There were five of them, all with banana-guns. The officer stepped forward. He was mid-twenties, had a low brow and wolfish teeth; his eyes looked vaguely oriental. On the breast of his uniform was a name badge in Gothic script: Hauptsturmführer Rottman. Even before he spoke, Burton guessed his type.

As the Reich had expanded ever further into Africa, Germany ran out of native-born citizens to control its colonies. So a new

189

breed of 'ethnics' needed to be found in the conquered territories of Europe: Serbs, Slovaks, Baltics, even Poles and Russians – anyone who could prove some German ancestry and was willing to swear an oath to the Führer. They were produced in their thousands by the SS colonial academies of Grunewald and Oranienburg, filled the lower ranks. Men who were insecure about their backgrounds; insecure, obedient, ambitious. Always ready to crack open a skull.

Rottman held out his palm. 'Your weapon.'

Burton's eyes scanned the cellar – narrowing as they met the Greek's – but he knew it was impossible. He handed over his pistol.

Rottman took it. 'A Browning HP, "the King of Nines",' he said, turning it over. 'I've not seen one of these since Muspel. Where did you get it from?' He had an antiseptic voice.

Burton made no reply.

Rottman resumed his examination, running his fingers over the barrel. Burton's gut twisted as if someone had their hand on Madeleine's leg. He thought of her husband, his fingers scraping her inner thigh and for a crazy moment Burton was ready to take all of them on, punch and kick and blast his way out of the cellar.

His thoughts must have shown on his face: the soldier with the BK against him pressed harder.

'And what do these mean?' asked Rottman, examining the engravings on the handle.

Burton continued to stare forward.

'Hmm. No matter.' Rottman tucked the weapon into his belt. 'Check him for ammunition and cuff him. The other one too.'

They took his extra clip, the gold coins, then bound his wrists; Patrick was dragged out next, had his handgun and pipe confiscated. Neither of them looked at each other.

'As for you,' said Rottman, turning to the Greek. 'Harbour illegals again and I'll have you and every low-life customer in this dump on a chain-gang for the next ten years. Now get out of my sight.'

Rottman led them upstairs. Outside there were four lorries waiting for them, more troops. A short distance away a man was face down in a pool of blood. The quayside was deserted.

'Split them up,' said Rottman. 'The old man at the front, this one in here.'

Burton was marched to the rear vehicle and shoved in. It was a steel cage on a flatbed lorry with hard wooden benches on either side and no cover from the sun. There were at least thirty men crushed into it; some were sobbing. Burton took his place at the back, two guards climbing in next to him. They pulled the cage door shut – but didn't lock it.

Engines started. Burton caught a mouthful of diesel fumes, and the lorries pulled away.

They drove through Otraco, over the Giesler bridge. For an instant Burton thought their destination was SS headquarters. Then they turned down the Avenue of Victory (a scale version of Germania's) and he realised they were leaving the city. On either side marble columns topped with sculptures flashed by, alternately eagles and the bronze heads of the party leadership: Hitler, Himmler, Goebbels, Göring. Followed by the conquerors of Africa: Rommel, Arnim, von Hulsen. There was no bust of Hochburg.

The convoy continued southwards out of Stanleystadt.

Burton's mind was racing. He'd wait till they were driving through the jungle: the trees would offer better cover. Then back to the city and that one bunk to Neu Berlin. And Patrick? Burton felt a squirm of guilt but pushed it from his mind. Reminded himself of the American's words in prison.

Every man for himself.

They were on a slip road. The outskirts of the city – a VW plant, rice mills and soap factories – were giving way to trees. Soon the jungle was rising again. Burton glanced at the two guards. One was smoking a cigarette, the other watching the cathedral sink beneath the tree line.

Burton arched his spine, began tightening and releasing his thigh muscles to relax them. Buttocks, shoulders, arms and neck. The looser his body the better. He pulled at the cuffs just in case they hadn't been secured properly.

With each second the jungle was thickening. Through the foliage he glimpsed the old road to Ponthierville; he'd heard it was a ghost town now, another Belgian outpost left to moulder through Nazi spite.

Burton took a deep gulp of air, checked the road behind them. It was empty. His heart was hammering in his throat. He'd go on three: the way he used to in the Legion before leaping off dunes steep enough to break your back.

Another deep breath. *Un . . . deux . . .*

This was going to hurt.

Trois!

He shot up. Kicked the cage door open. And hurled himself out of the lorry.

Burton landed hard, his body crashing on to the road. Blinding white pain shot up his leg like a chisel rammed into his kneecap. He rolled once. Twice. The ground tore a gash in his forehead.

The convoy screeched to a halt.

Burton dragged himself to his feet, vision spinning, and bolted towards the jungle. Limp-run, limp-run, limp-run. If he could just make the tree line . . .

Behind him there were shouts. Whistle blasts.

Each step sent another bolt of agony searing through his leg. Burton stumbled, forced himself back up. He had thirty feet to go.

There was a volley of gunfire above him: it chewed into the trees. Some of the other prisoners were cheering him on.

Twenty feet.

Burton tripped again, held his cuffed hands out to cushion the fall. Pain burst through his wrists. He staggered but maintained his footing. His knee was putty.

Limp-run, limp-run.

Fifteen feet.

A rifle butt slammed into his back.

Burton dropped.

The butt came again. Another joined it, and another. The cheering had stopped. He tried to thrash out with his feet. Something cracked against his skull. Spots of fire swam in front of his eyes, threatening to overtake him.

'Stop!'

The voice seemed to come from a long distance away.

Burton was yanked to his feet. His mouth swilled with blood. Rough hands dragged him back to the convoy; his boots trailed the ground.

Rottman was waiting for him. 'The only reason you're still alive is that I need my quota of workers for the day.'

Up close Burton noticed his hair. It was greasy black, the roots showing ginger. He dyes it, he thought, and almost laughed. He could hear Madeleine: *hail the Master Race!*

'But try that again,' continued Rottman, 'and I'll cripple you for life.' He yanked Burton's head back. Burton felt the nerves in his neck grind between vertebrae, his windpipe was horribly exposed. 'Understand?'

Burton refused to reply.

'Understand? Or do I have to break the fingers of every last prisoner?'

It was a bluff: he'd already told him he needed the workers. 'I understand,' croaked Burton.

'Good.'

Rottman swung his fist into Burton's chest. Hit him full in the solar plexus.

Burton collapsed to his knees and puked violently: a mess of mango juice, strudel and blood. Some of it splattered Rottman's boots; he took a sliver of satisfaction in that.

'Hmm. This one's exactly what we need at the tunnel,' said Rottman to the guards. 'A tough bastard. Chain his ankles, make sure he doesn't escape again.' He headed towards the lead vehicle. 'Let's get rolling.'

Once clear of Stanleystadt the convoy joined the PAA.

The Pan African Autobahn.

It had been one of the crowning achievements of the Casablanca Conference: a joint Anglo-German enterprise to link the continent from Cairo to the Cape, Neu Berlin in the west to Roscherhafen (formerly Dar es Salaam) in the east. The 'Friendship Road' they called it. Six lanes wide, more than six and a half thousand miles long. Hitler had taken a personal interest in the project, poring over the plans, insisting the camber be at least twenty-five centimetres thick. The German section, built by the SS using forced labour and secret construction methods, had been finished in record time, opened that March; the British were still years away from completing theirs. Further proof of the 'superiority of the National Socialist model' as Goebbels was fond of reminding the world. The Nazis were outpacing the British in every aspect of economic and techno-logical development.

Burton sat hunched and bound, watching the PAA flash past him. A blur of white concrete. His whole body was turning numb and purple; dark patches had soaked his trousers around the knees. His mouth was parched, tasted of bile and copper. Above him the sun beat through the mesh of the cage, slowly boiling his brain. Either side of him the two guards had parasols to shield themselves from the heat. Pink, ladies' parasols. In their other hands they clutched their BK44s.

It took them three hours to reach the town of Kasongo where the autobahn split. Burton glimpsed clean pavements and a branch of Deutschebank; settlers who turned away as the convoy passed. There was also a massive white road sign in German and English:

PAA (South) INTERNATIONAL TRAFFIC

Ankoro	200 km
Bukama	425 km
Elisabethstadt (border-control, N. Rhodesia)	700 km

Lusaka	1250 km / 775 miles
Salisbury	1650 km / 1025 miles
Cape Town (opening 1957)	4100 km / 2550 miles

PAA (South-West) PROHIBITED, AUTHORISED TRAFFIC ONLY

Lusambo	325 km
Sandoa	800 km

The lorries turned south-west in the direction of the lowering sun.

An hour after dusk they reached a checkpoint. The guards got out, visited the latrines and mess hall. Burton heard the sound of a football being kicked about. Later one of the Unterjocher came round with a bucket of water and ladle. He dipped it and let each prisoner take a few gulps. When he got to Burton he laughed and spat into the water. Burton drank eagerly, held the warm liquid in his mouth – a Legion trick to fight off the sensation of thirst. He ignored the lump of phlegm that bobbed against his tongue.

The lorries refuelled and drove through the night, heading due south now. Occasionally they overtook lines of stationary tanks (Burton noticed the skull and palm tree insignia of the Waffen-SS); other than that the road was empty.

Empty and completely straight.

It reminded Burton of a childhood picture book: of the endless road Jack had to walk to find the ogre's castle.

Eventually the jungle began to thin out, giving way to open grasslands dotted with boulders and dembos. In the moonlight Burton glimpsed vast banana and pineapple plantations. Nowadays every German – from Aachen in the west to the furthest garrisons of the Urals – expected tropical fruit on the table. It was one of the rights of conquest.

The Reich Farm Laws of 1933, which awarded land to farmers on a hereditary basis, were extended to the colonies following the Casablanca Treaty in a bid to 'Germanise' Africa. Thereafter anyone who could prove Aryan ancestry back to 1800 was eligible (including the emigrant communities of America and Brazil). Free tracts of land – five hundred, a thousand, five thousand hectares – were parcelled out along with a limitless supply of native labourers. For the first few years profits were high and life, on comfortable haciendas, easy. Then came the Windhuk Decree and all the blacks were sent north. Drudgery followed for the plantation owners. But when complaints reached Himmler he issued a typically disparaging rebuke: the racial hygiene of the continent was paramount. If settlers needed extra farmhands, let them bear children. A dozen per family. The more Germans born in Africa the better. It would secure the future.

Burton watched the plantations till they dwindled and the landscape became so monotonous the convoy might have been standing still. The Nazis may have developed the cities but this was frontier country, as untamed as Germany's eastern empire in Russia. Without the insulation of the trees the temperature plummeted. Burton sat shivering and tried to calculate where they were.

Along with his Browning the Lebbs had taken his watch in the cellar. That had been – what? – seven hours ago at least; they were travelling at fifty, sixty miles per hour. Which meant they must be almost four hundred miles from Stanleystadt now. Burton pictured his map – the one he had left in the Ziege – the one with its spider web of black lines. They should be somewhere between Luluaburg and Kanda-Kanda, on a latitude with Loanda.

Loanda: Ackerman.

Was he there now? Burton imagined him tucked up in bed – in warm, freshly laundered sheets. Could almost smell the starch and citrus cologne. Did he know about Rougier yet? Was Ackerman the one who had betrayed them like Patrick said? Or was he simply

a stooge for some Angolan spy? Why had British intelligence wanted
to assassinate Hochburg? What about Peace for Empire?

And why, of all people, had they wanted Burton to do it?

That last question puzzled him the most. Yet no matter how
Burton looked at it, he couldn't find a solution. He decided that
if he got out of this he'd be paying a visit to Her Majesty's
consulate in Angola.

There were too many questions pecking away inside Burton's
head. The shackles were burning his wrists and ankles. Never think
at night, son, his father used to tell him. It will only bring *makabere
Gedanken*. Ghoulish thoughts. But he had nothing else for company.

Burton's mind wandered from Ackerman to Hochburg. He
dredged his heart for some type of feeling. All he found was his
mother's cold, abandoned room. Killing him hadn't brought her
back, hadn't answered the mysteries that dogged his past. Hadn't
atoned for all those others Hochburg had murdered. It had simply
added to a pile of corpses. Lapinski, Nares, maybe Dolan and
Vacher. Maybe Patrick. All the men he'd killed in the previous
few days. All those before that: a lifetime of bloodshed to soak
away the past.

How many more had to be slaughtered to make up for it?
When would there be enough to let go?

When he could cobble an entire square from their skulls?

Ghoulish thoughts for sure.

Madeleine had been right. He remembered their conversation
on the farm, their final night together: *there's nothing for you in
Africa . . . Hochburg's a ghost . . . Don't bring him back to life.*

She was always right.

Now every second, every mile, was taking him further from her.

After their exchange in the arbour they had wandered indoors.
Burton made her a mug of Ovaltine (two sugars) and they lay
silently in bed, listening to the wind-chime outside.

'Do you remember what I told you about my family?' said
Madeleine after a long time. 'About Madagaskar.'

He pulled her close. 'Of course.' It was part of the special bond he felt towards her. He recognised the sadness that some-times emptied her smile, the private moments of staring into space. They both knew what it was like to have family stolen. To be left with unanswerable questions.

'After they were shipped there, I heard nothing. No letters, no Red Cross reports. *Gornisht*. At first I was desperate, visited the embassy and Foreign Office every day. No one could tell me anything. Nobody even cared. It was like they had disappeared, four names among ten million.' She stared into his eyes. 'I learned to live with it, Burton.'

He considered her words. 'Because you're stronger than I am.'

'No. Because I realise the truth can be worse than not knowing. That you don't need the truth to live your life—' she kissed him, her cheeks damp '—or be happy.'

If only he had listened to her. He'd give anything to go back there, to cast Hochburg and his parents from his mind for good. Never leave her. Revenge hadn't given him a future, it robbed him of one.

Burton hung his shoulders, breathed on his hands to warm them. The night was growing colder. Then a realisation.

'Oh, Maddie,' he whispered to himself, 'I've been asking the wrong question.'

It wasn't how many he had to kill to atone for the past. It was how many more to secure the days ahead. The answer was obvious.

Enough to get back home. Enough so he could join Madeleine again in their mildewy bed. Wrap himself around her, feel her soft, naked body against his, hot as a coal. Cup her belly with his calloused hands, feel the struggles of the child inside her.

That was how much blood he had to spill. There was rage enough in him yet.

And when it was done he'd fill the holes in the driveway. Harvest his quinces, plucking each one by hand, precious as any Kassai diamond. Never yearn for anything beyond the fireplace and farm again.

The convoy continued south, vanishing into the darkness.

Chapter Twenty-Two

Lulua River, Kongo
16 September, 22:30

'YOU hear that?'

In the darkness Neliah caught the panic in her sister's voice.

They were drifting with the current of the Lulua River. Zuri was the stronger swimmer but each stroke brought new dangers to her ears. Below them was ten metres of murky water, below that the tunnel they had come to destroy. Neliah pictured it: the fallen stone and earth, slaves toiling to move it. Somewhere in the night she heard the echo of pickaxes on rock.

And the sounds of the river. There had been a loud splash in the water ahead.

'Did you hear that?' whispered Zuri again, she kicked against the current until they were side by side. 'What was it?'

'Nothing,' replied Neliah.

'It sounded like a crocodile.'

'There aren't any here.'

'You promise?'

'You should have stayed with the others. Waited for the scouts.'

Her sister fell silent.

'Keep swimming,' said Neliah. 'Not much further now.'

They continued with the current, Neliah following the glimmer of the German lights to judge their position. She was using only her legs to swim, her hands held out of the water to keep the haversack dry. Her panga was sheathed on her back like a metal fin.

Finally she reached out for Zuri. 'There,' she said and they headed towards the shore, wading through thick papyrus on to the river bank. Neliah felt the mud between her toes. There was a stench of rotting vegetation.

When they were clear of it, she crouched down and opened the haversack. Inside were the bundles of dynamite. Despite Penhor's orders it had been simple enough to vanish from the camp. Neliah had clumped Ligio on the back of the head with a log, left plenty of *caporotto* for the boy-guards to get drunk on.

'They're dry,' breathed Neliah as she lifted out the first bundle. Each one was made of eight dynamite sticks and a radio detonator. Neliah turned the priming switch: a red lamp came on.

'What does that mean?' asked Zuri. Water dripped from her long hair. The night air had the breath of *tarazu* in it: she was shivering.

'It's working. You turn this switch and when we're ready, press this.' She lifted a box from the haversack. 'This is the detonator. It works by radio.'

Zuri wrinkled her nose. 'Are you sure you know what you're doing?'

'Trust me. *Papai* used the same thing.'

When they were growing up their father wanted his girls to be as well schooled as any Portuguese senhora. He even talked of taking them to Lisboa and startling people with his bright little *meninas*. Zuri was taught Latin and history and mathematics. But by the time Neliah was old enough, the rich days in marble had come. There were no more lazy afternoons for lessons. So Neliah's special treat was to go with *Papai* when he was blasting new quarries. He would show her the dynamite, the reels of 'det-chord' like thin white worms and, best of all, the plunger. At the end of the day he would let her push it down. She approached it as solemn as a priest, *Papai* chuckling. Then silence for that terrible moment. The first explosion had made her scream and cry. Later they would be the happiest moments of her life.

Neliah reached for the next bundle of dynamite. This time the lamp didn't illuminate. She tried another, and another. 'I told them,' she said, her fury rising. 'But none listened.'

'What?'

'Not to trust the British. They're snakes – this is trick-stuff.'

'Then why are we here? Destroying the tunnel is to help them.'

'Only to save ourselves. We can't let what the *Nazistas* did in the south happen to all Angola.'

Neliah checked the remaining charges. Only eight from twenty worked. She reached into the haversack for some twine. 'We tie them together. Make bigger bundles.'

'Will that work?'

'I don't know,' replied Neliah irritably. 'Yes.'

When they were done they put the charges back in the haversack and continued up the bank of the river until they reached a bush of barbed wire. They picked their way through it to the rim of the tunnel. There was a drop of ten metres, a ledge a dozen paces wide, then another ten metres of brickwork to the road below.

Neliah and Zuri peered over the edge at a door in the rock. 'That outcrop,' said Neliah, 'is where the escape-holes are. There's a passageway leading to them. That's how I got in last time.'

'What about soldiers?'

Neliah stared into the darkness. There were three tanks on the road outside, patrolling skull-troops, but the door to the passage was unguarded.

Neliah turned to her sister. 'You go first. I'll keep watch.'

Zuri cautiously lowered herself over the edge.

'The faster you go, the easier,' said Neliah.

'I'm trying,' her sister hissed back.

'When you get down, stay close against the wall.'

'What about the door?'

'Don't! Wait for me.' Neliah scrambled after her. She had almost reached the bottom when Zuri pulled the handle.

Neliah smelt it at once: the smoke of tobacco.

Startled, the skull-troop spat the cigarette from his mouth. Grabbed his rifle and shoved it into Zuri's belly.

'*Wer zum Teufel bist du?*'

Neliah leapt, crashed down on the soldier's back. They hit the ground, rolled close to the edge. In one movement Neliah stood and kicked the German. He tumbled backwards, through the door into the passageway. There was a flash of steel. The middle of his chest opened red.

Neliah fell on the soldier. Drove the panga through his heart. Twisted the blade till it dug into the ground. Then she pushed herself away, panting.

'*Ich schwöre dir . . . mein Führer . . .*'

The skull-troop was speaking his final words.

'What's he saying?' whispered Zuri, face full of fear like she was being cursed.

Ina had known the tongue of the Germans. When there was no time for Neliah to be taught Latin, she gave her lessons in the other to make up for it. Neliah spoke for the soldier in Herero: 'It's an oath. I swear . . . to you, my leader . . . to obey till the death . . .'

The breath vanished from him. He said no more.

Zuri crouched next to the wall, her eyes rain clouds ready to burst.

Neliah knew she hated the *Nazistas* as much as she did, but she lacked the *rungiro* – that hunger to avenge, to taste blood. *Papai* had made her heart too gentle.

'Now you understand why I didn't want you to come.'

For a long moment Zuri said nothing, just stood there wringing her plait. When she spoke, her voice was thick. 'None of this. None of this will bring them back.'

'I know.'

Zuri spoke on. 'I always think of that day when we hid . . . the screams . . . the smell of the cesspit. It still lives in my nose.

You were sick, remember?' She looked up, brushed away a tear. 'I want to fight. Just as much as you.'

'If you're scared, think of the north. Of *Ina* and *Papai*. All the others.' She rubbed her scar. 'It gives me the rage of a lion.'

'I'm not scared.'

Neliah squeezed her shoulder and knelt by the dead skull-troop. She dragged the panga from his body, re-sheathed it without wiping the blade. Next she picked up his rifle and went through his kit. She found bullets, grenades, cigarettes, some bonbons. She took the ammunition and grenades, offered the sweets to Zuri.

She shook her head. 'What do we do with the body?'

'I don't know. Dump it in the river. It'll look like the crocodiles chewed him.'

'You said there weren't any.'

'It's a joke.'

Zuri frowned, just like their *ina* used to.

Neliah took out the dynamite. 'The escape-holes are for if there's a fire in the tunnel. There are three of them along this passage, with ladders to the road below. You go to the far one, I'll do the other two.

'Why have I got to go to the far one?'

'Because it's safest. The skull-troops are at this end.' Neliah handed over three bundles of dynamite. 'Climb to the bottom and hide two there, leave another at the top. Turn on the switch like I showed you.'

Before she could tell her to be careful, Zuri was gone. Neliah watched as she scampered along the passage, her long tail of hair swishing behind her.

Then Neliah slung the haversack over her shoulder and followed till she reached the second hole. It was in the middle of the tunnel, was cut from the rock itself. Metal ladder rungs jutted out from the side. At the bottom, where she should have seen the opening to the road, there was nothing but debris. Somewhere she could hear the hiss of water.

Neliah took a fistful of dynamite and began to climb down. Gonsalves's voice was in her head: *she's a cook-girl. A negra. How could she know what she was doing?* This time the tunnel would come crashing down. She swore it.

By the time they got back to the others the scouts had returned.

They were on a rise above the tunnel, hidden by *enga*-grass as tall as a man. The night was still. After Neliah and Zuri planted the explosives they had swum back to the far shore, pulled their boots back on and silently made their way to the rest of the women.

They were a band of seven, all of them Herero or Bantu. All of them with their own tales of murder and families vanished to the north, the hunger for vengeance in their guts. For the Herero that hunger went deeper: back to their parents' parents and earlier. Long before the *Nazistas*, other Germans had come to the Herero lands, men with huge whiskers and strange hats. They had butchered their ancestors. Driven them out into the desert, poisoned the wells. If all the generations of Herero dead rose from their graves their number would be so huge that no German army could defeat them.

'I want to press the detonator,' said Zuri, making sure her plait was tight.

Neliah kept the haversack close to her chest, in her hand was the rifle she had taken from the dead skull-troop. She turned to Ajiah, one of the scouts. She was from Benguela with spindly legs that could run and run. They spoke in Bantu, the common tongue. 'Did you find the camp, the place of chimneys?'

Ajiah nodded. 'Not many Germans there.'

'Tanks?'

'No.'

'Prisoners?'

'Many many.'

'Portuguese? Angolans?'

'And others. Many tongues, all colours of white.'

All colours of white. Neliah gazed down at the tunnel. She was thinking, trying to plan for the future the way *Papai* used to. They would need as many fighters as possible when the Germans invaded Loanda. From high on the ridge she could see inside the tunnel, see the men working to remove the debris. They were passing out rocks in a chain of bodies. For a heartbeat she thought they were her people. Then she realised their skin was black only from dirt and toil. Skull-troops were guarding them.

'Give me the detonator,' said Zuri. 'It's time.'

Neliah was bewitched by the scene below. Every last man would be crushed to death when the dynamite exploded. Killed by her. 'We have to wait,' she replied.

'Wait for what?'

'They're digging by hand, the *Nazistas* always use machines. If we wait till they bring them we can destroy both. After that, they'll have nothing to clear the rocks with.'

She turned to the north towards the chimneys, could see fleeces of smoke glowing in the night sky. When the tunnel exploded the Germans would send more soldiers to hunt them down. Neliah made up her mind. This was the more dangerous place to be.

'Do you really want to fight, Zuri?'

'I'm not scared.'

'Go with Ajiah and two others, she knows the way. Close to here is a chimney-camp—'

'We said *pamue*. I want to stay with you.'

'It's what your Alberto wanted.'

Zuri shook her head. 'He said wear a white dress, stay at the camp. Cook.'

'Please, sister. Do as I ask. There will be danger enough. Go to the chimney-camp, find a place to hide where you can watch it. When we blow the dynamite they'll send skull-troops from there to help. That's when you attack. Free as many prisoners as you can, get them to join us. I will wait till high-sun tomorrow for the digging machines. If none is here by then . . .' Neliah patted the haversack.

'Ajiah said they're white. Why will they come with us?'

'Promise them your pork stew! Tell them how good it is.' When her sister didn't laugh, Neliah became grave again. 'You rescued them, they're far from home, they'll follow. If not, let the savannah have them. We meet back at Terras de Chisengue.'

'And then?'

'We save our land, like *Papai* wanted. Go to Loanda. There will be many Germans to kill in the city.'

Neliah handed her the gun from the dead soldier, the bullets and one of the grenades. Zuri took them and reached out to hug her. Neliah allowed her a brief embrace, curled her fingers round her sister's plait, brought the tuft to her mouth. It was smooth and prickly against her lips, smelt of mafuta oil. Memories of home. Then she pushed her away. 'Go! And remember what I said: think of Muspel and your heart will roar.'

Ajiah strode off through the grass, the other two followed, finally Zuri.

Neliah watched her sister go, the rifle looking awkward in her hands. She moved with the same short, rolling stride as their mother.

A sudden feeling wrenched at Neliah's chest, the feeling she would never see her sister again, never hear the comforting swish of her hair. With it came the urge to touch her one last time, to feel the smooth skin of her cheek against hers. To grasp her hands. She wished she hadn't pushed her away.

'Zuri,' she called after her. 'Zuri!' But there was no wind to carry her voice.

Her sister vanished into the grass and was gone.

Chapter Twenty-Three

PAA, Kongo
17 September, 08:50

N the horizon: stacks of poisonous smoke. It was then that Burton guessed what their destination would be. He felt a plunging wave of dread.

The convoy had continued south throughout the night. Somewhere along the road Burton drifted off into a shivering sleep. He dreamed fleetingly: saw the driveway back home, the potholes he kept promising Madeleine to repair. They had been filled with skulls.

When he awoke the sun was glinting on the autobahn; the shimmer of pink tarmac. His eyes felt raw, joints and muscles set like concrete. Several of the other prisoners had pissed themselves during the night. Now the lorry stank of urine. Urine and despair. Burton tried to flex his limbs but the chains around his wrists and ankles were too tight. Movement had returned to his knee though. He imagined *harba-dogo*, the *dambe* kick to the head. Rottman tumbling backwards.

An hour after dawn the lorries stopped to refuel once more. The guards got out, stretched their legs. Himmler had insisted that all members of the Schutzstaffel start their day with a breakfast of raw leeks and mineral water (Apollinaris, no doubt), a diet to fortify the new masters of Africa. But it seemed the Unterjocher paid little heed: there was the smell of coffee, cigarettes, bacon frying. Burton's stomach howled. Then another ladle of water for the prisoners, no phlegm this time, and they were back on the road.

Craning his neck, Burton glimpsed the first of the chimneys. They were caged inside girders and walkways, built on a scale that only an inferiority complex could conceive. The smell of the smoke reminded him of those final days in Tana – when the Luftwaffe bombed the city into powder. Tana: it had been his first job as a soldier of fortune. But whereas the Legion offered hardship and discipline, a regime to fill the void left by his childhood, the mercenary's way was chaotic. There were no rules to cling to, just violence. Even as he prospered in Madagascar, then the wars of central Africa, Burton knew he was emptying out again.

Ten minutes later the convoy rolled through a barbed wire gate into the factory complex. A rusting sign by the entrance read: *Deutsche Erd & Steinwerke GmbH Afrika* – the German Earth & Stoneworks Company; part of Department W, better known by its acronym: DESTA.

This then was to be his fate: worked to death in some Nazi labour camp. The price of revenge. Unless . . .

Burton looked to the other lorries trying to find Patrick. By his calculation they had travelled far enough to be near the border with Northern Rhodesia; it couldn't be more than fifty, sixty miles away. *Une petite promenade* they would have called that in the Legion. A stroll.

If only he could get out of these chains!

Rottman leapt out of the lead vehicle and was met by a hulking SS officer twirling a baton. They exchanged words, the officer gesturing to the trucks, to the factory – a furious swipe of the baton – over to the south.

Eddies of dust swirled up from the ground.

Rottman gave a Führer-salute and ran back to the convoy, blowing his whistle. The guards unloaded the men, all except Burton who remained chained to the lorry. Rottman selected twenty of the brawniest prisoners and ordered them back on.

'Punishment detail,' Burton overheard one of the guards say as the cage was shut. Rottman climbed on board; the engine started.

The captives who had been left behind were led away towards the factory. Burton scanned their shuffling forms. Whatever had happened on the quayside or cellar, they couldn't be parted like this.

'Patrick,' he yelled, trying to stand. 'Patrick!'

He glimpsed his old friend towards the rear.

Rottman leaned out of the cab. 'Shut him up!'

'*Chef!*'

Patrick hesitated, cocked his head as if he might turn back. Burton caught a hint of his face in profile.

A scowl.

'I'll get you back to Hannah.' It was the only thing he could think to say. 'I promise—'

A rifle butt slammed into Burton's stomach.

He doubled up, dropping back on to the bench with a crash of chains. The lorry pulled away. By the time he had enough breath to look up again, Patrick had turned to the front, was continuing with the other prisoners. Soon he was swallowed by the swirling dust.

The lorry drove for another twenty minutes before reaching its destination. It parked on a siding next to a tank.

Burton was unchained and herded out with the rest of the prisoners. He moved like an old, arthritic man; pins and needles screamed down his legs. When he couldn't climb off the lorry a hand shoved him out. He landed hard – a jolt to the knee – and tasted dirt. Rottman flashed a disapproving glare at the guards.

They had reached a tunnel.

Ahead was a fast-flowing river, a tributary of the Kassai, guessed Burton. The Lulua or maybe Lukoshi – which meant he was right about Rhodesia. As the PAA approached it the autobahn narrowed to four lanes and disappeared below into the tunnel. The tunnel itself appeared to have been damaged: the brickwork around the entrance was cracked, and Burton could see scorch marks. Inside a construction gang was at work.

His eyes roved over the rest of the site, calculating his chances of escape.

There were three tanks: two Panthers and a FP5 armed with a flamethrower; a sandbag emplacement with MG48 machine gun; at least twenty Waffen-SS soldiers. Their uniforms looked out of place in the sunlight. Near the entrance of the tunnel were several tents. From the largest emerged a man in a white coat. He pulled off his swastika armband, replaced it with a Red Cross one.

Behind him came two soldiers carrying a cast-iron cauldron. The cauldron was smoking.

I hope this means food, thought Burton. Some soup, any old slop. His belly was hollow.

The prisoners were made to stand in rows, the guards casually aiming their weapons at them. Rottman climbed on to the tailgate of the lorry and addressed the crowd. In his hand was a jambok: a hippo-hide whip, the favoured tool of discipline when the Germans had colonised DSWA in the previous century.

'*Arbeit macht frei*,' he said in his carbolic voice. 'Work brings freedom.

'As illegals in German Africa commandeered by the Unterjocher you are now officially chattels of the SS. RAD-Afrika laws stipulate you must work for the benefit of the Reich for the period of a year and one day. After such time you will be granted official papers and may choose your own employment.'

Burton suppressed a grim laugh, glanced at his fellow prisoners. Most were staring at Rottman dumbfounded; he doubted they spoke enough German to understand what was being said. They were men from the fringes of Europe, who had come to Africa with false dreams of getting rich or living unmolested.

'Prior to that happy day,' continued Rottman, 'and to dissuade you from escape, you will be marked as press-ganged workers.' He nodded to the two soldiers with the cauldron. They took off the lid.

Burton's heart shrivelled. Not soup.

A brazier.

Rottman was still speaking. 'Terrorists have attempted to destroy the tunnel behind us. Naturally they failed. Part of the PAA has been blocked, however. You are the relief gang; your task will be to clear the debris before the heavy machinery arrives.' He raised the whip in his hand. 'Any man found shirking will be punished. Severely. Take that as your sole warning.'

Rottman jumped off the lorry and nodded to the Red Cross man. 'Continue.'

The soldiers carried the brazier to the prisoners. Inside coals burned scarlet, orange and white. Several branding irons were buried in the heat.

The first prisoner was made to kneel and hold out his left arm, palm upwards. The two soldiers held him down while the Red Cross official shoved a wooden bit into his mouth.

Rottman wrapped a cloth round his hand and withdrew one of the branding irons from the fire. He lingered for a moment, then pressed it against the prisoner's forearm, halfway between the wrist and elbow.

The smell of charred flesh. A scream to silence the blood.

Rottman released the brand. The prisoner collapsed to the floor, writhing in agony. Cauterised on his arm were an inverted triangle and two letters: UJ.

The Red Cross man dabbed the wound with an iodine rag before wrapping it in a bandage. They moved on to the next prisoner.

Burton stared straight ahead, fought to control his lungs. In the gloom of the tunnel he saw men working, saw their exhaustion as they hacked away at the rockfall. Even if they survived the press gang they were all marked for life now.

Another agonised yell, more smoke.

There would be no easy escape to Rhodesia. Even if he managed to break out, even if he stole an SS uniform or found fresh papers, one look at his arm and he was finished.

He had to get away before they burned him.

Burton's eyes searched for an escape route. Anything. Above him was a ridge hidden in grass, beyond that the river. He saw the sunlight shimmering on its surface, indigo and brown. In front, tanks; behind him the endless road to Stanleystadt.

And everywhere black uniforms. BK44s. He'd be pumped full of holes before he took a dozen paces.

Rottman continued down the line. A steady process of bit, brand and iodine. He didn't seem to register the screams.

The air smelt like pork spitting on a barbecue.

Rottman had reached the prisoner next to Burton. He shook uncontrollably. The guards grabbed his arm, exposed the skin.

Burton tried to blank his mind . . . but for some reason kept fixating on the chest of drawers in his bedroom. Maddie had this annoying habit of leaving them open; it drove him to distraction sometimes. Now, though, Burton saw himself dash through the house opening every drawer he could find, pulling out the contents till it was raining socks and stockings and woollen scarves.

Rottman was standing over him.

Burton glimpsed the ivory handle of his Browning poking out of Rottman's trousers, felt a prickle of fury.

They forced him to kneel. His left kneecap jarred as it crunched into the ground. The Red Cross official reached for the bit. Burton could see the other men's saliva glistening on it.

'Wait,' said Rottman. 'This one's a tough bastard. He can do without.'

The official shrugged.

The soldiers forced Burton's arm out. Held it in place. He felt their grip tug at the hairs around his wrist. His tendons bulged.

Rottman tightened the cloth covering his hand, reached for a fresh brand, pulled it out of the fire.

Burton smelt its black, volcanic heat at the back of his throat.

For an instant he closed his eyes, tensed his jaw. Then they were open again. He wasn't going to give Rottman the satisfaction; first chance he got he swore he was going to break the fucker's neck.

The letters blazed before him.

UJ.

Chapter Twenty-Four

PAA, Kongo
17 September, 09:15

FROM the air it was even more impressive. A miracle of German engineering and Hochburg's genius.

Kepplar was in the passenger seat of his master's helicopter, marvelling at the scene below him. He had spent the last sixteen hours ransacking Stanleystadt for Cole and the American, working through the night to check every last tavern, flophouse and festering brothel. Nothing. He was resolute he wouldn't return empty-handed again; had never seen the Oberstgruppenführer so agitated. Then came a report of an incident with the Unterjocher the previous afternoon. A prisoner had attempted to escape from one of the convoys to Wutrohr 161.

Now Kepplar was heading south, on his lap a dossier supplied by the Gestapo.

He had intended to use the flight to catch up on some sleep but as soon as the PAA came into view, the fatigue left him. His heart swelled. What they had achieved in Kongo in a single decade the Belgians failed to do in a century. Even the British in India – before the Hindoos kicked them out – couldn't compare. The triumph belonged to the SS! They had put the niggers to good work in the years before Windhuk. Under Hochburg's auspices new cities and mining towns were built, hydroelectric dams across the Rivers Klara and Rufiji, even an opera house in the jungle near Gerberstadt designed by Brinkmann. The key had been transport. *Without it*, Hochburg declared on the day he became Governor General, *Kongo isn't worth two pfennigs*.

So: the Matadi lock system (largest in the world); ultramodern ports at Pythonhafen, Neu Berlin and Stanleystadt; the north–south railway network linking the colony to Muspel; a hub of airports to carry Germans back home or to the beach resorts of Kleine Küste and Strength-Through-Joy holidays. None of these achievements, however, stirred Kepplar as much as the Pan African Autobahn.

It was as straight as any Roman road, bisected the continent with its gleaming white lanes – arteries to pump the blood of German civilisation – with neither forest nor desert, river nor mountain allowed to stand in its path. The Kongo section had opened only a few months earlier. Along here the panzers of the Waffen-SS would thunder on their way to victory in Northern Rhodesia. But it was more than simply a triumph of civil engineering. The masterstroke of the PAA, at least for the German legs, was the material it was constructed from: a unique blend of concrete that would ensure the presence of National Socialism in Africa for millennia.

The idea was Hochburg's.

When he presented it to Himmler only two things were demanded of him. One, that work begin immediately. Two, that no one outside the SS must ever know its secret. Later, Hochburg told Kepplar, the Reichsführer had danced a jig at what they planned.

The pilot's voice came over the comlink. 'Two minutes, Gruppenführer,' he said, pointing to the horizon.

Kepplar opened the dossier on his lap, studied the photos in it, before returning his gaze to the grasslands below.

Already he could see the billowing chimneys of the Wutrohr labour camp. Although not of the magnitude of DESTA's complexes in Muspel, Wutrohr 161 was still a considerable achievement. Built in the deep south of Kongo – far from prying eyes

– it had risen from the bush in a matter of months to manufacture the cement for the PAA. This time not a single black hand had contaminated the construction: on Hochburg's insistence every last brick and girder was laid by the SS.

The Flettner landed and was met by a small contingent of troops. Kepplar climbed out of the helicopter, ducking against the wind, and hurried towards them. He was greeted by the camp commandant, Uhrig.

'Heil Hitler!' said Uhrig, snapping to attention. He was a gorilla in uniform.

Kepplar regarded the man with distaste: he knew the accusations against him. 'Heil!'

'This is an unexpected honour, Herr Gruppenführer,' said Uhrig as they strode away. 'But let me assure you I am doing everything – *everything* – in my power to clear the tunnel for the Governor. I've doubled the work-gangs, sent another across the river to dig from the far side. Told my men to whip any shirkers—'

'I'm sure the Herr Oberst will appreciate your efforts.'

'I also sent out patrols to hunt down the niggers that did it. When we catch them, they'll wish they'd been shipped off to Muspel.'

'I've not come to check on the progress of the tunnel,' said Kepplar. 'Two convoys of Unterjocher travelled here yesterday. Where are they?'

A flicker of disappointment. 'The last arrived thirty minutes ago. They're being de-loused ready for branding.'

'Assemble them immediately for my inspection. All of them.'

Uhrig chewed his lip. 'All of them?'

'Just do it.'

Ten minutes later Kepplar was standing in the parade square at the back of the camp. Chimneys towered above him casting shadows on the dusty ground. The sky was grey from smoke, had a tang of fire and dust.

Uhrig was running around barking orders at his men, shoving the assembled prisoners into place. The first dozen had been shaved, their heads white with disinfectant, the rest were as they had arrived. They were all still cuffed. Uhrig punched one who didn't move fast enough.

'Line up, you fucking pigs!' screamed Uhrig. 'A shoulder width apart. Make yourself presentable for the Herr Gruppenführer.'

He's desperate to impress, thought Kepplar, anything to get out of Wutrohr. Uhrig was a one-time hero of the Einsatzgruppen, had been among the first into Russia, and later Kongo. With him the stench of scandal: Polacks in the East, outright miscegenation in Africa. He had been accused of raping a native girl. Kepplar's stomach convulsed at the notion. Nothing was ever proved, at least not sufficiently for a prosecution under the Nuremberg Laws for race defilement, but his career suffered. For a crack trooper like Uhrig, Wutrohr must have been purgatory. He wanted to be back on the front line especially with the prospect of Angola and Northern Rhodesia. Kepplar had seen several transfer requests pass over Hochburg's desk.

Finally the prisoners were assembled, a ragamuffin parody of troops on parade.

'Stand to attention,' said Uhrig. He was twirling a baton of wood. 'Come on, you pigs!'

Kepplar scanned their faces. They seemed a mean bunch. Slavs and Polacks mostly to judge from their physiognomy, escaped workers. The slime of humanity. Also a few migrant Germans foolish enough to have lost their papers. They might get lucky.

'I said: stand to attention!' To emphasise his order Uhrig brought the baton crashing down into the back of the nearest prisoner. He crumpled to the ground. The rest straightened their spines.

'That will do, Uhrig,' said Kepplar.

'Sorry, Gruppenführer.'

Kepplar glanced at the Gestapo dossier then began walking down the ranks, examining the faces, looking for Cole and the American.

A Slav: Category Four skull.

Another Four.

216

And another.

Four.

Three/Four.

Four again.

Four—

Kepplar came to a halt, scrutinising the face in front of him. 'And he arrived today?' he said to Uhrig.

'This morning, Gruppenführer.'

Kepplar turned back to the prisoner, leaned in closer. He was a Category One/Two, in another life could have joined the SS. His head was bowed.

'Look at me,' said Kepplar.

The prisoner glanced up, eyes fixed on a point beyond the parade ground. He was in his fifties, lean and wrinkled, with thinning grey hair. His nose bent to the left. A scab on the bridge of it.

Kepplar beckoned Uhrig over. 'This one.'

They can't know it's me, Patrick kept telling himself.

They can't know it's me.

A Gruppenführer – a fucking major general – was walking down the line examining the faces before him. In his hand was a red folder. As he approached, Patrick saw part of his ear was missing: it looked as if it had been bitten off. He came to a halt in front of him. The faint smell of mint, like chewing gum that had been in your mouth all day.

Patrick averted his eyes. Steadied his breathing.

They only knew what Burton looked like. There was no way they could pick him out unless he gave himself away.

'This one.'

Patrick felt a choking sensation, fought to control his throat.

The camp commander, Uhrig, came over, a leer on his face. He had stopped twirling his baton, was now gripping it so hard his fist had turned crimson.

The Gruppenführer spoke. In English. 'You are Patrick Whaler, an American.' He spoke the last word with particular scorn; it dripped with Goebbels's taunts of capitalists and yellow-belly isolationism – the exact reason why Patrick had joined Burton at Dunkirk. It made sense at the time, though now . . . His idealism had long since withered away.

Patrick remained silent, kept his eyes straight ahead. He conjured up an expression of reverence, fear, bafflement.

'Three nights ago you and a team of assassins tried to kill our beloved Governor General. Do you deny it?'

Still Patrick said nothing.

Uhrig pushed his baton against Patrick's neck. 'Answer the Gruppenführer, you pig.' He shoved him backwards.

Patrick stumbled but kept his footing. 'Please, monsieur,' he said in his legionnaires' French, head bowed, 'I don't understand.'

The Gruppenführer raised his eyebrows. 'We can speak French if you prefer, we can even hang you in it.'

'I'm just an old man, monsieur, a worker. I didn't have the right papers. I don't understand what's going on, all I want is to get back to my family.'

This time the Nazi replied in German, raising his voice so everyone could hear. 'You are a criminal and a terrorist. Your fellow conspirators have all been captured or killed. Lapinski, Vacher, Dolan. You have no hope.'

Patrick swallowed hard, felt the currents in his stomach shift. He forced his expression to remain blank but even he couldn't help reacting to the next statement.

'Your mission has failed. Failed entirely. Herr Hochburg is alive. Alive and well – and as I speak planning his next move against the enemies of peace in Africa.' The Gruppenführer leaned in closer; for a second Patrick thought he was going to embrace him. His voice dropped to a whisper. 'You killed his decoy.'

It's a bluff, thought Patrick. All a bluff to get me talking. Remember: they don't know what I look like.

I'm a blank.

The Nazi stepped back, gave a signal to Uhrig. The camp

commander slipped his baton into his jackboots and withdrew his pistol. Patrick recognised it at once: a Luger P08, nine mil. The muzzle was placed against his forehead.

Patrick fell to his knees, cupped his hands. 'Please, monsieur, I don't know what you're talking about. I haven't killed anyone. I just want to get back to my daughter.'

Uhrig kept the pistol trained on his head.

'I have two daughters,' replied the Gruppenführer. 'Two daughters and a son. I haven't seen them for a year.'

'Then you understand, monsieur. I only came here to work, for money, for my family. We're very poor.'

'Where are you from?'

'Marseilles.'

'A Vichy. And what do you think of your Monsieur Laval?'

'He's a good man. I don't know. I'm not interested in politics.' Patrick looked up into the face above him: he could see the doubt in the Nazi's eyes. They were shockingly blue.

'What about Westmark? *Every* Frenchman has a view on that.'

Westmark: previously Alsace-Lorraine, 'a jewel we won't give back', as Hitler described it. It had been subsumed into Greater Germany in 1940, was now the seat of the Council of New Europe. Its loss remained a fiercely contentious issue in France.

'It will be ours again,' proclaimed Patrick, 'you'll see.'

The Gruppenführer considered this for a moment, then motioned to Uhrig to remove the gun.

'Shoot the man next to him.'

Uhrig twisted his Luger to the prisoner on Patrick's right. Patrick looked over to him. He was pleading in a language that—

Uhrig fired.

Blood sprayed Patrick's face, hot and thick. It splashed his mouth. For an instant he was standing over Nares again. Poor Nares . . .

The man slumped to the ground, blood continuing to spurt from his skull.

'And the next one.'

Uhrig moved along the line.

Hannah, he thought. *Concentrate on Hannah*. She's all that matters now. Getting out of Africa and back to her. Let them kill as many as they want. In prison he had memorised the picture she'd sent him, every last grain of film. He focused on her smile, the turn of the skin at the corner of her lips; the way the light caught her eyes – just like her mother.

A second shot.

The Gruppenführer was staring at him, eyes as unflinching as a mesmerist's, watching for any tick or tremble that might give him away.

'Please, monsieur . . .'

'And the next.'

There was a third shot. The ground was turning black.

Uhrig moved to the next prisoner, raised his gun again and looked over expectantly. His sleeve was sprayed scarlet.

The Gruppenführer turned to the folder in his hand and removed a photograph. Patrick could only see the back of it, glossy white paper.

'Perhaps you're thinking, Major Whaler, that we don't know what you look like. Perhaps you are pinning your hopes on this. Let me assure you nothing is further from the truth. I have your face here. Yours and Cole's, from a Gestapo file.'

Patrick used the back of his hand to wipe away the blood on his face. This was the interrogators' game. Another bluff.

Whoever blinked first, lost.

The Nazi was growing agitated. 'There are—' he estimated the number of prisoners, frowning as he did so '—ninety-five, a hundred men here. Must every one of them die?'

Patrick returned his gaze to the ground. Blood was trickling around his knees, soaking into his pants. A hundred men: at least the same number of children. Sons, daughters. Orphans-in-waiting because of him. He tried to push the thought away. Was that all Hannah was now? An orphan-in-waiting? The last time he'd seen her she was four years old. He had picked her up and she cried. She's not good with strangers, Ruth told him.

The Gruppenführer sighed. 'Very well.' He nodded at Uhrig.

He checked the mechanism on his Luger, then went down the line. One shot. Two. Three. He seemed bored.

The prisoners were staring at Patrick. Begging. Wailing. He'd heard that sound after battles, men with missing legs and open bowels pleading to be saved. It was the type of sound you never forgot. He had woken in prison with it gnawing his ears.

Four. Five. Six.

Patrick got to his feet, swayed. 'Promise me you won't kill any more?' he said in German.

'Uhrig has lost nine strong backs because of you. He doesn't have enough workers as it is.'

'I'm Whaler.'

'Kepplar.' He clicked his heels, saluted.

'How did you know?' asked Patrick.

'Your friend Dolan.'

'I knew he'd blab.'

'I had him squealing in minutes. It was easy enough.'

Patrick thought of the Welshman, his booming voice and armour-plated arrogance; he was just a kid really. 'Is he still alive?'

'For now. His court martial is tomorrow. You'll be taking the stand with him.'

'And the photo? It was blank, wasn't it?'

A spark played in Kepplar's blue eyes. He glanced down at the picture, slipped it back into his folder, snapped it shut. Patrick caught sight of the markings on the front. *Gestapo, Department E: TOP SECRET.*

'Enough chit-chat,' said Kepplar. 'Where is Burton Cole?'

Patrick hesitated. 'I haven't seen him since the Schädelplatz. Somebody double-crossed us, our plane was destroyed.'

'Get involved with British intelligence and what do you expect?'

'So it wasn't the Angolans?'

Kepplar shook his head.

'Ackerman?' asked Patrick.

'We knew from the start.' A thin smile. 'You never had a chance.'

221

'But why? What did he hope to gain?'

'Major Whaler, it's not for you to ask the questions. Now, where is Cole?'

'We split. After that I don't know.'

Kepplar sighed. 'You're an American, you like the movies. Cole too.'

'What?'

'You were seen *together* in Stanleystadt, fleeing across the rooftops. Paid an unexpected visit to Fräulein Riefenstahl's latest masterpiece.' He spoke up so Uhrig and the rest of the guards could hear him: 'I've met her, by the way. Charming woman.' He returned to Patrick. 'I'll ask one more time, or does the good Standartenführer here have to reload his Luger?'

Patrick tilted his face to the sky; let the sun warm it for a few moments. The heat was dry here, like the desert, the kind he loved. He could hear the flies already buzzing around the corpses either side of him. 'I don't know. We were put on separate trucks. When we got here he was driven away.'

Kepplar turned to Uhrig, raised his eyebrows. 'Is this true? How many trucks were there?'

'Four, Herr Gruppenführer.'

'Thirty prisoners per truck . . . and there are only a hundred here. What happened to the rest?'

Patrick watched Uhrig chew his lip. 'Sent on a punishment detail, to clear the tunnel.'

'From the same convoy as the American here?'

'One of my deputies dealt with it, Gruppenführer. When I find out who I'll have him whipped.'

Kepplar spoke deliberately: 'From the same convoy?'

'Yes.'

'Prepare my Flettner for immediate take-off. I'm going to the tunnel.'

Uhrig clicked his fingers and a guard scurried off. 'And the prisoner?' he said, withdrawing his baton from his jackboot and pointing it at Patrick.

'We may need to interrogate him further,' said Kepplar. 'Keep him alive, but make sure he'll be more ... amenable to questioning.'

He gave Patrick a final, piercing look with his blue eyes and headed in the direction of his helicopter.

'Very good, Herr Gruppenführer,' said Uhrig, watching him stride away. As soon as he was gone he turned back to Patrick. Unbuttoned his tunic and began rolling up his bloody sleeves.

Chapter Twenty-Five

Lulua Tunnel, PAA
17 September 09:45

DURING those first months as a boy soldier in the Legion all Burton seemed to do was brawl: scuffles in barracks, fist-fights in the drinking holes of rue de Daya. He wanted recompense for what had happened to his parents, for the childhood he'd been robbed of. If Hochburg couldn't pay then other people's blood seemed the best currency. One night, in Bar Madagascar, his nose had been broken and jaw dislocated; Patrick refused him any treatment. Years later, back in England, he snapped his wrist while training at the Exton Depot. He had been beaten black and yellow, been slashed with a bayonet, had shrapnel pepper his flesh but nothing – nothing – compared to the pain of the brand.

Burton screamed through his teeth as it pressed harder; spit bubbled in his mouth.

'Not so tough any more,' said Rottman.

Burton struggled to pull away but strong hands clamped him to the spot.

Rottman gave the iron a final dig, twisting it into the forearm. Burton screamed again, the sound exploding from his throat, raw and animal.

Then the brand was gone, Rottman moved to the next man.

Burton slumped forward, gasping; his forehead grazed the dirt.

If it still hurts, it's not that bad: Patrick's mantra at Sidi Bel Abbès. The Red Cross doctor splashed his iodine rag against the wound and bound it with a meagre bandage. A numbness was chewing at Burton's arm, spreading through his body. He felt it in his gums: a deep, burning throb. His arm was still smoking.

Rottman branded the rest of the prisoners before giving them a few minutes rest. The bucket and ladle came round again, followed by hunks of rye bread. Burton was too queasy to eat. In his mind he was with Maddie. Often when they lay between the sheets she would trace the scars on his body. Other women he'd known had been impressed, sometimes horrified, by his exploits. Not Madeleine. She simply accepted them, as she did all his wayward past; there was great solace in that. What would she make of the triangle and its two letters? Reminders were important to her: they taught you to value the present. She still kept her Star of David armband, even though her husband had told her to throw it away. It was hidden on the farm, in an empty jewellery box beneath their bed; the same place he stowed his Browning.

Guards went down the ranks of prisoners undoing their hand-cuffs. Picks and shovels were tossed at their feet.

Rottman scooped up one of the shovels. 'There are more than twenty soldiers here as well as the Unterjocher. You can't escape, but should you be tempted . . .' He brought the shovel down against a rock, hard enough to shatter concrete. 'Now move out!'

The prisoners were herded into the tunnel, past the tanks parked on the roadside.

Burton's arm felt as if it were ballooning with molten lead. He could barely grasp the spade he'd been given. Rottman had dropped the shovel, had picked up his jambok again. It was coiled in his hand, a sleeping viper.

The autobahn continued inside the tunnel for several hundred feet before it was blocked by a wall of fallen rock. The interior was lit by Klieg lights; there was the *chug-chug* of generators. Burton saw men working at the rock face, struggling to remove chunks of stone with bloody hands, and suddenly thought of Halifax's eulogy on losing India. *Civilisations cannot be built on the servitude of others.* What did he mean by that? Was it a prediction for the future of Nazi Africa . . .? Huge iron props held up the roof. The place smelt like a mineshaft, of deep earth and rushing water.

There were guards everywhere.

Another Hauptsturmführer came to meet Rottman and led him up the rock face to where several prisoners were working. There seemed to be a gap through the debris. A worker, shirtless and grimy, emerged from the hole and collapsed with exhaustion. Rottman nodded, pointed back to his own contingent of labourers and climbed down to them.

He addressed his captives. 'My orders are to get this road reopened in the next twenty-four hours. Remember what I told you.' His face stretched into a ghastly smile. 'Work brings freedom.' The guards began leading the men away. 'You: come with me.'

The prisoners looked pityingly at Burton.

'I've got something special for you.'

Burton felt a BK44 prod him in the back. He was led to the hole in the rock face above.

'Him?' said the other Hauptsturmführer. 'He doesn't look so hard.'

'Hmm. This one thinks he shits steel,' replied Rottman. He forced a miner's lamp on to Burton's head and shoved him backwards. 'Get in there. We're almost through.'

Burton crouched by the hole. It was no more than a man's width, two or three feet high and quickly narrowed. The roof seemed to be shifting constantly, tiny fragments of rock pattering down from it.

'And if I don't?'

Rottman thumped his forearm with the jambok.

Beneath the bandage Burton felt the brand flare and scream. The urge to grab his spade and swing it into Rottman's head was almost overwhelming. Only the number of soldiers dissuaded him.

Burton lowered himself to the ground, rolled down his sleeves to protect his arm and began crawling into the hole. Almost at once he heard the rock groaning and creaking; the hiss of water.

'Stop!' said Rottman. He took a manacle, clamped it around Burton's ankle and attached it to a chain. 'Just in case you get any stupid ideas.'

Burton continued crawling into the hole, his spade pushed ahead of him. He was soon in a cavity barely big enough to move in. His lungs felt crushed. Each wriggle forward chaffed his forearm against the ground. But already his mind was whirring: if he could get through to the other side . . .

The rock around him grew damper. He could see rivulets of water flowing down the sides. Then a whisper of air. Fresh air. The passage widened till Burton was able to get back on his knees again, then his feet. He was standing in a hollow.

There was a tug on the chain around his ankle. 'Have you found something?' Rottman's voice echoed round the rock.

Burton ignored it.

'Why have you stopped?' There was a tug on the chain, dragging Burton back.

'I've reached the end of the passage,' Burton shouted. The sound of his voice caused a shimmer of dust. 'I'm going to dig.'

The pressure on the chain eased.

The wall in front of him was riddled with tool marks. The previous worker had been close to breaking through. Burton wondered how long the unlucky bastard had toiled for. There were tiny holes letting in air, the sound of the wind beyond like men's voices. Burton took the spade and began scraping at the rock. As he dug he kept glancing down at the chain around his ankle. Would he be able to break it with the spade? He chipped away at the wall.

Suddenly a pickaxe came crashing through above him. It missed his face by inches. The roof of the hollow shuddered. Pebbles tumbled down.

'Stop!' yelled Burton.

The pickaxe was prised out. Came smashing down again.

'Stop!'

From far away Rottman's voice: 'What's going on?'

The chain snapped rigid, dragging Burton to the ground. He was pulled backwards.

The pickaxe above broke through the roof again. The sound of groaning rock. Tiny fissures were opening in the ceiling.

Then another noise, from the direction of the tunnel. Tinny and distant. For an instant Burton couldn't decipher it.

Gunfire.

Long after their screams rolled away, the stink of roasted meat hung in the air.

Neliah had spent the night on the ridge overlooking the tunnel. She stayed awake while Tungu and Bomani slept, watching the moon disappear into the earth, whispering *kumbus* for her sister. Trying not to let the words of Gonsalves haunt her mind. She was more than just a cook-girl! She would destroy the tunnel, show them all. Destroy the tunnel and smile. Finally the sun had climbed in the sky and with it a new-born thought. A trickster thought about Penhor and the dynamite . . . Then the lorries had arrived below and the men were seared like heads of cattle.

Now the prisoners were stumping towards the tunnel to be worked till their backs broke. They would be killed with the others when she fired the explosives. More skulls around her neck.

As if guessing her thoughts, a voice spoke in her ear: 'If we make explosion now they will live.' It was Tungu. She was Herero, a mountain of flesh with heartbroken eyes.

Neliah looked at the height of the sun. 'It's too soon. Zuri won't be at the chimney-camp.'

'She's had plenty time.'

'The plan was to wait,' said Neliah. 'Wait for the *Nazista* machines.'

'And if no machines come?'

Neliah turned her eye back to the men being herded into the tunnel. She could still smell their burned skin. 'My family deserved to live. So did yours.' She looked from Tungu to Bomani. 'And yours. We wait.'

The other two women nodded and resumed their silent watch. They were still hidden in the *enga*-grass. To the east the waters of the Lulua rippled in the sunlight.

'I hear something,' said Bomani.

Neliah listened. There was a noise like bees – coming from the direction Zuri had taken. Not bees . . . a machine.

She lifted up her head from the grass and stared down the road. It was empty. Her eyes rose to the sky. 'Stay down! Stay down!'

They pressed their bellies to the earth.

A *zenga-zera*, a whirr-bird, roared overhead.

'Did it see us?'

'No,' said Neliah, watching the helicopter swoop low over the river.

The *zenga-zera* made a circle as if coming in to land. Then bore down on them.

The ground burst upwards. Shreds of grass and smoke.

Down by the tunnel a whistle blew. Soldiers pointed towards them, some already climbing upwards.

Neliah reached for the haversack and took out the detonator.

'The *Nazistas* are coming!' said Bomani.

Neliah pulled the detonator aerial. 'Tungu, get your bow.'

Tungu took up position on the edge of the grass, stabbed a dozen arrows in the ground ready to be picked up and fired. The first went in the string of the bow. She pulled it back, her chest swelling.

The whirr-bird had landed, the wind from its engines blowing the tents over. A man dressed in black was running from it, pointing at them, screaming.

Neliah turned a switch, breathed in, waited. Her fingers nervously brushed her scar.

A red lamp came on above the detonation button. She looked

at the others. 'Cover your ears, open your mouths. The blast will tear the breath from you.' She thought back to when she was a girl, *Papai's* beaming face: *Go on*, menina, *you can do it* . . .

Neliah hunched up against the explosion. Pressed the button.

Nothing happened.

Neliah pressed it again.

Still nothing.

Silence except for the whirr of the helicopter, the sound of boots scrambling up rock.

A roar emerged from her throat. 'Penhor!' The scream echoed and swirled around her.

She hurled the detonator down, breaking it into a thousand pieces.

Bomani was on her feet. 'We go.'

Below them the sound of an engine starting. Fumes belched from one of the tanks.

'No,' said Neliah, her chest heaving. She was thinking of Gonsalves. Gonsalves, Penhor, all the white soldiers laughing at her. Of *Ina* swinging from the tree. 'The tunnel. We *must* destroy it.'

'But nothing happen.'

'If I can get to the dynamite . . .' Neliah held up the grenades she had taken from the dead skull-troop. She could use them as a detonator. 'Tungu, watch us with your bow. Bomani, follow me.'

'I'm scared.'

Neliah reached over, clasped her fingers. 'We go together.'

In Bomani's other hand was a spear, the point was shaking.

'Think of Muspel,' said Neliah. 'Think of your brothers and sisters. Make your heart roar!'

Neliah grasped her panga, the steel singing as it left its sheath. She glanced to the sky, whispered a word to the god Mukuru.

And ran.

Chapter Twenty-Six

IT was like being at the bottom of a well. A well of stamping boots.

Blows rained down on him: his head, back, legs. His Dunkirk scar felt like it was going to split. Patrick curled himself into a ball, arms protecting his skull, and let them work him over. He'd had worse. During the Spanish Civil War, when he'd still been idealistic (or stupid) enough to go fight the Fascists, he was captured by the Condor Legion; had endured several weeks of interrogation. It was there he learned the most valuable lesson of being tortured: if you gave no reaction, if you tried to tough it out, they beat you harder. The dodge was to look weak, pathetic. Somebody not worth the effort.

And all the while you hid inside your mind.

With each kick Patrick whimpered and begged for them to stop. He thought of Hannah. Thought of Ackerman, how he'd betrayed them: the Rhodesian was going to pay for this.

They couldn't have beaten him for more than five minutes before Uhrig stopped them. 'Enough, enough,' he said, sounding bored. He pushed through the assembled soldiers and dragged Patrick up by his hair. 'What do you think this is? The fucking Spielhaus? Goethe?'

Patrick couldn't focus properly: Uhrig was a blur in black uniform. 'Please, no more,' he sobbed.

'You think I'm falling for this pigshit? You're clever, *Amerikaner*, but Uhrig – Uhrig's got brains for ten. An old soldier like you needs to be broken a different way.' He picked his teeth, hawked, then broke into a wide grin. 'I've got just the thing.'

He strode off, twirling his baton. 'Bring him!'

A BK44 was shoved into Patrick's back and he was led away into the factory. He moved stiffly, joints bawling. They passed a shuddering conveyor belt covered in ballast; huge rotating pipes. The air felt thick in Patrick's nostrils, smelt of quicklime and something sickly sweet, almost like candyfloss. They were heading into the factory's interior.

'You should have seen the production levels when I was first sent here,' Uhrig said, ducking below a girder. 'We were at the bottom of the DESTA tables. I doubled things in a month. Quadrupled them in six. And what thanks have I got? Fuck all.'

He stopped, turned to face Patrick. This close Patrick could see the pockmarks in his face; his cheeks looked like they had woodworm. His skin was pasty white.

'You're my ticket out of here, Major Whaler. I find this friend of yours, they'll put me back where I belong: on the front line. Just in time for Angola, or maybe Rhodesia.'

'Rhodesia?'

'You'll see. Myself, I'd prefer Angola. More niggers to deal with there.' He laughed. 'They're blacker too.'

They resumed their journey into the heart of the factory, Uhrig humming snatches of the 'Pilgrims' Chorus' from *Tannhäuser* as they went. Finally they reached a door marked STRICTLY AUTHORISED PERSONNEL ONLY.

'You're very lucky, *Amerikaner*,' said Uhrig, reaching for a bunch of keys. 'No one outside the SS has ever seen inside.'

They entered a cylindrical chamber. It was dim, cool, still. From somewhere came the steady hum of condensing units. The guards seemed spooked. But what struck Patrick most was the stench. He breathed through his mouth.

'Ah!' said Uhrig, drawing in deep lungfuls. 'Just like Russia, the autumn of '42, when we turned the tide against the Bolsheviks. You fight in the East, *Amerikaner*?'

Patrick shook his head.

'Lucky you. I still have nightmares.' Uhrig snicked a light switch.

They were on a metal gangway suspended in the air. Below them a pit of—

Patrick forced his eyes upwards, struggled to control his breathing.

I'm dead, he thought. *I'm dead*.

The guard next to him vomited.

Uhrig spun on him. 'Get the fuck out of here.'

The guard scurried away, clutching his mouth.

'I've been setting up my own commando unit,' Uhrig said to Patrick. 'The SS Wutrohr Wolves. Anything to fight off the boredom. But I can't find enough men here. Too many useless cocksuckers like him. "Ethnics", not proper Germans.'

'My heart bleeds,' said Patrick.

Uhrig peered over the edge. 'You know, I've never met an *Amerikaner* before. Is it true what they say? That your country is full of pacifists.' The word came out with a mix of contempt and bewilderment, as if he couldn't comprehend the idea. 'Jews and gangsters. That every woman is a slut.'

Patrick saw his house in Las Cruces, the rolling desert hills. 'You tell me. I've not been back for a long time.'

'That your President was a cripple.'

'A long time.'

'Know what I think, *Amerikaner*? I think you stayed out of the war because you knew you'd lose. Were no match for us.'

'Maybe.'

'Is that why you didn't fight the Japs?'

'You got it. We're the United Cowards of America.'

Uhrig searched his face for any sign of sarcasm, then turned back to the pit below. 'You're not looking.'

'I already saw enough.'

Uhrig grinned and cracked his baton into the small of Patrick's knees. He dropped. Next moment Uhrig had him by the hair, forced his face downwards. 'See some more!' The Nazi's breath was hot in his ear, reeked of salami.

The meagre contents of Patrick's stomach came bursting out.

Uhrig let go of him and laughed. 'Uhrig will get you talking yet, *Amerikaner*.' He looked at the mass below him. 'Truly one of the Governor General's greatest ideas!'

Patrick wiped the puke from his mouth, the cuffs grazing his chin. 'Is he really still alive?'

'How the fuck am I supposed to know? Yes. Someone like Kepplar doesn't come all this way without an order.' Uhrig peeled off his tunic, then reached for some chains hanging from the ceiling. 'At least I hope he's still alive. The Governor's a generous man. Rewards hard work. I find this friend of yours, he'll get me out of this shit-hole.' He placed his jackboot on the back of Patrick's neck and forced him to look downwards again. 'So what do you think?'

Patrick felt the bile rising in his mouth again. 'I think you're fucking crazy. You. Hochburg. Every last one of you.'

Below him was a mass of dead bodies. Thousands of them: naked, white, hairless. Some appeared fresh, others were bloated with decomposition.

'Crazy?' said Uhrig. 'No, no. A stroke of genius. We take the bodies of our fallen heroes – the Waffen-SS, the Afrika Korps – grind them up, mix them with lime and gypsum and make a cement for the PAA unlike any other.' Uhrig pulled the chains above him till they were suspended over Patrick. 'We're literally Aryanising the soil of Africa. Can you believe that, *Amerikaner*? The autobahn is a knife, a pure white blade, through the heart of the black continent.'

Patrick wished his hands weren't cuffed. He wanted to put them to his ears: block out this lunacy. It was totally fucked up. *Sick*. If they knew about this back home, surely they'd fight; even Washington couldn't ignore it.

Uhrig attached a butcher's hook to the chains. 'Tie his feet.'

Two guards approached Patrick with another piece of chain. He struggled – till another swipe of Uhrig's baton had him flat on the floor. His legs were bound; the butcher's hook skewered through the chain around his ankles.

Uhrig had stepped over to the side of the gangway and was turning a handle. There was the *click-click-click* of a ratchet and the chain began to move.

Patrick was hoisted into the air.

The guards pushed him out till he was over the pit. Dangling head first. Thirty feet below: more dead bodies than he had ever seen. More than after they bombed Guernica, more even than Dunkirk.

Patrick felt the blood rushing to his head. He shut his eyes tight. Squirmed to free himself. One of the guards snickered at the sight.

'Shut the fuck up,' said Uhrig. 'Or you'll be next.' He turned back to Patrick. 'There's only one way out of this, *Amerikaner*. Talk. Now, what was the name of your comrade? Cole, wasn't it?'

Patrick saw him again on the truck. Their last glimpse of each other. *I'll get you back to Hannah . . . I promise.* 'Yeah, Cole. Major Cole.' He didn't care any more.

'So tell me something I don't know.' Uhrig released the ratchet. *Click-click*.

Patrick dropped two feet. Jerked to a halt, pain tearing through his ankles.

'Where is he?'

The hum of the condensing units.

'Where?'

Click-click.

'You're cheating,' said Uhrig. 'Open your eyes.'

Patrick kept them squeezed shut.

'Open them! Or I swear I'll let the chain go now.'

He can't kill me, thought Patrick. The Gruppenführer had forbidden him to. Then his mind was back on the parade ground.

He was convinced Kepplar had no idea what he looked like – and yet he'd been plucked out as easy as one of Burton's quinces.

Click-click-click. Another drop.

Patrick opened his eyes.

'Better . . . You know, we SS, we're hard. As the Reichsführer says, we know what it is to see five hundred corpses or a thousand. But you *Amerikaners*, you're like the British – anything not to fight. You want the easy life. Fat dinners and soft whores. So tell me what I need and you're back outside.' Uhrig breathed in deeply again. 'Imagine it: the sun, fresh air.'

'I already told you. Told the Gruppenführer. I don't know.'

Somewhere an alarm began to sound. Uhrig glanced up with annoyance. 'Find out what's going on,' he barked to one of the guards.

Click-click.

'I don't know!' shouted Patrick again.

'Pigshit. You're lying.'

'I don't owe Cole anything.'

'You *Amerikaners* never do.'

'It's his fault I'm here.'

'Kepplar said you were in Stanleystadt. That's where Cole is now, isn't it? Hiding somewhere.'

Click-click.

Patrick dropped again; tried to lift his body up and away. Pale, rigid limbs were reaching out for him. He could see grasping fingers locked with rigor mortis. See wide-open mouths and blank eyes. The smell was overpowering. It burned at the back of his throat. Putrid. Sour.

'He was on the truck,' said Patrick. His ears were pounding. 'The one you sent away with Rottman.'

'Very convenient.'

Click-click.

'I swear.'

'I've spent thirteen months in this cesspit. I don't expect to spend another day. Where is Cole?'

The guard burst back into the room. 'Standartenführer! They're attacking the tunnel again.'

'What?'

'The rebels.'

'Summon all the troops. Everyone. Get them down to the tunnel immediately. We'll catch those niggers this time. Skin 'em alive.'

Uhrig reached for his tunic.

'What about him?' asked one of the other guards, pointing at Patrick. 'Shall I haul him back up?'

'He's not going anywhere.'

Patrick's head was bulging with blood, eyes watering. He looked at the gangway, away from the mountain of dead.

'Last chance, *Amerikaner*. I might be gone for some time. Where's your friend?'

'I already told you. On the truck.'

Uhrig snorted, finished doing up his tunic. He checked his Luger in its holster and stormed towards the door. Then he paused, glanced back at Patrick.

He strode back to the ratchet – and set it free.

Patrick screamed.

Clickclickclickclickclickclickclickclickclick—

Chapter Twenty-Seven

NELIAH tore into the ranks of skull-troops, her panga slicing left and right. Circles of blood sprayed the grass. Close to her heels Bomani had screamed herself into a rage. The point of her spear was red.

A soldier fell, grabbed at Neliah's leg. She spun, hacked at his arm, and tumbled to the ground, the breath knocked from her. She pushed herself up – as another skull-troop aimed his rifle at her.

There was a hissing sound.

The German toppled over, an arrow in his face.

Neliah snatched up his weapon and raced after Bomani. The breath of the wind was in her feet, the hunger of the *rungiro* urging her on. She would kill for the ancestors, those massacred by the grandfathers of the *Nazistas*. Kill for those who had lain in the pit back home and been torn open by grenades, for the screams that still visited her at night. But most of all she would kill for *Papai*. For *Ina*. Their spirits would protect her now.

Neliah and Bomani reached the road.

From above them Tungu's arrows whipped through the air, striking the troops down. Deadly as any rifle. The Germans took cover, raked the ridge above with gunfire. Neliah could already see inside the tunnel. Between it and her – three tanks. One was

238

trundling towards them, another to the tunnel. The ground shook beneath her feet.

'Take this,' she said, thrusting the gun into Bomani's hands. 'I need to get to the tunnel.'

'What will you do?'

Neliah reached for the two grenades she was carrying. 'All it takes is one. It goes, the dynamite goes with it.'

The rifle drooped in Bomani's hands. 'But who will look after Zuri?'

'She's the oldest, remember.' Neliah pushed the rifle back against Bomani's chest. 'Kill as many as you can.'

With that her feet were flying again.

She reached the first tank, leapt on to the turret and pulled the hatch. The driver looked up, startled, went for his pistol. Neliah pulled the pin from the first grenade, threw it between the feet of the driver and slammed the hatch shut.

Behind her Bomani shot at the soldiers, her bullets pinging wide.

Neliah jumped off the tank. One stride, two, three. A loud crump. The tank shook like some great monster belching. Smoke poured from it.

The second tank continued towards the tunnel. Neliah caught its tail, her mouth filling with fumes, and clambered upwards.

'Neliah!'

She spun round to see Bomani drop. For a single moment their eyes met – *help me!* – then the skull-troops were gathered around her crawling body. They emptied their rifles into her.

Neliah hid her heart in rock, she would weep later for Bomani. She swung her panga, the blade glistening, and pulled open the turret. Gunshots screamed past her face.

One of the crew climbed out. Neliah drove the panga into his chest, twisted and withdrew the blade. She pushed him out of the way and dropped into the belly of the steel beast.

Behind her the third machine had started its engine. Was already chasing after them.

Neliah closed the hatch. Inside the tank was like an oven, the air hot with grease and sweat and gunpowder. At the front, close to the ground, was the driver. Inside the turret, the gunner. He looked over at Neliah, mouth wide open.

She speared the panga into his thigh.

He screamed. A fountain of blood.

Neliah pulled the blade back out and hooked it round his neck. '*Los!*' she shouted to the driver below.

'Do it, do it,' begged the gunner. Blood was pumping from his leg.

The driver hesitated, then pressed the pedals. The tank rumbled forward.

'Faster,' said Neliah. 'Head for the—'

There was a huge blast from without.

The tank shook. Stones rained down on them, a thousand wild hands beating at the roof.

Neliah pulled the blade harder against the gunner's throat. 'What is it?'

His face seethed with pain. He pointed a bloody finger from his eye to a box in front of him. 'Periscope.'

Neliah didn't understand the word. She chanced a look, putting her face to the eye-hole – and found herself seeing outside. They were near the tunnel. Guards were whipping the workers as they ran. There was a swarm of skull-troops.

And the third tank.

It had roared ahead, the turret pointing backwards at them. A burst of lightning spat from its gun.

Neliah pulled away from the eye-hole.

The shell blasted into the side of the tank. There was a deafening bang. They lurched hard to the left. Neliah thought they were going to roll over, then the tank thumped back to the ground. It filled with smoke and sparks. Neliah's eyes stung.

'Fire back!' she yelled at the gunner.

He sat slumped against her, his mouth foaming. The blast had pulled the panga through his windpipe.

Neliah was fighting to breathe. She ordered the driver to slow them.

Another shell punched into the rear of the tank.

'Slow down!'

She looked at the driver. He was crushed into his seat, the controls gory.

Neliah's throat was burning. She coughed, trying to draw breath, heaved the hatch above her head. It didn't move. In the smoke she searched blindly for some way to release it.

Above her knee she found a trigger.

Coughing as if her lungs would split, Neliah pulled it. There was a roar. The smell of petroleum. But no explosion, no kick-back. She pulled it a second time.

From outside came the screams of men. Crackling. Loud enough to hear over the engine.

The last of her breath was leaving her.

Neliah struggled with the hatch again. Pushed her neck and shoulders against it with all her strength. Called on the spirits to help. Unseen hands banged with her.

The hatch came free.

She burst through it, sucking in gulps of burning air.

She was in the tunnel. The walls, the ground, everything was on fire. The other tank had stopped outside, the skull-troops held off by the flames. Ahead – a solid wall of debris.

The tank surged towards it.

Neliah scrambled out of the hatch, panga in hand, and jumped.

The pickaxe fell again, this time breaking a hole in the ceiling. Burton covered his head as shale peppered his eyes. By the time his vision had cleared a face was peering down at him through the gap.

'Looks like we've broken through,' said the man above; his voice was Polish. 'We'll help you up.'

A hand was offered.

Burton reached out and grabbed it. It felt cool and rocky; reminded him of Ackerman's handshake.

At that moment Burton felt a sharp tug on his ankle-chain. He struggled to keep hold of the hand – was yanked to his knees. Another tug and he fell flat on his front.

The face above him vanished.

The chain was being pulled hard. Burton was dragged across the floor . . . back into the passage . . . the damp taste of stone in his mouth.

He held out his hands, clawing at the walls to grab hold of something. The sides tore at his branded arm. Shards of electric pain. He dug his fingers into the rock. Felt it crumble away beneath his nails. There must have been several men pulling on the chain: he couldn't fight them.

His head banged against the rock, smashing the miner's lamp. Instant darkness.

Another haul. And another.

Beyond the passageway he heard Rottman's voice. 'Faster!'

'But, Hauptsturmführer, what about below?'

'There are enough soldiers to deal with it. I don't want this prick to get away.'

The retort of gunfire again. And a new sound.

Tank tracks.

In the cramped space Burton managed to twist himself over so he was on his back. He spread his legs, jammed his boots into the sides. The chain pulled tight, sending a bolt of pain through his knee, up his spine. The rock was disintegrating.

From the darkness behind him came the Polish voice again. 'Hey! You still there?'

Burton stretched forward with his hand, frantically searching for the ankle cuff, trying to prise it from his leg. It was impossible. The chain was pulled hard again.

Burton lost his footing.

He was dragged through the hole, hands scrambling for any purchase.

Next moment he was back outside. The roof of the tunnel flickered red and black. From ground level came gusts of heat.

He could see the FP5, the flame-tank, chugging towards the rock face. It moved erratically, fire spewing from its turret. Men like human torches tried to flee it.

Rottman loomed over him, narrowed his slanty eyes. He seemed indifferent to events below. 'What did I tell you if you tried to escape again? Hold him down.'

There were two soldiers and the other Hauptsturmführer. They pinned him to the floor. Rottman lifted up a pickaxe. Aimed it at Burton's kneecap.

From the hole behind him came a ghostly cry: 'You still there?'

Burton snatched one of his legs free. Lashed out – but not fast enough.

Rottman swung the pickaxe.

Neliah landed on her belly, her jaw cracking the ground. She tasted blood.

The tank crashed into the rock-wall. Erupted in a ball of flame.

Neliah felt it whip the skin on her neck. She forced herself up, pulled out the last grenade and ran towards the escape-hole where she had planted the dynamite.

'No!'

It was hidden in fire.

She tried to move forward. The heat was too savage. But she could see the flames snaking round the hole and ladder. They would soon find the dynamite, catch it alight, do the grenade's work for her. The tunnel would come crashing down.

Neliah picked up the panga. Her eyes flew around her for a way out. The other escape-hole was blocked by a wall of orange and red. The main exit also. Outside, the skull-troops had retreated from the blaze. Neliah stepped towards the back of the tunnel, realising she was trapped between the fire and rock. Already she could feel her skin roasting, the road was melting beneath her boots.

She held the grenade tight in her fist – it would serve her still. Better a quick death than to burn alive.

Then a final thought.

Penhor.

What had he told her? *There's no more dynamite left, we've taken it all. Need it for the battle ahead.* But Neliah had found the crate hidden in the strongroom. It had been easy. Easy because Penhor wanted her to. He knew she would go back to the tunnel. Knew the detonators were useless.

It wasn't the British equipment – it was him.

The flames tightened round her.

Neliah stumbled and fell. Pulled her knees close like a little girl.

She thought of her mother and father, how once *Ina* had given her a handful of honey-almonds as a treat and told her not to tell Zuri.

'Be safe,' she whispered to her sister. 'Wherever you go.'

Neliah squeezed her eyes shut, they were too scorched for tears, and put the grenade against her heart.

She reached for the pin.

There was an explosion as the FP5 hit the rock face below, a huge ball of fire rushing past them to the roof. Everything shook.

Rottman was hurled forward, the pickaxe lodging in the ground.

Burton lashed out again with his free leg, cracked it into the face of the other Hauptsturmführer. He rolled over, throwing his entire weight behind the movement, freed one of his arms. The soldiers were scrambling to grab him. Burton buried his hand into the crotch of one of them. Found his balls. Squeezed to burst them.

The soldier shrieked in pain, clamping his groin.

Burton rolled again. Found the other soldier's leg. Sank his teeth into it. Tore out a mouthful of cloth and flesh.

Then he was on his feet, mouth like a vampire.

Burton grabbed the soldier still clutching his crotch and hurled him off the rock face. He watched him plummet into the inferno, bouncing off crags as he fell. The FP5 had crashed into the wall of debris below. For a second he thought he saw a girl – a *black* girl – sitting among the flames. Then she was obscured by a veil of smoke.

Burton turned to the other soldier, the one with the gushing leg; watched him scurry away and hide.

A shovel slammed into Burton's ribs.

He staggered, winded, and spun round. The other Hauptsturmführer rushed at him. Burton managed to duck out of his way. *Gwiwar* – an elbow into chest bone – *gwiwar yarfe*. The back of Burton's hand slammed into his nose. Slammed again, leaving a lump of blood and gristle.

Suddenly Burton fell to his hands and knees.

Someone had tugged the chain round his ankle. It was Rottman, aiming his Browning at him.

Burton tugged back.

Rottman stumbled. Misfire.

Burton snatched up a rock from the ground. Smashed it against Rottman's shin. Smashed it again even harder. Felt the tibia snap.

The Browning clattered to the ground. The German cupped his jackboot, face streaming.

Burton was back on his feet. He charged Rottman, using his head as a battering ram. Both men collapsed to the ground. Burton lassoed his leg-chain around Rottman's neck. Tightened it. Tightened it. *Tightened it*. Rottman hissed and spat, his slanted eyes bulging. He reached round, clawed at the letters burned into Burton's arm.

Burton ignored the pain. Pulled tighter still. Thought of what men like Rottman had done to Maddie in Vienna. He was lathered in sweat.

The scratching at his forearm became weaker.

Finally Rottman went limp.

Burton let a grim satisfaction dance in his chest. He shoved Rottman off and searched his body. He found the keys to the ankle cuff, the extra clip, Patrick's pipe and lighter: his lucky pipe! Working its magic again. He unchained himself, searched for his pistol. It had fallen several feet away.

Burton picked up the Browning, clutched it to his mouth and kissed it. The handle came away bloody.

He stood and peered over the edge: below, the tunnel and autobahn were a furnace. He saw men staggering around, their bodies ablaze. Smelt skin and hair burning. He thought of his parents' orphanage on the night it had burned down. The screams of the children as they were trapped inside. His father unmovable as the flames took him . . .

Burton slipped the pistol behind his back, making sure it was secure in his belt, and dived into the hole once more.

Something landed in front of Neliah.

It was a skull-troop, bloody and broken from his fall.

She looked up, her fingers letting go of the grenade pin.

On a ledge above her men were fighting. A prisoner and guards in black. The prisoner fought like a *diaboli*, snarling blood. She recognised the *rungiro* at once – it beat in his breast just like hers. He killed the *Nazistas*.

And vanished.

Where had he gone? Neliah sheathed the panga on her back, scrambled up the rock-wall after him. Then she saw it. Her heart roared.

There was a hole in the stone.

She began climbing as fast as she could.

Beneath her the flames surged into the escape-hole. Found the dynamite.

Burton was much quicker this time. He crawled through the darkness to the hollow. There was no sign of the Pole but a sallow light shimmered through the rent above him. Burton felt the breeze on his face. It smelt of dank rock, and also something sweeter.

Air warmed by sunlight.

Above him the roof scraped and shivered. There was a rushing sound, like a subterranean waterfall.

Burton grabbed the sides of the hole and pulled himself up.

He was in a burrow, beyond it another opening smashed though the rock. He shimmied forward . . . into the light.

And out.

Something moved in front of Burton, blocking his path. Two black columns.

He looked through them to the scene below. Another avalanche of fallen debris, more workers toiling to remove it, the white surface of the PAA . . . Burton followed its path to the grasslands outside. Another fifty miles and he'd be at the border with Northern Rhodesia.

Rhodesia!

He felt a tingle of freedom.

His eye returned to the columns blocking his path. They were the colour of night, shiny but scuffed. Made of leather.

His heart sagged.

Jackboots.

Chapter Twenty-Eight

AFTER the Casablanca Conference handed western Africa to the Nazis, Churchill started telling a bitter joke. If you wanted to get rich on the continent forget diamonds or copper or gold. Invest in jackboots.

It was going to be *the* growth industry.

Burton hoped never to see another pair again.

Very slowly, very carefully, he stood up, keeping his arms wide of his body to show he wasn't carrying a weapon. He could feel the Browning hidden against his back. He stared at the Lebb in front of him. This one's name-badge read: Untersturmführer Schenka. Another 'ethnic German', another drone off the SS production-line. Behind him were several guards with BK44s, exhausted workers. He glimpsed the Pole whose face he had seen earlier; his head was bowed.

Burton made his voice authoritative, urgent; put on his best Prussian accent – something to intimidate Schenka's yokel background. 'My name is Sturmbannführer Kohl. I'm Gestapo.'

He was useless at this type of thing, aware of how he must appear – the filthy trousers, torn shirt, blood-soaked face – but it was all his flagging brain could muster. Hierarchy was everything to the Nazis.

Schenka looked him up and down, placed his hand on his holster.

Over his shoulder Burton could see the PAA continue its journey south. He thought of Lusaka, Northern Rhodesia's capital, with its airport and flights to Europe. On their first night in the country he and Patrick had stayed at the Grand. Crisp sheets, air-conditioned restaurant, swimming pool. How civilised it all seemed. How normal.

'Bullshit,' said Schenka. 'Guards!'

Burton fixed him with a stare, raised his voice so everyone could hear; there was the slightest tic in his jaw. 'Listen to me, *Unter*sturmführer.' He made the word drip contempt. 'A team of commandos has attacked the tunnel, the same commandos who assassinated the Governor General. You must have heard the shots. I need your help to stop them.' He gestured towards the hole behind him. 'Through there.'

Schenka's face creased. 'I wasn't told of any operations.'

'Of course you weren't!'

'I'll have to radio back to—'

'I haven't got time for this. Help me now and I guarantee you promotion. Fuck up: and you'll spend the next five years in Muspel.'

'Gestapo?'

'Department A4.'

'How do I know you're not one of the terrorists? Or escaped from the Unterjocher?'

'Guarding sand dunes will give you plenty of time to reflect on it.'

Schenka hesitated. 'Check his arm,' he said to the guards.

Before they reached him Burton had tugged up his sleeve and showed off his unblemished skin.

'Sturmbannführer: the mark is always on the left side.'

'Of course.' Burton began to roll up his other sleeve. Schenka stepped forward to inspect it.

Kai duka. Dambe's most savage move.

The headbutt.

Schenka dropped, hands clutching his face. Blood streamed between his fingers.

The guards rushed in. Burton floored the first, but there were too many. He'd never fight his way past.

He hit the deck, rolled backwards and did the only thing left to him.

He crawled back into the hole he'd emerged from.

Burton moved fast, praying that none of the guards would stuff a BK after him, praying for a way out of the firestorm on the other side. He felt hands snatch at his boots.

Suddenly there was a face in his way.

A black girl was trying to push past him. Burton smelt smoke in her hair. She looked straight through him, struggled forward. '*Avanca! Agora!*'

'No,' he said, not understanding her. 'There are Germans. Nazis.'

Before he could say anything else, Burton was dragged backwards. He held out his palm to ward off the girl but she crawled after him.

Above them a patter of dust and falling stone.

Burton was pulled out of the hole, banana-guns trained on him. Schenka stepped forward still holding his bloody nose. 'Unterjocher scum. You're fucking dead. Tie him!'

'Untersturmführer,' said the guard by the hole. 'There's another one. A . . . a darkie.'

'It can't be.'

The guard dragged her out by the ears. Burton saw that she was young, no more than a teenager, with a cruel scar down her temple. Her eyes were wild, flashing like onyx – just like Maddie's did when she was angry.

She snarled at the guard, struggled to free herself.

Schenka looked down at her, his mouth curling with disgust and fury. He kicked her in the chest. She fell backwards, head bouncing against the rock. Schenka raised his foot to stamp on her skull.

'No!'

Burton hurled himself at the Untersturmführer, knocking him off his feet. He felt a boot crack into his kidneys, blows to the back and head. Then the muzzle of a rifle between his shoulders. He was forced to his knees, next to the black girl. There was a gash on the side of her face, a line of blood running from her nostril.

Schenka ran his sleeve across his own bleeding nose, dredged his lungs and spat a gob of phlegm on the black girl. 'There's only one thing I hate more than niggers,' he said, turning to Burton, 'and that's nigger-lovers.'

The girl was saying something in her strange language. It sounded familiar to Burton, wasn't an African tongue.

'Since he likes her so much, tie them together. We'll take them back to Uhrig. I'm sure the Standartenführer will know what to do with them.'

The guards bound a rope round Burton and the girl's wrists. Pulled it tight. Burton felt the blood slow in his arm.

The girl was still talking. '*Tenos que correr.*'

'Quiet!' said Schenka.

Burton realised she was talking to him. He concentrated on what she was saying: it sounded like Spanish; Patrick had taught him a few phrases after his time in the Civil War. *Correr.*

To run.

Her eyes were fixed on the road below. No, not the road – the wall of the tunnel. Carved into it Burton saw a doorway, some type of emergency exit. She tugged on the rope around their wrists, looked straight at him, bobbing her head up and down in encouragement. '*Agora,*' she whispered, tugging on his wrist again. She was lifting off her knees to run.

Schenka pulled out his Luger and aimed it straight at her. 'Say another word and—'

From deep within the rock there was an explosion.

A sound so loud Burton felt rather than heard it, a boom pulsing through the nerves in his jaw. His ears popped, then a high-pitched whine.

Dust cascaded from above.

A beat, a beat and a half, and Burton was blasted off his knees. Either side of him the Nazis and workers fell to the ground.

The rock beneath him began to vibrate and crumble . . . gave way. He tumbled downwards in a landslide of rubble, the black girl still bound to his wrist.

They landed in a tangle of limbs, black and white.

Burton was on his feet instantly, the girl next to him blinking as if she had just woken. He pulled her up, urged her to follow, half dragged her along with him.

Schenka struggled to stand, his face a furious mask of blood and dust. He fired his Luger, the bullet sparking on the ground near them, the sound muffled in Burton's ear.

And then something else.

A terrible cracking noise. Fissures were appearing in the roof of the tunnel. Jets of hissing water. And with them a new sound.

A rushing gurgling. The stamp of a hundred horses, like a cavalry charge. Five hundred. A thousand.

Ten thousand.

They reached the emergency exit; there were rungs in the rock. Burton began to climb, his free hand grasping the treads, the one tied to the girl held low so she could follow. Her eyes were wide open now.

The tunnel collapsed.

The river flooded in. A ferocious wave of unrelenting water.

The ladder shook beneath Burton's grip. He was climbing in slow motion. Could hear his mother reading from the Bible: *and God said unto Noah, the end of all flesh is come, for the earth is filled with violence.*

He glanced down. The bottom of the shaft was already a whirlpool. He looked into the eyes of the black girl expecting terror. The water was tearing at her waist.

She seemed to be smiling.

The water surged over her. Burton managed a final, clawing breath. A lungful of metallic air.

Then everything went black.

Part Three

NORTH ANGOLA

The White man's salvation lies in the furnace . . . Let the flames redeem our souls, let the flames wipe Africa clean

WALTER HOCHBURG
Private Journal, 1932

Chapter Twenty-Nine

Wutrohr Labour Camp, PAA
17 September, 10:25

A flashlight pierced the gloom.

'I can't see him.'

'He's got to be there.'

The light scanned the dead bodies more studiously.

'Nothing.'

'Pull up the chain.'

Click-click-click-click-click . . .

Patrick watched the guards above him as they wound the ratchet. He was tearing off his clothes: boots, pants, blood-spattered shirt. Everything. He yanked the shirt over his head down to his wrists, ripped the last bit over his handcuffs. Then he took his boots and hurled them towards the darkest corner of the platform above.

'What was that?'

The light spun wildly before making another pass over the corpses. It flashed right over him.

Patrick stopped dead, his naked body pressed against the corpses around him. He could feel their icy flesh, feel the heat leaching out of his own skin.

Dropping into the pit had been like plunging into a lake of frozen limbs. At first he screamed, the horror almost impossible to control. The stench of putrefaction filled his lungs till they were solid. Then the detached part of his brain took over, saw an opportunity for escape. The corpses were supporting him: the chain around his ankles had gone slack. He eased himself off the hook, managed to untie his feet and slithered deeper into the bodies until he was hidden from sight. His skull was pounding with blood. He began to take off his clothes.

His nakedness would be his camouflage.

Click-click-click-click-click.

The guards continued to wind the ratchet until the hook was level with the gangway.

'He's gone!'

'He can't have escaped.' Another pass of the beam. 'We'll have to go down there, find him.'

'Fuck that.'

'Or would you rather tell Uhrig we lost his prisoner?'

Silence, then one of the guards shouted out. '*Amerikaner*, there's no way out. Stop fucking us around and show yourself.' His voice echoed around the chamber. 'We promise not to hurt you.'

Patrick pushed himself deeper. His body was growing colder by the second, his breath vapour. All around glassy eyes stared right through him.

A rattle of chains. The ratchet began clicking again. One of the guards was lowered into the pit, his feet supported by the hook.

Click-click-click.

Patrick glimpsed upwards, saw the soles of the soldier's boots as they descended. He clutched a BK44, the muzzle trembling.

From outside, the retort of gunfire.

The chain juddered to a halt. 'Did you hear that?'

'It's nothing.'

'What if the rebels are attacking us too?'

'Just keep lowering me.'

Click-click-click.

The guard descended until he skimmed the surface of the bodies. He fumbled with the flashlight, trying to penetrate the dimness of the chamber.

Patrick was twenty feet away. He reached for the corpse next to him, tried to straighten its arm but it was locked with rigor mortis. He pushed harder, heard the elbow joint snap as he straightened it. Patrick held it up – a dead man's salute to the Führer.

Catching the movement, the guard started. Fired off a few rounds.

Patrick heard the dull smack of bullets burying into flesh. The smell of cordite and ground meat.

'What are you doing?' shouted the guard above.

'I saw something.'

'You crazy? Shoot him and Uhrig will stick you in the crusher.'

'What the fuck am I supposed to do?'

Patrick slid closer to the soldier above him. Raised another corpse's hand. Let it drop.

The guard swung round; the clink of chains.

'There! Something moved.' He flashed his light. 'Lower me down.'

Click-click.

Patrick became still, held his breath – one more motionless body among many. He used to have nightmares about all the men he'd killed, now he couldn't even remember their faces.

'Perhaps we should get some back-up,' said the guard on the platform.

'You heard Uhrig, everyone's gone to the tunnel. No, we do this alone. He's one old man.'

Patrick leapt up, grabbed the guard and dragged him into the bodies. A flurry of bullets. Patrick felt a blaze of heat across his shoulder.

The chain swung wildly. The beam of the flashlight bouncing off the walls.

From above: 'What's going on?'

Patrick chopped hard against the guard's wrist, making him drop the BK, then shoved the whole of his hand into his mouth. Fought against the gnashing teeth. Pulled down with all his force.

The Lebb's jaw snapped instantly. He made a strange *aw- aw-* noise.

'*What's going on?*'

Patrick turned his finger to a point and drove it into the German's eye. Twisted it like a key.

'Jenzer, what's happened?'

The voice from the platform sounded frantic.

Patrick reached for the hook and fastened it to the guard's tunic. Killed the flashlight.

Darkness.

'Jenzer?'

Click-click, click . . .

The dead soldier was yanked upwards. Body twitching, eye streaming jelly. Patrick grabbed the fallen BK44, hugged it to his chest and resumed his face-down position among the dead.

Click-click-click.

Somewhere in the complex more gunfire, the distinctive clap of a grenade exploding.

Click-click-click—

A gasp.

'You bastard!' The guard opened fire.

Bullets thudded around Patrick, inches from his exposed back and buttocks. He counted off the rounds till the magazine was spent, heard the guard panting. Next moment footsteps rang out on the platform above him, the door opened. Clanged shut.

Silence except for the hum of condensing units.

Patrick remained still for several minutes expecting more guards. His whole body was gooseflesh.

None came.

So much for Uhrig's Wolves!

Once he was sure it was safe he stood and crawled towards the platform, felt his kneecaps squash into faces. He hauled himself up, BK over his shoulder, and rolled on to the gangway.

Patrick checked the wound on his shoulder. It was a burn mark, no bleeding. His hips and ankles were acid; the rest of his body covered in bruises from the kicking he'd taken outside. When he was younger they would have healed in no time, now they'd be with him for weeks. The swelling was worst around his ribs and the half-moon scar on his abdomen.

His Dunkirk scar.

Burton had sewn up the wound as they hid from the Lebbs. Hands messy and red. The stitch-work was bad, but it had saved his life.

Patrick shivered. Refused to let the thought take hold. He grabbed the chains and pulled the dead guard in, stripped his uniform, put on his trousers. They fitted as bad as the pair he'd stolen in Stanleystadt. This is becoming a habit, Patrick mused grimly: wearing strange men's pants. Next he began to search for his boots.

You can lose your clothes, he used to tell new legionnaires, *lose your weapon, even lose your mind – but* never *lose your boots*. To prove the point he'd march them ten miles through the rocky dunes of Bel Abbès, barefoot. No one forgot the lesson. Patrick saw them now, feet raw and blistered. Saw their expressions turn from pain to utter disappointment with him, as if they knew he was going to ditch Burton.

You didn't leave your men behind, they seemed to say. Your comrades. *Your friends.* You went looking for them. It was the code of the Legion.

But Patrick had been clear that day in prison. This was for Hannah. If things fucked up he wasn't going to die in Africa. He'd wasted too much of his life for that, fighting for pointless causes when he should have been with his family. Idealism was a pay-cheque he had long since spent.

He found his first boot, yanked it on. Then the other one.

Burton could be anywhere – back on the highway, the tunnel. Maybe he had escaped, was already heading to the border. Maybe Kepplar had caught him . . .

Patrick banged the wall in frustration. His fist came away cold. He lashed out again.

Then became still.

He concentrated on that moment in Stanleystadt when the Lebbs had dragged him from the cellar, Rottman taking his pipe. That dread of never seeing his daughter again, never making up for all those lost years. It was like being forced to stare over the edge of a deep pit.

There was nothing he could do for Burton; if he tried he was dead. But he might still be able to keep his promise to Hannah. Get out of this place, head for—

Close by, the clang of a door.

Patrick snatched up the BK44, moved stiffly to the entrance of the chamber. He heard another door open ... then close. It sounded like somebody was checking all the rooms along the corridor.

Patrick snicked off the safety.

Footsteps. Another door being heaved open.

Angola. That was his plan. He'd head for Angola.

He'd worked it out on the long ride from Stanleystadt, crushed in the back of the truck, eyes closed but not sleeping. If he escaped there was no point heading south. With his hobo clothes and Yankee accent the Rhodesians would never let him across the border. Even if he got lucky, then what? It was hundreds of miles to Lusaka or Salisbury and both were landlocked; he had no identification, no money to buy an air ticket. But Angola ...

The door clanged shut.

The guard must be checking to see if he'd escaped. More footsteps. The grind of hinges as another door opened.

The Angolan border was porous. He spoke enough Portuguese to get by, knew the terrain from when he'd been there in '49 and the Waffen-SS invaded the south (another mercenary mission where the only right side was the one that paid best). He'd make for Loanda and the Atlantic, stow away; an American was always drawn to the west coast of Africa. There was also the promise of Ackerman. Some payback. The chance of putting a bullet through the sonofabitch's head for what he'd done.

The door closed, near enough to send vibrations along the walls. More footfalls, a breath away now. Patrick watched the handle in front of him turn. It opened cautiously, the muzzle of a BK44 poking through.

He grabbed the rifle and pulled hard.

A figure stumbled into the room. Patrick cracked his elbow into his face. The figure tumbled to the ground. Patrick was on him in an instant, aimed his gun at his throat.

Then lowered it in disbelief.

The figure's eyes flickered. 'I came looking for you . . .'

The gunman passed out. But not a gunman.

A gunwoman.

A girl, not much older than Hannah, with a long plait.

Patrick lifted her arm, rubbed at the skin to wipe away the camouflage paint. But his first instinct had been right.

He shook his head in disbelief again.

She was black.

Chapter Thirty

Lulua River, Kongo
17 September, 10:30

OW they survived he never knew. His father would have said it was the hand of God; Patrick luck. But Burton believed it was Madeleine. The need to hold her again, to bury his face in her black, honeysuckle hair; the life they could live together. It forced him on. Let him drag that final fistful of air from his lungs.

All around him darkness, the rumbling roar of bubbles, the suction of the water dragging him down like Jonah. The black girl was still tied to his wrist. Burton could feel her fighting the torrent. Both of them kicked upwards.

Upwards.

The gullet of his throat pulsed for oxygen. His boots heavy as gravestones.

Upwards . . .

They broke the surface.

Burton sucked in a lungful of air and water. Started choking.

The river around him was a cauldron. Churning white, khaki, brown. The girl burst through it, retching. She fought to stay above the foam. Burton hauled her up. He could just make out the shore, kicked towards it. For once he was grateful to Hochburg: he had taught him to swim.

Finally, as his muscles were turning to pulp, his feet found the bottom. Burton struggled through the waves, dragging the girl. Through a wall of papyrus. And collapsed into the mud.

They both coughed and spluttered.

Water burned through Burton's nose. He let his head drop and squinted into the brightness of the sky.

The brand on his forearm was throbbing, had been brought alive by the river. But it was good to have been submerged – the sweat and grime of the past few days had been washed from him. The blood sluiced from his mouth.

He felt new.

Burton snapped upright, his eyes searching the sunny spots of the bank. He tugged at the girl. 'What about crocodiles?'

She shook her head, and started to laugh uncontrollably.

Soon Burton joined in.

He laughed till tears ran down his face, just like they had done in Hochburg's office, laughed till his chest was raw and hollow. He saw his mother's empty room again and realised that the air in his lungs was more precious than any truth.

Then his head dropped into the mud and he lay there like a shipwrecked sailor.

In the distance he heard men shouting.

The sound was muffled, his ears were still ringing from the explosion in the tunnel.

Burton sat up, alert again. He scanned the undergrowth for movement, realised he was on the wrong bank for Rhodesia. The voices surged . . . then faded till all he could hear was the black girl breathing next to him and the rush of the river. Debris floated in it. Upturned bodies.

He leaned back and let the sunlight warm his face, the way Patrick did. His old commanding officer always loved the sun – even the hellish glare of the Sahara – no wonder he wanted to settle somewhere like New Mexico. He had described his hacienda there many times: the mustard-coloured walls and cool rooms, an icebox full of beer. Outside, a terrace with easy chairs, a garden of lime trees and cacti, and then the desert itself, stretching into the mountains. A place where a man could live out his final years.

Burton rolled the thought round his mind, pushed it away. Concentrated on the girl's breathing instead. It was slumberous and deep, strangely comforting.

He studied her face. Apart from the scar on her temple, it was completely symmetrical with a broad nose and the type of skin his father would have marked as *gemischt* – mixed – on the orphanage ledger. Her hair had been brutally chopped. But it was her age that struck him most.

She was so young.

Suddenly Burton was overlooking the Schädelplatz again: its unholy square. Something slithered inside him at the memory. What would Hochburg have done to the girl? What would any Nazi? It made him want to reach out and touch her, feel the warmth of her scalp. The sanctity of her skull.

The girl opened her eyes and caught him staring at her. Burton glanced away and reached for his Browning. He checked it over, released the clip before sliding it smoothly back in place; opened the exhaust port and blew through it to discharge the water. Then he wiped it dry.

The girl said something he didn't understand.

He shook his head.

She tried again, this time in German. 'What's your name?'

'Burton.'

She repeated it. Her accent made it sound like *Burtang*.

'And you?'

'Neliah. Neliah Tavares.'

He looked at her face again, noticed how clear her eyes were. And in the darkest part of the pupil, something else. A void. A place emptied by brutality. He'd seen it many times before – in soldiers, refugees; caught it in his own eye when he stared in the mirror.

Burton held out his hand, the one the Nazis hadn't tied. After a brief hesitation she gripped it and they shook. Her skin felt supple, but the bones were like nuggets of steel.

'I owe you my life, Burton—'

He raised his palm to silence her. 'No blood oaths,' he said, thinking of Patrick again, of Dunkirk. 'You don't owe me anything.'

He reached over and began to untie the rope that bound their wrists together. The knot was as tight as if it had been welded. As he worked he saw Neliah staring at the brand on his arm; his sleeve was in tatters.

'You will always be marked,' she said softly.

When Burton didn't reply, she reached out and traced the inverted triangle. He pulled away. 'You escape from somewhere? I haven't seen a black face in all of Kongo.'

'I am Angolan, one of the *Resistencia*.'

'But you speak German.'

'My mother taught me. Said it was wise to know your enemy's tongue. Her *ina* came from Damaraland. Escaped to Angola after the *Blutbad*.'

Blutbad. The blood bath.

Burton's father had often spoken about the massacres in South-West Africa. They had been committed at the turn of the century, long before the Nazis, by the first Germans to settle DSWA. Three-quarters of the black population wiped out. A dreadful stain on our conscience, he used to call it. That was after his mother had left, after Hochburg. Years later Churchill raised the subject with Halifax before he flew to Casablanca. 'The German can't be trusted,' warned the former Prime Minister, 'murder is in his veins. War the only diplomacy he understands.' The public has spoken, Lord Halifax was reported to have replied. Peace for Empire, Mr Churchill. Peace for Empire.

'You are Herero?' said Burton.

She nodded.

'I know the Herero. They are a brave people. Warriors. Always ready to fight.' *Which is more than can be said for the British*, he thought.

A sparkle of pride. 'And you, Burton—' *Burtang* '—you are German?'

265

'I speak it.' He gave her a cautious smile. 'It's wise to know your enemy's tongue.'

Burton went back to unpicking the rope.

'I watched you arrive at the tunnel,' said Neliah. 'What happened to the other men you came with?'

'Dead, I guess.'

Her face darkened. 'They were your friends?'

'No. My friends are . . .' Burton concentrated on the knot. 'I'm heading for Rhodesia.'

'Then you must be fast. The *Nazistas* will soon invade.'

He looked up sharply. 'Impossible!'

'That is why I blew up the tunnel – to stop them.' She rubbed her scar. 'They are at Matadi also, will attack Angola.'

'Where did you hear this?'

'Orders from Loanda. From Penhor. He's our *comandante*.'

Burton considered her words, then what Rougier had said in Stanleystadt. 'Do you know someone called Ackerman?'

She shook her head.

'Are you sure? He's a British agent, works with the *Resistencia*.'

'Penhor has allies with the British. They supply him weapons. But I have never heard this name before. Who is he?'

'He's the one who sent me here. To Africa.'

'Why?'

'To kill a man.'

'Why?'

'If only I knew.'

Voices. Close by.

They ducked below the papyrus.

Burton pulled his Browning, hoped it was dry enough to fire. He pressed himself flat against the mud, gestured at Neliah to do the same. Along the top of the bank appeared a patrol of SS soldiers. Furious faces. BK44s. An officer harried them on, his eye darting everywhere.

Next to Burton, Neliah reached behind her back. For the first time he noticed she was carrying a panga. She withdrew the blade from its sheath. The slice of metal on leather.

'No,' hissed Burton.

The troops were directly ahead now. No more than twenty feet. He saw she was tensing.

Burton slid over to her. Grabbed her panga hand and pressed it into the mud.

'I didn't survive the tunnel for this,' he whispered. 'There are too many.'

For a few seconds she struggled against him – she was strong – then nodded her head. Let go of the weapon. Burton remained where he was, his hand still on top of hers. This close he could smell her skin. It had no scent, only the coldness of the water.

Once the patrol passed he released her.

'They would have killed us,' he said.

Neliah snatched up the panga, swung it towards Burton and cut the rope between them. 'I have to go. Now.'

'Back to Angola?'

'My sister. There is chimney-camp near here. She needs my help.'

'It's a labour camp. SS. You understand what that means?'

'You were there?'

'My friend is.'

'Come with me then. My sister goes to fight, to free the prisoners.' She stood up – was almost as tall as Burton – and riffled through her pockets. Pulled out a hand grenade.

'No. I have to get to Rhodesia.'

'But your friend. We can save him.'

Burton hesitated, tried not to think about his final words to Patrick, that pledge to get him back to Hannah. It had been parting bravado, nothing more. The easy vow of a condemned man . . . Except now he had a choice.

Yes, Burton reminded himself, *just like Patrick had one on the quayside in Stanleystadt.*

'Goodbye, Neliah Tavares.'

He splashed out into the river, held his Browning over his head to keep it dry. He could be in Lusaka by tomorrow.

She gave him a curious frown as if his actions were unfathomable. 'Your friend,' she called after him.

Burton waded out deeper, began to swim through the flotsam. He was halfway to the opposite bank when he hesitated. Stopped, trod water.

He was still thinking about his promise to Patrick. Then his promise to Madeleine. The baby, their future on the farm. The quinces that would soon need harvesting. It was all within his grasp again. Before Maddie life had been brutish. If he ever considered the days ahead all he saw was an early grave, or maybe an old man: arthritic, alone, undone by the past. But now . . .

He thought of the promise his mother made him: *I'll never leave you, Burton. Never.*

Cross your heart, Mama?

Cross my heart. And hope to die.

Those words haunted him. Why had she needed to declare what should have been evident? He saw her now, splashing in the river by their home. Hochburg had taught her to swim too. He loved the water; promised she would never drown while he was there. Soon she was as confident as a fish.

So many promises.

Burton pushed himself around, facing the way he'd come.

He saw Neliah climbing through the papyrus, poised like a leopard, panga held in front of her. Her limbs flexed hard and muscular. She would reach the labour camp in no time. His father would have urged him to follow, to offer his protection: *she was but a child in the kingdom of Moloch.*

Next moment she was gone from sight.

Burton made up his mind, turned away, and resumed his swimming: a steady front crawl to the opposite shore and the prospect of Rhodesia. The water was still choppy from the explosion. Splintered lumps of timber bobbed past him, ends of machinery. Dead bodies.

He ploughed through them.

Chapter Thirty-One

Schädelplatz, Kongo
18 September, 11:55

DOLAN was allowed two minutes with the British attaché. He was a runt of a man, sweaty suit, slab of paperwork under his arm. The type of pencil-pusher who had worked on some minor sub-clause of the Casablanca Treaty. He didn't bother to introduce himself or shake Dolan's hand.

'They treating you well?' he asked.

'How does it look?' replied Dolan, failing to keep the bile from his voice.

After Hochburg finished interrogating him he had honoured his word, sent his own doctor to treat him. Dolan's leg was now in plaster – but no amount of ice packs or ointment could hide the swelling to his face or missing teeth. The whites of his eyes had turned puce from the chilli. He had spent the last two days in a prison cell, clutching his groin, unable to combat bouts of shaking.

'Frankly, there's little we can do for you,' said the attaché. 'Berlin is screaming blue murder—'

'Germania.'

'What? Oh, yes, I never got used to the change. We're trying to avert an all-out war. The Rhodesian reserves have been called up. Bombers are flying in from England. As if there weren't enough problems with Angola. Now it looks as if Casablanca itself might be nullified.'

Dolan thought it should never have been signed in the first place. 'What about me? Any chance I'll get out of this?'

'My advice is admit nothing, respect the court no matter what a farce and for God's sake—' he dabbed his forehead '—there's *no* conspiracy.'

'But will I get out?'

The attaché refused to meet his eye. 'I suppose there's no physical proof as such . . .'

Moments later Dolan was escorted to court. Hochburg's doctor had refused him crutches, fearing he might use them as a weapon: two guards supported him.

He took the dock.

The court was dominated by a huge eagle and swastika seal. Beneath it was the judges' bench, to the side a small gallery crammed with SS uniforms and what Dolan took to be journalists. The GG they called them, Goebbels's *Geiers*. His vultures. Lounging at the front, not a drop of sweat upon him, was Hochburg. The courtroom had a smell of lacquer. Although fans whirred overhead the air was stifling.

More men in uniforms arrived. The British attaché took his place in front of the judges' bench. Technicians from Rundfunk Afrika, the Nazi broadcaster, busied themselves with radio equipment. Dolan felt a loosening in his chest: at least they couldn't hurt him again, not with so many witnesses. Finally the clerk of the court called order.

'All rise for Herr President Judge Freisler.'

An excited murmur.

Roland Freisler – 'raving Roland' – the personification of Nazi blood justice. He had served as the President of Hitler's People's Court, the Volksgerichtshof; been one of the architects of Jewish resettlement to Madagaskar. Now a senior SS dignitary, he only presided over trials of national importance, and had flown to Africa at Hochburg's request.

The court stood.

Dolan watched the judge storm in. He wore burgundy robes

over a black uniform and bow tie. Was balding, had a sour mouth, hooded eyes. After a terse Führer salute, he assumed his place, introducing the two other SS judges at his side and a neutral observer from the Council of New Europe: Señor Aguilar, the Spanish consul.

At least there's one independent voice, thought Dolan. Maybe I've still got a chance.

Freisler flicked through the notes in front of him, wrote something, then looked up and pierced Dolan with his eyes.

'Are you a pervert?'

Dolan shifted awkwardly. His leg was already throbbing, he wanted to sit down. There was no chair in the dock. 'Sir?'

Freisler raised his voice. It was shrill and phlegmy. 'It's a simple question. Are you a pervert? A homosexual?'

'No.'

'Maybe you think my court is some Jewish lavatory?'

'No.'

'Then why do you keep fiddling with yourself?'

Dolan's torn and bloodied combat fatigues had been taken from him that morning. In their place a coarse grey suit with trousers several sizes too big; no belt or braces, no underwear. He had to keep hoisting them up to maintain his dignity.

Dolan let go of the waistband, felt his trousers sag.

Amused whispers from the gallery.

Freisler returned to his notes. 'You are Lieutenant Owen Dolan, of the Welsh Guards, Great Britain. Serial Number 2200118.'

Dolan hesitated, glanced at the British attaché. He was scribbling notes.

'Yes.'

'Speak into the microphone.'

Dolan dipped his head. 'Yes.'

'Louder!'

'Yes.'

'On September 14th, at approximately zero one hundred hours you and a team of British and Rhodesian criminals, backed by the governments in London, Lusaka and Salisbury, attempted to assassinate the Governor General of Deutsch Kongo. How do you plead?'

For an instant Dolan considered claiming insanity. Then he looked at all the faces watching him and realised no one would notice.

He said nothing. Probed his remaining front teeth. They were loose.

'Are you deaf? How do you plead?'

'Not gui—'

'I have your full confession in front of me. The names of your co-conspirators.'

'Sir, this confession was obtained under torture.'

Spittle flew from Freisler's mouth. 'There will be no such lies in my court! Admit the truth and there *may* be leniency. Were you part of the team that attempted to assassinate Governor General Hochburg? A tool of Anglo-Rhodesian aggression?'

'Sir, I was not part—'

'Yes or no!'

'No.'

'Did you attempt to blow up the Schädelplatz?'

Dolan felt a tug of professional pride. A half smile. 'No.'

'Wipe that lousy smirk off your face. Let it be noted that the prisoner appears to find these proceedings a joke. Did you attempt an illegal crossing of the Kongo-Sudan border?'

'No.'

Freisler hurled down his pen. 'Quit this drivel! You were captured at Doruma. Over a hundred witnesses saw you, including the Governor General and his deputy. We have testaments from the British guards at Muzunga. You deny all this?'

Dolan tugged at his trousers again. Said nothing. Faces peered in his direction. Part of him wanted to beg for mercy – what would Patrick say? – but he knew he was already dead. And if he was dead, he might as well go down with a bang. He summoned the last of his fight, wished he had his boxes of tricks with him to wreak merry hell.

Freisler was growing impatient. 'Were you captured at Doruma?'

'I was there on leave—'

'Yes or no.'

'Visiting a whorehouse. Your German *mädchens* are so much cheaper than the girls back home.'

'The accused will shut his filthy mouth.'

'And ten times dirtier.'

'You degenerate!'

Dolan felt a knot of triumph, like when Kepplar had failed to make him talk. He forced a ribald laugh. 'The things they'll do for the Fatherland.'

Freisler snatched up his gavel. Hammered it in a frenzy. He glared at the radio technicians: 'Stop the broadcast! Stop the broadcast!'

Hochburg stood.

'Herr President,' he said calmly. 'We must continue. I would hate for our enemies to accuse us of holding a show trial.'

The judge next to Freisler leaned over and whispered into his ear. He ceased his banging, straightened his back. 'You are quite right, Oberstgruppenführer. For the record, the accused has refused to co-operate. Shown *contempt* for these most serious of proceedings.' He adjusted his bow tie. 'We call a witness.'

The clerk of the court hurried out. Dolan watched him go. Could they have captured the major? The old man? But no, they'd be in the stand too. It was going to be some stooge. He looked towards the gallery, caught Hochburg's attention.

Hochburg rolled his eyes in boredom.

The clerk reappeared, and held the door open.

An SS officer hobbled in, supported by a cane. In his other hand was a red folder marked *Department E: TOP SECRET*.

Dolan felt the floor surge towards him. He sucked in a lungful of air to clear his head.

The officer continued into the court, his cane tapping the floor. As he passed Dolan he flicked him an apologetic look. A scent of onions and boot leather.

'You bastard!' shouted Dolan, lunging forward, indifferent to the pain in his leg now.

The guards pulled him back. Freisler was banging his gavel again.

The SS officer took the witness stand.

With barely contained glee the judge spoke into the microphone: 'Please state your rank and name for the court.'

The officer gave Dolan another look. 'Sturmbannführer.' His voice filled the room. 'Sturmbannführer Lazlo Rougier. Gestapo.'

'I must apologise for my appearance, Herr President,' said Rougier. Around his neck was a collar-brace. 'But I had an accident in Stanleystadt.'

'We're all sure you were doing your duty, Sturmbannführer,' replied Freisler.

Dolan leaned forward in the dock, supported himself against the rail. The courtroom was suddenly much hotter. His scalp was trickling.

'The accused will show due respect. Stand up, you slovenly pig.'

'My leg.'

'Carry on, Sturmbannführer.'

'Thank you, Herr President. I work for Gestapo counter-intelligence. For several months we have been monitoring the activities of Donald Ackerman, a senior British intelligence officer operating from Angola.'

Dolan glanced at the attaché, expecting him to refute the claim. He kept his head down, was still writing furiously.

'Ackerman, along with aggressors in the British and Rhodesian governments, planned to assassinate Governor General Hochburg.'

'What was their motive?'

'Under the Casablanca Treaty, all foreign mining rights in German territory were guaranteed until 1950, when they would revert back to the Reich. LMC, a Lusaka-based syndicate, agreed

a three-year extension to the Kassai fields with Oberstgruppenführer Hochburg. They assumed this would be an ongoing arrangement. However, when they learned that the Governor General
intended a new company to take over production – DESTA no
less, our SS Earthworks – they decided to have him removed.'

'Where does Ackerman fit into this?'

Dolan shook his head. It was like the pantomimes his mam
used to take him and his brother to see: the actors knew their
lines by heart. He wished his brother was with him now, his
ruddy face jeering at the court. *Give 'em two fingers, boyo.*

'LMC like to regard themselves as a reputable organisation,'
continued Rougier. 'They wanted no blood on their hands so
contracted British intelligence to do the job for them. In return
the British would get twenty per cent of their annual diamond
production. Approximately, nine hundred thousand Reichmarks.'

There was a gasp in the courtroom.

'An extraordinary sum, Sturmbannführer,' said Freisler. 'And
why did the British need this money?'

'To fund the Angola Resistance, supply them with weapons.
Allow them to wage a guerrilla war against us.'

The gallery erupted.

Amid the commotion Dolan looked at Hochburg. He didn't
even blink.

When the furore had died down, Freisler turned to the British
attaché. 'What do you have to say to these charges?'

'I'm still waiting for instructions from London, Herr President.
But Her Majesty's Government is opposed to all acts of aggression or terrorism no matter who—'

'What were the details of the conspiracy?' Freisler had turned
back to Rougier.

'Ackerman recruited a team of ruthless professionals to carry
out the assassination. Fanatics.' Rougier raised the file in his
hand. 'With the Herr President's permission?'

The file was passed to the judges, then Señor Aguilar, the
British attaché, finally Dolan. He opened it, flicked through some

photographs: Lapinski, Vacher, himself. They were mug shots from their ID papers, had been blown up full size, the images grainy.

Dolan shook his head again. A drop of sweat fell from his brow, splashed the pictures.

The fight was pooling out of him. He just wanted to sit down.

Freisler addressed him. 'Can you identify these men?'

'No.'

'Idiot!' His voice was shrill with contempt. 'You can't even identify yourself.'

Dolan turned to the next photo. It was of Burton Cole and Patrick. They were perched on a bath tub. The old man looked desolate, his face towards the floor; the major seemed to be scrutinising himself as if gazing into a mirror.

'Well?' said Freisler.

'Yes.'

'Speak up!'

'I can . . . I can identify them.'

'Their names.'

'Myself, Lapinski, Vacher, Cole . . .' He hesitated. 'Whaler.'

Freisler leaned back with a look of poisonous satisfaction.

But Dolan realised there was still a glimmer of hope. He stared at the British attaché, willing him to get to his feet. State the obvious.

In the end it was the Spanish consul who came to his defence.

'Herr President, with respect, although this demonstrates the link between the accused and the other men, it doesn't prove a conspiracy to assassinate Herr Hochburg. Speaking on behalf of the European Council, and given the gravity of the charges and their consequences, we would expect more.'

Freisler nodded. 'Let it never be said that our courts are anything but fastidious. Sturmbannführer, I understand there is further evidence.'

Rougier was talking to one of the RFA technicians. He nodded to a colleague. Next moment there was a hiss of speakers. Then a thud as a recording started. A rushing sound, like a water-fall.

A voice, French accent. Echoey but distinct. Then others:

What do you say?
I can't see it matters any more. We're assassins.
Our mission was to [distortion] the Governor General.
Remove . . . Remove how?
With extreme prejudice. I killed Hochburg with my own hands.
You strangled him?
Knife . . .

A click. The recording ended.

Silence.

Dolan felt a prickle of hopeless tears. He looked at Aguilar. He was shaking his head. By his side the attaché dabbed himself.

Firing squad, thought Dolan. Quick, efficient. He wouldn't feel a thing. Or maybe the guillotine. Anything. As long as it wasn't hanging . . . He'd heard how the Nazis would keep the rope short so your neck didn't break. It could take up to fifteen minutes until you were strangled, legs thrashing, tongue blue. Then there were the nightmare stories about piano wire.

'Do you recognise those voices?' asked Freisler.

Dolan bowed his head.

Rougier answered for him: 'They are the voices of Majors Cole and Whaler.'

Freisler gathered his papers together, tapped them into shape. 'Thank you, Sturmbannführer, you may step down.'

Rougier climbed off the stand and, leaning on his cane, left the courtroom.

'The conspirators Lapinski and Vacher have already been neutralised by our security forces,' said Freisler. '*In absentia*, I find Major Burton Cole and Major Patrick Whaler guilty.' His eyes turned to Dolan. 'I also find the present-accused guilty. Sentence: death.'

Whispers of agreement in the gallery.

Not hanging. Please, not hanging.

Dolan suddenly burst into song. In Welsh. He didn't know where it came from, the lyrics just emerged from his lips, voice booming, like his dad: '*Lord, lead me through the wilderness*—'

'Shut up!' shouted Freisler. He banged his gavel. 'Shut your stinking mouth!'

'*Me, a pilgrim of poor appearance*—'

'Silence him!'

One of the guards kicked Dolan's plaster-cast.

He stumbled in the dock, the song shrivelling in his throat. Through his tears he saw someone rise.

'With your permission, Herr President.'

Hochburg took the stand, addressed the court.

'Perhaps it would be best if someone fetched Lieutenant Dolan a chair.' He adjusted the microphone, began speaking in the same soft baritone he had used while slicing the chilli. In the gallery some of the journalists leaned forward to hear better.

'We Germans are a peace-loving nation. Witness the stability we have brought to Europe, or the Casablanca Treaty. In Africa we have forged a society based on the principles of trade and technology. Racial hygiene. Harmony. But what we call peace others view as weakness. We have enemies everywhere, those who would ruin our progress for their own ends.

'First Angola. We sued for peace . . . then they attacked Kongo. Just yesterday an army of Angolan criminals committed a terrible act of sabotage on the PAA. The Road of Friendship!

'Now the British and Rhodesians threaten our Africa Reich.'

Dolan watched as Hochburg's black eyes smouldered. There was still not a drop of sweat on him.

'They sent their assassins to kill me. They failed. But this blatant act of aggression cannot go unpunished. Were we to resort to diplomacy this would only encourage the British further, goad them on. So much for their hollow promise, "Peace for Empire". They have forced our hand.' His voice soared. 'Theirs is a declaration of war!

'And so to protect Deutsch Kongo, its citizens and resources, I shall order units of the Waffen-SS to Northern Rhodesia to repel our foes. I do this with the Führer's full blessing, I do it as he ordered our forces into Russia in 1941. With reluctance, with the heaviest of hearts. But there come moments in every country's history where it must act decisively or surrender its way of life for ever. As with the Soviets, we will prevail.

'In the meantime, our noble Field Marshal von Arnim is already leading his Afrika Korps to crush the terrorist regime of North Angola. A regime we now know is funded by the British.

'There is, however, still hope.' Hochburg offered his hands. 'We know that Cole and Whaler remain at large. Let me assure you they will be hunted down. Hunted without respite. Even as I speak my deputy, Gruppenführer Kepplar, is closing in on their trail. Perhaps, though, someone is harbouring these assassins, someone listening to this broadcast right now. If that is the case, I urge you to surrender them at once; there will be clemency.' His voice dropped again. 'The fate of a continent may rest in your hands.

'Long live German Africa. Heil Hitler!'

The gallery – SS and journalists alike – stood as one.

'*Sieg Heil! Sieg Heil!*'

Hochburg motioned for them to sit as if he found their outburst an embarrassment.

'Words worthy of Bismarck himself,' said Freisler. He turned his attention back to Dolan. 'Your sentence is to be carried out immediately.'

There was a pressure building inside Dolan's head. The judge's words seemed muffled.

'Normally you'd be put in front of a firing squad.' A malevolent smile. 'Due to the severity of the crime, however, not to mention its personal nature, I think the manner of your execution should be at the Governor General's discretion.'

Hochburg nodded.

Hear me God, thought Dolan, *not the gallows*.

'Let this be a warning to all the enemies of peace in Africa.' Hochburg pronounced his sentence.

Not hanging. Worse.

Worse than anything Dolan could have imagined.

His knees buckled.

Chapter Thirty-Two

Terras de Chisengue, North Angola
18 September, 13:25

'TURN it off,' said Patrick. He couldn't stand any more.

I think the manner of your execution should be at the Governor General's discretion.

Nobody moved. They were all engrossed, listening to the simultaneous Portuguese translation.

'Turn it off!'

Let this be a warning to all the enemies of peace in Africa, said Hochburg.

There was horrified silence at the sentence. Hands covered mouths.

Patrick moved towards the radio set. He wanted to hurl it to the ground. The thought of Dolan – booming, arrogant Dolan – dying like that made him want to plug his ears. Scream.

Ligio blocked his path. Pulled his pistol. 'You're one of them, aren't you?'

Patrick stared at the lieutenant. He was a punk, phoney tough with a flop of greasy black hair and eyes that wouldn't sit still. There was a bandage around his head where Zuri's sister had clumped him.

'I'm nothing,' said Patrick.

'Keep your hands where I can see them, old man, and sit down. Slowly.'

If Burton had been with him they would have charged the lieutenant, taken on the other Angolan soldiers – but alone there were too many.

Patrick raised his hands (they were still cuffed) and resumed his position next to Zuri. Her expression was impossible to read: curious, protective, peeved. They were sitting on hard barrack benches in the *octógono*. Huddled nearby were the other prisoners that had come with them from the labour camp.

'Which one are you?' asked Ligio.

'*Amigo*, I'm nothing to do with this. I swear.'

Keeping his gun aimed at Patrick, Ligio snapped the radio off. 'I'm not your friend, and I know you're lying. Zuri told me what happened at the camp. She saw it all from her hiding place. Saw a dozen men shot dead because of you.'

'It was nine. I counted every one.'

'Which is why I went to find him,' said Zuri, her plait swishing. 'He's on our side.'

Ligio flicked the gun in her direction. 'You and your sister have caused enough trouble. Should have stayed in the kitchens where you belong.'

Zuri went to rise but Patrick put out a restraining hand. He didn't need her defending him. He let out a weary sigh and offered his response to her rather than Ligio.

'I'm Whaler,' he said. 'The American.'

'Why didn't you say before?' she asked.

'Rougier said it was the Angolans who set us up. I didn't know what to believe.' For an instant he was holding him face down in the toilet again. He'd been mistaken about Ackerman; should have kept that French sonofabitch under water till he went limp.

'But you still came with me.'

'I thought you might be able to help me. I also . . . I also felt bad about whacking you.'

Zuri traced the swelling on her lip where he'd hit her the day before, then turned to Ligio: 'He tried to kill the German, their chief,' she said. 'He's got to be with us.'

Ligio made no response.

'She's right,' said Patrick. 'I was part of the team hired by Ackerman.'

'So?' replied the young lieutenant.

'You heard the trial: Ackerman's the one supplying you. We're on the same side, *amigo*.'

'I've never heard his name before. It's just Nazi propaganda.'

'What?'

Ligio addressed the rest of the soldiers. 'Anyone else know this Ackerman?'

They all shook their heads, every last man.

Patrick went to reply, then closed his mouth. Outside he could hear the chatter of parrots. His brain was too worn to keep up with this. Maybe one day, sitting at home with Hannah, they'd puzzle it out together.

'What do we do, Lieutenant?' asked one of the Angolan soldiers. They were what the Legion called *bleus*: boy soldiers, goggle-eyed and toting guns that were too big for them.

'I don't know.'

'Set him free!' said Zuri.

Patrick looked at her, unsure why she was so eager to safe-guard him.

She was five years older than Hannah and he couldn't help wonder how different their lives must have been. At least Zuri had known her father. She'd spoken about him as they travelled to Angola; told Patrick about his death as if he could right it – at least that's what he felt. Or maybe it was guilt. How many pleas had he ignored last time he'd been in Angola? How many fathers and daughters had he abandoned when the Nazis invaded the south? All because they couldn't pay a mercenary's wage.

'Do you still think about him?' he had asked.

'I try not to.' A long silence. 'I think of his voice. The smell of his room, like man-skin and tobacco. How his face became bright when he lifted me up as a girl. That I will never see him again . . .'

'I'm sorry,' said Patrick, squeezing her shoulder. His throat felt jagged: he wondered what Hannah would say if a stranger asked the same question. He probably deserved whatever his daughter's reply.

Later, Zuri told him about her younger sister, Neliah. How they would journey to Loanda to fight with the *Resistencia*, that Zuri was just as brave: *see what I did at the chimney-camp!* There was something about her that reminded him of the girls he'd helped in Guernica: shoeless orphans who wanted to chatter. Her familiarity, her intensity, unnerved him. He wasn't used to women, had been confined to the world of uniforms and killing for so long that it was all he knew.

In turn she asked him why he was in Africa, why the Nazis were so interested in him. Patrick had skirted her questions, avoided any mention of Burton even though he was still wondering if he'd done the right thing by him. Instead he talked about Ruth, how they never should have married or had a child; about Hannah and getting home. How he wanted to make up for the past.

When finally they arrived at the rebels' camp Zuri had been summoned to a fuming Ligio. The rest of the Herero women, Patrick and the prisoners were sent to the *octógono* and guarded by the Angolans. Patrick's BK44 was confiscated. In one of the corners a soldier was fiddling with a receiver in an attempt to pick up news about the German invasion of the north, but on every frequency there was only one broadcast. Dolan's trial.

'What do we do?' repeated the soldier.

Ligio took a step forward, raised the pistol again until it was level with Patrick's head. 'We hand him over to the *Nazistas*.'

Patrick remained impassive.

'How could you?' said Zuri.

'You heard the radio, "the fate of Africa is in our hands". We have to do it.'

'My father did what the *Nazistas* said. They murdered him.'

'Lieutenant,' said Patrick. 'You're part of the Resistance. To

German eyes that makes you a terrorist too. Hand me over and they'll shoot us both.'

'They said there'd be an amnesty.'

Patrick gave a dismissive laugh. 'Yeah, right. The Krauts are famous for them.'

'It's *you* they want, not us.'

'True . . . but then what? The invasion's already started, there's nowhere for you to go. Angola's finished—'

'We can still beat them back.'

Another dismissive snort. 'That's what Stalin said.'

'So we head for Mozambique.' Ligio raised his voice so the rest of the soldiers could hear him. 'We'll get a hero's welcome there.'

Patrick shook his head: another kid warrior who had never tasted battle. Hadn't they heard Dolan on the radio? That shattered voice. Thirty seconds of enemy fire and spilled guts and nothing would ever seem heroic again. *I got to get out of here*, he thought, *before they do something stupid*. He hoped Zuri was with him.

Patrick offered his cuffed wrists: the lieutenant would be on the floor before he knew what hit him. 'You'd better hand me over then, *amigo*.'

Ligio kept his gun arm straight but didn't move.

'He's right about Mozambique.' Zuri was on her feet, trying to soft-pedal the lieutenant. '*Una salus victis nullam sperare salutem.*'

'What?'

'"There's no safe place for the defeated." Nowhere for us. You can't give him up.'

Ligio kept his eyes on Patrick. 'Since when have the kitchen girls been in charge?'

'Alberto wouldn't do it.'

'While *Comandante* Penhor is in Loanda, I'm in command.'

'And where were you when we raided the chimney-factory?'

Patrick saw Ligio's neck flush pink. 'Obeying my orders, unlike you.'

'Orders! We're all on the same side. We . . .' Zuri's voice withered in her mouth. Her face paled.

Patrick turned, followed her gaze.

She was staring out of the *octógono*'s entrance. Somebody was coming up the stairs. A huge black woman with the saddest eyes Patrick had ever seen. Forgetting Ligio, Zuri took a few steps towards her.

'Tungu. Tungu, where's . . .?' Zuri looked past her, to the stairs and empty camp beyond.

The woman called Tungu trod slowly into the room. She was streaked with mud and held a bow in her hand.

'Where's Neliah?' asked Zuri.

'She was very brave,' said Tungu. Her words were flat and slow. 'Blew tunnel to Mukuru like she promised. Kill many skulltroops.'

'Where is she?'

Zuri's voice reminded Patrick of his wife's after Hannah was born, when they'd wake to silence and she was petrified that their daughter wasn't crying.

Tungu reached out for Zuri's shoulder, bowed her head before she spoke again. 'With the ancestors now. They will sing *yimbira* to her.'

Zuri snatched her shoulder away from the other woman. Let out a rasp of air, her face turning hard. She tugged at her plait. For several moments she did nothing. Then she buckled, falling to one knee. Clasped her stomach.

Nobody moved. Everyone was watching her.

Patrick saw Zuri struggle to breathe. It sounded as if a bone were lodged in her throat. He pushed past Ligio and went to her side. Placed his hand gently against her neck, crouched down beside her. She clutched hold of him. He couldn't remember the last time a woman – a child – had embraced him.

Patrick looked up at Tungu. 'There was a man, a white man, sent to work on the tunnel. Blond hair . . .' He struggled to describe Burton.

'There many prisoners.'

'What happened to them?'

Tungu shook her head. 'Tunnel blown. None escape.'

Patrick swallowed, nodded. It couldn't be . . .

Fearless, dangerous, stupid Burton: gone.

He heard his last words shouted from the truck at the labour camp again. *I'll get you back to Hannah, I promise.* Patrick wished he'd turned round. Wished he'd faced him. Wished he'd never said those things in Stanleystadt.

He stood up, his hand still resting on the nape of Zuri's neck. She was weeping softly.

Then another sound. From outside. Patrick strained to make sense of it.

The clink of webbing.

He stared out of the door, into the dappled brightness of the trees. Saw black shapes darting towards the stairs. He spun towards Ligio.

But it was too late.

One of the *octógono*'s walls exploded inwards. A slingshot of splinters and smoke.

Stormtroopers poured in through the hole. They were flying up the stairs too. The pounding of boots on wood. The *clunk-click* of machine guns being readied. The Angolan soldiers dropped their weapons, boys who no longer wanted to play.

They were surrounded.

Patrick saw a familiar figure climbing the steps. 'No tears,' he whispered to Zuri, gently helping her to her feet. 'Not for these bastards.'

Next moment the point of a gun was in his back. 'I'm sorry, Major,' said Ligio. 'It's best for my men.'

'You idiot. We're all dead now.'

Uhrig reached the top of the stairs. Gone was his black SS uniform, instead tropical combat fatigues, a blur of khaki, sage and brown; paratrooper boots. Bandoliers of ammunition criss-crossed his chest. Over his shoulder was a thick coil of rope. Uhrig's eyes scanned the room, hovered briefly over Patrick, then wandered up to the rafters. He smiled to himself.

A gallows' smile.

Ligio stepped forward, pushed Patrick in front of him. 'Senhor Sturmbannführer—'

Uhrig frowned. 'Sturmbannführer?' He slapped his shoulder flashes. '*Standarten*führer, I think.'

'Senhor Standartenführer—' he struggled to mouth the word '—I am Lieutenant Carlos Ligio of the Portuguese Colonial Defence Force. This is one of the fugitives you are searching for. Whaler, the American.'

'No!' said Zuri. Her cheeks were stained with tears.

Ligio batted her away.

Patrick caught Uhrig's expression and felt a twist of revulsion. The Nazi was eyeing Zuri the way a starved man looked at a steak.

Uhrig turned back to Ligio, saluted. 'Thank you, Lieutenant.' He pulled Patrick towards him by the cuffs; the metal gouged his wrists.

'Your Governor General he . . . he spoke of clemency,' said Ligio.

'Of course.' Uhrig pulled his Luger: shot him dead.

The roar of the pistol bounced off the walls.

'Round up all the soldiers,' Uhrig ordered his men. 'Take them outside. Shoot them—'

'They're just kids,' said Patrick.

'You think I give a shit?'

'What about the others, Standartenführer?'

'The workers we'll take back to Wutrohr. The niggers . . . they can watch.'

The Herero were forced to lie on the ground, muzzles against their heads. All except Zuri.

Uhrig re-holstered his Luger, took a step closer to Patrick.

Slammed him in the gut.

Patrick dropped as if he would never breathe again. He sensed stormtroopers groping around him, half heard Uhrig's barked commands. A thick cord of rope was threaded through his cuffs. Then whipped over his head. Over the rafters.

'You see that?' said Uhrig. 'It's mountaineering rope. From when I climbed Kilmanscharo. The finest SS weave, strong as anything. Strong enough to take a pig.' He hawked and spat. 'Pull him up!'

Patrick was yanked off the ground.

He heard Zuri cry out again, prayed she'd shut her mouth. Two soldiers heaved on the rope. He was lifted into the air until his boots were dangling five feet from the floor.

His arms screamed in their sockets: he could feel the ligaments slowly ripping. His abdomen was stretched tight enough to snap.

'Now, *Amerikaner*,' said Uhrig, 'where were we?'

Chapter Thirty-Three

OUTSIDE there was a volley of gunfire.

'Ah . . . farewell, sweet youth,' said Uhrig. 'There's no one to save you, Major Whaler. So you'd better start talking. Where is he?'

Patrick's arms were on fire, his chest so tight he could barely breathe.

'Where's Cole?'

Patrick said nothing.

Hide, he thought, *it's the only thing left. Hide!*

He barricaded himself into his mind. Tried to picture his hacienda in Las Cruces. The arches that shaded the front door, the terracotta tiles in the kitchen. Hannah in a new dress, tanned and happy, calling him Dad. The baking sun.

But the more he concentrated on the image, the more his thoughts kept tumbling back to Burton.

He saw him that first day at Sidi Bel Abbès, barely old enough to volunteer. Something about his insolence, that scowling, forsaken spark in his eyes, reminded Patrick of himself at that age. He had told the boy to go back home to his parents, that the Legion wasn't for him. It only made Burton more determined to take the coin of Madame la République.

Outside there was a second volley. Uhrig looked bored. He was pacing up and down, boots ringing on the hollow floor.

'I can't hear you, *Amerikaner*,' he said. 'Or perhaps you need something more persuasive.'

His eyes lingered on Zuri.

Another memory: drill on Les Grandes Dunes. Endless miles of sand hot enough to blister the feet of a camel. One by one the other rookies had dropped, all except Burton, driven on by his inner fury. Patrick had never seen such grit. That night he invited the boy to his quarters. Poured them both a cup of rough fig wine, drank a toast: *the Kaiser!*

Soldat 2ième Classe Cole had become one of the best soldiers Patrick had ever known. Had that rare hunger to survive, no matter what.

And now he was dead.

The rope creaked above Patrick, his shoulders agony. The half-moon scar on his stomach felt as if it were going to rip open.

If I get out of this, I'm going to find Madeleine. Tell her everything. I swear it.

But what? That Burton had failed to kill Hochburg, failed to learn the truth about his mother. Had died in some nowhere tunnel, crushed or drowned for nothing. Should never have left home. That Patrick, his oldest friend, the only man he trusted, had fled into the savannah with some girl he'd just met rather than save him?

Patrick hung his head.

Below, Ligio was curled up on the floor, an oval of blood spreading around him. Zuri was on her knees between two stormtroopers, hands on head. She kept glancing at him, eyes brimming with anguish. He willed her to look away.

Uhrig stopped pacing. Sighed.

'You know the worst thing about you escaping, *Amerikaner*? Having to listen to Kepplar when he got back from the tunnel. *Find him, Standartenführer*,' he mimicked. '*Don't fail me again.*'

Patrick struggled to heave himself up. Anything to ease the pressure on his shoulders.

'Lucky my Wolves spotted the big bitch.' Uhrig cocked his

head in Tungu's direction. 'Allowed us to track her all the way here. Now, where's Cole?'

Patrick remained silent.

'It was a long journey,' continued Uhrig. 'Plenty of time to think, and one question kept playing on my mind. You're clearly not one of those isolationist pussies: you got some fight in you. So how to get you talking, *Amerikaner*? What about a bayonet through the kneecap? Pop it out from behind, nice and slow. Or slitting your fingertips open? Of course in an ideal world we'd have your daughter.'

Patrick felt a cold trickle of horror in his gut. 'I don't have a daughter.'

'Uhrig has a good memory. Heard your blabbing to the Gruppenführer. You seemed genuine enough.'

'Any old bullshit to shut him up.'

Uhrig snorted. 'On the eastern front, when we interrogated the partisans, I always found having a man's daughter worked best. Sons they cared less about – but that's just the way of the world. I remember my own father beat me once in the streets of Hamburg. In full view of everyone. And nobody raised a finger. If I'd been blond and pretty I'm sure they'd have dragged him in front of the magistrate . . .' He mused upon it before resuming. 'But daughters. Daughters always get results.'

Uhrig grabbed Zuri by the hair, hauled her to her feet. In his hand was a dagger. He pressed it against her windpipe. She stood rigid and shaking.

Patrick kept his face blank, focused on the pain in his shoulder sockets. 'You think I care about some black monkey? Go on. Cut her throat.'

'Here we go again! Just like your performance in the parade square. Quite the thwarted actor, aren't we, *Amerikaner*? But I saw the two of you together. Saw how much she wanted to save you from the lieutenant.'

Uhrig slowly ran the knife from Zuri's neck, between her breasts to her stomach before poking it against her crotch. She tried to pull away but Uhrig wrapped her plait around his fist.

'In Russia, when my Einsatzgruppen reached a new village do you know what the women did? Killed themselves. Even the crones. They'd rather be dead than indulge us. There were never enough to go around – so we had a rule. Ten men to one girl, no more. Otherwise—' he rocked his hips obscenely '—you're just fucking offal.'

The magma was bubbling up in Patrick. He fought to show no reaction. One word and Zuri was dead.

Uhrig looked around. 'My Wolves, we're twenty-five men. She's going to be a real mess by the time we're finished with her, *Amerikaner*. Blancmange . . . Pity it's not your little girl.'

Patrick let out a roar.

'I'm going to fucking kill you! I swear it.' He jerked and spun on the rope. Above him the rafters creaked as if they were about to break.

'Good,' said Uhrig. 'We're getting somewhere. Now: Burton Cole?'

'He's dead.'

'Don't give me that pigshit.'

'He was killed in the tunnel. Ask Tungu.'

Uhrig ripped down Zuri's pants. Patrick noticed her legs – they seemed so thin, so bare. She struggled away from him but Uhrig grasped her plait more firmly, tugged on it like a leash. Zuri's forehead stretched tight around her skull. The dagger played up and down her thighs.

'Where?' demanded Uhrig.

'Let her go!'

'Where's Cole?'

'He died in the explosion.' Patrick pulled at the rope again, oblivious to the pain now. 'It was your fault, you sent him there.'

'You're lying.'

'Let her go!'

Uhrig grinned. 'If you insist.' He flicked the knife.

Zuri tumbled to her knees.

Uhrig stood over her, swinging her severed plait in his hand.

He brought the hair to his face, sniffed. 'I always like a souvenir,' he said, stuffing the braid into his pocket.

Zuri desperately clawed the back of her head. She was crying and struggling not to; tears pooled in her eyes.

Uhrig kicked her over, put his boot on her back to stop her moving. 'You,' he said to the nearest stormtrooper. 'Come do your duty.'

'How many times,' shouted Patrick. 'Cole's dead!'

The trooper edged forward, regarded the sprawled figure beneath him with distaste. 'But, Herr Standartenführer, she's . . . a negroid. The Nuremberg Laws—'

'This isn't Germany.' Uhrig stared Patrick in the eye. 'Just get on with it. Pretend you're banging some Aryan schoolgirl if it helps.'

The trooper fumbled with his belt, then stopped. 'I can't, Herr Standartenführer, I can't—'

Uhrig turned purple. 'You limp-dick cocksucker. Get the fuck out of my sight.'

Patrick allowed himself a moment of bleak satisfaction.

Below him Zuri was struggling to crawl away. Uhrig pushed the heel of his boot down harder. 'Volunteers!'

Several men stepped forward.

'Better. You first.'

The stormtrooper set aside his BK44, rolled Zuri over and unzipped his pants.

'Last chance, *Amerikaner*. Where is Burton Cole?'

Zuri stared straight into Patrick's face. Eyes imploring.

'Stanleystadt,' he blurted. 'He never left, is still hiding there.'

Uhrig hesitated, wagged his finger. 'You're clever, *Amerikaner*, but I told you before. Uhrig has brains for ten. You're going to have to do better than that.' He nodded to the trooper.

He knelt between Zuri's legs, ran his eyes over her body. Then he was on top of her, smothering her face with bites as she hissed and squirmed. The other stormtroopers gathered to watch.

'Not as sweet as Fräulein Whaler, I'm sure,' said Uhrig. 'But she'll do.'

Patrick thrashed around, his face a contortion. He focused on the rafters.

Then a scream.

High-pitched. Like an animal being speared.

Oh, Jesus, what were they doing to her? Patrick forced himself to look back, his eyes blurred.

The trooper was trying to stand, hands clasping his crotch. Blood spewed everywhere.

On the ground, between Zuri's thighs, a hole had been punched through the floorboards. Patrick glimpsed a rusty machete disappearing back into it.

Bewilderment on Uhrig's face.

A Mills-bomb was tossed out: a hand grenade. It rolled across the floor towards the stormtroopers.

Zuri pushed herself away, curled into a ball. Patrick heaved his body upwards with all his strength.

'Run!' bellowed Uhrig.

Three-two-one . . .

Burton counted down the final seconds of the fuse.

The grenade exploded.

A lightning flash. Screams.

He kicked away more slats, pushed Neliah through the hole. 'Go!' She was trembling with rage, the panga bloody in her fist.

Burton stayed behind, scurrying beneath the stilts of the *octógono*. In each hand was one of the BK44s they'd stolen from the perimeter guards after slitting their throats. He peered up through the floorboards. Fired wherever he saw boots.

Shards of timber shot upwards. Bullets ripping through feet and ankles. More screams. Gobs of flesh.

He moved forward, kicking up leaves. Fired.

Move, fire. Move, fire.

The first BK emptied. He tossed it away.

Above him Uhrig was shouting. 'Flame units! Get the flame units!'

More troops were running towards the building, one with a tank on his back. Burton dived into position opposite the stairs. Waited till their boots were thundering up the steps. Locked his finger on the trigger.

This time the bullets chewed into shin bones. He aimed higher. Hit the soldier with the flamethrower.

Phwum. A ball of fire.

Burton buried his face into the dirt. Felt the hair on his arms shrivel, ears blister. The stench of petrol.

He crawled away from the burning staircase back to the hole. Heaved himself through it, took in the *octógono*.

It was strewn with bodies. The walls ablaze. Burton saw Neliah kneeling by her sister, a huddle of black women around them. Patrick had been cut down. He clutched a BK, his hands shaking as if he could barely lift the weapon. His face was screwed up, bloodthirsty. A mesh of livid wrinkles.

'Uhrig!' he roared. 'You're a dead man. You hear me? A fucking dead man.' Patrick spun round, blasted at everything.

Stopped solid.

Stared at Burton.

He had an expression of such astonishment that Burton almost burst out laughing; *tout bouleversé* they called that face in the Legion. 'Major Whaler,' he said, 'get down below and cover our escape.'

No response.

'Major!'

Patrick gave him another startled look, his mouth agog ... then he clambered down through the floorboards.

Burton turned to Neliah. She was pulling up her sister's trousers. 'Can she walk?'

'Yes.'

'Back through the hole.'

He helped them down.

The flames had reached the rafters. Through the fire he could see shapes moving towards him. The flash of bullets.

Burton returned fire till his magazine was spent. He pulled out his Browning and dropped to the ground below.

'We need more weapons,' he said to Neliah.

'The strongroom.' She was cradling her sister, the panga held protectively over her breast. 'This way.'

They darted through the smoke to a squat brick building. The flames from the *octógono* were spreading to the other huts. The crackle of wood and thatch. Burned leather. Someone was pleading for help in German.

'Down there,' said Neliah, sheltering inside. 'Tungu, go with them.'

A massive Herero woman disappeared down the stairs. Burton and Patrick followed into a storeroom. There were some old Enfield .303s, a Thompson submachine gun. Crates of ammo, canteens, medical supplies.

Burton slung the Thompson over his shoulder, thrust the rest of the rifles towards Tungu.

'Go!'

She flew back up the stairs. Patrick was shoving phials of morphine into a haversack, syringes, bandages, water bottles. Burton joined him, picked up an ammo case, checked it for rounds.

'They told me you were dead,' said Patrick. 'Killed in the tunnel.'

'Not yet.'

Patrick suddenly threw his arms around him.

Burton felt the roughness of his stubble against his cheek. Shoved him away. 'We have to move!'

'My hands.' Patrick placed his cuffed wrists against the ground, twisted his face away.

Burton aimed his Browning at the middle of the chain. Fired a single shot. A deafening boom.

The cuffs broke free.

Patrick stuffed the last of the supplies in the bag. 'Wait. There's something else. Hochburg. He's alive.'

'What?'

'He's alive.'

Burton froze.

It was like that moment back on the farm among the quince trees. The strongroom seemed to close in around him, grow darker. The air at once too thin, but thick enough to choke. Burton tasted blood and tears. His voice was a whisper. 'No.'

'I heard him on the radio. With Rougier – he sold us out, not Ackerman; I got it wrong.'

'But I killed him.'

Neliah's voice echoed down the stairs. 'Hurry!'

'You got his decoy,' said Patrick.

From above: gunfire, heavier calibre weapons. MG48s. *Hurry!* Neliah called again. Her voice seemed to come from a great distance. For an endless moment Burton did nothing. His tongue felt heavy and dry in his mouth. He couldn't swallow.

Hochburg was still alive ...

Then he grabbed the last of the ammo crates and tore up the stairs, Patrick at his heels.

They reached the top. Standing over the Herero were some white men. Burton raised the Thompson.

'No,' said Neliah. 'Their arms.'

They were marked with UJ; their faces bewildered, scared. Escaped prisoners.

Burton peered out of the door frame. Flame units were moving through the camp. Roaring plumes of orange and red devoured everything. Behind them more troopers.

Nobody needed telling.

Patrick and Neliah reached to carry Zuri. She shrugged them both off, snatched one of the guns from Tungu and ran. For a second Burton thought she was going to attack the Germans, but she veered off. Was swallowed by the grass. Neliah and the other women followed, then the prisoners, finally Patrick and Burton.

The camp was engulfed in flames.

Chapter Thirty-Four

Schädelplatz, Kongo
19 September, 06:38

AWN.

When the guards came he was going to make a break for it. It didn't matter about his broken leg now, didn't matter if he got shot. A bullet in the head was preferable to the barbarism that awaited him.

Even the gallows and a short rope would be better.

Dolan tried to control himself, forced his body rigid . . . but almost at once the tremors started again. Tremors travelling from his chest, into his belly and limbs. His remaining teeth chattered.

He still couldn't believe this was happening. It all seemed hazy. Unreal.

Somewhere he heard a door open. Then the echo of boots, heading towards his cell. He squeezed his eyes shut. Readied himself. His muscles felt sapless.

He had expected the night to rush by, but it seemed endless. Earlier a guard arrived with Hochburg's compliments, asking him to choose his final meal. Dolan wanted something to fox them, something a German chef would scratch his head at. One final, futile gesture of defiance. It was all he had left.

'Old English trifle,' he blurted out. Just like his mam used to make at Christmas.

Several hours later the guard returned with a silver spoon and a bowl of the stuff. It was the most delicious trifle he'd ever tasted, better than anything at home. Slivers of fresh strawberry and mango, sherry sponge, golden custard. The sweetest, thickest cream. As soon as he finished eating he puked in the corner.

The footsteps reached the door. Locks turned.

'It's time.'

Guards entered the cell.

Dolan's heart thundered. He tensed, rolled his fingers into fists – found himself too weak to act.

They dragged him to his feet, carried him above ground. The sky was full of dense, mauve-grey clouds, the skulls almost shimmering in their light. At the far end of the square – the scene of his execution. He couldn't bear to look, twisted his head away. Dolan began shaking more violently despite the balmy morning air.

'*Lord, lead me through the wilderness,*' he mumbled to himself. '*Me . . . me, a pilgrim . . .*' He remembered singing it at school.

A small crowd had gathered to watch: the bureaucrats and torturers of the Schädelplatz, secretaries in pencil skirts, a yawning Señor Aguilar, the British attaché. Someone had brought his children. Dolan watched two young boys in Pimpf uniforms chase each other. They stopped as he approached, sidled back to their father.

The guards led him through the crowd, his plaster-cast scraping the ground . . .

And there it was.

How many times had he studied the plans of the Schädelplatz, never once imagining this is where it would end?

There were three of them.

'*A pilgrim of poor . . . appearance.*'

Three pyramids of wood, each with a stake protruding from the centre.

They took him to the left pyre, round the back, up a short flight of steps to a platform hidden among the logs. The stink of petrol was overpowering.

Dolan was chained to the stake. Then left alone. Somewhere he heard the tinkle of a wind-chime.

'*I don't have strength . . . strength or life in me . . .*' The lyrics were in his head now. His windpipe too tight to sing.

At the far end of the square, from the direction he had just been carried, three men appeared. Two carried swastika banners. The one in the middle a flaming torch. All were wearing black hoods. They marched solemnly towards him. Behind them came a drummer rapping a heartbeat tattoo.

Dolan stared into the crowd, eyes beseeching. *Please!* Someone had to stop this. It was 1952, not the fucking Middle Ages. In the front row, flanked by bodyguards, he saw Hochburg, dog at his feet. He was gazing beyond the pyres at some invisible point. His face seemed locked. Cold and cruel. Eyes black.

Will they be the last things I ever see? thought Dolan. Two pinpricks of darkness.

He began convulsing. His mind a thunderflash of images. He struggled to make sense of them – as if somehow they might offer salvation.

Home . . . the dank wallpaper in his old bedroom with the floral pattern he hated so much . . . a girlfriend who loved boiled sweets, always tasted of cough-candy and peardrops when he groped her . . . his brother, polishing his boots, always so bloody cheery . . .

He had died at Dunkirk, bombed into the water as the Expeditionary Force attempted to flee. A hero, so the dispatches said, an example to live up to. Survivors told of the sea foaming red. How could the country have surrendered after that? It wasn't peace, no matter what the politicians claimed – it was defeat.

The torch and swastikas were close now, close enough for Dolan to smell the burning pitch of the flame. His breath came as rapid as a machine gun. The crowd parted to let them through.

A sponge cake, white icing and glitter . . . Dolan saw himself blow out six candles . . . the recruitment depot in Newport on his eighteenth birthday, Mam all tears again . . . Drill instructors

*yammering in his ear . . . His box of tricks crammed with TNT
. . . Evac training . . . the whirr of helicopters—*

Helicopters! That was it.

They would save him. A team of commandos brought in by chopper, abseiling into the square, led by Patrick and the major, guns blazing. They wouldn't let him die here, not like this, not all alone. Dolan scanned the clouds, expecting to see a helicopter at any second.

The executioner had reached the base of the pyre. He turned to the crowd, presented the torch. They raised their arms in a wordless Führer salute. Even Aguilar and the British attaché.

The drum fell silent. Hochburg nodded.

The executioner lowered the flame into the wood. It caught instantly.

Dolan stared into his masked face. Then at the crowd. The two Pimpf boys were watching him intently, timid smiles playing on their lips.

He turned to the sky again, ignored the smoke flooding his nose and mouth. The reek of fuel. He could already feel his plaster-cast melting, fusing into his flesh. Through his tears he searched for the rescue helicopter.

Any second now. *Any second.*

The horizon remained empty.

The Welshman screamed. And screamed.

Hochburg watched the flames spiral up his body; felt nothing – the way he used to when he was a boy and would burn scorpions under a lens. He knew there were some who disapproved of his methods, men like Arnim, but only retribution of such severity would deter their enemies in the future.

Dolan writhed, the tendons in his neck standing out like metal wires beneath his skin. His flesh blistered and popped. Not once did he close his eyes; they were riveted on the heavens.

The crowd around Hochburg murmured, stepped back from the spectacle. Some of the women wept and began to leave.

Hochburg saw two boys refusing to be dragged away by their father. The air smelt of crackling – sweet, rich, purified. The same as that first time . . .

And still Dolan screamed.

Next to him were two other pyres: one for the American when he was captured, one for Burton Cole. If he was still alive. Hochburg prayed he hadn't been cheated that satisfaction. This whole ritual was for his sake.

Was long overdue.

He had used fire as his instrument of justice before. It was reserved for the lowest traitors, for those who would destroy the glories he had brought to Africa. Once, after an uprising in Muspel, he had burned enough niggers to make the midday sky black. *Black* – the Reichsführer had approved of the irony. The first time, however, had been twenty years earlier, before he wore the swastika, on a desolate beach in Togoland, on the night he had finally forsaken God.

Two days after he buried his Eleanor.

She was curled up when he found her, facing away from the ocean; the waves were flat, the sun white and low. Her face was split, clothes torn to rags. The sand around her body stained a dark brown.

The rage burned from Hochburg's chest into his throat. His exhaustion evaporated. It was like that moment he found his parents, brother and sister. When he had crawled from his hiding place and found them spread across the ground. Eviscerated.

'My God. Eleanor!' He dropped to his knees and gently scooped her up. Smelt copper and saliva. 'Who did this to you?' he said in English. 'Who did this?'

Her eyelids flickered. 'Walter? Is that you?' She sounded as if she'd bitten her tongue.

He took in her injuries: the cuts, claw marks, bruises. Her thighs were soaked with blood. 'Who did this?'

'I knew you'd come after me.'

'I haven't stopped since you left.' He wiped the sweat from his hair. 'Haven't slept or eaten . . .' His eyes dissolved in tears. 'What have they done to you?'

She didn't reply – simply offered her hand. He gripped it so hard she gasped. It felt tiny in his, fragile enough to crush, like the very first time they met and she held it out so formally. They had both been shy then. He had never forgotten that first touch: the warmth of it, that instant sense of belonging. Now her skin was icy, the cold seeping into his own flesh.

'Why?' he asked. There was a savagery to his voice. She had run away three days earlier. 'Why did you leave?'

She tried to pull her hand away but he refused to release it. 'How many times do I have to tell you? Burton.'

Hochburg made no reply.

'I keep seeing him . . . all alone. Confused. Crying.' Her breath came in shallow, broken gulps. 'I can't get that picture out of my head. Can't live with it any more . . . can't live with myself. I promised I'd never leave him. I promised . . .'

'And what of your promise to me?'

'Oh, Walter . . . I had to go. We both knew it was time.'

Hochburg felt a bitter pang, looked away, out across the ocean. It was one of those sunsets where the sky turned to steel rather than blood. 'What were you going to do?' he said. 'Wait for a ship? Sail to Lomé. They'd never have seen you.'

Eleanor managed a smile, nodded at a stack of wood further down the beach. 'I was going to light a fire.'

'A fire,' said Hochburg. '*And as the fire burneth a wood, so persecute them with thy tempest . . .*'

'*And make them afraid with thy storm.*'

Psalms 83:14.

She had whispered it in his ear after that first, frantic time they made love, as they mopped the sweat off their bodies and dressed to go to evening prayer. Would often repeat it after their couplings in the orphanage. He never knew why. The words haunted him. Mocked him.

For a long moment Hochburg was silent, he breathed in time

with her. Eleanor let her eyes close, rolled her head against him; she was fading away. He spoke in a rush. 'Eleanor! Wake up. I have an idea.'

She was blinking at him again. Porcelain-blue eyes, flecked with grey.

'Burton can be with us,' continued Hochburg. 'We'll live together as a family.' He fought away his jealousy. 'I was a fool never to think of it before.'

'It's too late now, Walter.'

'No!'

'Too late for me.'

'You shouldn't have gone alone. I told you this was wild country.'

'I had to get back.'

'I could have protected you.'

She tried to loosen herself from his grip again. 'If I'd told you what I was going to do . . . that I was going back home, you'd never have let me leave.'

'But look what they've done . . .' His voice broke.

'It's God's judgement.'

'No.'

'His tempest . . . Punishment for my weakness.'

Hochburg bowed his head, his hair falling lankly around his face. 'No God – no true, loving God – could allow this to happen.'

'We've sinned . . . I've broken my little boy's heart. My husband—'

'No!'

'You have to find them, Walter.' She swallowed, a dry, blood-less click. 'Beg them my . . . forgiveness.'

He pulled her face to his, felt the swollen grey skin of her cheek. 'You can't die, Eleanor. I won't allow it.'

She finally freed her hand. It seemed to take the last of her life-force. 'Promise me.'

'I forbid it.' He rocked her back and forth.

'I'm scared . . . Walter . . .'

Hochburg hugged her tighter. Felt her pulse slow and fade,

like a scream echoing in the darkness to nothing. He held her till she was cold. Behind him the waves silently lapped the shore. Night fell.

Hochburg dug her grave with his bare hands, in a sheltered spot by some palms with an unbroken view of the ocean. He dug in pitch blackness. Three cubits deep, the sides made smooth; ignoring his nails as they split. Laid her body gently in the sand at the bottom. Tasted her lips one final time. Slowly packed the soil back on top of her, sobbing with every handful. Marked the spot with a crude wind-chime made from raffia-string, wood and seashells. Then he slumped by her grave, watched the sun rise and fall.

Rise and fall.

They called this stretch of shoreline the Slave Coast. Along the beach there was no sign of human existence, nothing to mark the twentieth century. It might have been the beginning of time. Or the end.

Images laid siege to his mind. He saw the savages that had done this to her; this could only be the wickedness of the negroid. Heard their animal grunts and laughter, the slap of their hands against her face. Black against white. Heard Eleanor call out for her son.

Her son, not him.

And all the while his body was racked with weeping. He held his palms in front of his face wanting to hide. When they butchered his family, his innards had shrivelled and died. But this – this was far worse. There had to be something to blot out this pain.

Something.

Hochburg knew what.

He had resisted it – the Sixth Commandment – for so long. But the time for talking, for endless deliberation in his journal, was over. He must act now, as he should have done after they slaughtered his parents. If he had shown more resolve then, Eleanor might have lived.

It only took him a few hours to find the niggers responsible. There were three of them. He split the first one's skull before his

companions were even aware of him. Overpowered the other two
– they were brothers – and dragged them back to the scene of
their crime.

Night had fallen again.

At first they refused to admit it, claimed to be fishermen. Knew
nothing about a white woman. He had beaten and slashed them,
screamed brimstone threats in every native tongue he knew. And
still they denied it, wept and begged for mercy. Then he dragged
them to the driftwood Eleanor had gathered, built it into a larger
pile and staked the younger brother to it.

Hochburg clutched a flaming torch. 'You murdered her,' he
roared at the elder.

'*Sarki*, please, I beg you—'

'Murdered her. Tell me!'

'No!'

Hochburg plunged his flame into the tinder.

The screams were loud enough to be heard across all of Togo.

He grasped the other brother's hair, made him watch every
last spasm of the burning. Drink down lungfuls of human smoke.

Only then did the nigger avow his guilt.

For this confession Hochburg built a second pyre. Watched the
fire rage till it was nothing more than ash and bone. Felt purged
of the agony within. Only after the flames died down did his
loss begin to creep back; it needed more flesh.

Burton.

If it hadn't been for him, if Eleanor hadn't wanted to see her
son again, she would never have left. Would still be alive. Her
choice had condemned her as surely as if Burton had slit her
throat. He was to blame! He was the source of all Hochburg's
anguish. The thought raged in him like darkness in his blood.

He stretched his limbs, breathed deeply. The air smelt crisp.
Purified.

Vengeance is mine and I will repay.

And then a vision, as clear as the distant horizon and the light
breaking over it.

He fell to his knees and searched the remainders of the pyres, rooting through the ash, indifferent to the smouldering debris that seared his fingers. His nose filled with smoke. Finally he found what he was looking for. It was scorched but still intact. He held it aloft in the direction of the rising, red sun.

A skull.

Hochburg examined its structure, pushed his thumbs into the eye sockets, pulled at the remaining teeth. Stroked the cranium. And in that moment he saw his future, his salvation, an end to his pain, not only for himself but all of Africa. No white man must ever again suffer the loss he had endured. His eyes gleamed.

But first: Burton Kohl.

He began collecting more wood.

The crowd had departed. Hochburg stood alone except for two Leibwache and his dog, Fenris. He roused himself from his introspection: it served no purpose. After all those years his grief was still there, clamouring to be numbed.

Only retribution could satisfy it.

Dolan was dead. A blackened husk. Occasionally a limb would still twitch.

He had been brave, thought Hochburg, hadn't begged for mercy despite his screams. The SS could do with more hearts like his, instead of all the 'ethnic Germans' he kept being fobbed off with.

The flames continued to crackle around him, sending a plume of smoke across the skull-cobbled square. Hochburg followed its trail. Saw Kepplar marching towards him; he looked exhausted, his face pricked with spots. 'Heil Hitler!' he said, snapping to attention. There was a stale odour of peppermint.

Hochburg gave a languid wave of the wrist. 'I see you are empty-handed. Again.'

'I managed to track Cole and the American to Wutrohr. There . . . there I lost them. Whaler escaped, Cole was sent on a punishment detail—'

'To the tunnel?'

'Yes, Herr Oberst.'

'The tunnel which is now ... how shall we put it ... not a tunnel.'

Kepplar shifted his shoulders as though his shirt were made of hair. 'No one could have survived the explosion.'

'Did you recover a body?'

'No, Herr Oberst.'

'So there is the possibility he survived.'

'A possibility, yes. I sent Standartenführer Uhrig to search the area, to track down anyone who might have escaped.'

'Uhrig?'

'The camp commander at Wutrohr.' Kepplar's lip curled. 'The miscegenist.'

'You're not jealous, are you?' Hochburg roared with laughter, felt the smoke parch his throat. He closed his eyes. 'Burton was a boy when I knew him. I wonder what the man is like ...'

'A criminal, the worst kind of degenerate—'

Hochburg tutted. 'Spare me the diatribe, I wasn't asking the little Doctor.'

He ran his hand over his head – he was a near-perfect Category One – felt the smoothness of his scalp. His hair had started to drop out in the weeks after Eleanor; had never regrown. 'I would say obstinate, like his mother. A survivor.' He breathed in deeply again, sucking in the heat of the embers, the past. 'He's still alive. I know it.'

His eyes snapped open again. He signalled to the Leibwache. 'I think it is time I took over the pursuit of young Burtchen personally,' said Hochburg.

'But Northern Rhodesia, Herr Oberstgruppenführer, the invasion.'

'My generals are more than competent, they can deal with it for now.'

'But *you* must lead. You must—'

The Leibwache grabbed Kepplar's arms, tore at his swastika armband.

An expression of white panic.

'What did I tell you, Derbus?' said Hochburg, his voice soothing. 'Don't fail me again. And yet once more you have returned without Burton Cole.'

The guards dragged Kepplar towards one of the pyres. He kicked helplessly at the ground. Fenris barked.

'But Herr Oberst . . . I've been halfway across Kongo for you, haven't slept—'

'You should have gone back to Germania when I told you.'

'I wanted to continue our work, be at your side.'

'A year is too long for a man to be away from his family. If it were me I would miss my wife terribly.'

They were binding him to the stake. Sparks flared from Dolan's pyre.

'Herr Oberst. Walter. Please!'

Hochburg strode away, across the skulls.

Behind him Kepplar's yells continued: 'Herr Oberst, please. Herr Oberst!'

Chapter Thirty-Five

Quimbundo, North Angola
19 September, 10:00

THEY smelt them long before they saw them.

The stench came through the miombo trees, burrowed into Neliah's nose. Made her belly lurch. It reminded her of the barrels of salt-cod *Papai* used to import from Lisboa. Buzzards circled above.

They had fled from the camp until the roar of the flames was distant and the *ndeera*-grass silent. Then the long trek to the railway at Quimbundo, walking through the night till the savannah became woodland. All the time Burton urged them forward, fearful of resting in case the *Nazistas* caught them. But the trees were noiseless, except for once when Neliah heard an elephant rustling among the leaves.

They were thirteen now, everyone else lost or dead. Herself and Zuri, Tungu, Ajiah and two other Herero. Five prisoners from the chimney-camp. Burton and his friend, Patrick. Patrick reminded her a little of *Papai* – his grey hair, gruff voice, the manner in which he walked in the world. When Neliah scolded her sister for finding *yet another* old white man, she replied there was no eye-lust in him, that he was good of heart.

As for Burton, she didn't know. He hated the *Nazistas*, but she didn't know.

He had spoken few words on their journey from the river to

the empty chimney-camp and then Angola, not even why he had changed his mind and was following. He was a soldier, but different to the *comandante* or Gonsalves or any of the *Resistencia*. *Ina* would have called him *omu-potu*. Skin-blind. He had saved her life in the tunnel, helped save Zuri – but there was also a devil in him. Something that made Neliah wary, even if she recognised the same *rungiro* in him as in herself. He was only with them now to get to Loanda and a boat home.

She told him that there would be no train at Quimbundo, that Penhor and his soldiers would have taken it to the capital.

'It doesn't matter,' he replied. 'We can follow the tracks.'

She liked the softness of his voice. 'We Herero go also. Get to Loanda to join our army.'

'They allow blacks?'

'They don't want to. But we must all fight to save Angola. That is what my father believed.'

Neliah led the group, Burton and Patrick at the rear, their guns watching the trees. Her hand was curled into Zuri's, the other gripped the panga. She kept looking at her sister's hair, missed the swish of her plait.

'It will grow back,' said Neliah.

Zuri shook her head.

'It will, I promise. But even more long. More beautiful.'

'I don't want it to grow.'

'You must! Remember how much *Papai* loved it.'

'From now on I'm going to keep it cut, like yours.'

Neliah glanced at her sister and wondered if a smile or a girl-look would ever light her face again. She moved as if her hip bones were stuck. Her trousers were stained with blood, there was a bite mark on her cheek. But it was her eyes that chilled Neliah most. They were staring ahead, empty. It made her think of a tale *Ina* would tell when they were children, of the Kishi – a creature that came from the forest to steal the souls of women. Its face was said to be ugly and white, like all evil spirits.

Neliah squeezed her hand harder. 'I was wrong to send you to the chimney-camp. You should have stayed with me. *Pamue*.'

'You were doing your best, sister.' Her voice became gentler. 'Since our parents, you've always taken care of me, even though it should be the other way round. *Ina* named you well, Neliah. Truly you are strong of will, vigorous of spirit, level of mind.'

'No. I must earn it. The *Nazistas* will never touch you again, Zuri, I swear. I'll die first.'

'You mustn't die. Not ever.' Her eyes swelled. 'I don't want to be left on my own.'

'Then we must run, hide, go some place where they cannot find us.'

'I don't want to hide either. I told you in the tunnel, I want to fight! Want to kill as many skull-troops as possible.'

'I know.'

'Find the one named Uhrig.' The words came out like irons from a forge.

Neliah looked at her again. She had been wrong, her eyes weren't empty, they were full to the brim. Full of *rungiro*. A hunger for revenge.

'And when you're face to face with him?'

'What do you think?' She laughed joylessly but for a heart-beat Neliah glimpsed the old Zuri. '*Vindicta nemo magis gaudet quam foemina*.'

'You know I don't understand.' For once she wasn't irritated.

'No one rejoices more in revenge than a woman.'

'Or a sister,' replied Neliah in a whisper. 'When the time comes the panga is yours.'

After that they walked in silence till the air began to stink.

'What is it?' asked Tungu.

'I know that smell,' said Zuri, her eyes darkening. She put her hand to her nose.

Burton joined them. 'Where are we?'

'We must be near the railway now,' said Neliah. 'Very near.'

They continued through the trees, the smell thickening all the time. The air buzzed with insects. Finally they emerged into a clearing.

Quimbundo.

There was a half-built brick building with no roof, a wooden workshop, water tower, piles of coal like huge termite hills. Everything was itching with leaves. *The forest is hungry,* thought Neliah, *wants to bite back what man has taken.* There was also a *tyndo*, a steam-train, its engine cold and silent. The tracks vanished into the trees.

In front of the *tyndo* a tent had been pitched and long tables set for dinner to feed Penhor's soldiers. Bowls of food, tin trays, metal cups. The stench was coming from the tables.

Quimbundo was one of the far outposts of the Lunda Railway (more commonly called the 'Salazar Line' after Portugal's President) situated less than ten miles from where the tracks abruptly ended. For decades Angola had been dominated by the Benguela Railway in the south, but the discovery of diamonds in the north-east led to prospectors demanding a link from the interior to Loanda, and from there to the markets of Europe and America. President Salazar, always keen to bolster Portugal's fortunes and wanting a project to prove himself the equal of German achievements, obliged. And so three hundred and seventy miles of track, viaduct and tunnel were constructed, mining communities sprouting along its furthest leg.

Then the Germans had occupied the south, the Benguela Railway coming under Nazi control to connect the copper belts of Kongo to the Atlantic. Fearful of a similar fate, the prospectors abandoned their new diamond mines and left the eastern section of the Salazar incomplete. Since then the *Resistencia* had used it to ferry troops back and forth.

Neliah was bewitched by the tables. They were throbbing with flies.

'What happened?' said Zuri. Her voice rose. 'Alberto . . .'

Burton stepped closer. Neliah saw that his expression was blank.

'There's no blood, no bullet cases,' he said, picking up a bowl of rice. He sniffed it. 'Poison?'

'It'd have to be something quick,' said Patrick. 'Like cyanide.'

Burton pulled the rice away from his nose. 'Or sarin.'

There were three tables, sitting at them the soldiers *Comandante* Penhor had led from Terras de Chisengue.

All of them dead.

Their mouths twisted in agony, bodies starting to stink and rot in the heat.

Chapter Thirty-Six

NELIAH was unable to drag her eyes away from the tables. 'They're not all here,' she said. 'Where's Penhor?' Her lips tightened. 'Where's Gonsalves? There are others missing also.'

'Stay here,' said Burton, pulling his gun. He began to search the buildings with Patrick.

'Alberto,' Zuri whispered again, her brow knotted. She looked around the clearing. 'Why would the *Nazistas* do this?'

'It wasn't the *Nazistas*,' said Neliah. 'They have guns, tanks. Don't need poison.'

'Then who?'

She hesitated. For some reason she was thinking about Gonsalves. Then Penhor, how he wanted her to find the dynamite because he knew she'd go back to the tunnel. Knew the detonators were useless. 'I don't know,' she said at last. There would be no satisfaction in sharing her thoughts – Zuri didn't need any more pain.

Neliah turned away from her sister and stared into the face of the nearest soldier. She remembered serving him in the kitchens, his name was José. He had a wife and a little boy in Lisboa, sometimes drank too much *caporotto* and sang Fado songs that made the other soldiers cry—

A gunshot.

Neliah pushed Zuri to the ground, held out her panga. The others ducked under the table with them. The sound rolled away into the trees.

Silence except for the *zumm* of flies. They were feasting.

Then footfalls.

Burton walked back from the direction of the workshop. He was leading someone at gunpoint: a man in overalls and a cap, covered in black, babbling in Portuguese.

'I don't understand him,' said Burton.

Neliah translated. 'He's says don't shoot him.'

Burton lowered his pistol, kept his other hand clamped on the man's shoulder.

'He's the train driver . . . Says that one of the soldiers did the poisoning.'

'How did he manage to escape?'

'He was working on the engine, didn't eat . . . Afterwards he hid in the coal.'

'Which soldier? Does he know who?'

'He doesn't know his name . . . He was scared, there was shooting also . . . One of the Portuguese, he thinks, with black hair.'

Burton looked at her. 'Any ideas?'

'It could be any of them.'

The driver was speaking again.

'He says later a plane landed close to here. Took off again after a few minutes. Flew west.'

Burton chewed on this, let go of the driver. 'Ask him if he can get the train running. Can he get us to Loanda?'

The driver didn't need translating. He nodded his head. '*Loanda, sim.*'

'Burton!' Patrick was calling from the trees. 'You'd better see this.'

Neliah and Zuri followed Burton to behind the roofless building. They found Patrick staring into a shallow ditch. There were more bodies. Zuri glanced down, then covered her mouth.

'The sooner we're out of here the better,' said Burton. 'Me and Patrick will help the driver. Get the train going.'

'What about the bodies?' said Zuri. 'We can't leave them. Not like this. The smell. Animals will find them . . .'

'There are too many,' said Burton.

'I don't care about the others. Just these here.'

'Don't worry,' said Patrick, reaching out for Zuri. 'We'll bury them for you.'

'We don't have time,' said Burton, but Neliah saw the struggle in his eyes.

Zuri grabbed his hand. 'Our parents were left like this. Please, Burton.'

'Your parents?' He gave a long sigh, his breath coming from deep within. 'We'll check the train first, then find some spades.'

The two soldiers walked away, leaving Neliah and her sister alone.

Neliah gazed into the ditch below. There were four or five men, it was difficult to tell. They were a pile of arms and legs, lying face down, the back of their skulls torn open. They'd been shot in the face. Among the bodies was a blue uniform and red sash.

She looked at her sister. 'I'm sorry.'

Zuri's eyes were dry. 'Whatever you thought about him, Neliah, he loved our country. The same as *Papai* did. Didn't want the *Nazistas* to own it.'

'Who will tell his wife in Portugal? His children?'

'Someone will bring them news.'

Without warning Zuri leapt into the ditch. Grabbed Penhor's red sash and climbed back out. The whole time she kept her eyes away from the gaping, bloody heads.

'Did . . . did you love him?' asked Neliah.

Zuri crushed the sash between her fingers. 'Not real love.'

'Then why did you do it?'

'To protect you, sister.'

'I don't understand.'

'If I hadn't shared his bed what would we be? Out in the forest, always running from skull-troops.' She rubbed the bite mark on her face. 'Just another two *negras* that nobody cared about.'

Neliah felt her throat grow thick.

She cupped her sister's cheeks and kissed her.

The ground was sandy, easy to dig.

Burton flicked a pile of dirt into the ditch, thinking about the other soldiers he'd buried over the years. And those who'd just been left. At Bel Abbès he always volunteered for burial duty, perhaps because he never got to lay his parents to rest. It was something else to curse Hochburg for. A cloud of insects rose from the corpses.

Patrick had come across the spades in the workshop. While he searched for them Burton got on his hands and knees, checked underneath the tables of rotting food. Finally he found what he was looking for.

Neliah's mouth creased with disapproval. 'You mustn't!'

'He doesn't need them,' said Burton, pulling off the dead soldier's boots. 'I do.'

They were a decent fit, cushioned his throbbing toes and heels. When Neliah had gone he also took a shirt to replace his tattered one. There was a superstition in the Legion: the clothes of dead men would protect you.

Burton and Patrick continued to dig. Breathed through their mouths.

Gradually the corpses disappeared beneath a layer of earth. From nearby came the lilt of women's voices; the hiss of steam.

'I got to stop,' said Patrick. 'My arms.' He rolled his shoulders, inhaled sharply.

Burton rested his spade in the ground. His face was dripping. He took a swig from his canteen and offered it to Patrick. The American shook his head. They stood in silence, staring down at the grave like two mourners deep in thought.

'How come you came back?' said Patrick eventually. They'd only passed a few words since the rebel camp, mostly about

Dolan, God rest his soul. Neither wanted to talk much or knew what to say. Now Patrick's voice was tentative, self-conscious.

'Because I promised,' replied Burton. 'Said I'd get you back home, to Hannah.'

'When I heard you at the labour camp, I wanted to turn round.'

'But you didn't.'

'There was dust in my eye.'

Burton gave a knowing smile. He took another mouthful of water, sluiced it round his mouth. 'Well, before you get too sentimental, it wasn't the only reason. I also did it for Madeleine.'

'And how was saving an old fool like me going to help?'

'You may be a fool, but you're also the only friend I've got left. The closest thing to family.' He picked up his spade and began to dig again. 'If I'd left you it would have been like my mother: the same not knowing, always wondering what happened. And I'm tired of looking back, Patrick. I want a future. Me and Madeleine, not ghosts. I had to at least try and find you.'

'But Stanleystadt. I was going to get on that boat.'

'Every man for himself, eh?'

'I shouldn't have said that.'

'You never meant it, *Chef*. Not really.'

'I did.'

Burton laughed, a worn-out aching laugh. He shook his head. 'No. There's some *honneur de la Légion* in you yet. If you'd really wanted to lose me you could have done it. Just vanished. I'd have woken up in that doss house alone.'

Patrick considered his words. 'So you came back for me.'

'No more ghosts.'

'What about Hochburg?'

Burton's spine stiffened; he drove his spade hard into the earth. 'I can't believe he's still alive. I swear the man's the devil himself. But I don't care.'

'And your mother? That truth you wanted so bad?'

'What does it matter now? What does any of it matter now: the truth, revenge? I'll never get back inside the Schädelplatz.'

Burton swiped a fly from his face. 'Don't want to. I've wasted a lifetime on this stuff.' He was thinking of Maddie and how she'd found peace despite her family's fate in Madagaskar. He admired her acceptance – it offered him a different way to live.

'You sure?'

'Madeleine told me you don't need the truth to live your life. She was right. All I want now is to get home to her.'

'Home,' repeated Patrick. 'You'll invite me, won't you? To the farm.'

'Of course! You can meet Maddie. We'll have tea and cake, scones with quince jam.'

Patrick smiled. With his white stubble and watery eyes he seemed older than ever. 'That'd be swell.' He picked up his spade again.

After that they worked in silence till their shirts were plastered to their backs and the soldiers were buried. Once they were done Burton reached for his water again, swallowed a mouthful, offered it to Patrick.

This time he took it, but didn't drink. 'When Tungu said you'd been killed, I . . .' He stared into the canteen. 'I'm glad you're still with me, Burton.'

For a long moment Burton didn't reply. Then: 'We made it this far, *Chef*. We'll do the rest. It's four hundred miles to Loanda.'

'Then what? Do we go find Ackerman?'

'If we take Rougier at his word, he'll be at the consulate. Maybe he can help us out of here, maybe not. At the very least he's got some explaining to do. I want to know why me. Who am I to British intelligence?'

'And after?'

'The first boat to anywhere. I never want to see Africa again.'

Patrick laughed. 'I'll drink to that.' He raised the canteen to his lips. 'The Kaiser!'

Burton took it back – 'The Kaiser!' – and drained the bottle. The water tasted earthy, warm, sweet.

They picked up their guns and walked to the train.

The locomotive was a black Beyer-Garratt. It pulled a tender brimming with coal, two cattle-trucks and at the rear a platform mounted with an anti-aircraft gun. The prisoners and most of the Herero were already on board, their legs dangling over the side through the open doors. Neliah and Zuri stood by the engine. It towered over them, smoke coiling from the funnel. An aroma of coal. The smell reminded Burton of foggy London streets, of Hampstead: Madeleine's family home. Servants tending fireplaces, wall-to-wall carpets, gilded furniture. He shuddered inside.

How distant England was. That's why people hadn't balked at the Nazis' conquest of Africa, thought Burton, or when they deported the Jews to Madagaskar; why they nervously laughed off Windhuk and its legacy of rumour. It was all too remote to care about. Too far away to imagine – or even want to. Better to get on with your life and enjoy the good times that peace had brought.

Patrick stepped over to Zuri. 'It's done.'

There was a red sash tied around her waist. She looked in the direction of the ditch, then stood on tiptoes and whispered something in Patrick's ear. He nodded, gently touched her elbow.

'We gathered more guns,' said Neliah, 'and some food. We also found this. I don't know if it works.' At her feet were two wooden crates. She opened one of them.

Patrick whistled.

Burton knelt by the box: it was packed full of dynamite and timer-fuses. 'We should stow it at the back, with the AA gun. That'll be safest.' He fastened the lid. 'How long to Loanda?'

Neliah shouted up to the driver. He was checking dials in the engine, seemed chirpier now they were about to leave.

'He says eight or nine hours – if the tracks haven't been bombed again.'

'Is that likely?'

Neliah translated. The driver shrugged.

'Tell him if he sees any Germans – on the ground, in the air – to sound the whistle at once.'

Moments later the pistons began to chug back and forth. The

wheels turned. Burton watched Quimbundo slide away. He had a final glimpse of the tables: the putrefying soldiers, their grimaces. From a distant they could almost be laughing. The stench was still livid in his nose. Then the trees obscured them.

He sat down next to Patrick. Cool air rushed in through the open cattle-door. The beat of the train.

Burton felt exhausted, his muscles like they had been wrapped in barbed wire. He put aside the Thompson, rolled up his sleeve and checked his burn-mark; it was throbbing, the U and J a vivid burgundy colour.

'Another scar for the collection,' said Patrick.

'One I could have done without.'

'Let's make sure it's your last.' Patrick leaned his head back, closed his eyes. 'Try and get some rest, boy.'

Burton held his arm towards the open door, let the breeze soothe the brand. He smelt coal again: thought of Madeleine at home in London, living the perfect little life her husband had decided for her. He wondered how he would react when she told him about their affair. Wondered how his own father felt after Mama vanished; he had never spoken a word about it. Then Burton lay down and let the rocking of the train lull him to sleep.

A hundred miles later he was still awake.

Chapter Thirty-Seven

Schädelplatz, Kongo
19 September, 12:40

BEFORE him lay all of middle Africa.

Hochburg was in the operations room of the Schädelplatz, hands behind his back, pacing up and down. There was a hum of conversation, the *cht-cht-cht* of telex machines.

He was waiting for a radio call.

In front of him: a ten by four metre table map of the region marked with black triangles. Heading from Matadi towards Loanda was the Afrika Korps (90 Light Division, 6th Urwald Panzer), their exact position unknown because Arnim refused to send updates to the Schädelplatz; everything on Operation Nelke had to be relayed via Germania. To the south and south-east, the armies of the Waffen-SS bound for Northern Rhodesia. Military engineers were building a pontoon over the Lulua River ready to transport the first panzers. So much for the field marshal's threat not to help! The Wehrmacht liked to delude itself, but in the end would always surrender to the will of the SS. *Der Elefant*, the fabled conqueror of Africa, was nothing more than a circus animal.

Meanwhile another SS battalion had been diverted from the Lulua to the PAA at Elisabethstadt to join the second column attacking from the east. Lusaka would be crushed between two pincers. Soon the whole country would be his and the Einsatzgruppen could begin the process of racial cleansing: the negroid threat to Kongo's southern border eradicated.

Everything was proceeding as Hochburg had planned.

Everything except for the photos he'd been handed that morning. They were from Schwarzflügel aerial reconnaissance. His generals murmured when they saw them. Thirty miles from the Rhodesian side of the border, at Solwezi, was a mass of enemy tanks hidden beneath netting. Hochburg dismissed the pictures: *a training exercise. Coincidence. The Rhodesians haven't had time to prepare.*

Besides, they would be no match for the SS: Britain and its colonies had grown fat on peace.

'Herr Oberstgruppenführer!'

The radio operator held up a phone. Hochburg snatched it from him.

A burst of static. 'Heil Hitler!'

'Yes, yes,' said Hochburg. 'Is he still alive?'

'Yes, Herr Oberstgruppenführer.'

It was Uhrig.

'I saw Cole with my own eyes. The *Amerikaner* too. Over.'

Hochburg felt the blood surge into his throat, cold and exuberant. He gripped the phone till the Bakelite creaked. 'Where is he now?'

'I tracked them to Quimbundo, part of the Salazar Railway. North-east Angola. Over.'

Hochburg scanned the map in front of him. 'I have it.'

'Something happened here. We found lots of bodies. All of them poisoned. Over.'

'What about Cole?'

Another crackle of static.

'There was no train. I assume, Herr Oberstgruppenführer, he's headed for Loanda. Over.'

'Standartenführer, assemble a dozen of your best men. I shall meet you at Quimbundo.' He detailed his instructions.

'My Wolves will be ready. Over.'

'Make sure they are rested but hungry.'

'Yes, Herr Oberstgruppenführer.' A hesitation. 'With respect, Herr Oberst, I was wondering if . . . I want to be re-assigned back to the Einsatzgruppen. Over.'

Hochburg gave an icy smile. 'Get me Cole – *alive* – and I'll promote you to a full general. I'll be with you in three hours. Be ready. Out.'

He turned to the radio operator. 'Send word to Kondolele. I want my Walküres to leave immediately.'

Hochburg walked briskly from the operations room to his study. On his desk were the remainders of the mango and straw-berry trifle he'd eaten for breakfast. Fenris, his Ridgeback, was dozing by the veranda. The dog looked up as he came in. Shook his jowls in greeting.

Hochburg changed out of his dress uniform into a vented black shirt, camouflage trousers and smock; belt with grinning skull buckle, boots that laced up to the shin. To the belt he buckled ammunition pouches, holster and Taurus pistol (another of his Brazilian imports).

In the corner of the room, nestled among the bookshelves, was a gun cabinet. Hochburg unlocked it and took out his BK44. It had been given to him by the Reichsführer himself, a gift for all his efforts in Muspel. The stock was made of brushed steel, the words – *Good Hunting, H.H.* – engraved on it.

Hochburg checked the firing mechanism, took several of the banana-shaped magazines, then went to his desk drawer to retrieve his final weapon: the knife Burton had tried to kill him with, the one he had pulled from his decoy's corpse. It had been whetted to a deadly point, but he recognised it from the silverware Eleanor was so proud of.

After they eloped from the orphanage he had promised to buy her an even more splendid set, but never had the means. They had lived in a cabin near Keta, theirs a simple life of books and passion, swimming in the lagoon. Eleanor had been so happy at first, before the guilt began to gnaw at her. Before dreams of her son and husband woke her at night and she turned her back when Hochburg reached to comfort her.

He slid the drawer shut and knelt by his dog, tickled his chin. Fenris rolled on his side, baring his teeth, gave a growl of satisfaction. And as his fingers raked the animal's coat, a thought struck Hochburg.

His plan was to hunt Burton down ... but the boy was as hellbent on revenge as he was. He glanced towards the maps of Africa on the wall; the bloodstains had been scrubbed off but remained just visible. Faded streaks of vermilion. Burton had stabbed his decoy with a frenzy matched only by the rage in Hochburg's heart.

It had never occurred to him before: what if it was he, *Hochburg*, who didn't return from their confrontation?

He leaned forward, nuzzled Fenris's forehead, and left.

The dog barked as he strode away. A low, pitiful yelping.

Hochburg's helicopter was waiting for him in the middle of the skull-square. Not the Flettner he had let Kepplar use.

But his Walküre gunship.

The Walküre was Focke-Wulf's state-of-the-art attack helicopter; had been commissioned by Odilo Globocnik, the SS Governor of Madagaskar, who wanted a new toy to patrol his island domain. Built at a secret installation in Muspel, the Walküre was a decade ahead of anything the British had. It was capable of two hundred kilometres per hour, armed with a rotating barrel-gun and six Ruhrstahl X-7 rockets. The prototype tests had been completed two months earlier. A mock village was built in the desert and populated by blacks; they were even given rifles and told to defend themselves. Within the hour the Walküre had proven its efficiency.

When Hochburg heard the reports he was minded of Joshua 6:21, the battle of Jericho: '*and they utterly destroyed all that was in the city, both man and woman, young and old, ox and sheep and ass*'. He immediately ordered four of the machines, despite Globocnik insisting they were his helicopters and his alone. Conflicts between the Governors of Africa were not uncommon; in the end, Himmler had to settle the matter.

The pilot was completing his final checks as Hochburg approached. The rotor blades began to spin, were soon at full speed. Hochburg adored the sound, its raw power and fury. He clambered into the bubble cockpit.

Over the radio came a voice: 'Walküre Leader, this is Walküre One. We're approaching the Schädelplatz, over.'

Hochburg pulled on his headset. 'Walküre One, I see you. We're leaving now.'

The helicopter took to the sky.

Below, Hochburg watched the ash from Dolan's pyre swirl round the square, the charcoal stump of his body crumble to nothing.

From the direction of Kondolele came three more Walküres, behind them two other craft. They took up formation behind Hochburg's helicopter: a black arrowhead.

'What bearing, Herr Oberstgruppenführer?' asked the pilot.

'South-west,' replied Hochburg, loading his BK44. 'To Angola.'

Chapter Thirty-Eight

Salazar Railway, North Angola
19 September, 17:25

'I hope this means dinner,' said Burton. 'I'm starved.'

They were in the second cattle-truck. Outside, the trees had given way to grassland and abandoned cotton plantations. The sky was beginning to darken. An hour earlier, after skirting the mountains of central Angola, the train reached Malange. Burton had been in the locomotive with Neliah, shovelling coal into the firebox.

'He's asking, should he slow down?' said Neliah, translating for the driver.

'No. Keep going, as fast as possible.'

They hurtled through the station. Burton glimpsed a blur of Portuguese and Angolan troops – startled white faces – on their way to fight in Loanda. They were one hundred and fifty miles from the capital now.

Zuri handed them two heaped bowls. 'Slave food,' she said. It was a mass of rice and cassava. 'There was nothing else.'

'You never ate desert rations,' said Patrick. 'It'll be a banquet.'

Burton watched him take the bowl and thank her with a smile. She smiled back but her eyes had a distant quality, sad and shy.

When she was out of earshot, Patrick sniffed the food and said, 'What if it's from the same batch as Quimbundo? Poisoned?'

'I'm too hungry to care.'

There were no spoons, so Burton ate with his hands, shovelling the cassava in. It had been mixed with palm oil and chilli, tasted creamy, like the mashed yams his mother used to serve the orphans. He saw her and Hochburg stirring vats together, glancing at each other through the steam.

Patrick picked at his rice. 'I'm trying not to remember our last meal. In Stanleystadt.'

'Don't worry,' said Burton, his mouth full. 'The Lebbs can't find us now.'

'I hope you're right. I keep thinking about Hannah, I got so much to make up.'

'You'll make a good father.'

'Haven't so far.' Patrick chewed pensively for several moments. 'D'you think I should tell her about my life? What I've done? The things I've seen?'

Burton thought about his own unborn child, what he might have to confess one day. 'I don't know. It's what we are but . . . it doesn't make you a bad man.'

'Don't make me a decent one either.'

They continued eating.

'You never did finish your story in the tavern,' said Patrick after a while. 'About Hochburg and your mother.'

Burton felt the cassava clot in his throat. 'There's not much else to tell.'

'What about your father?'

'He was an old man, it broke him. He'd lost his wife and . . . surrogate son.'

'He still had you.'

'He faded away, not even his faith was enough. He prayed – but God didn't answer.'

'Does he ever?'

'Sometimes I'd visit his room and he'd just sit there, clutching my mother's picture, rocking back and forth. I tried talking to him, pleading, begging.' Burton put down his half-finished bowl.

'The orphanage ran wild. I got into fights with the other kids, "sinned" with the girls . . . but nothing roused my father.'

Burton halted, unsure what to say next.

How could he put that time into words? If there was a hell, he was definitely going there. He'd revelled in too much blood to escape that fate; it was the one thing Madeleine couldn't save him from. But he never saw the lake of fire and brimstone St John had promised. When he died he'd be fourteen again, trapped for ever with the familiar view of the Oti River and a hundred parentless kids. His father's silent sobbing in his ears.

'You don't have to say anything,' said Patrick.

'It's okay,' replied Burton. 'I should have told you this long ago. It was two years after my mother vanished that Hochburg returned. He was raving mad, wanted blood. He . . .' Burton hesitated over the detail. 'He chained the orphanage doors, torched the place. I barely escaped. My father didn't bother, just let the fire take him. Most of the kids were burned alive.'

'Jesus.'

'You never heard anything so terrible. That's when I knew what Hochburg was capable of, knew for certain about my mother. I wanted to kill him . . .'

Burton felt the moment again. The orphanage was an inferno, flames roaring and flattening in the wind. A crematorium for all those trapped inside. They had opened their home to Hochburg, given freely of their affection – and this was how he repaid them. Burton stood there limply, face and arms charred, tears scalding his blistered cheeks. And in his heart was a lone yearning. Not for Mama or Father. Not for the children whose screams continued to madden the air. But for Hochburg. Burton conjured up all the punishments of the Bible – Achan stoned to death, Samson's eyes gouged out, Jael hammering a stake through the head of Sisera – and wished them upon him. Wanted to stare him in the face and strike the fatal blow.

'. . . Except he was already dead. Burned with the rest. Or so I believed till Ackerman showed up.'

Burton fell silent, wondering how different his life might have been if he had searched the ruins of the orphanage. Found Hochburg. Instead he had run away, fleeing into the jungle before the dawn broke. All that remained of his past life was the clothes he wore and the few pieces he had salvaged from the blaze: a blackened wind-chime and some silver cutlery.

'I wish I'd known,' said Patrick, 'when you arrived at Bel Abbès. I would have been easier on you.'

'No. I needed what the Legion gave.'

After that they sat in silence, listening to the rhythm of the train. Each second was taking them closer to Loanda. Burton concentrated on that thought, stroked the stubble on his chin: felt comforted by it.

Loanda, home, Madeleine.

Patrick put down his food, stretched. 'I wish I had my pipe.'

'I almost forgot,' said Burton. He reached into his pocket. 'Courtesy of Hauptsturmführer Rottman. Your Zippo too.'

Patrick's eyes danced. 'And how is the good ol' Hauptsturmführer?'

'Let's say his Unterjocher days are behind him.'

Patrick grunted, popped the pipe between his teeth. 'Tobacco?'

Burton shook his head.

'Oh well. Good to have it back.' He tapped the bowl, sucked air through it. Leaned back contentedly. 'Maybe our luck's changing at last. Maybe Ackerman will be waiting with our diamonds and a couple of first-class tickets out of here.'

'That might be too much.'

'D'you think we can trust him?'

Burton shrugged. 'You tell me.'

'I'll admit he didn't betray us – but something still doesn't add up. If he was supplying the Resistance, how come they never heard of him?'

'Neliah said the same.'

'And why risk so much over some mines?' Patrick studied his

pipe. 'It's a high price for a war. Goes against the whole Peace for Empire thing.'

'We'll know soon enough.'

'If he talks.'

'We can always stick his head down the toilet if he doesn't.'

At the other end of the carriage the Herero were clearing away the cooking implements. Neliah helped Zuri with a pail of starchy water, picked it up and went to the open door. Burton watched her silhouette. Watched as the bucket suddenly went loose in her hand.

The shrill blast of a whistle. Once, twice.

Then over and over.

Burton snatched up his Thompson machine gun. Leapt to his feet.

Neliah faced him and yelled: '*Zenga-zeras!*'

'What?'

She pointed out of the train. Burton followed her finger. Cotton fields streaked past, deserted, overgrown. The sinking sun had turned the sky to fire.

Then he saw them: six black carbuncles on the horizon.

Growing by the second.

'What are they?' shouted Patrick.

The first helicopter roared overhead.

The sound mauled Burton's ears, caused him to duck. Hot air pummelled into the carriage. 'Walküres,' he yelled back. 'But I thought they were only prototypes.'

'Looks like somebody's been busy.'

The four gunships criss-crossed above them, their engines blurring the sky. In the distance were two other helicopters which Burton couldn't identify. They hugged the horizon, holding back for now.

Something flashed past the open door.

'Why are they jumping?' shouted Zuri. 'Why are they jumping?'

Burton saw two of the prisoners leap off the train to save

themselves; their bodies bounced off the ground. The others rushed in from the first carriage, faces pale and terrified.

The train was slowing.

He turned to Patrick. 'Major, get to the front and protect the engine. If the helicopters hit it we're dead. And see if you can speed us up, fast as possible. Take Zuri—'

'No.' Neliah stood in front of her. 'Zuri stays with me.'

Her sister pushed past, tied the red sash tight around her waist and joined Patrick. 'I want to fight!'

'Get up there,' said Burton. 'Give the spare guns to the Herero and prisoners. Tell them to aim for the cockpit or the rotor blades.'

Patrick and Zuri gathered a stack of rifles. Moved out.

'Wait!' Neliah reached to touch her sister, but she was already gone.

'Don't worry,' said Burton, hustling her and Tungu in the opposite direction. 'Patrick will keep her safe.'

They reached the end of the carriage and jumped across the coupling to the platform at the rear of the train. There was an anti-aircraft gun protected by a wall of sandbags. Burton recognised it as an old Breda 35, probably a relic from the desert war in North Africa a decade earlier; he prayed it still worked. Stacked up behind it, next to the crates of dynamite Neliah had found at the station, were strips of ammunition.

Burton grabbed one and, showing Neliah and Tungu what to do, loaded the gun. There was a reassuring *clunk*. Then he jumped into the gunner's seat, spun the wheel that rotated the base and squinted through the sight.

Neliah was staring at the horizon, at the other two helicopters. 'Why are they waiting?'

Burton ignored her, tracked the nearest Walküre.

He pulled the trigger. Let loose a ferocious barrage of shells. Burton's upper body juddered with the kickback. Neliah and Tungu clamped their hands over their ears.

Above, thick bursts of fire trailed the helicopter. Missed the target.

Burton swore. Wiped the sweat from his face with the back of his arm. Jettisoned the empty strip; each one carried a dozen shells.

'Reload!' he yelled at Neliah and Tungu.

They slammed more ammunition into the gun.

Another Walküre came in low behind the train, cannon blazing. The tracks clanged and flashed as the beam of fire surged forward. Bullets chewed into the platform and sandbags. The two Herero girls ducked behind them. Burton smelt hot steel and grit.

He lined up the helicopter in his sights. The pilot was swerving left to right. Burton followed the movement, a madman watching a pendulum. Unblinking.

Left to right. Left to right.

He fired. Two shots.

Missed.

Fired again—

The cockpit vanished in a ball of flame. Neliah whooped.

Molten debris whipped down on them. Burton felt his face burn as he swivelled the gun to follow another Walküre.

One flashed past, through a wall of smoke, close enough for Burton to see the cockpit clearly. Next to the pilot was a familiar figure. Bald head, black eyes boring into him.

Burton gave a raw, animal scream from deep in his chest. Fired. His finger welded to the trigger. A blaze of shells. Then:

Click.

'Reload!'

'Burton.' Neliah tugged at his shoulder.

'I said reload! Now!' Hochburg was soaring out of range.

Neliah pulled harder. He turned to her in a rage. Her face was pale, eyes like pinpricks. She pulled him one last time, before burrowing into the sandbags.

He looked up. Another gunship was almost upon them. It fired: a rocket ripping through the air.

Burton hurled himself on top of Neliah.

*

Patrick and Zuri reached the engine. Hot oily brass, steam. The driver cowered in the corner, hands over his head. Patrick yanked him to his feet. 'Get this thing moving!'

'I . . . I can't.'

The helicopters screamed through the air above, the smoke stack from the engine whirling like a tornado. In the first car the prisoners were taking pot-shots.

'Why not?' said Patrick.

The driver didn't give a reason, simply pulled away and squeezed himself back in the corner.

Patrick shoved his rifle into his face. 'Do it or I'll blow your fucking head off.'

The driver sank to his knees.

Zuri grabbed him, shoved him towards the control panel. '*Agora!*'

Hands shaking, he twisted a valve. Patrick felt the pressure in the engine build, the pistons pumping faster. Above them the stack began to thicken.

The driver checked some dials, glanced nervously at Patrick. He stepped back and using a metal hook lifted a panel in the floor to expose the firebox. There was a blast of heat, like a desert kiln. 'We need more fuel,' he said.

Patrick clambered on to the tender and began shovelling down coal. Zuri and the driver swept it into the firebox, re-stoked the engine.

An explosion.

Patrick stumbled on the coal, the shockwave almost knocking him off his feet. He looked up. Burton had taken out one of the Walküres. Was already tracking another, gun blazing; oblivious to the helicopter coming in from the other side.

A warning cry rose in Patrick's throat – but it was useless.

The Walküre fired. The back of the train erupted in fire and claw marks of smoke.

'Neliah!' Zuri scrambled up the tender next to him. 'Neliah!'

'No,' said Patrick, trying to pull her back. But she tore from his grip, down the coal and towards the first carriage, her red sash snapping behind her.

The Walküre that fired the rocket zoomed over the train before circling back for another shot. With it came the two helicopters that had been shying away from the battle so far.

Patrick's eyes shrank with dismay.

He flicked a glance over the side, wondered if he should try his luck and jump. He had his pipe back, might just survive. Then he leapt back into the engine, snatched up his Enfield rifle and returned to the tender. He lay flat, lumps of coal poking against his ribs, black dust in his nostrils. Patrick took several deep lungfuls of air. Steadied his breathing.

The two troop carriers came in low.

The first hovered over the near car. Doors opened on both sides. Patrick could see right through: a silhouette of stormtroopers against the fading orange light. Ropes were thrown out, the soldiers took their positions.

Began to abseil on to the train.

Patrick zeroed the V-notch on the pilot. He saw him clearly in the bubble of the cockpit: he was focused on the roof below, guiding the joystick, trying to keep his helicopter perfectly positioned. His eyes were hidden behind a visor.

At the far end of the train there was another explosion. Munitions streaked the sky.

Patrick ignored it, held his breath. Judged the wind velocity and downdraught. Fifty knots at about forty, forty-two degrees. He aimed high. Three and half feet to the right, well above the cockpit. Squeezed the trigger. Felt the recoil snap his shoulder.

Nothing happened.

The troops kept coming. Their boots inches from touching down.

Then he saw it.

Patrick exhaled. A black thread trickled from under the pilot's visor. Directly between the eyes. Burton's words echoed in his head: *you're still the best shot I know.*

The pilot slumped forward, driving the joystick between his legs.

The Walküre banked hard left. Some of the soldiers let go of their ropes, bounced off the roof over the sides, their screams snatched away by the wind. The others clung on. Were dragged with the gunship as it smashed into the ground.

There was a cloud of fire. Lethal spears of rotor blade exploded in all directions. Patrick buried his face into the coal, covering his head. Hot splinters lashed his arms and back.

Another Walküre descended on the tender, scouring it with cannon fire.

He had no choice but to throw himself backwards into the engine, use its walls for cover. Bullets zinged inches from his head, puncturing the metal. The driver curled himself into a ball, screaming one moment, silent the next: half his chest gone.

Patrick lifted his Enfield to take a shot at the helicopters – but the onslaught was too fearsome. Brass casings rained down on him.

Behind the Walküre, protected by its gunfire, Patrick glimpsed the other troop carrier. It hovered over the second carriage. Ropes were thrown out.

Next moment, stormtroopers began to descend.

The floor looked as if it had been mopped with blood. Everything rocked from side to side.

Burton could barely breathe, his lungs choked with what his father would have called *das Höllenfeuer*, hellfire. He pushed himself up, shook the sand from his hair.

The platform and sandbags were ablaze. The Breda gun a buckled wreck.

Neliah was hunched over Tungu, trying to lift her up. She failed, slipped on the blood-soaked floor. A jagged triangle of metal was buried deep in Tungu's back, blood spewing from the wound. Her eyes already glassy.

The Walküre that had fired the rocket was coming round to attack again.

Still dazed, Burton reached over for the crate of dynamite, struggling not to slip on the floor. He opened the box, grabbed one of the bundles and twisted the timer to twenty seconds. *Twenty, nineteen* . . . Shoved it back in with the rest of the explosives.

The Walküre was descending.

'Quick!' said Neliah.

He grabbed his Thompson and together they jumped through the flames on to the next carriage. Burton immediately got to his knees and reached for the coupling that linked the carriage to the platform. The ground thundered below him, inches from his hand.

He cranked the disconnecting rod, still counting the seconds in his head, *ten, nine, eight* . . . Next, prised up the hook that connected the two parts of the train. Released it. The buffers strained . . . then tore apart, snapping the vacuum pipe between the two. There was a hiss and the brakes fired automatically.

The gun platform began to fall back. The Walküre honed in on it.

. . .*Five, four, three* . . .

Burton and Neliah watched the pilot bring the gunship level with the platform. The wind from the rotors flecked the air with Tungu's blood.

The Walküre fired another rocket.

. . .*Two, one.*

The dynamite exploded, igniting the rest of the munitions like a huge Roman candle.

Bolts shot into the air, glowing red and white. A sound that burned Burton's ears. He thought of Dolan, how much he'd have enjoyed the spectacle, could almost hear his chortle of approval: BOOM!

The fire rained down on the Walküre, catching its engine. The pilot pulled away. Smoke trailed from the gunship's exhaust port. It spun wildly, clipped the ground, bounced once, twice, crashed into the railway line.

There was no whoop from Neliah this time. 'Tungu,' she whispered next to Burton. He glanced at her. There was a livid burn on her forehead; her face was set hard.

Suddenly another explosion at the front of the train. Another helicopter reduced to fire and atoms. Its burning hulk streaked by spitting flames.

Burton turned towards the locomotive. One of the Walküres strafed it while another helicopter – a troop carrier – positioned itself above them.

'Move!' said Burton, pulling open the carriage door, thrusting Neliah in. They raced through it, knocking over the food bowls. Overhead the deafening clack of rotor blades. The thud of boots landing on the roof.

Burton fired upwards. He heard a bloody cry. Saw a body plummet off the roof.

Then a gust of wind. The door at the far end of the carriage was kicked open.

In stepped a hulking SS trooper. Slaughterhouse eyes, face smeared with camouflage paint. He was gripping an MG48.

Uhrig.

Chapter Thirty-Nine

THE clatter of the helicopters faded as they pulled away from the train. In its place the wind rushing through the open door, the relentless thunder of the railway. Overhead, Burton heard boots tramp towards the back of the carriage. Several stormtroopers armed with BK44s stood behind Uhrig.

'So you're Cole,' he said, scrutinising him. He seemed unimpressed.

Burton showed no reaction.

Next to him, Neliah took a step forward, her fist tight around her panga. 'His shoulder,' she hissed. Wrapped around Uhrig's armpit was a ribband of plaited black hair.

Zuri's hair.

Burton could feel the rage emanating from Neliah. Red-hot, deadly. He held out his hand to ward her off.

Uhrig saw the movement. Sneered. 'I always prefer them with a bit of fight. Like that bitch at the camp. Pity I didn't get a go on her myself.'

Burton placed himself between Uhrig and Neliah, began treading backwards, pushing her with him. His boots squished the rice and cassava on the floor.

Uhrig raised his MG48. 'There's no way off this train, Cole. My Wolves have it covered. Put down your weapon, the nigger too.' The train rocked to the left. 'The Governor General wants you alive.'

There was a burst of gunfire from behind Uhrig. He snapped around. Two of his men fell back, their torsos erupting. Someone was shooting from the roof above.

'Zuri!' said Neliah.

Burton fired his Thompson, bullets ricocheting round the walls. Pushed himself and Neliah back. 'Go!' He thrust her towards the far door. Let off another round of fire and followed.

They burst out into the fading daylight, to the ledge at the rear of the carriage. The Walküres were circling at a distance now. Huge black hornets waiting for their honey. From the roof Burton heard the scuffling of boots. A soldier was climbing down.

In a single movement Neliah swung her panga into his calf. A spurt of blood. He screamed, dropped his rifle. Neliah prised her blade out of his leg as Burton grabbed him and hurled him from the train.

'Cover me!' he said, handing Neliah the machine gun and climbing upwards.

On top the savannah flashed past even faster. The edge of the roof was sticky with blood. Through the funnel of smoke he saw Zuri and several of the others on the first carriage firing downwards. Bullets flared back. One of the Herero was hit: she keeled off the train.

Burton offered Neliah his hand. She gave him the gun, then pulled herself up, spying Zuri and darting towards her.

'Careful,' said Burton.

The train was swaying from side to side. He followed, kept his weapon trained on the rear of the carriage, eyes alert for Hochburg's helicopter. Each step was like walking on greased flagstones. He felt too high up, the sensation somehow worse than the rooftops of Stanleystadt.

Something was tossed after him. A flash-grenade. Burton tried to swipe it away.

BANG!

His ears popped, vision flaring white and green. The train lurched to the side. Burton lost his footing. Landed on his front, spread his limbs and struggled not to slide off.

Bullets ripped through the roof close enough for him to smell sawdust and soot.

'Burton!'

He looked up, the wind beating his face. Neliah had slipped off the roof, was clutching the edge. On the other carriage Zuri had stopped firing. Stood and stared helplessly.

'Burton!'

From the corner of his eye he saw one of the Walküres dip its nose and hurtle back towards the train. Burton looped the strap of his Thompson around his neck, crawled towards Neliah. There was a handrail along the edge of the roof: her fingers were clamped round it. He held out his hand. Stretched as far as he could.

Another few inches, just another few inches . . .

Grasped hold of her.

Burton pulled, forced himself not to think of that long moment as Rougier had slipped from his grip. She wasn't heavy: was already back on the roof, her eyes bright with relief.

Suddenly Neliah was dragged down again, pulling Burton with her. 'He's got me,' she cried. 'He's got me!'

Through the roof Burton heard Uhrig strain as he tried to haul her legs inside.

The Walküre roared overhead, knocking Zuri and the prisoners off their feet. Smoke slapped into Burton's face: hot flecks of soot. He screwed his eyes shut, felt his arm muscles stretch to tearing point as he tugged on Neliah. She was kicking Uhrig. Burton heard her boots flick and thud against him. He pulled again. Used all his strength.

Without warning she was free.

Burton continued to heave, pulling Neliah on to the roof, sliding right across it to the other side. He let go of her. Tumbled over the edge. Just managed to hook his fingers round the handrail. The strap of the Thompson cut into his neck.

Beneath him the ground rushed past.

Neliah grabbed his collar. Struggled to haul him back on the roof. The force of the wind rammed itself into his mouth.

Then a splintering sound.

Uhrig was breaking the side of the carriage to get to him. A meaty hand smashed right through. Snatched at him. Burton kicked back. Heaved himself up. Kicked again.

The hand vanished. More splintering planks and Uhrig's face was in the hole: leering pockmarked cheeks. Burton raised his boot. Stamped down. Managed to lever himself back on to the roof.

He unwound the machine gun from his neck. Looked at Neliah. Tears streamed down her face; her shoulder was bulging from its socket, dislocated.

At the far end of the carriage more soldiers were clambering up. Burton fired a ragged salvo from his Thompson: clipped one, made the others duck. Then he ran with Neliah, leaping from the second carriage, tumbling into Zuri and the prisoners on the next.

Burton thrust Neliah into Zuri's arms. 'It's her shoulder. Get her to Patrick.'

Neliah squeezed his arm, stared intently into his eyes. 'Twice I owe you my life.'

'No blood oaths, remember.' He slammed his last magazine into the Thompson. 'Get to the front!'

With that Burton dropped into the well between the two carriages below. The sound of the tracks was deafening; smoke poured out of the first carriage. The soldiers Zuri had gunned down were sprawled on the floor. Burton knelt, began to untwist the coupling hook.

Someone kicked him from behind.

Burton tumbled forward, dropped the Thompson over the side. He felt hands round his neck, his windpipe being crushed.

Burton rammed himself backwards, smashed his assailant into the carriage wall. For an instant the grip round his throat slackened, then squeezed even harder. Burton choked. He was swept off his feet. His head thrust between the coupling.

The ground thundered past. Inches from his face.

A blur of sleepers and stone. The smell of a sandstorm.

Burton squeezed his eyes shut, fumbled for the disconnecting rod and spun it till it was loose. His jugular was turning numb.

'Standartenführer! I've got him!'

Burton grabbed at the fingers round his throat. Tore them back. Relished each joint as it snapped. A shriek. Next moment Burton was free.

He stood, vision swimming, spun round. *Duka.* The soldier tumbled back, his nose smeared scarlet. Burton grabbed him, hurled him head first between the carriages. He flew on to the tracks, skull bursting like a watermelon.

Burton released the coupling: the second carriage began to slow.

'Cole!'

Uhrig and another stormtrooper had reached the edge – but the gap was already too wide to leap.

Uhrig gave a murderous roar, as thwarted and furious as a dog on a chain. Next moment he was climbing on to the roof of the carriage. Burton thought he was going to jump after him. *He's crazy. He'll never make it.* But Uhrig was beckoning to the troop carrier. It answered his call, swooped down on the slowing carriage, ropes dangling from its side. Uhrig and the stormtrooper grabbed them.

Burton climbed on to the roof, pulled out his Browning. He was met by wild eyes and the barrel of a gun: Zuri.

The troop carrier lifted into the sky. Burton watched Uhrig swinging beneath its landing gear.

'Move!' he said to Zuri.

She ignored him, a guttural whine erupting in her throat. She fired at Uhrig, emptied the magazine. Bullets flickered on the underbelly of the helicopter.

'Move!' he said again, tugging on her arm.

Reluctantly she followed, glancing back at Uhrig as he cut through the air. They reached the end of the carriage, jumped on to the tender, crashing into the coal.

The troop carrier descended towards the first carriage, its down-draught swirling smoke everywhere. Soot stung Burton's eyes.

Uhrig's boots were twenty feet from the roof.

Burton jumped down to the coupling. Fought to release it.

Fifteen feet. Ten.

Five.

A single gunshot.

Patrick was squeezed in the corner of the locomotive, his rifle pointed towards the helicopter above. Eye squinting down the sight.

Another shot.

Burton watched a crack shoot up the glass bubble of the cockpit. The pilot pulled up sharply.

The stormtrooper next to Uhrig jumped. Almost skidded off the roof. Managed to hold on.

Uhrig's face was a snapshot of rage. He glanced down, saw his last chance was about to leave him. Let go of the rope.

He crashed on to the roof, his MG48 skittering over the side. He balanced himself, reached for his holster. Above him the troop carrier drew back into the sky. A Walküre swooped in its place.

Patrick fired at Uhrig. The Nazi grabbed the stormtrooper at his side, held him in front as a shield. Burton heard the bullets thudding into the soldier's chest.

The Walküre roared over, cannons blazing.

Patrick swung round, tailed the helicopter with his rifle. The second remaining gunship was already on its approach.

'Burton!' shouted Patrick. 'I need more firepower.'

Burton released the last carriage's coupling, scrambled over the coal. The carriage began to fall away.

'Set it free!' he shouted at Zuri as he leapt off the tender. He snatched up Patrick's spare Enfield, took up position on the opposite side of the locomotive. They both fired at the Walküres.

Shells whistled and sparked off the engine. The air was notched with steam.

Neliah reached over to help her sister. Zuri waved her away. 'I can do it.'

Burton looked for Hochburg as a Walküre soared over. He fired at the tail rotor. Worked the bolt to reload, glanced down at Zuri. She had unwound the rod, was about to unhook the link.

'Zuri! No!'

She was undoing it from the wrong side. Was still on the tender. An arm looped around her throat. She cried out, kicked back. But Uhrig held tight.

His face was grimy with coal and blood. In his fist: a pistol. Neliah moved to protect her sister.

'Forget it!' said Uhrig. He slammed his Luger against Zuri's skull, then snarled at Burton.

'Stop the fucking train.'

Chapter Forty

ELIAH stared into her sister's eyes. They were red-raw, held a tiny pebble of fear. But mostly rage. *Don't you dare*, they said. *This is what I want. I'm going to kill him. The* rungiro *will protect me.*

Uhrig's gun was digging into her head.

Nobody moved.

Either side the savannah rushed by – emerald, yellow, grey. The sky was turning to night. The two whirr-birds hovered above them like buzzards over carrion. Neliah smelt Quimbundo again, the tables of dead. She had forgotten the pain where her shoulder was pulled loose.

'I said stop the fucking train!' screamed Uhrig. 'Or the nigger's dead.' His face was streaked black with coal.

Patrick stepped backwards and reached for one of the turning-levers.

'No!' said Zuri.

His hand hesitated.

'Do it, *Amerikaner*.'

'No!'

'Shut the fuck up.' The *Nazista* pulled his gun away from Zuri's head, slammed it hard against her face where the bite mark was. The metal came away with a ribbon of blood.

Neliah was unable to control herself.

She dropped her panga, snatched Burton's rifle from him. Aimed it at Uhrig.

Suddenly it was as if the breath had been sucked out of the world. Everything moved like in a dream. Slow as slow.

Neliah watched Uhrig pull his pistol away from Zuri's head, aim it into the train, straight at her chest. The same moment, Zuri heaved backwards, pushed away Uhrig's gun. Sank her teeth into his arm.

There was an ear-burst bang. But the bullet missed.

She saw Zuri bite harder, Uhrig stagger to his knees. He fired again into the *tyndo*.

This time something sparked near Neliah's face. Flicked off the walls. She felt a hot bite in her cheek. Blood. She covered her face and through her fingers saw her sister wrestling with the German. Pride swelled in her heart. Pride . . . and then horror as she understood what Zuri was about to do.

The two sisters looked each other in the eye. Neliah's belly turned to flood water.

Zuri kicked against the joining-hook.

Immediately the coal-wagon was free. Began to fall away.

'Zuri. Jump!'

Her sister struggled forward.

'*Zuri!*'

The gap was no more than ten paces – but it might have been a mountain gorge. Neliah rushed towards the edge of the *tyndo*, wanted to leap after her sister.

Burton grabbed hold of her.

'Let go!' she yelled, fighting.

'You won't make it.'

'My sister!'

'She did it to save you.'

'Zuri!'

She was falling further and further away.

Uhrig stood, his arm wet and red. But Zuri was faster. She

kicked him between the legs, scratched his face. Uhrig swiped her away. Brought his fist smashing down on her collar-bone. Zuri's left side went slack, she dropped. Then lashed out again, unbalancing the *Nazista*. His gun fell from his grip. Neliah watched it vanish into the gloom.

Zuri was back on her feet, fighting to climb the coal-wagon. Uhrig followed.

Neliah felt like her insides were shrinking. Blood ran down her cheek.

Zuri reached the top of the coal, began to crawl towards the far end, her broken side clawing weakly to drag her over.

Jump, sister, thought Neliah. *Fly!*

Behind her Uhrig got to the top of the ladder. Slowly, deliberately, he pulled a dagger from his belt.

Burton's arms squeezed closer around Neliah. 'Don't look,' he whispered into her ear.

But she couldn't tear her eyes away.

Uhrig said something, his words whipped away. He was stroking the plait of hair tied around his shoulder. Zuri turned to face him, eyes fearful. And defiant. Uhrig towered over her, careful to keep out of reach of her swiping legs. He licked his finger, ran it over the blade of his knife.

The blood surged through Neliah's neck.

Zuri grabbed a lump of coal. Threw it at him. Uhrig laughed. She snatched up another, then another. Uhrig lifted his arm to block them. One bounced off his head. He took a step back . . . stumbled . . . lost his footing.

Zuri lunged forward. Kicked his shinbones.

For an instant he hung there – shock on his face – then he dropped from the coal-wagon. Fell into the grass below.

Neliah's heart roared!

'Jesus H. Christ,' said Patrick. He slammed himself against the edge of the *tyndo*, lifted his rifle towards the sky.

The coal-wagon was still slowing, Zuri growing smaller with every heartbeat. The two whirr-birds were circling around it.

Neliah saw her sister curled on top, Penhor's sash whipping round her like a red tail.

Patrick fired a shot. In the wind and smoke it vanished. He fired again.

One of the whirr-birds sank lower till it was the same height as the coal-wagon. Neliah could almost hear the greedy swallow of its guns as it prepared to fire.

'Zuri!'

Her sister glanced back at her. Stretched out her hand.

Neliah struggled in Burton's grip. Held out her own hand, fingers reaching across the tracks into nothing. One last touch, that's all she wanted. To feel the smooth skin of her sister's cheek. To grasp her hands. *Pamue*, together.

Neliah wailed.

The Walküre fired all its weapons. A blinding flash of cannon and rockets. A second later the tender was blown from the rails in a ball of fire.

Burton thought he glimpsed Zuri jump free.

Patrick fired a third shot.

Sparks flared around the rotor blades. Smoke began pouring out of the helicopter's engine. Patrick fired again and again, his mouth misshapen with rage.

The Walküre spun wildly, its tail jerking towards the ground. It caught the tracks, flipped over. And exploded.

Neliah was wailing in Burton's arms. He hugged her into him. Crushed her face into his chest. Felt her sobs shake him.

Patrick lowered the rifle from his eye. 'It's over.' His voice was lifeless.

The final Walküre soared over them and away.

Burton followed it, saw Hochburg again. There was a look of intense curiosity on his face, frustration and bloodthirsty rage. His eyes were as black as Burton remembered them as a child. Hochburg gave him a mocking wave.

Then the gunship headed west, into the sinking sun, becoming smaller and smaller.

Burton rested his head against Neliah's. Her hair felt coarse, skin feverish. She sagged in his arms.

Patrick reached for the control panel, eased the pressure on the engine. They began to slow. 'The prisoners jumped,' he said softly. 'Zuri saved them from the camp . . . but they jumped.' The wrinkles round his eyes seemed black in the twilight. 'What was the point?'

Suddenly he reached back for the controls. Spun them to full pressure. The train surged forward again, smoke roaring from the funnel.

Burton looked up.

Hochburg's helicopter had turned, was coming back, skimming low over the rails.

Guns blazing.

Bullets screamed round them, a blizzard of scarlet tracer fire. They tore through the metal work. Vents of steam scalded Burton's arms. There was a tremendous bang. The sound of ripping steel.

The train began to slow.

Hochburg was heading straight for them. The tracks ahead an inferno of cannon fire.

Burton felt his stomach shrivel. 'We have to jump.'

'We'll never make it.'

Even with the train slowing the ground was still a lethal blur. 'If we don't we're dead for sure.'

Burton raised Neliah's face. Her eyes stared right through him, chin crumpled. 'We're going to jump.'

No reply.

'Neliah! We're going to jump. Do you understand?'

She nodded blankly.

'This is fucking crazy,' said Patrick.

Shells continued to rain down on them. The locomotive glowed with each bullet.

Burton secured his Browning in his belt, then picked up Neliah's panga and moved her to the edge. Her head was twisted in the direction of Zuri. She was whispering something.

Patrick joined them.

'On three,' said Burton, struggling to keep the cassava in his gut from rising to his throat. 'Like in the Legion.' He curled his hand into Neliah's, tightened the other round the panga. Gripped the handle till his knuckles stung.

More gunfire. The train charged forward.

Oh, Maddie, he thought. He could smell the honeysuckle scent of her hair.

'One.'

The Walküre was almost on them.

'Two . . .'

Burton hesitated.

He never got to three.

Part Four

LOANDA

Hot over African ground, the sun is glowing
Our panzer engines sing their song . . .
The tracks rattle, the guns roar
Panzers roll in Africa!

AFRIKA KORPS MARCHING SONG

Chapter Forty-One

Salazar Railway, North Angola
19 September, 18:10

WHEN Hochburg found her she was still alive.
He had ordered the pilot to search the wreckage
of the train for Burton. The remains were strewn
along the track: several hundred metres of flame and twisted
metal. The helicopter's spotlight probed the mulberry darkness.

'There!' said Hochburg. 'I see someone.'

The Walküre set down and he strode through the wind of the
rotor blades. Smoke stung his eyes. He was in an overgrown
cotton field littered with debris and clumps of fire. White tufts
whorled around him like he was walking in a snowstorm. There
was a reek of scorched metal.

And crawling through the dirt – a nigger.

She was young and from the shape of her skull (the nasal
guttering, the angle of the prognathism) most likely Bantu-Herero.
There was a red sash tied around her waist soaked in blood.

Hochburg stilled his disappointment at not finding Burton.
Rolled her over with his boot to see her better. She was lacerated with wounds, her skin badly burned, leg broken, the femur
protruding through the flesh of her thigh. Tears mixed with blood
streamed down her face.

When she saw him she struggled to crawl faster. Failed. Curled herself into a crooked ball; she whimpered as her leg scraped the ground.

Hochburg squatted on his haunches next to her. Spoke softly in Bantu.

'Where's Burton? What happened to him?'

She seemed startled to hear him speak her own language, but made no reply.

Behind them the rotor blades of the Walküre continued to spin, whipping smoke around the wreckage.

'Where?'

Again she said nothing. Hochburg put his hand on her thigh, feeling the wet canvas of her trousers. Ran it along to where the bone poked out. Squeezed.

The girl screamed.

'Where?'

She tried to prise away his fingers, was shaking violently. Blood bubbled from her nostrils. Hochburg released his grip, conscious that such methods rarely worked with the blacks.

Years before, as the boundaries of German Africa swelled, the Reichsführer had become queasy at what Hochburg proposed, especially how the British might react if they discovered the truth. Deporting Jews to Madagaskar was one thing, but this . . . He therefore tasked him with writing a treatise on the inferiority of the indigenous races of Africa. It would form the legal and moral basis for the Windhuk Decree and their plans in Muspel. Hochburg's research, drawing on scholars such as de Lapouge and the craniologist Johann Blumenbach, showed that the negroid brain was substantially different to that of Europeans (Slavs obviously excluded). That their understanding of pain was particularly crude – more akin to that of apes or cattle.

He knew no amount of physical persuasion would get the girl to talk.

Hochburg moved his hand from her leg to her face, brushed her cheek with his icy fingers. 'I can make it go away,' he soothed.

'Make it all better, but you have to help me. I need to know where Burton is.'

She pushed him off. Then pointed to her mouth, beckoned him forward so she could speak. Hochburg leaned in till he felt her breath against his face. It was sweet, heavy with blood. She whispered something. He pressed closer.

The movement was slow. The girl grabbed a rock, tried to smash it against his skull.

It glanced off feebly.

Hochburg grabbed her wrist, dug his nails into her tendons. She dropped the stone.

'Stupid girl!'

'*Quamuis multos necaueris . . .*'

'What?'

She was saying something. It sounded like Latin.

Hochburg pressed his ear to her mouth. She was too weak to be a threat now.

'*Quamuis multos necaueris . . . successorem tuum occidere non poteris.*'

Hochburg pulled back, caught her eyes: a stare of pathetic defiance.

'"No matter how many of us you kill,"' he translated, '"you will never kill your successor." Seneca's advice to Nero.'

She looked crestfallen.

'An educated nigger, whatever next.'

His hand returned to her thigh, hovered over the bone. He saw ants teeming around the base of the wound, swimming through a river of blood. 'Tell me where Burton is.'

But the girl had closed her eyes. Her breathing rapid and shallow. She was murmuring something, over and over.

He leaned in again.

'I'm scared, *Papai* . . . so scared . . .'

In those whisperings Hochburg heard Eleanor's final words again. Felt that moment when she freed her hand from his. Over the years he'd played it endlessly in his mind. What did she fear?

The beckoning silence? God's judgement? That she would never see her son again? He had never felt so powerless.

Nearby Hochburg heard someone crash through the cotton plants, coming towards him.

He reached forward and covered the girl's nose and mouth with his hand. Her eyes flickered. He pressed harder, crushed her lips. Felt her last tugs of breath. Blood and saliva seeped between his fingers.

'Shhh, child,' he said as she struggled. My little black buttons, he used to call them at the orphanage; Eleanor always smiled at that.

He held his hand there till she was dead. Then stood, wiped his palms clean on his trousers.

The crashing was getting closer. Hochburg turned in the direction of the sound: saw a silhouette against the glare of the Walküre's searchlight. He pulled his pistol.

'Fucking black bitch!'

Uhrig lurched forward, dagger in hand. His head was a mess of congealed blood; flesh could be seen glistening through the tears in his uniform. The hand without the knife hung limply at his side.

He crashed down next to the girl and drove his knife into her again and again, the blade puncturing every part of her body.

'Enough,' said Hochburg.

The frenzy continued.

'I said: enough!'

Uhrig spun round, his mouth a knot of rage. For an instant Hochburg thought he was going to attack him. Then he lowered the dagger. 'Yes, Herr Oberstgruppenführer.'

'I need your energies elsewhere. How are your injuries?'

'They're nothing.' He spat a gob of blood on the dead girl. 'I can still fight, Herr Oberst.'

Hochburg gave him an indulgent smile. 'We'll make a general of you yet, Standartenführer.'

'And Cole?'

They began walking back to the helicopter. 'We'll never find him in the dark,' replied Hochburg. He felt a calm resignation, that moment of breathless silence before a flame ignites.

'Then what?'

'You said it yourself. These tracks lead all the way to Loanda.'

'But he could go anywhere in the city.'

'No,' said Hochburg. 'The only place that makes sense now is the British consulate.'

'How do you know he won't head straight for the docks? Get on a boat.'

'Have a little faith, Standartenführer. Wherever he goes, we will be waiting.'

They reached the Walküre. Behind it the remaining troop carrier had set down, a crack visible in its windscreen.

'Get on board,' said Hochburg, 'Tell the pilot to follow us. We'll see to your wounds at our next destination.'

He watched Uhrig limp away; then climbed into his own helicopter, took out a map and put on his headset. Static crackled in his ears.

'Schädelplatz, this is Hochburg.'

More static, then: 'Receiving you, Oberstgruppenführer. Over.'

'Where are my panzers?'

'Both columns are approaching the border with Northern Rhodesia. Will be in attack position by midnight.'

'Any resistance?'

'None reported.'

'And what of Operation Nelke? Have the Afrika Korps reached Loanda yet?'

'Germania says they're near the outskirts of the city, Herr Oberst. Plan to attack at first light the day after tomorrow. Over.'

'Why the delay?'

'It has been agreed between the Portuguese and Field Marshal Arnim. To allow civilians to escape.'

Hochburg curled his lip. 'Arnim the merciful. I hope it only extends to whites.' He scanned the map, tapped a point forty kilometres north-east of Loanda. 'I need more men and weapons. Send a company of Waffen-SS to Caxito. There's an airfield there; it should be in our hands by now.' He considered Uhrig's words about the docks, Burton escaping by boat. 'Some inflatables too, high-power.'

'At once, Oberstgruppenführer. Over.'

'Out.'

Hochburg buckled himself in, ordered the pilot back into the sky.

The gunship lifted off, its search-beam illuminating the scene below. Hochburg glimpsed the tracks vanishing towards Loanda, the dead girl. The light reflected on her skin: a kaleidoscope of blood.

Then the Walküre soared away and left her body to the jackals.

Chapter Forty-Two

Loanda, North Angola
21 September, 03:00

IF Burton could name it, it hurt.

His brain was pulsing in his skull, his jaw bone slack and swollen, lips split. There were welts on his arms, chest, shoulders. Bruises spreading like ink dropped in water. The knuckles on his right hand – his gun hand – had been split open, were now covered in a knot of bandages; it was excruciating to flex his fingers. On his legs: more bruising and cuts. The ligaments around his knee felt frayed. Each step jarred the bones in his feet. Even the hard lump of bone behind his ear, that place Madeleine loved to nuzzle so much, was tender.

He had been daydreaming of her for the past few hours. He was back on the farm lying in a cold bath, wounds turning numb, Maddie gently massaging his body. Fingertips and soap suds, black hair trailing in the water. The last time anyone else bathed him he'd been a child. He reached out for her, brushed the solid curve of her belly. The whole world seemed still, at rest. *Boy or girl?* she whispered.

Burton had never wanted her or his bed so much.

They had reached Loanda, were trudging through the Cita Alte district towards the British consulate. Founded in 1573, Angola's capital was the oldest European city in southern Africa: the Paris of the sub-Sahara. Currently it lay in darkness, almost every light turned off or blacked out. There was a haunted feel to the place, thought Burton. The streets were empty, nothing but dust and the occasional Ford Vedette screeching round corners. Packs of abandoned dogs roamed the gutters. Once they passed some black Angolan soldiers as they erected a barricade: planks and wooden crates to stop an army of grinding steel.

Just as Burton had been about to say 'three' Hochburg's gunship had blasted a hole in the railway line. A girder clanged against the locomotive. Next instant the train careered off the tracks and down an embankment, the cab rolling over and over.

Burton was slammed to the floor. Everything turned grey, blurry, misshapen. He felt scalding heat against his face. A physical concussion of noise: bangs, the shriek of metal, Neliah screaming. His body became a mannequin tossed in a storm. Lumps of coal thundered down on him. Finally, just when it seemed the maelstrom would never end, the train ground to a shuddering halt.

A sound: like sand running down a chute.

For a few dazed moments Burton thought he was back in the crashed Gotha, could hear Nares gasping.

He struggled to stand. Threw up. His whole face was limp, tendrils of blood and vomit dribbled from his mouth. In the distance he heard the whirl of Hochburg's helicopter. He groped around for Patrick and Neliah. Hauled them to their feet; they were ragdolls. They grabbed the medical bag and what weapons they could find and crawled out of the wreckage. The world lurched back and forth.

'Come on!' said Burton, his voice slurred.

They limp-ran through the fire and swirling cotton. Fled into the dusk.

By morning they had reached the town of Barraca, sixty miles south-east of the capital; it was burned out and deserted. Burton found a battered Pegaso lorry which he drove till the tank was dry. From there they walked, passing through a flood of refugees heading in the opposite direction. Nearly all the faces they saw were white.

'There's nowhere for my people to go,' said Neliah. 'Nowhere but Muspel. We must stay for the battle.'

Burton gave a weary, ironic laugh. 'A white city with only blacks to defend it.'

'A white country, a white colony.'

'Then why fight?'

'It's the last hope we have.'

Burton thought about her words, felt something sluice around his gut. 'Halifax could have stopped this, saved Angola.' Another ironic laugh. 'Saved the whole damned continent.'

'Who is Halifax?'

'Our leader. The great man of peace. There are plenty of troops in Rhodesia, he should have ordered them in.'

'But he did nothing.'

'No. He cared too much about Empire.'

'And those he leads?'

'It was easier to look the other way. Same with Windhuk – the deportations, the rumours about Muspel.'

'Why?'

'Because if we admitted what was happening we'd have been forced to act. And nobody wanted to fight or see British coffins coming back home. Not over Africa. Not over . . .' He couldn't finish the sentence, not in Neliah's presence: it was too shameful.

'It would make no difference,' she said. 'The *Nazistas* love death too much. It is the air they breathe.'

He glanced at her. She was rubbing the scar on her temple as if it stung; her other hand was welded to her panga, kept rapping it against her thigh. Her gaze was fixed, eyes puffy and listless. Ever since the train he had wanted to hold her, comfort her loss, yet he had done nothing more than silently rub some antiseptic into her wounds. Something made him shy of reaching out even though she had not hidden her tears from him, had kept close to his side the whole time. He sensed a red-hot fury inside her waiting to explode.

'Come with us,' he said. 'Back to England. You'll be safe there.'

'There is an old Herero saying, Burton.' Her voice sounded hollowed out. '*Those who lose their kinsfolk, must live among graves.* I'm not leaving Zuri.'

They trudged on, against the tide of weary, dust-caked bodies, sneaked through the German lines after nightfall, then the meagre Angolan defences, and into the darkness of Loanda.

Next to him Patrick was limping, his Enfield rifle held low against his side. He looked worn to the nub, his face piebald with bruises; the scab on his nose had opened up again. Burton saw him breathe in deep lungfuls of air. Beyond the dust of the city they could both smell it: the Atlantic.

Freedom.

The British consulate was at the end of Rua de Diogo Cão, nestled among palms and flame trees. A fragment of home, mused Burton. Just seeing its white stucco frontage, the Union Jack fluttering above, filled him with a guarded relief. He felt a lull in his muscles as if he could sleep for a month.

'It reminds me of the churches in Spain,' said Patrick.

With its tower and baroque windows Burton agreed. He checked the defences as they approached: eight-foot perimeter wall, barrier and wrought-iron gates, sentry box. A dozen marines on guard duty. Parked along the pavement was a line of cars, engines revving, ready to rush people away.

Opposite the consulate was the Ministerio de Saude building. The three of them huddled beneath its walls.

'Are you sure about this?' said Patrick.

Burton nodded. 'Ackerman might be able to get us out of here. He's also the one with the answers.'

'I still think we should be careful. He may not be overly thrilled to see us.'

'Me and Neliah will go in first. You stay here. Give us ten minutes.'

'Then what?'

'You'll think of something.'

'The docks are two and a half miles in that direction,' replied Patrick, jerking his head towards the bay.

'Very funny.'

'Don't worry. You don't give me the okay, I come in all guns blazing.'

'You sound like Dolan.'

Patrick considered his words. 'Actually, Dolan always sounded like me.'

Burton checked his Browning – he had only two bullets left – and gave it to Patrick for safe-keeping. Then he turned to Neliah and said, 'They won't let us in with weapons.'

She unstrapped the panga from her back, but didn't hand it over. '*Comandante* Penhor used to come here,' she said, staring up at the tower. 'To get weapons for the *Resistencia*. Once he came back with a dress for Zuri, white with lace. Nothing for me. She wanted to share it, but I always said no. I was so jealous.'

Burton didn't know what to say. He took her hand, carefully prised the panga from her fingers, and guided her towards the consulate.

'Be careful,' Patrick called after them.

The marines at the gate wore steel helmets, carried Sten sub-machine guns. Burton saluted the sergeant, gave his name and rank and asked to see Ackerman. The sergeant dispatched one of his men indoors. Several minutes later he returned with an official dressed in pinstripe trousers and waistcoat, sleeves rolled up. The waistcoat looked tighter than a straitjacket.

'Farrow,' he said, extending his hand. His face was a mixture of aristocrat and thug. He had a long forehead and retreating hair, fine cheek bones; boxer's nose, scars. He seemed that fixer-type the British were so fond of in Africa: as efficient as they were expedient, vaguely honourable. Men who did things without needing to ask why. 'Good to see you again, Major Cole.'

'We know each other?'

Farrow looked him up and down. 'You were slightly less battered last time. Stanleyville, 1944. You helped get some of our people out.'

Burton had a vague recollection. 'I remember the waistcoat.'

'I remember the price tag, got a rollicking for it back in London. Now it seems you're the one who needs the help. Understand you're looking for Lieutenant Colonel Ackerman.'

'*Lieutenant Colonel?* Yes.'

'You work for him.'

Burton hesitated. 'Do you?'

'Heavens no! I'm Colonial Office, have nothing to do with that end of the corridor. My job is to get everyone out, preferably safe and sound.'

'Is Ackerman here?'

Farrow eyed his injuries again. 'You'd better follow me, Major.'

He led Burton and Neliah through the gates and across a compound to a set of green double doors. Burton noticed the bulge of a revolver in Farrow's pocket as they followed. Their boots crunched on cinders. Once through the doors they were in a hallway that ran the length of the consulate. Polished wooden floors, an unlit chandelier. The air smelt of paperwork reduced to ash.

'Haven't arrived a moment too soon,' said Farrow, indicating the staircase. 'We're evacuating the place.'

Burton's knee blazed with each step. 'Where to?'

'HMS *Ibis*. She's a Royal Navy frigate moored outside the bay. Most of the staff and their families are already on board. We're just tidying up the last details here now.'

'Haven't the Germans blockaded the port?'

'Of course, even sent an aircraft carrier. The *Strasser*. But Kriegsmarine's instructions are only to stop reinforcements from coming in. As long as we beat the deadline, they're allowing everyone out.'

'Deadline?'

'Actually, have to say Jerry has been rather decent about it given the hullaballoo in Kongo. They could have pounded us into oblivion, but Field Marshal Arnim extended his amnesty to us personally.'

'When does the ship leave?'

They reached the top of the stairs, turned down a corridor.

'Zero six hundred hours, just before the attack starts. I chartered a tug at the docks to take the rest of our people out to her. If you work for Ackerman there'll definitely be a spot. Not so sure about the girl.'

'I don't want a boat,' said Neliah, staring ahead. 'I want to fight. Save Loanda.'

'Good luck! From what I hear you Angolans don't have a chance in hell.'

They had arrived at a door. It was made from polished mpingo wood, brass knob, no nameplate or markings. The typical entrance to an intelligence officer's domain, thought Burton.

Farrow knocked. No answer.

He knocked again and this time opened the door, ushering them through.

They were in an office that looked as if it had been burgled. The bookcases were bare, filing cabinets open and empty, the walls stripped of decoration except for a portrait of the last king. Only a few pieces of furniture remained: pedestal desk, some wooden chairs. On the desk were two flutes and a half-drunk bottle of champagne. The starkness of the room reminded Burton of Hochburg's study.

At the far end was another door, standing slightly ajar. Burton heard voices coming from it, a shout of laughter.

Farrow cleared his throat. 'Lieutenant Colonel.'

The voices fell silent. Seconds later the door opened wider. There was a familiar scent of citrus cologne.

Out stepped Ackerman.

He was wearing an olive-green dress uniform, a single pip and crown on the lapels. His silver hair was dyed jet black. If he was startled to see Burton he made no show of it. He straightened his cuffs.

'Major Cole,' he said, 'I must confess, I never expected to see you again.' He looked from Burton to Neliah. 'It seems your reputation is . . .'

The blood drained from his face.

Burton turned to the girl at his side. Her mouth was wide with shock. Then it tightened, her eyes flashing black and wild.

'*Bastardo*,' she hissed. '*Omu-runde!*'

And hurled herself at Ackerman.

Chapter Forty-Three

IF only she had her panga. She would have cut his balls off.

For a long moment Neliah had been too shocked to do anything. She stared at him as he came out of the second door and her breath stuck in her throat.

Then she leapt across the table, smashing over the bottle. Snarled like a mongoose dropped in a basket of snakes. She crashed into him, knocked him to the ground. Fists pelting his face. All the while hearing Zuri's heartbroken cries in her head. Beautiful Zuri. She should have leapt to save her. They should have died together. Neliah had failed her sister.

She slammed her fist into his nose. Saw blood.

A hand grabbed her arm from behind. 'What are you doing?' said Burton.

'He's a traitor!'

'No. This is Ackerman.'

'*Omu-runde!*' She pulled free. Let her fists fly again.

Then the click of a gun, close in her ear.

'I'd rather not shoot you – but I will if I have to.' It was the *vara*-man, Farrow. 'Get off the lieutenant colonel, and back away.'

She continued to struggle.

Farrow stepped closer. 'Major, tell her.'

'Neliah,' whispered Burton. 'Let him go.' He helped her stand, kept his fingers curled around her wrist. His face was a river of confusion. 'What are you doing?' he asked.

'Penhor,' she said. 'He's Penhor.'

She watched the *comandante* get to his feet and pick up the bottle, its contents foaming on the floor. 'I'd saved it to celebrate,' he said. 'It's a Pol Roger '39. What a damned waste.' He reached inside his pocket for a cloth and dabbed his bloody nose. 'You can put the gun away now, Farrow. Thank you.'

'Shall I call the marines?'

'No need, I'll take care of things from here. You get to the docks and make sure the charter is ready. I don't want to miss that Royal Navy ship.'

Farrow nodded, flicked a puzzled look at Burton and hurried out.

Nobody spoke. Neliah felt her blood still raging.

'You've got some talking to do,' said Burton.

The man she knew as Penhor ignored him, brushed down his uniform, picking off flecks. He didn't seem right in green – blue was his colour, blue with a red sash. 'It's good to see you again, girl,' he said. 'And where's Zuri?'

'What do you care?'

'Where is she?'

Neliah's chest shuddered. Her breath felt like the wind before the rains came. She tried not to think of her sister, twisted and broken in the carcass of the *tyndo*. Or Tungu blown to pieces. Or Bomani curled up in the dirt as the *Nazistas* shot her.

'Dead.'

Penhor's eyes slowly lowered, the rims glistening. 'How?'

When Neliah didn't reply, Burton spoke. 'The Krauts. She died trying to save us.'

'I told her to stay at the camp. Told both of you.'

'We're not just kitchen girls.'

Penhor let out a sigh. 'My poor Zuri.'

'Don't you say that,' hissed Neliah. 'Don't you dare speak her name again!'

'She was very special to me.'

Neliah thought of them together, a nest of black and white limbs. She wanted to throw herself at him again, smash his head against the wall. 'She hated you, Penhor. Thought you an old, leching cockerel. She only lay with you so we could remain at the camp. She was looking after me.'

'I never meant her to get hurt.'

'You know the worst? She wept for you. At Quimbundo. Wept for your wife back in Portugal, your children . . .'

Penhor turned away, wouldn't meet her glare.

Neliah felt sick in her belly.

Silence.

From far, far away came the rumble of aeroplanes. Somewhere in the room Neliah smelt tobacco – like the charutos *Papai* used to smoke when there were times to celebrate.

Suddenly she understood everything. Everything. She went to speak – but couldn't drag the words from her mouth.

'So are you British intelligence?' asked Burton. 'Or part of the Resistance?'

Penhor glanced at the second door before he answered. 'I work for the British . . . "encouraging" the Angolans. They're bloody useless these people. Need constant prodding to keep the pressure on Kongo.'

'And the diamonds?'

'It's true what they said at Dolan's trial. The British have been bankrolling the Resistance. You see, once the Germans controlled the quarries in the south they had no interest in North Angola. Were never going to invade – unless they were provoked. I just gave a helping hand.'

'But why would the British want the Krauts to invade? It doesn't make sense.'

Neliah found her tongue. 'It was you.'

Penhor turned from Burton. Fixed her with a look. 'What?'

'You. You killed them at the railway. Poisoned them.'

Penhor made no reply. He walked over to the thick curtains that blocked the window, parted them and stared at the street below. Neliah saw the ghost of his hand in the glass. Beyond the city was darkness.

'It was Gonsalves's fault,' he said. 'My plan was to return to Loanda with the troops. They would join the defence of the city, I would disappear: get back to the consulate and then Britain. Except Gonsalves wouldn't keep his mouth shut. Kept arguing about the tunnel. *How we must destroy it. That such a task should never have been left to a "nig-girl".*'

'So you fed them poison.'

'I wasn't going to let Gonsalves balls-up our plans. They'd taken far too long for that. Were too important.' Penhor turned back to the room. 'He kept whispering, twisted the others against me. Convinced them they should go to the tunnel. I had a bloody mutiny on my hands! Those who didn't eat the food I had to shoot.'

'But we saw your body.'

'You saw my uniform. Despite these barbaric times one still needs to exercise a certain caution . . . even if you're working for the greater good.' He ran his tongue between his teeth and top lip. 'It was better to cover my tracks. I'm sorry you saw it.'

Neliah stared at him without blinking. The filthy reek of his lemon-water skin filled her nose. Made her want to spit.

'Don't pity them, girl,' continued Penhor, 'especially not Gonsalves. He died cursing me and your sister.'

She knew he was trying to win her to his side. Neliah felt as if *dendes* were burrowing under her skin. 'They were Angolans!'

'They served a higher cause.'

'What about the dynamite?'

Penhor gave a little smile, nodded. 'I knew you'd disobey my orders, go back to the tunnel. The detonators were faulty. Same as the first time I sent you.'

'I still did it! Smashed it into the river.'

'Yes, and nearly ruined everything we planned. I underestimated you, Senhora.'

'I don't get it,' said Burton. He was frowning. 'What's so damn important about this tunnel?'

Penhor rolled his eyes towards him, but didn't reply.

In the end it was another voice that answered. 'Everything, Major. Everything.' It came from behind the other door. A man in uniform stepped out, blew smoke. 'It's why we sent you to Africa in the first place.'

On the sidewalk near the consular building was a palm tree, the lower half of its trunk painted white. Patrick limped over to it and slid to the ground. He was beat, his body like a sandbag that someone had split open and shaken loose. His ankle had been gnawing him since Barraca.

He put down the weapons he'd been entrusted with and checked the wound. His sock was soaked. He rooted through the medical kit, found some iodine and a bandage, applied them. The only painkiller was morphine: way too powerful.

Patrick rolled his sock back up and leaned his head against the palm. Fought the urge to close his eyes. Every time he shut them he saw Zuri again, reaching out, helpless. Accusing. *Why didn't you save me?*

Outside the consulate some of the marines were helping to load a truck. The rest scanned the street, kept giving him suspicious glares. Dogs scampered past. From somewhere came the sound of sawing. In the dark thoroughfares beyond, the city seemed to be holding its breath. He'd give Burton a few minutes more, then go find him.

Patrick reached for his pipe. Put it in his mouth, instinctively turning it upside down because of the blackout.

Pulled it straight back out again.

The bowl was cracked in half, part of it missing.

He'd bought it in Argonne during the Great War, a month before the Armistice. It had survived the trenches, the flu pandemic afterwards, the Legion, Spain, Dunkirk, the mercenary years in Africa – and never once a chip. It was his lucky mascot. As long as the pipe stayed in one piece, so would he.

He dropped it on the ground, shifted away from it as if it were a dead animal.

Don't be a dumbass, Patrick told himself. It's just a superstition. The port was less than three miles away, and afterwards – America, Hannah, a train west to Las Cruces. Father and daughter. In the years left to him he was going to take good care of her. She'd never want for anything.

At one of the consulate's windows, the blackout curtains parted for an instant. Patrick saw a glimmer of sickly light, a hand. Then they closed again.

Something uneasy stirred in his gut.

To ward it off Patrick concentrated on Hannah. The dread of never seeing her again had been replaced by hope. He pictured her greeting him as he finally stepped back on American soil. Curls of blonde hair whipping in the breeze, laughter and tears. Silence. He had no idea what her voice sounded like now that she was a young woman. It might be warm and folksy like his wife Ruth's had been. Or the leaden tone of his mother. What if he didn't like it? What if she had the type of giggling laugh that made him want to grit his teeth?

He thought of something Ruth often said, that homespun wisdom she was so fond of and he couldn't bear. *Pat, you're happy cooking the stew – but you don't wanna eat it.*

Something moved in the corner of his eye.

Patrick glanced down at his pipe. It was trembling, edging in his direction. He frowned. Reached out for it. Felt the ground vibrate beneath his hand.

Patrick stood, slung the medical kit and Enfield over his shoulder; put Burton's Browning down his belt, gripped Neliah's machete. The street was empty, even the dogs had fled. He began to walk away from the consulate, in the direction of the Governor's Palace.

Then he heard it – a low, faint rumbling.

The sound was growing louder, inside it another noise. A squeaking: high-pitched and mechanical. Patrick walked till he reached a right turn, came to a standstill. In front of him was a pink-painted wall, daubed with graffiti urging Loanda's citizens never to surrender:

DEFEND! FIGHT! WIN!

ANGOLA SHITS ON THE SS

SEE YA! I'M ON THE NEXT BOAT TO LISBOA

He could feel the vibrations in his feet now, rising up through the soles of his boots. His ankle recoiled.

Another sound: the growl of exhaust fumes.

He took a step back, his stomach tightening like a fist.

The wall in front of him collapsed.

'Holy shit!'

Patrick ran.

Ran back towards the consulate, legs pumping. The marines raised their Sten guns as he dashed towards them. For the briefest instant he was tempted to fly straight past to the docks.

'Don't shoot! Don't shoot!' he said, skidding to a halt. 'Let me in.'

The sergeant held up his palm. 'We can't do that—'

'I haven't got time to argue. Just let me through.'

One of the marines stared down the street, gun wilting in his hands. 'God help us . . . It's started.'

The others followed his gaze. Patrick saw his chance. Barged past them into the building.

'Stop!'

The nearest marine tore after him. Patrick whirled round, swung the butt of his rifle against him, knocked him for a home run. In the street: the first gunshots.

He tore into the vestibule. Above him the chandelier was tinkling, glass against glass.

'Burton!' he shouted. 'Burton!'

Patrick opened all the doors he could see. Found nothing but empty rooms and abandoned offices.

'Burton! Where are you?'

He spun around desperately; raced to the top of the stairs. Found himself in a corridor: a dozen wooden doors, all identical.

Began to kick down every last one.

Chapter Forty-Four

04:25

URTON recognised him at once, had seen his image in newsreels and papers. The grey uniform and Knight's Cross; pencil moustache and bald head, the ears. *Der Elefant*.

Field Marshal Hans-Jürgen von Arnim.

It was like that moment at Mupe when the plane had exploded. Burton felt as if he were dropping into some bottomless black vortex, limbs flapping. Was almost overwhelmed by disbelief, confusion. A primal urge to run.

Neliah seemed to sense his disquiet, edged closer. 'Who is he?' she whispered.

Burton spoke so the whole room could hear: 'His name's Arnim.'

'He's a *Nazista*?'

'No, a soldier. Commander of the Afrika Korps.'

There was a cigar in Arnim's mouth. He took a contemplative drag on it, the tip flaring red; held the smoke in his lungs. 'And you must be Major Cole,' he replied.

Burton turned to Ackerman, unable to hide his contempt. 'You were working for the Krauts all along.'

'Not for them, Major. *With* them.'

'Same fucking difference.'

'No. This was never about Britain or Germany. It's about Africa. The future. We've been at this together.'

'Together . . .' Burton suddenly felt an unspeakable weariness. He wanted to sit down, let his head droop. Couldn't even remember what had driven him to Africa in the first place. He tried to fit the pieces. 'Against Hochburg?'

'Precisely,' said Arnim. 'The man's a danger to us all. Is – how do you British say? – "a loose cannon". He won't be happy till the whole continent is drowning in blood.'

'But I thought he had Germania's blessing.'

'The Führer's mind has been twisted,' replied Arnim, his lips puckering. 'By Himmler, Hochburg. They're hoodlums. Crooks, murderers. The Führer has no idea what's going on in Africa.'

'No one cared for the last ten years.'

'Believe me, there are those of us in Germania, in the Wehrmacht, who have worried for a long time. Same with you British. Then came the news that forced us to act.' Arnim paused, took another deep draw on his cigar. 'Six months ago an officer of the Abwehr approached me about Hochburg. An intelligence report about the twenty per cent cut he was taking from LMC. Of course I already knew about that, but the officer had something else. Something the SS wanted kept *streng geheim*. Top secret. Do you know what Hochburg has been doing with his diamonds?'

Burton shook his head.

'He's been buying bodies.'

'Bodies?'

'Of fallen soldiers, German soldiers. Despite Hochburg's proclaimed mastery of Africa, we're still losing plenty of men. To the insurgents, disease. Here's a fact Herr Goebbels always omits from his weekly broadcast: eight thousand dead since 1950. Almost three thousand this year alone. And that doesn't even include the "ethnics".'

Arnim threw his cigar on the floor, crushed it under his boot. The bitter stench of ash.

'Meanwhile Hochburg has been using the diamonds to bribe officials. Bribing them to sign off empty coffins as they arrive in the Fatherland while the corpses remain here. To be defiled. Ground up into his autobahn.' Arnim's lips narrowed with disgust. 'He has this lunatic notion of "Aryanising" the soil of Africa. Making it white.'

Burton considered the Schädelplatz, the vista he'd been forced to admire. 'The man's a fanatic. What do you expect?'

'It's not ideology, it's madness. Desecration, pure and simple. I couldn't sit by and let this happen. A commander's duty is always to his men, and their memory. Hochburg had to be stopped.'

'But I failed,' said Burton. 'I didn't kill him.'

'Of course you failed,' retorted Arnim. 'What would Hochburg be to us dead? Another martyr to National Socialism? Another name to evoke on Heldentag? I don't think so! The plan was to destroy his myth, not build a new one. We always wanted you to fail.'

Burton looked from the field marshal to Ackerman. 'Then why send me?'

Neither replied.

Arnim flicked away the cigar butt with the toe of his boot.

'A lot of people have died for this,' said Burton. 'Dolan, Vacher, Lapinski. Nares. Men under my command.' His eyes pierced Ackerman's. 'Your "special" Zuri. The least you owe me is an explanation.'

For a long moment he was met with silence.

Then Arnim spoke: 'Very well, Major, as one soldier to another.' He straightened the Knight's Cross at his throat. 'It should all have ended in '43, at Casablanca. The treaty was a good one. Returned the colonies we'd lost after Versailles, extended our territories; guaranteed yours. Brought stability to us all. Prosperity. But Hochburg never thought so. He believed Africa was Germany's by right. Was so obsessed with the blacks that he wanted dominion over them all, the whole continent. Worse still, he's cunning, patient—'

381

Yes, thought Burton, *like he was with my mother*.

'—won over Germania with his so-called achievements: the mineral wealth, new cities. The Windhuk Decree, what he did in Muspel.' A derisive snort. 'Helped build up the SS till its tentacles were curled around everything: trade, agriculture, labour. Created an army to rival the Afrika Korps. Then he bided his time. It's no coincidence that all this is happening now – in the same year that the German sections of the PAA have been completed. When he can finally move his forces with ease.

'But it's hubris. What with the insurgencies in Aquatoriana and western Kongo we can barely maintain the territory we have, let alone further conquest. And exactly who is going to settle all this new land? Or work it? Peace is the only viable future.'

'You still found enough men to invade Angola,' said Burton.

Arnim made a dismissive gesture. 'What's going on here is a necessary sideshow. Nothing on the scale Hochburg envisions. His war will plunge us into chaos, destroy everything we have in Africa. North Angola is merely part of our strategy.'

'And how do the British fit into all this?'

'Forget the charade for the cameras, all those joint communiqués and Halifax's smiles. Secretly, your Colonial Office has been fearful of Hochburg's territorial ambitions for years. The whole of southern Africa could be drawn in. Imagine the destruction, how many would be killed – and I'm not just talking about the blacks. It might even spark new hostilities in Europe.'

'So Ackerman came knocking on your door.'

'There are others who share my views in the Wehrmacht, in Germania. Discreet men. Men with the right channels to London. When we learned that LMC wanted rid of Hochburg, and that British intelligence was prepared to do the dirty work, we saw an opportunity for us all. So we devised a plan together: stage Hochburg's assassination, let it be a disaster. Then leave a trail back to Rhodesia and Britain. Pander to his paranoia, his ridiculous sense of destiny. Provoke him to invade like he so desperately wanted.'

Loanda

Burton put his hand to his face, felt his calloused fingers against his eyes. This was insane! 'What if I'd succeeded?' he said. 'Killed him instead of his decoy.'

'Why do you think there was a decoy in the first place? Or that the Waffen-SS were waiting for you at Mupe?'

'You warned him.'

Ackerman answered. 'That Vichy shit Rougier. I knew he was Gestapo, so used him to arrange the jeeps and weapons. It followed he'd expose the plot.'

'But they might have arrested us as soon as we arrived in Kongo.'

'No. They needed to catch you red-handed. Only that would give them the full . . . "justification" to act.'

'I saw panzers along the PAA,' said Burton. 'Waffen-SS markings.'

'Hochburg's army,' replied Arnim. 'Ready to roll into Northern Rhodesia.' He glanced at Neliah, smiled at her the way he might a kitten he was about to drown. 'Which is why we needed the tunnel left intact. Which is why engineers from the Afrika Korps have already built a new bridge across it.'

'And when they reach the border?'

'Four squadrons of Typhoons have been flown in from Britain. They'll pick off Hochburg's panzers one by one. Afterwards, your 8th Army is waiting in Solwezi. They bloodied our nose at El Alamein, this time it will be a knockout punch. Hochburg doesn't expect any resistance. We can stop him before he starts.' Arnim smiled again. 'It will be a personal pleasure to watch him limp back to the Schädelplatz, bowed by his own ambition.'

Burton was struggling to make sense of it all. He gave a sardonic laugh. 'You really think this will finish him?'

'For fifteen years the Reich has known nothing but victory. Defeat will taste all the more bitter. They won't be able to pin this one on Versailles.'

'It might rally them to the cause.'

'I doubt it. More likely those plumped-up pheasants in Germania will be falling over each other to blame someone. Who

383

better than Hochburg far away in Africa? If I know Himmler he'll gladly offer him up to save his own worthless hide.'

'But you won't have got rid of the SS.'

'Its grip will be weakened, that is enough. The Führer will start listening to men like me again.'

'It'll never work.'

'What would you prefer, Major? That we do nothing! Hochburg wants all of Africa, won't rest till it's one huge, smouldering graveyard. At least this way gives us a chance for peace. You should be thanking us, Major. Holding your head high. You've done the world a great service.'

Burton thought of Madeleine. Saw them together in the arbour, overlooking fields, unable to talk. Would she share Arnim's view? Or think him a skivvy for the swastika? He'd not realised it before, at least never so clearly, but he wanted her to be proud of him.

'What about Peace for Empire?' Burton turned to Ackerman. 'You've started a fucking war.'

'A limited border skirmish. For too long Britain has been seen as spineless; this will remind Germany we're still a force to be reckoned with. Once Hochburg has been defeated, we stop. Reaffirm our commitment to Casablanca – only this time as equal partners, not an ailing power. Consider it a little "payback" for Dunkirk.'

'You want my approval?'

'I couldn't care less, Major Cole. This has always been about the greater good. Keeping the empire strong. There is no better guarantee of peace. For all our sakes.'

The field marshal nodded his agreement.

There was a drawn-out silence.

'What about Angola?' It was Neliah who spoke.

Arnim contemplated his boots. 'My biggest mistake was not leading the initial invasion for the quarries. In the south. I handed it to the Waffen-SS, which only emboldened Hochburg.'

'I meant now. The north.'

'A *yambo*,' said Ackerman apologetically. 'A pawn. Once the Germans had the marble in the south there was no reason to invade the north. But we needed the Afrika Korps diverted, to make sure there could be no reinforcements for Hochburg's army. So I was tasked with getting the *Resistencia* to attack Kongo. Provoke it so that the field marshal would invade North Angola. Once his troops were engaged, there would be no one to save the Waffen-SS in Rhodesia.'

'And after?'

Ackerman gazed beyond her at the empty office, shrugged. 'There were never any plans. I'm sure one day the Germans will withdraw.'

Neliah flared her nostrils. 'I wish Zuri was here. To see what you really are.'

'Don't be stupid, girl. The field marshal's right, you should be grateful. If Hochburg isn't stopped all you blacks are dead.'

'All my family are. All my friends,' came the spitting reply. 'And for what? So you whites can pick over our graves.'

Outside there were some gunshots.

Ackerman moved over to the window again, parted the curtains to check outside. 'Nothing.'

'What about my team?' asked Burton. 'Were we ever going to get out?'

'You were supposed to be . . . "de-activated" at Mupe. Blown up with the aircraft,' replied Ackerman. He let the curtain drop. 'But you got lucky. The Germans were a little too keen, fired before they should have.'

Burton took a step towards the table, curling his bandaged hand into a fist. 'I'll show you lucky.' He glanced around the room for a weapon. Something to batter Ackerman's head with. His eyes came to rest on the bottle of champagne.

Ackerman retreated behind his desk.

'Not so fast, Major Cole,' said Arnim. 'We're all men of honour here. You've helped us immeasurably, and since you've managed to get this far the least we can do now is speed you on your way.

385

I'm sure there'll be a place for you on that Royal Navy vessel.'

'Unfortunately not, Field Marshal,' said Ackerman. 'My instructions from London are quite explicit. *No* member of the team must return alive.'

He pulled out a gun from the desk. A Webley revolver.

Burton calculated the distance between himself and the champagne bottle. Nine feet. Ackerman could get off at least two shots. His only hope was to keep him talking long enough for Patrick to arrive.

'Sorry, Major.' Ackerman cocked the trigger. 'Orders.'

'Wait! There's one last thing I have to know. Why me?'

'What?'

'You could have chosen anyone to kill Hochburg. Didn't I say there were plenty better? So why me? Dolan was picked to lead the mission. Then at the last moment you changed to me. Why?'

Arnim looked blankly at him. 'I had no hand in it.'

'It wasn't me either,' said Ackerman. 'It came from higher up.'

'Who?'

'He sent me to your farm. Was rabid. I've never seen him like that. Normally he's self-control itself.'

'Who?'

'Insisted we change from Dolan to you. No explanation given.'

'Who?' demanded Burton.

'My superior. Cranley.'

Burton felt his blood turn to ice, soak his spine. 'Jared Cranley?'

'Yes. You know him?'

For a long moment Burton did nothing. He stared past Arnim and Ackerman at the wall behind them. A picture had been removed, the plaster where it once hung paler than the rest of the room. He heard his father on the night he died, screaming as the flames consumed him. *And Ahab said to Elijah: hast thou found me, O mine enemy?*

Hast thou found me . . .

His injured knee gave way.

He stumbled. Reached to Neliah for support, squeezed her

arm as he bent forward, like a runner at the end of long race. She stopped him from falling.

Ackerman's brow furrowed with curiosity. 'You know him?' he repeated, the revolver faltering in his hand.

From somewhere came the sound of doors slammed open and shut.

'Burton!'

Patrick's voice echoed along the corridor. Breathless and desperate.

'In here,' shouted Neliah. She pressed closer to Burton. Helped steady him.

'Cranley,' he mumbled to her. Tears of desperation welled in his eyes. He should have stayed at the farm.

'I don't understand,' she whispered back. 'Who's Cranley?'

The door burst open.

Ackerman's gun snapped towards it.

It was Patrick, rifle in one hand, Neliah's panga in the other. 'Burton. We gotta split. Now!'

There was a roll of thunder. The building shook.

Keeping his Webley aimed at Patrick, Ackerman moved back to the window, parted the curtain again. 'The attack.' His voice wavered. 'It's started.'

'Impossible,' said Arnim. 'My ceasefire lasts till zero six hundred. There can be no—'

A blast hit the consulate.

Burton saw the window explode inwards. Ackerman shredded by a storm of fire and glass.

The lights went off. Smoke flooded the room.

Burton's ears pinged and went flat. He felt Neliah clasp hold of him. Patrick close by in the darkness.

There was another blast.

The ground collapsed beneath their feet.

Chapter Forty-Five

British Consulate, Loanda
21 September, 04:40

'HIT it again!' shouted Hochburg.

A cold elation prickled around his throat. He'd seen the American dash inside the building. Burton must surely be in his grasp now.

Hochburg stood in the turret of a Panther tank, its gun elevated towards the consulate. There were two other panzers pointed at the building; a truck full of Waffen-SS commandos pouring on to the street. Uhrig spurred them on.

The gunner fired, the whole panzer shunting backwards. Hochburg clamped his hand on the hatch to steady himself.

There was a roar. A fog of smoke.

Then the cacophony of collapsing masonry and glass. It reverberated around the city, past the Governor's Palace, up to darkened hills. Somewhere a klaxon began to scream. Others took up the cry. Next moment pockets of gunfire, the distant shriek of mortars.

When the smoke cleared Hochburg could see the consulate: its white façade was caved in, like a skull that had been smashed with a crowbar. Dead marines littered the ground, the pavement flowing red.

Hochburg pulled out his Taurus pistol, leapt to the ground and gathered the commandos around him. They were dressed in black – almost invisible against the night – BK44s eager in their grips.

'I want everyone dead,' said Hochburg. 'But not Burton Cole. We take him alive. Anyone accidentally kills him and I'll have your wife shot. Wives, parents, brothers, sisters, neighbours, anybody you ever passed a pleasant fucking word with. Am I understood?'

'What about the rear of the compound?' said Uhrig. 'They could escape that way.'

'Take ten men, Standartenführer. Make sure nobody gets out. Have one of the Panthers go with you.'

Hochburg turned his attention back to the assembled soldiers. 'Inside are the men who tried to kill me. It is time we repaid them in blood. Don't fail me.'

The troops gave a war cry, shook their weapons above their heads, and stormed the building.

In his ear a muffled, high-pitched whine. The air was thick with brick dust. He struggled to breathe, each lungful like a bag of flour being poured down his throat.

Burton tried to move.

Failed.

He opened his eyes: darkness, swirling powder, great blocks of broken stone. Where once there was a ceiling now he saw chinks of sky. He was lying on the ground, no one else with him.

Burton reached out to push himself up. Failed once more. He couldn't move his left arm. It was caught above his head at an odd angle. He checked it, running his eyes from his shoulder to the elbow, past the burnt UJ triangle to the wrist.

His breath came in short, sharp gasps.

He got to his hand.

It was crushed between two huge slabs of concrete.

Burton studied it with a detached curiosity, unable to comprehend what he was seeing. He pulled, tried to free himself. A shard of intense white pain: a dagger thrust into his armpit. Behind it a sodden numbness. He tugged again. Nothing. Blood was spreading around the hand, trickled down his arm – but slowly, as if there were no pressure in the arteries.

He could feel nothing beyond the elbow joint.

The whining in his ears began to subside. He heard the clatter of rubble, cascades of dust. And behind it another sound, a scurrying sound. Like rats in the attic. They got into the roof of the farmhouse sometimes, scratched on the bedroom ceiling. The sound never stirred Madeleine but he would lie there all night listening to it. This wasn't rats though.

It was the scurry of boots.

Burton pulled harder. Still his hand didn't budge.

He scrambled around for something to defend himself with. All he could find was a lump of brick; he clasped it in his free hand.

Then a cry to still his heart.

'Fee-fi-fo-fum, I smell the blood of an Englishman . . .'

Burton pulled at his hand more desperately. Thought he was going to black out with the stabbing in his armpit. The hysteria threatened to overwhelm him.

'Burton!'

Hochburg's voice rang out like that night he returned to the orphanage, when the flames devoured everything.

The whole of Burton's left side was turning to meltwater. He pulled again, was becoming too weak.

Footsteps, close by. Heavy and shuffling.

'Fee-fi-fo-fum . . .'

He felt rough fingers slip round his neck and lift up his head. Saw the inverted face of a clown: dusty white, blood-red lips.

Patrick.

'On your feet, legionnaire,' he said. 'We got to move.'

'My arm,' replied Burton. His tongue felt heavy, mouth full of crumbled stone.

Hochburg's voice rang out again. There was a spurt of machine gun fire.

'Where's Neliah?' said Burton. 'The others?'

Patrick didn't reply. He was staring at Burton's trapped hand, his eyes dull. Hopeless.

'See if you can release it,' said Burton.

He shook his head.

'Come on!'

Patrick reached for the concrete, heaved, every crease on his face thickening. The rock wouldn't shift. He tried again, failed, then gripped Burton's wrist. 'Best you look away, boy.'

He pulled.

Black spots swam in Burton's eyes. He bit his tongue not to scream. Felt his nose fill with bubbling liquid.

Patrick released him. His cheeks were wet. 'It's impossible.'

Burton understood. It was that moment all soldiers pretend not to prepare for. 'There's a boat,' he said. 'At the docks. It'll take you to a Royal Navy vessel, the *Ibis*—'

'No.'

'You've got till six hundred.'

'I'm staying.'

'Find Farrow, he knows us from Stanleyville. He'll get you on board.'

'I said I'm staying.'

'There's nothing you can do. One of us has to get away.' He grabbed Patrick, pulled his ear close to his mouth. 'Find Maddie. Tell her what happened. Tell her I love her.'

'No. No.'

Burton shoved him off. 'Now get out of here. Back to Hannah. You deserve it.'

'So do you.'

'No. I should have listened to Madeleine. I got what I deserved.'

'Don't say that.'

'This is my revenge, Patrick. My truth. Right here.'

His old friend stepped back, peered into the whirling grit as if some miracle might be hidden there.

The scurry of boots again, much closer now.

'Go!' said Burton.

Patrick turned, ducked beneath a fallen lintel, and began to crawl away.

Then he stopped. His hand went to his stomach, to where his scar was.

'I won't leave you, boy, not this time.'

He scrambled back, fell to his knees and tried to prise apart the concrete jaws that held Burton's hand, groaning with the effort.

'Please,' begged Burton. He gritted his teeth, tried to push him away. 'You can't save me.'

'You stayed at Dunkirk. Now it's my turn.'

'But we'll both die. For what? Think of Hannah, think of—'

Suddenly a movement. So close neither of them had time to react.

Burton glimpsed another chalky face. Eyes that begged forgiveness.

There was a flash of steel.

A ringing sound. Metal on stone.

And his hand was free.

Burton felt nothing.

He tumbled back, sending up a cloud of dust. Lifted his arm. And stared at the place where his left hand used to be.

It was a clean cut, straight along the wrist.

He couldn't tear his eyes away. Counted the squirts of blood. *One . . . two . . . three . . .*

Automatically he hoisted the stump above his head to reduce the blood flow. Like he was back in Bel Abbès, raising his hand to ask one of the *sous-officiers* a question.

'It feels lighter,' he said to himself, his voice calm and utterly level.

Patrick undid his belt and wrapped it around Burton's forearm. Pulled it tight. The skin bulged around the leather.

'Burton. Look at me. Look at me!'

Patrick stared into his eyes. Checked the pulse under his jaw. Behind him Burton saw Neliah. Her face was caked with dust. She held the panga low in her hand, the tip barely above the ground. He smiled at her. She refused to meet his gaze.

Patrick reached into the haversack around his neck. Pulled out a bottle, loaded a syringe with morphine.

'There's no need,' said Burton. 'It doesn't hurt. We can go now.'

He went to stand and collapsed, the world spinning around him. He heard the thump of boots, the sound so loud he was convinced they were inside his head.

A stormtrooper broke through the rubble. Bullets sparked.

Neliah charged him, brought her panga down on his head like an axe. 'More are coming!' she yelled, snatching up the fallen banana-gun.

Patrick hesitated with the syringe. Then punched it into Burton's shoulder and pressed the plunger. Burton felt the liquid enter him, a cool thread lacing its way through his bloodstream. Next moment Patrick and Neliah had raised him to his feet. The three of them stumbled forward, dipped beneath a concrete beam and found themselves in a maze of masonry and pulverised stone. Burton looked over his shoulder, wanted a final glimpse of his hand.

They turned left. Then right. Then right again. Rubble groaned above them. Trickles of dust.

'This way!' said Neliah.

Another left turn. They crawled through a hole.

Next moment Burton was breathing lungfuls of fresh air. His brain felt swollen with oxygen. 'The docks,' he managed to say.

Patrick was spinning round, trying to orientate himself.

'Quick!' said Neliah.

The sound of boots on tarmac rang out along the street.

'Help me,' said Patrick.

He slung Burton's arm over his shoulder. Neliah took the other side and they half ran, half staggered into the darkness. Towards the port.

Behind them came the rumbling of tank tracks.

'Oberstgruppenführer! Oberstgruppenführer!'

Hochburg followed the cries through the building. He felt dust patter down on his bald head, grit chafe against his collar. The air smelt like a mausoleum.

In the city beyond: more gunfire, artillery pounding the sky. His little incursion had lit the touchpaper for the battle of Loanda.

'Oberstgruppenführer!'

Hochburg ducked into a partially collapsed chamber. Buried in the rubble was a picture of George VI, the canvas ripped, his face torn in pieces. At the back of the room a stormtrooper stood over a body.

'Is it Cole?' asked Hochburg, stepping forward eagerly.

The trooper moved aside.

Beneath him was Arnim: his body buckled and broken, uniform in shreds.

Hochburg's disappointment turned to curiosity, then rancour. *Arnim!* He dismissed the stormtrooper; gave a mock bow to the figure below him. 'An unexpected pleasure, Herr Field Marshal.'

'Get me a medic.' He spoke with his usual starched, superior accent – except now each syllable cost him a mouthful of blood. It was congealing around his mouth and cheeks.

'I wonder what your court martial will make of this,' mused Hochburg, stroking his chin. 'You. The British consulate. The man who tried to assassinate me.'

'I'm sure your friend Freisler will make—' he grimaced '— whatever you want of it.'

Hochburg stepped over him, squashed his boot against Arnim's chest. 'On the belts of my Waffen troops is a simple motto: *Meine Ehre heisst Treue.* My honour is my loyalty. You Wehrmacht should learn from it.'

'We have our own motto: *God is with us.*'

'God?' Hochburg ground his heel in. 'God is dead.'

The field marshal squirmed, veins bulging in his face.

'You're a traitor to Africa,' said Hochburg. 'And to Germany.' He bent forward, snatched the Knight's Cross from his throat.

'Take it. It's the only medal you'll ever get.' Arnim forced a sticky black laugh. 'You're finished, Hochburg. You, the SS. All your deranged ambitions.'

'We'll see. My panzers are already in Northern Rhodesia. Are fighting their way to victory in Lusaka.'

'They'll never make it. See what Germania, what the Führer, thinks of you when you're routed, when your invincible troops are slaughtered. Turn tail. Our first defeat since Versailles.' He laughed again. 'I'm told the Rhodesians even have a company of black troops – ready to cut you down.'

Hochburg raised his pistol. Aimed it directly at Arnim's forehead.

'You can't shoot me.'

'I'm not going to,' replied Hochburg. 'You were already dead when I found you, crushed by the collapsing building. And your own treachery.'

'They'll find my body. See the bullet hole.'

A glacial smile spread across Hochburg's face. 'Trust me, there won't be much of you left.'

'What are you going to do?' said the field marshal. 'Grind me into your road?'

'Don't flatter yourself.'

Hochburg pulled the trigger: felt the blood spray his face.

Chapter Forty-Six

05:00

'STOP,' said Patrick. He was breathless, his ankle like a wet sponge. In his free hand he gripped the BK44 Neliah had picked up in the consulate.

They crashed to a halt, Burton slumping between them. Across the road to their left was Loanda's central post office, in front a wide plaza and the Cathedral of the Redeemer. Patrick recognised a boarded-up café from when he was last here, sipping beer and giving whores ten Angolar bills to leave him be. They were a mile and a half from the docks.

Burton was pale and feverish, his stump tucked protectively under his armpit. Next to him the dust on Neliah's face had dissolved into a sweaty mask.

'We must keep going,' she said.

Beneath them the ground shook with *whap-whap* of tracks on tarmac. It was impossible to tell how close they were.

Patrick ignored her. Checked Burton's tourniquet: it was still tight, the blood flow reduced to nothing. He quickly bandaged the wound.

'The first Book of Kings,' said Burton. '21:20. *I have found thee: because thou hast sold thyself to work evil in the sight of the Lord.*' He was staring at the domed towers of the cathedral. 'It was Cranley, *Chef*. Not Ackerman. Cranley all along.'

'Cranley? Who the fuck is Cranley?'

Burton closed his eyes and smiled. One moment he seemed lucid, the next drowning in his dreams.

Patrick turned to Neliah. 'What happened in the consulate? What's he talking about?'

'I don't know.'

A whistling noise.

Something flashed overhead, like an incandescent gull.

The cathedral exploded, one of its towers toppling down. The clatter of falling stone, a bell rent in two with a terrible clanging sound. It cut through Patrick's bones.

He yanked Burton to his feet, put him over his shoulder in a fireman's lift. They sprinted across the plaza –

Another tank shell. Then another.

– out of the square, down a side alley next to the cathedral. More shells. The walls crumbled to brick and plaster around them.

They emerged on to a main thoroughfare. Patrick snatched a glance at the street sign: Rua de Salvador Correira. It should lead directly to the port. He looked up the road and almost buckled under Burton's weight. Rumbling towards them was a Panther tank.

It fired. The shockwave blasted them off their feet. Flames whipped through the buildings on either side.

Behind them another tank gouged a path down the alley.

Patrick whirled round: there were no side streets, no other escape routes. They were going to be crushed like tomatoes in a vice.

Another shell landed, punched a hole in the road. There was a stink of methane.

Through the smoke Patrick glimpsed troops in the darkness, the fire glinting on their helmets. He struggled to his feet. The street seemed to be closing in.

'Look,' groaned Burton.

Patrick followed his gaze. There was a crater in the ground.

Neliah ran to it, tripped, landed on her belly. She crawled the final few feet. Peered downwards. Instantly she pulled her head back up, retching. She spat bile, covered her mouth with her hand. Patrick and Burton joined her. Below them was a main sewer, a river of excrement flowing in the direction of the bay.

The tanks fired again. Debris thundered down on them. Burying into their scalps. Patrick hunkered low, covered his head. His hands came away bloody.

'We don't have a choice,' he said. He pushed Neliah into the hole, helped lower Burton in after her.

The tanks had come to a halt, their turrets searching the street. Troops fanned out around them. Suddenly Patrick felt the breath splinter in his throat. Leading the troops was a dead man.

Uhrig. Somehow he'd survived his fall off the train.

For an instant he thought of Zuri; wanted to rake the sono-fabitch's body till it was chock-full of lead. But it would give away their position. Patrick ducked below ground into the sewers.

The stench hit him like a fist in the nose. The shit of ninety thousand people. He gagged.

Ahead, Neliah was supporting Burton, her hand clamped over her mouth. They were on a narrow walkway with barely enough room to stand. A dozen feet below them, the effluent river.

'Keep going,' said Patrick over the rush of the water. 'Follow the current.'

They pressed forward, trod carefully, kept slipping. The walkway was like goose fat, the walls dripped. Patrick heard the squeals of rats around his boots.

They reached a corner and turned into complete darkness.

'We mustn't go further,' said Neliah. 'We'll fall. Break our necks.'

'Wait,' said Patrick. He tore at the arm of his shirt, ripped it off, then searched his pocket for his Zippo. He flicked the lighter. A triangle of flame glowed in the darkness.

Behind them, voices echoed along the tunnel. Orders barked in German.

They must have gone down there. Into the hole! Move it!

Neliah's body went taut, her hand falling from her mouth. 'It can't be . . .' she said. In the flame Patrick saw her eyes blaze with madness. She stepped towards the voices and brandished her panga. 'Uhrig.'

Patrick barred her way. 'We need your help to get out of here. Burton needs you.'

'But my sister!'

'It won't bring her back.'

'I promised no one would hurt her again.'

'She's past that now.'

Neliah tried to push him out of the way.

Patrick grabbed her by both arms, hated himself for what he said next. 'What would Zuri do if she was here?'

She pulled herself free.

'What would she do?'

Neliah glared at him, seemed ready to fight, then grudgingly lowered the blade.

Patrick handed her his lighter and torn sleeve. 'Cut it into strips. Wrap the first around the end of your machete, keep the other pieces dry till you need them. Light it only when I tell you.'

'What about the skull-troops? They will be able to follow us.'

'Just go!'

With that he doubled back to the corner and flattened himself against the ground. He scooped slime off the walls and rubbed it into his cheeks and forehead to blacken his face. Then he aimed his BK44 along the walkway in the direction of the hole.

He saw soldiers climbing down.

'Come on, you pigs: move it!' shouted Uhrig as he shoved them through the opening. 'I want Cole!'

As soon as the last man had descended, Uhrig followed.

Patrick watched as they crept unsteadily along the walkway. Their flashlights pointed to the ground in front of them, a harsh sickle against his eyes. There were seven or eight of them.

'Faster!' screamed Uhrig.

Patrick waited till they were inches from his face before firing. Each shot shredded boots and kneecaps. The soldiers tumbled over each other, blocked the walkway. One plunged into the sewer, splashing filth into Patrick's face. Flashlights shot up at crazy angles. Ignoring the screams in his ears, Patrick pushed himself off the ground, let go another burst of bullets, and ran, struggling not to slip.

'*Amerikaner!*'

Patrick twisted round, fired blindly, ran again. Bullets splintered the walls round him. He felt something whack against his side, a flash of heat spread across his flanks. No pain. He stumbled, then continued into the darkness.

'Now,' he shouted to Neliah. 'Light it!'

Ahead he saw a flicker of flame. It expanded as the material from his shirt caught fire. Burton and Neliah were further in front than he expected. Patrick chased after them, every hundred yards spinning round to point his BK into the darkness.

For the moment no one was following.

He trailed the firefly for ten minutes before it halted and he caught up with the others.

'Which way?' asked the girl, swiping the torch from left to right.

The sewer split into two.

'Main tunnel,' said Patrick. He took Burton from Neliah. He was wan but blissful: the morphine had kicked in. Patrick clicked his fingers in his face.

Burton's eyes opened. 'You hear that, *Chef*?'

'What?'

'Listen. A wind-chime.'

'You're imagining it.'

'No. It's close. Same as the one at home.' Burton stared into the darkness, his mouth wide. Then his expression hardened, grew sad. 'It's gone . . .'

'I'm gonna put you on my back, boy. Keep your eyes open. Watch behind us.'

They continued along the walkway.

Patrick's hair was dripping with sweat, his eyes stung. On his shoulder Burton seemed to grow heavier with each step. He felt a wet patch spreading around his midriff where Uhrig's bullet had nicked him.

Another few minutes and Neliah stopped again. She held her flaming panga to the wall: 'See here.'

There was a rusty ladder bolted to the bricks, the rungs disappearing upwards into a manhole.

Patrick tried to calculate how far they'd gone. 'Keep going,' he said. 'Underground will be safer. We need to get as close to the docks as we can.'

They had only travelled another two hundred yards when Patrick got a whiff of fresh, salty air. The walkway ended; below them the sewer flowed into an outlet pipe. It was large enough to crawl through. Patrick eased Burton off his shoulder and splashed waist-deep into the sludge below, waded over to the outlet. It was blocked by a grille. He shook it, struggled to wrench it open, feeling the rust and filth burn his hands.

It was welded shut.

'What can you see?' asked Burton.

Patrick pressed his face against the bars. They had gone past the bay to Loanda's northern beach. Palm trees rustled in the darkness. To the left he saw cranes rising above the docks and beyond that the ocean – close enough to breathe.

'We have to go back,' he said, hauling himself up on to the walkway. 'To the ladder.' He reached for Burton.

Burton shrugged him off. He held his severed hand under his armpit. 'I can manage.'

Patrick led the way, skimming his palm along the wall till he found the rungs again. He looked up: it was thirty-five, forty feet to street level.

'Can you climb?' he asked Burton.

'I think so.'

'Someone's coming,' said Neliah.

Flashlight beams danced along the roof. Below them deformed, lurching silhouettes, growing larger by the second.

'I can hear you, *Amerikaner*,' shouted Uhrig. 'Hear you, Cole. There's no escape. Give yourself up, a sewer is no place for a white man to die.'

'Go,' said Neliah, stepping away from them. 'Climb!'

'Not without you,' replied Burton.

'I stay.'

'No.'

'*I stay!*'

'Neliah, please . . .'

She turned to face him, lifted the burning panga to see him better. Patrick watched as she gently put her fingers to the stump of Burton's bandaged hand; he didn't flinch. They came away red and she touched them to her lips. 'No blood oaths,' she said.

Burton went to embrace her – but she kept her distance. He held her eye for a final moment. Then began to climb.

'You don't have to do this,' said Patrick, gripping the ladder. 'You can come with us.'

'This is right thing to do.'

'He'll kill you.'

'He already did,' said Neliah, 'on the train.'

Patrick nodded. Offered her the BK44. She pushed it away, swung her panga. It flared in front of his eyes. Then the flame was gone.

'Zuri,' he whispered in the darkness.

'Zuri,' came back the ghostly reply.

Chapter Forty-Seven

E'D been wrong to let Burton go first.

'Keep trying,' shouted Patrick, his neck craned upwards.

Burton heaved again, but was too weak to shift the manhole cover.

Below them came the echo of gunfire. Screams.

Burton looked down. 'Neliah.'

'There's nothing we can do for her, she made her choice. Try again!'

Burton screwed up his face; it was sopping. Another heave. Patrick saw the cover lift an inch.

Then drop back.

'Something pushed against it!'

'I'm coming up,' said Patrick. He waited until Burton had squeezed himself tight against the wall, then climbed the final rungs. There was barely enough room for both of them. The BK on his shoulder scraped bricks. He smelt something gangrenous on Burton's breath.

There was a second burst of gunfire below . . . A sound like a heavy stone dropped in a well.

Patrick struggled to get into position.

'What if the boat's already gone?' said Burton.

'It won't be.'

'What if it is?'

Patrick put both palms against the cover. Pushed with all his strength. A wedge of fresh air. Suddenly something pushed it back down, bent his wrists. He pushed again, elbows straining as if the sockets would pop – and the cover was off.

Patrick slid it to one side and climbed out into a torrent of legs.

All around him people were rushing past. Somebody tripped on the cover, crashed to the ground cursing in Portuguese. In the distance the blare of artillery fire: howitzers by the sound of it.

Patrick helped Burton out and they both gulped down lung-fuls of air. It was like that moment when they emerged from their hidey-hole in Dunkirk, except this time the air was balmy.

They were in Largo Diogo Cão, the square in front of the docks. Rising above them the monolithic structure of Customs House: gateway to the quayside itself. A barrier and sandbag emplacement had been erected across the entrance but failed to hold back the crowds. The guards had deserted their posts, crushed bodies lay strewn all round.

Patrick looked up at the clock-tower: 05:30.

'Come on!' He slung Burton's arm over his shoulder and they joined the throng, staggering past railway sidings and on to the main pier. It was flanked by cranes and warehouses. Total chaos.

'The far end,' said Burton, fighting for breath. 'Boats.'

The distance seemed longer than the entire length of the PAA.

They ploughed through the mass of bodies, Patrick jostling people aside. The air stank of sweat and hysteria. One woman refused to move: Patrick shoved her to the ground without a thought; pulled the BK44 off its strap and held it in front, finger on the trigger.

At the edge of the quay a line of soldiers struggled to maintain order. Patrick saw Portuguese troops, British marines, even the familiar white kepis of legionnaires. There were only four boats left, engines chugging violently. Gangplanks being pulled up.

'Which one?' shouted Patrick.

'Find Farrow,' said Burton. He swirled on his feet like a drunk.

'But which boat?'

Burton pointed to the furthest one. A tugboat. It flew a Union Jack.

Was casting off its ropes.

Patrick lifted his BK, cut a burst above the mob, bullets skimming heads. People screamed. Ran. A ragged corridor opened up through the crowd. He hauled Burton through the mêlée.

They stumbled, almost dropped. Kept running. Patrick ignored the agony in his ankle.

The last of the ropes were free. Marines stood by the gunwale, waving Sten guns to ward off the foolhardy.

'Stop!' yelled Patrick.

He saw the water around the tug churn white. Its engine throttled up.

They skidded to a halt on the edge of the harbour. Fell to their knees.

'Wait! Please!'

People were hurling themselves into the water in an attempt to get on board.

The marines lifted their weapons to defend the boat. In between them was a man in a tight waistcoat giving orders.

'Farrow!' shouted Burton. 'Farrow!'

But the boat was already pulling away – out towards the open sea.

In the darkness, Neliah let the *rungiro* flow through her. Promised to let it gorge. She saw herself win back the plait of Zuri's hair. Kill Uhrig. Then she spoke a prayer to Mukuru – asked him to give her the strength of the heavens. To still the fear if it should beat in her heart.

The lights of the *Nazistas* were getting closer. She heard the clink of their weapons. And above them, in the city, another sound – the boom of big guns. The walls trembled.

Neliah pulled off one boot and threw it on to the path, gripped her panga and slid into the dung-river. The filth came to her chest, the current tugged on her legs. It made her think of the Lulua, swimming with Zuri. She could hear her voice again, fretting about crocodiles.

It was the only place Zuri lived now – in her memory. The only place they all lived, *Ina*, *Papai*, Tungu, Bomani. If Neliah died their memory would die too. There would be no trace of them, nothing to hand on to those who came after. She whispered more words to Mukuru. She had to live for their sake.

'Cole! *Amerikaner*!'

The skull-troops were almost upon her. There were three of them, Uhrig leading. In the light of the torches his face was scarred with shadows. His gun swayed in front of him. Neliah saw the loop of precious hair around his shoulder.

Her heart roared, hungry for blood.

She sank into the water till it touched below her mouth. The stink made her want to empty her belly. It was worse than when they hid in the cesspit back home. This was the shit of strangers. Lumps of wood floated past, the body of a dead cat.

One of the *Nazistas* tripped. 'Standartenführer, I found something.'

Uhrig stopped, spun round.

The skull-troop picked up Neliah's boot. 'Is it Cole's?'

Neliah pushed herself against the walkway till her eyes were level with their toecaps. She lifted the panga out of the water. Pulled her shoulder back. She could hear the blade drip.

Uhrig snatched the boot. 'Not unless he's got girl's feet.'

Neliah swung her arm.

The panga sliced right through the first *Nazista*'s leg. He toppled on to Uhrig, his finger catching the trigger. For a heart-beat the tunnel was the colour of day. Uhrig shoved him off – back into the other skull-troop. Another burst of fire, a heap of thrashing arms and howls, the smell of guts. Only Uhrig remained standing.

Neliah leapt up from the dung-river, swiped her panga at him, an arc of metal and brown water. The blade lodged in his ankle. He dropped his rifle and grabbed the wound, face seething. Neliah twisted the panga, pulled it out to strike again.

Then a dazzling flash. Burning circles of red and white in her head.

Uhrig clubbed her with his torch. Neliah felt her neck snap backwards, nose flatten. She tumbled into the filth below, was dragged away by the current. Her mouth and nostrils bubbled with shit.

She broke the surface, retching. Heard a loud splash as Uhrig jumped in after her. Went under again, rolling over and over. Neliah kept her fist knotted around the panga. She scraped the bottom, found her feet. The toes of one sinking into mud, the other heavy inside her boot.

Neliah coughed and spat, tried not to swallow. She had reached the end of the tunnel where they had turned back a few minutes before. Through the bars she saw the sea, rippling like the black fur of a *barungue*. She waded to the walkway and reached with both arms to pull herself up.

A hand crushed her throat. Thick, brutish fingers. Another went around her wrist, shook the panga from her grip. It landed on the walkway with a clang.

She was dragged back down into the filth.

Neliah fought, legs thrashing. She opened her eyes but it stung worse than wasps. Next moment she was back in the air, Uhrig's breath chewing her ear. They stood in the dung-river, below the walkway, waves chopping around them.

'Where's Cole?'

She said nothing. Felt the fingers crush harder round her windpipe. Her blood was becoming stone.

'*Where's Cole?*'

'Gone . . . safe.'

'And left the poor nigger down here on her own? Pigshit!'

The *Nazista* thrust her back into the filth. Neliah thought her neck was going to snap. She scrambled around, hands reaching between his legs, tried to crush him there.

Uhrig pulled her up, laughing. 'We can play later. I already told you I like a bitch with a bit of fight. But first, Cole.'

'You'll never find him.'

He punched her in the belly. Neliah fell in half, her insides screaming.

Uhrig's breath was hot in her ear again. 'Listen! You hear that? Above us.'

All Neliah heard was her body fight for breath.

'That's the German Army. We'll crush this pigsty of a city in hours. And behind the army, the Einsatzgruppen. That's where I should be.' His fingers were tight around her throat again. 'All I need is Cole and I'm back with them. Give me what I want and I promise you'll get special treatment.'

'My sister. You killed her.' Through her blinking eyes she saw Zuri's hair tied round his shoulder.

'You think I give a fuck? I've killed a hundred niggers. A thousand.'

'I swore to die first. It should have been me.'

'If you're lucky I'll send you to meet her. Now, last chance. Where's Cole?'

'Zuri – *nydi zembira!*' Forgive me.

'Where's Cole?'

This time, she made no reply.

With a roar of frustration Uhrig thrust her deep into the filthy brown river. Neliah felt his arm lock straight. She kicked her legs, clawed the bottom, tried to fight back. Her breath grew thin and venomous.

Her hand found his boot. She fumbled from his shin to the ankle, fingers seeking the place that had tasted her panga.

All she felt was unbroken leather. She had the wrong leg.

Neliah's head was whirling. She saw dark shapes against her eyes, saw the spirits of the dead beckon her to join them. There were so many. She groped for his other leg, his other ankle. Found the wound.

Drove her fingers into it like a spearhead.

Above water, she heard Uhrig yell. The iron ring around her neck slackened. Neliah burst through the shit, gulped air.

Uhrig was clutching his leg. His teeth bared white.

Neliah charged, smashed him over. Waves of scum exploded around them. Then she was on top of him, burrowing her fingers into his windpipe. She held him there, saw that moment on the *tyndo* as Zuri stretched out her hand. Saw the terror in her sister's eyes.

Neliah roared till her throat was dry. Let the *rungiro* feast.

Uhrig thrashed like a demon, beat the water in a frenzy. Ripped at her fingers. Not once did she loosen her grip. Time had no meaning.

And then the water was calm except for the hissing of foam.

Neliah dragged Uhrig out and carefully undid the braid of Zuri's hair from his shoulder. She cupped it in her palms, pushed the *Nazista*'s body away. She wanted the rats to eat it. Gnaw on his face.

Neliah waded back to the walkway, placed Zuri's plait down, then put out her hands to pull herself up. Her fingers brushed her panga.

Behind her a surge of water.

Uhrig exploded through the surface.

Neliah spun round, snatched hold of her panga, brought the blade swinging down with all her strength. It struck him in the centre of the head, buried through to his nose.

Split his skull in two.

His face disappeared in a mask of blood. Two white eyes staring at her – a look of rage and disbelief. And finally the emptiness of death.

Neliah prised the panga from the bone, let him drop back into the water. The current pulled him away, dragged him to the bars at the end of the tunnel. His body bobbed up and down.

She climbed out of the dung-river, sat and pulled her knees

close. Ran her hand along Zuri's tail, picking off pieces of dirt. She would wash and clean it, scent it with mafuta oil like *Ina* used to do when they were girls. Would keep it close to her skin for as long as she lived.

'I swear it, Zuri,' she whispered, hiding the hair away. 'I'll die first.'

Inside her head a familiar voice answered – *I know, Neliah, I know*.

Neliah. It was an old Herero name, her mother had given her it. *Strong of will* it meant. *Strong of will, vigorous of spirit, level of mind*. She would live to be worthy of it yet.

Something rumbled overhead – the noise of tank wheels. The tunnel shook. Elsewhere in the city she heard machine guns, grenades. The booming of artillery. Getting fiercer, spreading into every street and building and home. Loanda needed an army to defend it. Not an army of whites or men like Penhor and Gonsalves. But an army that understood the fear of Muspel – whose hearts would roar like heroes.

Neliah spoke a final word to Mukuru, asked him to watch over Burton and Patrick, speed them home.

Then she joined the battle.

Chapter Forty-Eight

05:35

BURTON was laughing. A laugh of crazy jubilation. His whole body felt warm and rested. If Maddie had been there he'd have snatched her up, danced a waltz around the quayside. Asked her to marry him. She was all tears and giggles. Yes! She reached for his hand, pulled it to her lips. Then her eyes ballooned in horror.

Deep inside his head Burton heard a voice, hard and cautionary, like his father's: *It's just the morphine. Be careful, son, stay alert.*

Otherwise you'll never get back to her.

He shouted over to Patrick, beckoned to him. He had fought his way to the French ship, was begging the legionnaires to let them on board.

There was no need. The tugboat was turning back.

Burton laughed again. Saw Farrow shout up to the bridge, order the captain to reverse. Some of the marines climbed down into a dinghy tied to the starboard side of the tug.

Patrick limped back, helped Burton to his feet. Seeing the boat return, the crowd pressed around them: a swarm of panicking bodies. More people threw themselves into the water.

'We can't come all the way,' shouted Farrow. 'You'll have to jump, Major. Swim to the right side, to the dinghy.'

The tug stopped twenty feet short of the quay, its engines turning the harbour to froth. Burton and Patrick leapt.

The water was cold, chewed on Burton's stump, blunted his euphoria. He swam, feeling no resistance against his left hand, only marrow-numbing pain every time it slapped the waves. There seemed to be hundreds of people around him: a frenzy of thrashing arms, wild faces. Hands snatched at him, pulled him down. Water flooded into his mouth and nostrils. He fought back to the surface. Saw Patrick reach the dinghy, clamber on board.

The marines opened fire, blasting the swimmers around him. The foam turned red, just like at Dunkirk. Burton kicked hard, fought against the fingers that tore at his body. He was almost there when he was dragged under again. A man was clawing his back.

Burton used his elbow to dislodge him, *gwiwar*, but the movement had little force in the water. He raked the man's eyes. Broke the surface – a gasp of air – was pulled back down. Bubbles gurgled in his ears, the fizz of bullets, distorted screams. He had no more breath, no more fight—

An oar cracked the man's head. He let go, drifted off helplessly.

Burton felt a hand on his collar. Patrick dragged him out of the water, his face crucified with the effort.

As soon as they were both on board Farrow shouted to the captain. The engines powered up again, swamping the swimmers below.

The tugboat pulled away.

'Jesus wept,' said Farrow when he saw Burton's arm. 'What happened?'

Burton was too exhausted to reply, simply shook his head. There were a few civilians on the boat – a matronly young woman, men in suits and panama hats – who regarded him with a mixture of curiosity and alarm.

'What about Ackerman? I heard the consulate was hit.'

Another shake of the head.

'Lying Jerry scum,' said Farrow. He curled his knuckles into a fist, pounded his other hand. 'I knew they'd break their cease-fire.' He stared at Burton's injury again. 'It won't be long to the Royal Navy ship. They'll fix you up.'

'Thank you,' Burton managed to say, his chest heaving. 'Thank you for turning around.'

'Couldn't very well leave you, Major. Another few minutes, mind, and you'd have been swimming home.' He marched off.

Burton buried his stump beneath his armpit and sank to the ground. His brain kept issuing commands to his hand. He could feel them pulsing from his head to his shoulder, feel the tendons in his forearm ripple. Then nothing.

Patrick slumped down next to him. They were both too exhausted to speak, just sat there and watched the city slowly recede. A squadron of Heinkel bombers roared overhead, their jet engines lacerating the sky. Then a second wave. They would have flown up from the huge Luftwaffe bases in DSWA. Tracer fire from ack-ack guns pursued them. Missed.

How many cities have I seen like this? thought Burton. Dunkirk, Tana, Stanleyville, Douala. How many more would there be? The Nazis would change Loanda's name – as they did with every place they conquered, as if victory alone was not enough. History had to be expunged. Soon Angola's capital would be just another Hitleropolis: a city dedicated to an ageing dictator who no longer cared about Africa. The quayside continued to writhe with bodies, their wailing keener than the bombs: the anguish of those with no hope left.

Patrick covered his ears. 'Those poor bastards.'

'Fat days for mercenaries,' replied Burton mirthlessly.

'We left so many behind. All because they didn't have nickel to pay.' He shook his head in disgust. 'Will God ever forgive us?'

'God gave up on you and me long ago.' Burton turned to face his old friend. His skin was pale, lips a purplish blue; he clutched his side. 'You hit, *Chef*?'

Patrick pulled back his shirt to reveal his Dunkirk scar, and further along his flank a new wound daubed in blood. 'I'll live.' Tucked into his waistband was Burton's Browning. He pulled it out. 'You?'

Burton took the weapon. 'Remember what you used to tell us in the Legion. "If it still hurts, it's not that bad."' Tears welled in his eyes. 'It doesn't hurt.'

The tugboat continued across the bay.

Burton felt consciousness slip from him, like he was sinking into warm mud. He thought of the farm, the orchards. Saw the quinces on the trees, fat and golden and ready to pick. Next his mind wandered to Neliah. He heard her say his name. *Burtang.* She was so young. So fierce. He remembered something Madeleine had once said: girls make the best soldiers; aren't as hysterical or irresponsible as men.

He hoped Neliah was still alive, that she would flee the city, maybe get to Mozambique . . . even though his heart told him she'd stay. Fight to her dying breath. Her pledge to Zuri was as strong as the SS oath to Hitler. Stronger in fact: it was born of love, not hatred or fanaticism.

Burton felt himself drift off further. He needed to stay alert. Forced himself to sit up, spoke to keep lucid. 'You were right. It was a set-up from the start,' he said.

'You mean Ackerman.'

'It went higher than that. Right to the top. The British, Germans—'

'Germans?'

'Field Marshal Arnim himself. Arnim, Cranley, I don't know how many others.' He gave a bitter laugh. 'All for the greater good.'

'Who is this Cranley?'

'He wanted me dead. All of us.'

Burton suddenly grabbed Patrick by the shirt, pulled him close. 'I have to get back to London.' His breath tasted feverish. 'Need your help, friend, one last time. Need to find Cranley before . . .'

The words died in his mouth.

*

On the jetty a new scream rose from the crowd. People surged forward like wildebeest fleeing a predator.

Burton struggled to his feet to see better.

Next instant he was lurching towards the front of the boat, the adrenaline flowing again, Patrick at his side. They reached the wheelhouse, climbed up the bridge ladder to the top deck.

'Speed her up!' Burton shouted at the captain. He was white Angolan, unshaven with a huge paunch, sucking on a kola-nut.

'Who are you? Where's Senhor Farrow?'

'Do it!'

'I'm already at ten knots. It's too risky to go faster till we're clear of the bay.'

Burton shoved him aside, grabbed the throttle-lever and rammed it to maximum. The chugging of the engines became an angry growl; they surged forward. He turned to Patrick. 'Will it be enough?'

'I don't know, boy, I don't know.'

Two panzers had appeared on the quayside, on their turrets the skull and palm symbol of the Waffen-SS. Behind them was a lorry full of troops. The tanks' guns were being cranked up to the maximum elevation.

The captain crossed himself, kept the throttle at maximum.

Burton watched, waited. The guns were still rising. He caught his reflection in the bridge window. A stranger stared back – lacerated face, skin clogged with filth and blood. Dark, half-dead eyes.

There was a blast from one of the tanks. The sound caterwauled across the bay.

Then a boom.

The waves erupted in front of them, whipping water against the window. Burton flinched.

A second blast. Close enough to rock the tugboat this time.

'*Mais rapido!*' shouted the captain. His hand was jammed against the throttle now. He spun the wheel through several revolutions. Burton and Patrick tumbled to the starboard; climbed back down to the deck.

'Fuck is going on?' demanded Farrow.

The marines were gathered round him, mouths grim, jittery. A few were taking shots at the quays. Burton wanted to grab one of their Sten guns. There was a third blast. More water showered down on them, close enough to drench Burton.

On the jetty, the troops had climbed out of the lorry. They opened fire, mowing down the crowd, cleared a path for two inflatable rafts to be carried to the water's edge. In the flare of the gunlight Burton saw Hochburg. He tore off his smock, hurled it to the ground. Even from this distance the elation on his face was clear.

The first boat was put into the water. The rasp of an outboard motor starting.

'Faster,' Burton yelled to the captain, even though he knew there was no more power left. 'Faster!'

There was a flash of smoke from one of the tanks. A second later, the other fired.

Burton tried to track the first shot against the flaming background of Loanda. It was a streak of movement, almost invisible. But he could hear it: a whistle that grew deeper with every second, filled his ears with shrieking iron.

It clipped the boat: on the port side, below the bridge. A burst of splinters, followed by a geyser of seawater.

The tug rocked violently, knocking everyone off their feet.

Then more whistling. Closer and closer.

The second shell hit.

It ploughed right through the middle of the boat. Spat out whole planks. Giblets of steel and wood.

Burton was spun over, caught his stump. He felt his stomach twist inside out, bile fill his throat. Splinters stung his face and arms. There was no fire, just billows of choking smoke. The civilians he'd seen earlier – the woman, men in panamas – lay slopped on the deck. Some of the marines were also dead.

The tug began to yaw horrifyingly, tipping the port side towards the waterline. Burton struggled to stand.

The second inflatable was leaving the quay, Hochburg at the prow, a BK44 held across his chest. The first one was already halfway across the bay.

Burton's brain was yawing like the boat. He pinched the bridge of his nose, forced himself to focus. The uninjured marines were taking up position around the gunwale, were already firing. He shouted to Farrow: 'Check the dinghy. See if we can still use it. Patrick, with me.'

They staggered back towards the wheelhouse, met the captain climbing down the ladder.

'Where's the spare fuel?' demanded Burton.

'My boat . . . my boat.' Tears streamed down his beard.

Burton grabbed him with one hand, ripped at his shirt till their faces were touching. 'Where's the fucking fuel?'

'There are some drums. On the aft.'

Burton and Patrick got to them. The tug was tilting further and further to the left. Slowly sinking. They thrust aside the empty barrels till they found a full one. Rolled it to the side of the boat where some marines were firing. The effort was almost too much for Burton.

'I need your bayonet,' he said to the nearest marine, who handed it over without looking away from his gun.

The first inflatable was approaching the port side of the boat, ten feet below them.

Burton rammed the blade into the barrel, gouged open a hole. *Tonneaux de Roumis* they called these in the Legion, a technique for defending forts.

Patrick ripped off a shred of his shirt. Burton soaked it in diesel then he plugged up the hole with it, making a fuse. They took either end of the drum and prepared to lift it on to the gunwale.

'One. Two. Three.'

They heaved. It was too heavy.

Burton shouted over to the marines. 'Help us!' One of them took the middle of the drum. They heaved again, raising it several feet in the air . . . before it crashed back down. Patrick howled, slumped over, his face scarlet. He clasped his toecap.

The inflatable was just below them, the stormtroopers swinging grappling hooks. Burton heard German voices: *Erschiessen!* Shoot them!

He drove the bayonet back into the barrel, tore the metal open. Diesel gushed out, spread in a milky film across the deck.

'You mad?' yelled the marine.

Burton lifted the drum to increase the flow, judged its weight till it was light enough. 'Now!'

Patrick managed to get back on his feet and the three of them hefted it on to the edge of the boat. Burton held out his hand to Patrick. 'Lighter.'

'Neliah.'

'What?'

'Neliah had it!'

Stormtroopers were climbing up the side.

Burton shoved the barrel overboard. It hit one of the troopers, knocked him back on to the inflatable, his legs and arms flapping either side of it. The raft sprang upwards, then crashed back into the water.

Burton grabbed his Browning, aimed at the barrel through dripping hair. Pulled the trigger.

The blast punched him back.

He felt his nose and cheeks shrivel, hair frazzle. Debris rained down around him. Ignited the fuel on the deck. He rolled across it, through the inferno, out of the flames, feeling his clothes and skin fuse. Patrick crashed into him, his body smoking, hands orange and blistered.

The whole port side of the tugboat was ablaze. Men thrashed about. Hurled themselves into the sea. Screams in German.

Then gunshots – from the starboard. Sten guns mixed with BK44s.

Burton turned towards them. Saw the marines there being blasted back; grappling hooks clatter over the edge. He bowed his head.

Hochburg's inflatable.

Chapter Forty-Nine

05:45

THERE would be no escape for Burton this time.

Hochburg clambered on to the sinking tugboat. It was pitching at forty-five degrees, the far side ablaze. He breathed in the flames, a heady bouquet of tar and wood and flesh. Tasted that first burning in Togoland again. The deck was littered with injured men. One snatched at Hochburg's boots, begged for help. Hochburg slid him away with the muzzle of his BK44. His eyes searched the boat.

He found Burton and Whaler by the wheelhouse. They were climbing the ladder to the bridge as the flames snapped around their legs; a marine helped them. Burton looked beaten: his skin streaked with blood, clothes smoking rags. Each movement agony.

For a moment Hochburg almost pitied him, the way he might a wounded dog when the kindest thing was a bullet in the head. Then the fire filled his nostrils again.

He turned to the stormtroopers in the inflatable below. There were six of them.

'Hauptsturmführer, get your men and the MG48s on board. Concentrate all your fire on the wheelhouse. We'll flush them out.'

One of the commandos began to climb; the rest stayed where

they were, the Hauptsturmführer among them. They swayed anxiously, the fire glimmering on their faces.

'What are you waiting for?'

'Herr Oberstgruppenführer, the boat's sinking, it's suicide!'

Hochburg aimed his BK at the inflatable, raked it with bullets. There was a burst of air and immediately it began to sink. The stormtroopers scrambled out.

They took up positions along the slanting deck like gunners on a mountain slope. There was no cover – everything had slid to the port side, was in flames. Hochburg crawled to the front, watched the MG48s being loaded. The water was licking around their boots. Burton had disappeared into the wheelhouse.

'Oberstgruppenführer!' The trooper next to him pulled at his sleeve, pointed to the far end of the tugboat.

Below the wheelhouse, a man in a waistcoat clambered into a rowboat.

'Forget him,' said Hochburg. 'All I want is Cole.'

He gave the order to fire.

There was a marine at the top of the ladder. 'Come on, mate!' he said. 'Almost there.'

Burton climbed towards him – but clumsily, as if he had never climbed anything in his life, his stump banging on every rung. Fresh spots of blood had appeared on the bandage, were beginning to spread and join. The morphine was ebbing. He felt an itchy numbness, the bones in his forearm throbbed. His skin stank of cinders. Behind him Patrick wheezed and cursed.

With the marine's help they dragged themselves on to the bridge. Everything was at a giddy angle, creaking. The floor awash with blood. The captain was face down, impaled on a spear of decking.

Burton dragged himself through the room to the window at the far side; it had been upended, was more like a skylight now. He lifted it, jamming it open, and looked out. Below was the hull of the tugboat, risen out of the water. Below that, the dinghy.

'Farrow!'

He'd found some oars, was sliding them into place. 'Fit to go, Major.'

'Get ready, we're coming—'

The wheelhouse exploded in gunfire.

Burton threw himself down. Heard the distinctive rattle of MG48s. The cabin walls ruptured and snapped, the windows disintegrating. Burton shielded his face, felt like his eardrums were going to burst.

The marine stood up, scythed the deck outside with his Sten gun. Was blown back, his ribcage torn open. Burton crawled over his body, through the hailstorm of glass, towards Patrick.

The MGs stopped.

Burton heard the clink of magazines and hot metal. They were reloading. He snatched up the marine's Sten gun, kept himself flat to the ground and fired through the window. Screams. Then the MGs again. Bullets ripped through the wheelhouse, turning it to sawdust.

'Patrick,' shouted Burton. 'We have to get to Farrow. Next time they reload. You go first, I'll cover.'

Patrick didn't move.

'Major Whaler!'

This time Patrick rolled over, gave a snort of laughter. His face was all creases, nostrils flaring, pupils tiny pinpricks. He clutched his stomach, holding in his intestines.

Burton felt his breath turn to thorns. '*Chef*! Can you move?'

'There's life in the old fool yet.' Blood flowed down his chin. 'I'll cover you.'

Another gut-sopped laugh. He took the Sten from Burton's grip. 'Not with one hand. You first.'

'No.'

'I'm the better shot, remember?'

The tugboat suddenly lurched downwards. There was a sound like steel rods snapping.

'Major!' It was Farrow calling. 'For heaven's sake, man. Come on!'

Patrick pushed him away. 'Go, boy.'

Burton didn't move.

'I'll follow, I promise. Got to get back to Hannah. But you first . . . chancers before age this time.'

Burton knew he was lying. He slid away, kept glancing back at his friend through the haze of shrapnel. Patrick raised the gun to his eye, began to fire in rapid bursts. Lethal as ever.

Then silence.

The MG48s had stopped again.

Burton heard the crackle of fire as it continued to devour the tug. Men groaning below; Patrick panting over his weapon. Back on shore, the constant *crump-crump-crump* of bombers. But there was no sound of reloading.

A voice cried out, a voice that had haunted Burton for decades. A raw baritone.

'My men are all dead, dead or wounded. Useless pricks. It's just me now, Burton. You want the truth about Eleanor, you want to kill me – here I am.'

'Go!' hissed Patrick.

Every muscle in Burton's body had turned to stone.

'I even have your silver knife,' continued Hochburg, 'ready to plunge into my heart.' He laughed. 'Didn't we once read a fairy tale together like that? Some trite little fable of beanstalks and revenge.'

'Go!' said Patrick again.

Burton pulled out his Browning. He had one bullet left. He thought of his mother. Thought of Madeleine, the baby. It was going to be a girl, a sister for Alice. Somehow he knew it.

Patrick shook his head. Swallowed. Each breath caused him to grimace.

'I'm waiting, Burton,' came Hochburg's voice.

Burton pushed himself up to his knees, crouched below the window. Body tense.

'If you go out there,' said Patrick, 'we all died for nothing.'

Burton lifted the Browning.

'Go out there and I'll shoot you myself.' He twisted the Sten gun in his grip. 'I swear it.'

Neither of them moved. There was just the whipping sound of the flames. The boat sinking.

Burton raised his pistol, clicked it and released the magazine. He tossed the clip to Patrick, then he leaned in, gently kissed his forehead and whispered a single word.

'Home.'

Hochburg tapped the knife against his thigh, eyes focused on the door, waiting for Burton to emerge.

He held his other hand low, gestured to the gunner to hold his fire. They were both struggling to stay upright as the boat continued to yaw. The rest of the men lay lifeless or bleeding, their bodies listing in the water. The level was above Hochburg's knees now. Rising fast.

In front of him there was a clattering of wood against wood, half-heard voices. Then nothing more.

'You risked everything in the Schädelplatz to find the truth,' Hochburg shouted, trying to goad Burton out. 'Now I'm giving it to you. All you have to do is walk through that door.'

'How can I trust you?'

A shiver ran through Hochburg at Burton's voice. No longer the girlish pitch of a child, but the intonation of a man. He imagined it screaming as the flames seized him. Just like Dolan, just like the niggers.

Hochburg sheathed the knife, then reached for some flotsam and tossed it away. It landed noisily. 'You hear that? That's your knife. I am unarmed. We fight like men.' He lowered his mouth to the gunner. 'Remember, I want him alive. Aim for the legs.'

They waited. Hochburg felt a single drop of sweat trickle down the ridge of his spine.

The door burst open. A volley of shots.

The gunner returned fire, then crumpled over his weapon. Bullets strafed the deck, spat splinters into Hochburg's face. He raised his arm to protect himself and watched as someone crashed through the side window of the wheelhouse; he couldn't tell if it was Burton. The figure scrambled down the hull, flopped into the waiting rowboat.

The pull of oars.

Hochburg kicked away the gunner, lifted up his MG48. Fired at the rowboat, then charged the wheelhouse. Another volley came from the door – but this time the bullets flew wide. Hochburg felt them vanish over his head. He was invincible now.

He reached the ladder, roared as he emptied the last of the magazine into the bridge. The fire had encircled it, was spreading up the walls. He climbed, the rungs burning his hands, and wrenched the door open.

Hochburg pulled his Taurus. Cocked the trigger.

Inside, the bridge was a mosaic of blood and shattered glass. He entered without caution, boots crunching on the floor. There was a dead marine, a fat man skewered on a spike of wood. And closest to him a third body, lying face down, arm at an awkward angle beneath its chest.

Hochburg aimed his pistol, rolled the body over.

It was Whaler. Dead.

He'd spent his final moments clearing a shape in the broken glass beneath him. A ragged letter H. Hochburg stared into the American's face. There was a faint, ironic smile on his lips. It seemed to mock him.

The bridge was a box of fire. Hochburg pulled himself out through the window on to the roof and stared across the bay. He saw the rowboat heading towards the darkness of the ocean; could barely make out the rower and next to him Burton Cole.

Hochburg let out a sob of inconsolable rage and frustration. The anguish of an executioner cheated, the world not righted. He fired his pistol – but Burton was already out of range. Then his mouth twisted cruelly.

There was one last way to wound the boy.

*

Burton was shivering, slumped at the back of the dinghy. He held his Browning weakly in front of him. The ivory felt solid in his hand, the last bit of reassurance he had.

Farrow was rowing hard, shoulders bulging beneath his waistcoat. 'I can see her, Major. The *Ibis*.'

Burton twisted round: saw a flotilla of vessels, ensigns of various nationalities, twinkling lights. As welcome as the candles Madeleine burned on Hanukkah.

He turned back to the tug. It was almost submerged now, only the roof of the wheelhouse left above the water. It was burning, the diesel floating on the sea around it also ablaze. A halo of flames. And in the centre: Hochburg.

'You want the truth, Burton?' he yelled. 'Want to know what happened to your mother?'

Burton covered his ears, felt the cold metal of his gun against his skull. But the other hand – his stump – couldn't block out Hochburg's voice. It reverberated across the water, louder than the bombs dropping on Loanda.

'Eleanor died because of you. Raped, beaten, left to perish on some lonely beach. Her blood is on your hands, Burton. Not mine, not the niggers. Not God in all his knowing brutality. Yours! The truth is she died because of you.'

The words tolled in Burton's head. No how, no why, just an accusation. *Because of you.* A procession of voices clamoured it: his father, Patrick, the rest of the team, Cranley. *Because of you. Because of you.*

He felt numb, tearless. Kept his Browning pressed to his head.

The tug was sinking beneath the waves, the fire dissolving into coils of steam. Hochburg was up to his chest. He seemed not to notice; had always loved the water, been a strong swimmer. His mouth was a ring of hatred.

'I'll find you, Burton. Wherever you walk on this earth I will find you. You have my word.'

The boat vanished in a cauldron of foam. Left nothing but a film of burning diesel and lumps of wreckage. Burton had a final glimpse of Hochburg. The skeletal head and contorted features. The black eyes. Exactly how he remembered them in his nightmares.

Black as the devil's hangman.

Chapter Fifty

HMS Ibis, *Atlantic Ocean*
21 September, 05:55

THEY carried Burton Cole aboard. Farrow and five sailors, like pallbearers. The hands of strangers gently supporting his body, laying him down on the deck, his Browning resting on his chest. The morphine had worn off, his stump throbbed. It wasn't the agony he expected, more like a day-old burn . . . but growing in intensity. He felt a sense of irreparable loss. His face was livid and charred.

'I'll fetch the surgeon,' said Farrow. He vanished with one of the seamen into the throng of passengers.

Burton levered himself into a sitting position. A blanket was thrown around his shoulders, a mug of black tea put in his good hand. The vessel was crowded: men with sweaty, creased faces, haggard women with children at their skirts – every one of them white. The smell of stale perfume and unwashed bodies. They kept their distance from Burton, as if he were contagious, but their voices were clear. English mostly, but also Portuguese, Afrikaans, the occasional American accent. Everyone seemed to be talking at once, as if somehow it would keep them safe. A babel of rumour and half-heard news:

The Krauts have invaded Northern Rhodesia . . . been beaten back at the border . . . the lads of the 8th Army, Montgomery brought out of retirement . . . we've already crossed into Kongo itself . . .

*are threatening to continue all the way to Stanleystadt if we have
to ... that'll teach the bastards to mess with us ... Germania is
demanding an immediate ceasefire, Hitler's raving ...*

Burton was no longer interested; let them slaughter each other
if that's what they wanted. Africa had always had an insatiable
thirst for blood. He didn't care whether they tore up the
Casablanca Treaty. Whether Hochburg triumphed or failed. Lived
or died. As for his parting words, Burton refused to consider
them: they were nothing but lies.

Lies!

All he cared about now was getting home. Home and Cranley.

He felt the engines begin to pound below deck, the vibrations
running up his body to the tip of his wrist bone. Pain seeped
through him. He swallowed some tea, gagged. It was so sweet
even Maddie would have poured it away. He put down the mug,
leaned his head back and gazed at Loanda.

The horizon was streaked pink and pearl-grey with the dawn,
the city itself still hidden in darkness. Bombers continued to
rumble overhead, the light of the new day burnishing their wings.
Explosions flared among the buildings. Palls of smoke. A screen
to hide the vivisectionist's work. The bay was mostly empty; only
a few remaining boats hurried across it. Seagulls darted and
wheeled over the water. There was no sign of the tug or Hochburg.
Burton tried to pinpoint where it had sunk, the *Chef*'s final resting
place. If he ever met Hannah he'd describe the spot. He wanted
it to be peaceful, but all he saw were the reflections of Nazi
conquest.

Burton searched inside himself for an emotion. Found nothing.
He was too exhausted, too emptied out. He would mourn Patrick
later. When Africa was a distant smudge on the horizon.

For the moment his thoughts were back in Ackerman's office,
that look of bewilderment on the Rhodesian's face.

'*He sent me to your farm. Was rabid. I've never seen him like
that. Normally he's self-control itself.*'

'*Who?*' Burton had demanded.

'*Insisted we change from Dolan to you. No explanation given.*'

'*Who?*'

'*My superior. Cranley.*'

Ackerman had been the bearer of *Hiobsbotschaft* all along. *Hiobsbotschaft*: from the Old Testament, Job's news. The type of news you didn't want to hear.

The tremor of the engines grew more insistent. There was a waft of salty air . . . and the frigate began to head into the Atlantic.

Burton snatched at the legs of a passing sailor. 'How long?' he demanded. 'How long back to Britain?'

The sailor recoiled, aghast at the bloody handprint on his trousers.

'How long?'

'Seventeen days.'

Burton urged the ship on faster.

The whole time he had been in Africa, chasing ghosts, the real danger was at home. Cranley had set his trap: sent Burton to Kongo and an inevitable death. What revenge had he reaped back in England?

Jared Cranley: Madeleine's husband.

Burton pictured Maddie on the farm. Wrapped up in bed, hugging her pregnant belly, every lock, door and window bolted. He'd get back to her, squeeze her hand again just as he had done on their last night together. Trembling with tenderness. Her soft, delicate fingers entwined with his.

He held the image for as long as he could – but waves of blackness were rolling over him. He struggled to keep his eyes open. The pain in his arm was spreading now, pooling in his chest. There was a sulphurous taste at the back of his mouth.

Burton buried his wounded wrist beneath his armpit. Clutched his empty Browning.

The frigate sailed away from Loanda, away from the rising sun, and turned west. Back towards the darkness and the long journey home.

AUTHOR'S NOTE

Although *The Afrika Reich* is based on documented plans the Nazis had for the continent, it is foremost a work of fiction. To that end I have simplified certain aspects of the history (alternative and otherwise) for the sake of the narrative.

The Nazis' first significant overture towards Africa was in May 1934, barely a year after seizing power, when they established the Colonial Policy Office – Kolonialpolitisches Amt (KPA). Its objective was to agitate for the territories Germany had lost after the Versailles Treaty and, in Hitler's words, 'to press energetically the preparatory work for a future colonial administration'. Systematic planning began in the spring of 1939.

Despite this Hitler didn't see himself turning to Africa till 1944 at the earliest – after the Soviet Union had been defeated and a large surface navy built. It was the fall of France in June 1940, when the Reich seemed invincible, which accelerated events. That summer colonial fever gripped the Nazis. The Wehrmacht selected ten battalions for the conquest ahead (a forerunner of the Afrika Korps), designed tropical uniforms and weapons. Training courses for the Colonial Service began at Hamburg University. Elsewhere plans were afoot for pre-fabricated garrison towns; a 'multi-terrain automobile' was developed that could be used anywhere in Africa.

The KPA, along with the Foreign Ministry and Kriegsmarine (Navy) began to circulate secret memoranda detailing Nazi ambitions for the continent. Common to all of them was the reacquisition of Germany's former colonies and creation of 'Mittelafrika' – a solid bloc of territory stretching from the Atlantic to the Indian Ocean. It was hoped that this land could be obtained through negotiation, if not force would be necessary. As early as 1937 there was discussion of Angola being 'appropriated'.*

The most comprehensive of these secret documents is the Bielfeld Memorandum of 6 November 1940. This proposed the seizure of Belgian and French Congo, Equatorial French Africa and a large portion of French West Africa; there was also some suggestion of incorporating Nigeria, Kenya and Northern Rhodesia. Naval bases were earmarked for Dakar, Conakry and the Canary Islands, while Madagascar was reserved as a future 'dumping-ground' for Jews. This vast area was to be exploited for its natural resources, upon which Germany's European empire would be built.

Of course none of this would be possible if there was conflict with Great Britain. From the pages of *Mein Kampf* onwards Hitler hoped for an understanding with the British and made repeated overtures to that effect. He was genuinely surprised and disappointed when Britain declared war in 1939.

Could there have been a different outcome? In the seventy years since the outbreak of the Second World War the 'finest hour' myth has taken such a hold on the British imagination that it's difficult to conceive of an alternative. Events at the time were far less certain. In November 1939 the (opposition) Labour Party advocated negotiations with Hitler to guarantee the British Empire; Prime Minister Chamberlain's postbag ran three to one in favour of peace. Of the five members of the War Cabinet, two were in favour of a peace settlement with Germany. Most prominent was the Foreign Secretary, Lord Halifax, who only narrowly missed becoming Prime Minister after Chamberlain resigned. Given a different set of circumstances it is possible to imagine Halifax and Hitler meeting to agree 'a division of the world', as the Führer hoped.

Hitler's attitude towards Africa was characteristically schizophrenic. Sometimes he made grandiose declarations (such as the epigraph to this book). On other occasions he was dismissive:

* See Hossbach Memorandum

'the only colony I'd like to have back would be our Cameroons – nothing else'.

More ominously, in January 1941 he permitted Himmler to establish a training centre for the colonies in Berlin, with a second set up in Vienna the following year. At this point the Reichsführer made it clear that the SS would be responsible for policing Africa with the KPA sidelined. It is impossible to know the full progression of events but if we take occupied Europe as a model it seems inevitable that Himmler's blackshirts would come to dominate at the expense of the civilian administration and military. The governors general would possess almost unlimited power. In such an environment someone like Walter Hochburg would have thrived.

The new masters of Africa planned cities that adhered to Himmler's 'string of pearls' theory: kernels of civilisation amidst the wilderness, linked by autobahn. The SS Economic Department would control labour, industry, agriculture, forestry and mining. Finding enough Germans to settle the land was an acute problem – but by 1940 SS racial experts were scouring the globe for 'ethnics' (5.5 million descendents were identified in the US and South America alone). As for the native populations of Africa, their fate remains ambiguous. The KPA planned a relatively benign system of mandatory labour. The SS wanted an end to 'soft negrophilism'; promoted 'ethnic reallocation and consolidation' with those 'unsuitable for hard labour to be completely eliminated.' I will return to this subject in subsequent books.

Those looking for a more detailed account of a possible Nazi Africa should read Wolfe Schmokel's *Dream of Empire: German Colonialism, 1919-45* (Yale, 1964). I would also recommend *Hitler's War Aims, Vol II* by Norman Rich (Andre Deutsch, 1974) and Gerhard Weinberg's *World in Balance* (University Press of New England, 1981). Mark Mazower's *Hitler's Empire* (Allen Lane, 2008) is a vivid depiction of Nazi Europe and offers a glimpse of the bureaucracy, chaos and horror that might have been elsewhere.

ACKNOWLEDGEMENTS

Writing is a solitary profession so I am lucky to have had the encouragement of many people during the years spent on this book.

For their support, advice and inspiration at key stages in my writing career I'd like to express my gratitude to: William Boyd, Linda Christmas & John Higgins, Julie Gray, Nigel de la Poer, Joanne Saville, Mike Shaw, Sol Stein and John Whitcombe. Sadly, some on this list are no longer with us – I like to think, however, that their influence lives on.

For their technical help, I thank: Colne Valley Railway, Susan Curtis, Elizabeth Ferretti for double checking my translations, Harry Hine, Pedro Jacinto, Peter Rosenfeld of St Mary's Hospital, London for answering my questions on amputation, John Smith of the French Foreign Legion, and SOAS Library. For all things American: Norm Benson, Dick Custin, CL Frontera and Alan Hutcheson. I am especially indebted to Jennifer Domingo, librarian extraordinaire who helped me track down various obscure texts; Dominique Hardy for all her work in Luanda (present day Loanda); and Lieutenant Colonel Kenneth Mason for his exhaustive study of Congo in the 1940s. As is *de rigueur* on such occasions, any errors in the text are mine.

Thanks also to: Tom 'Peanuts' Bolon, Bob Burke, Andreas Campomar, Robin Carter, Sheila Dalton, Andrew Dance, Katharine D'Souza, Samar Hammam, Douglas Jackson, Peter Jones, Laura Macdougall, Lorraine Mace, Sara O'Keeffe,

Sarah-Jane Page, Edward Parnell, Robin Porter, Lexi Revellian, Gemma Rougier, Susan Sellers, Edward Smith at youwriteon.com, Justine Windsor and everyone at Writers' Centre Norwich / Escalator Literature 2007, in particular Katy Carr, Chris Gribble and Leila Telford. Special mention for Sarah Bower and Alex Scarrow.

This book was written with the assistance of an Arts Council England grant.

Finally, a big and heartfelt thank you to: Katharine McMahon for her insight and guidance; Jonathan Pegg, my agent, for his unflagging commitment to this project; Lorrie Porter for always finding time to read the manuscript when there was no time for anything else; Nick Sayers for championing the book at Hodder; and last but not least, Alice Louise Tilton without whom I would never have gone back to Africa.

GS